Singles, Set and Match

By

Elaine Spires

Printed and bound in the UK by KnowledgePoint Limited, Reading.

Print Edition
ISBN: 978-0-9928672-4-9
Published by Elaine Spires July 2019

To Indie Authors

To your faith and belief in yourselves

You know how hard it is

THE DAY BEFORE

'. . . AND SO HAVING exchanged rings and their vows I now declare they are husband and wife.'

Eve felt a lump rising in her throat and sudden, hot tears flooded her eyes with the wave of emotion the words brought on. She bit her lip and tried to smile, aware that she was probably gurning a scary, hideous grimace while blinking furiously to dispel the tears without having to dab at her eyes and draw attention to the fact that she was crying.

'You may kiss your bride.'

The registrar beamed at the couple who took a tentative step forward and reached towards each other, nervously bumping noses before finding each others' lips. Egged on by the cheers from the small congregation and swept away by the moment, his confidence and sense of the romantic reaching a giddy crescendo, the groom doubled his new wife back over his arm, tango-dancing style with a little too much enthusiasm and she crashed to the floor, pulling him with her.

Two young men rushed forward to help the hapless pair

to their feet as gales of laughter caught the breeze and wafted from under the wedding gazebo, past the multi-coloured bougainvillea onto the sandy cove where the tables stood ready for the wedding breakfast before floating away over the sea.

'You clumsy old sod!'

The bride giggled as she chided her groom and pulled her floral garland straight on her head.

'Aye, well, you're heavier than you look,' he parried.

'Murray!'

Every woman present groaned and many of the men gasped his name in disbelief at what they'd just heard. Eve's tears were now of laughter. She watched as Eileen gave Murray a playful slap on the arm and a pretend dirty look, causing him to envelope her in a huge hug and plant a smacker on her lips. Watching them, Eve welled up again as wedding guests gathered around them offering congratulatory kisses and handshakes. She was so pleased for these two Travel Together stalwarts; she'd grown immensely fond of them, especially Murray. And if anyone had told her that when she'd first met him on a holiday to Antigua several years earlier she'd have laughed in their face. But miserable, moaning Murray had mellowed and much of that was due to his new bride, Eileen, who'd met him on a tour of India that Eve had also worked. Eve liked Eileen very much; she was a sensible, sensitive woman who'd had her fair share of problems but never let them get her down. And it looked as if her relationship with the two young men who'd just helped her back onto her feet, her sons, Luke and Jason, was cordial and loving once again. Not so long ago it had been a bit rocky so Eve understood. One had gone off to live with his father who ran a bar on mainland Spain and the other one hadn't got on with Murray. But today she was glad to see they were letting bygones be bygones and were supportive of their mum's new-found happiness.

She stepped forward and kissed Eileen on both cheeks.

'Congratulations! You look absolutely gorgeous.' Eileen's pretty face glowed with a real happiness that turned it stunningly beautiful.

'I decided I'd have an Ad Lib dress as we were getting married in Ibiza,' Eileen said. 'I hope I don't look like mutton.'

'Don't be silly! It really suits you,' Eve said truthfully, admiring the layered, handkerchief-hemmed dress that skimmed Eileen's curvy hips before falling to her mid-calf. 'Well done, Murray!' Eve turned to the groom in his cream cut-off trousers and pale blue shirt that matched his bride's outfit perfectly.

'Thanks, Eve.'

'You decided not to go for Scottish traditional dress? I was looking forward to seeing you in full highland regalia,' Eve teased.

'Not in this heat! It's too warm for woolly socks.'

'And the only one seeing his sporran is me!' Eileen said, making them all laugh.

'Thank you for coming to our wedding and thank you for your part in our first meeting up. And getting back together,' Murray added, kissing Eve's cheek and clutching her hand in his. 'You're a good woman, Eve.'

His eyes were filled with unshed tears.

'I'm not really sure I did anything,' Eve protested, swallowing the lump in her throat then kissing him again. 'But I couldn't be happier for you. For both of you.'

They were interrupted by the popping of corks as two waiters began to fill glasses and the group made its way from under the gazebo onto the nearby sandy cove where the tables were now being covered with plates of the most delicious looking tapas. Eve took the hand of the gorgeous toddler who'd stood patiently by her side during the ceremony; a beautiful fairy in a cloud of pale green and lilac tulle.

'Let's go and get some food, shall we?' Eve asked. The child's face lit up at the thought and broke into a huge grin.

'You okay?'

Eve felt the arm around her waist and turned to look into the deep, dark eyes of her son Michael. She knew what he was referring to and she'd tried not to think about it. It wasn't too long ago they had imagined the next wedding they'd be going to would be Eve's. She squeezed her eyes for a second to rid her mind of the thought before smiling at Michael.

'I'm fine, Michael. Fine. Wasn't it a beautiful ceremony?'

'Oh, it was lovely! I felt myself getting all choked up,' Natalie said, letting go of Michael's arm and giving Eve's hand a pat. 'Did you like the bride, darling? The pretty lady?'

Felicity nodded and smiled, offering her other hand to her mother.

'And she was such a good girl! She sat still and didn't fidget.' Eve beamed with pride at her grand-daughter as Natalie placed a tender kiss on the child's head.

Michael took his wife's arm to steady her pregnant waddle, as the four of them went to join the others at the wedding breakfast.

Eve had seen some of her ex-clients among the wedding guests. There was Dave with his live-in girlfriend Penny who he had met on a Travel Together Christmas break. Dave had also been on an Antigua holiday with Murray and the two men had kept in touch. And Frances from the Indian holiday with Eileen and two holidays with Murray. They were great people and Eve was delighted to see them again. And, of course, Michael and Natalie were also her ex-clients as well as being her son and daughter-in-law. Fate had brought them all together on a singles' holiday and Eve couldn't be happier. She smiled and waved at them all but turned her attention to her little grand-daughter who tugged her hand.

'I want no shoes,' Felicity said.

'We'd better ask Mummy or Daddy.' Eve was always the diplomat.

Natalie had agreed and so Eve helped Felicity to slip her sandals off and watched as the child sat down on the sand and squealed with delight as she dug her toes into the cool grains and picked up a handful and let it run through her fingers. For a split second Eve allowed her thoughts to take a *What If Route…*

Shaking her head, Eve cleared the thoughts from her mind and along with them all thoughts of her not-to-be-wedding: the wedding that might have been, should have been but now would never be.

No regrets!

She gave herself a stern rebuke knowing she had made her decision, carefully, painfully but pragmatically.

Eve was brought back to the present by Felicity's chuckling; she thought it the sweetest, most beautiful sound in the world. She looked at her grand-daughter and felt a love for her that was fierce, whole and unconditional. She threw her arms around the child and pulled her close, kissing her halo of tight, black curls.

'No, Grandma! Squash me!' Felicity protested.

'Squashing you? I'm loving you, Pickle.'

She tickled Felicity's belly making her squeal with loud laughter. Eve adored the time they spent together and was never happier than when she was babysitting for Michael and Natalie, who needed her help more than ever with a second baby on the way. They had decided as soon as they knew Natalie was pregnant again against a CVS and amniocentesis agreeing that the chances of another child with a chromosome abnormality was low.

'And I don't care if we had ten more children with it, there's no way I'd get rid of any of them,' Natalie had declared. 'It would be like saying we regretted having Felicity and that we loved her less or that her life wasn't worth as much as a non-Downs child's.'

Since Felicity's birth, not quite three years earlier Natalie had started up classes for differently-abled children at her stage school and they'd been a roaring success. At her last show those children had brought the house down and Eve's heart had totally melted at the sight of Felicity in her tiny tap shoes and gold sparkly dress dancing to We're in the Money.

'Grandma no shoes,' Felicity said, pulling at Eve's sandals. Eve bent and undid her own straps and slipped them off and Felicity promptly tried to bury her feet in the sand. Eve pushed her feet deeper to help her.

'So, 'ow come you've got time off to be 'ere?'

Eve looked up to see Dave and Penny standing beside her, each holding a glass of cava.

'I'd've fought Travel Togevva would've bin working you to the bone in 'igh season,' he continued.

'Well, I'm actually here on a job. I was offered a holiday here on Ibiza. The group all arrive tomorrow so the timing of the wedding was perfect.'

'Oh, that's good!' Penny said. 'It's nice you can mix social occasions with work.'

'It doesn't happen that often, but for once the gods were on my side.'

'She's a little smasher, ain't she?' Dave kneeled next to Felicity and offered her his hand. She shook it formally.

'Please meet you,' she said.

'Oh she's gorgeous! Aren't you, poppet?' Penny said.

'You two aren't getting broody are you?'

Frances burst out laughing as she joined the group, long gold and green earrings jangling.

'I wouldn't mind one like our little Felicity, eh, pet?' Penny said, tickling her neck.

'You've gone quiet, Dave,' Frances teased.

'Shall I get anuvver round in?' Dave said, helping himself to two glasses of cava from the tray that was being offered. 'Baby talk makes me nervous. And firsty!'

✦ ✦ ✦

MICHAEL SAT BACK in his chair, threw his napkin onto his empty plate and exhaled loudly.

'Well, these Ibicencans can certainly put on a decent meal. I am stuffed. Well and truly stuffed.'

'And an ice-cream profiterole wedding cake was a superb choice,' Natalie said, patting her belly. 'Of course, I had to have a large slice as I'm eating for two,' she added, giggling. 'I shall be the size of a house if I carry on like this.'

'As if! Three weeks after you had Felicity you looked like you'd never been pregnant,' Eve said.

'I've found it harder keeping off sweet things this time, though. Oops!'

She reached and picked up Felicity's spoon which had fallen onto the dazzling white table cloth, rubbing at the dark blob with her own napkin making it worse.

'No more!' Felicity said, shaking her head before whipping it round in the direction of the top table where Eileen's son Jason was tapping a spoon against his glass to get everyone's attention.

'Thanks, Ladies and Gentlemen. I hope you've all enjoyed the meal. I just wanted to say on behalf of Luke and me, erm, thanks for coming out to Ibiza for Mum's wedding. We're both proud of her today. She looks really nice. I didn't recognise her when she first came out of her room this morning.'

'Oh, thanks, Son!' Eileen faked being miffed. 'There's a compliment there somewhere I think."

There was a chorus of laughter and cheering from the guests.

'What I mean is you scrub up all right.'

'Jason! Stop digging!' Luke pulled his brothers arm, theatrically provoking more laughter.

'Anyway. Murray's bloody lucky to have you is what I'm trying to say. And I know we haven't always seen eye to eye, Mum, and I know a lot of that was down to me. I didn't make it that easy for you to love me, let alone like me. But you did. I know now how much you struggled, like, doing two jobs and that. You always did what was best for me and Luke. You always put us first. I can see that now. And you had Nan on at you most of the time, too. And I can just imagine what she'd say seeing you today. You gave up a lot of your own life for us… But you never gave up on us." His voice quivered and he looked down at the table for a moment, composing himself. He gave a little cough and swallowed.

'And now it's your turn, Mum. It's time for you to be happy. And that's what we really want you and Murray to be. So, can I ask everyone to raise their glasses and toast Mum and Murray. Be happy always!'

'Be happy always!'

There was a thunderous round of applause and a blushing Jason sat down, his brother giving him a congratulatory thump on the back, Murray shaking his hand and Eileen leaning across her bridegroom to give her elder son a kiss on the cheek.

Then is was Murray's turn.

'Well, those of yous who know me know I'm a man of few words…'

'But lots of opinions!' Dave heckled.

'Aye. Well, mebbe I am. And I'm of the opinion that I am the luckiest man in the world that this wonderful woman is now my wife. When we met on a singles' holiday in India I could never have hoped or dreamed that this day would come. Och, yes, we've had our ups and downs and for a wee while I thought I'd blown my chances with her. And mebbe giving her a box of party poppers on New Year's Eve when she'd been expecting an engagement ring wasn't my best ever move…'

He paused as the guests erupted into gales of laughter.

'…But I'm overwhelmed with gratitude that our love for each other has overcome my occasional lack of sensitivity and that she gave me a second chance. Jason, Luke, you heard me make vows to your mother earlier and I promise you I will keep them. I will love and cherish her always.'

Eve felt weepy again at Murray's unexpectedly tender words. She looked at the Bride and saw that she was dabbing her eyes.

'Eileen, you have made me happier than I ever thought possible. Today you look gorgeous, but then you are beautiful every day. Inside and out. So, my toast is: to my beautiful bride. To Eileen!'

'To Eileen!'

'And now, Murray and Eileen are going to have their

first dance as Mr and Mrs Sneddon!' Jason announced.

The opening notes tinkled, then Gladys Knight's golden voice rang out as Murray took Eileen by the hand and led her onto the dance floor.

'I've had my share, of life's up and downs…'

A stiletto was thrust sharply into Eve's heart. She sat motionless, goose pimples running the length of her arms and back, waves of nostalgia, of what-might-have-beens, of bliss and of pain washed over her. Blazes Club in Windsor; Melv; their separation; their reunion; their song. Their song.

'You'd be there in every line of pain and glory…'

The wedding party sang and swayed along as Murray swept his bride around, her dress floating behind her, before singing the title line to her, gazing lovingly into her eyes.

'You're the best thing, that ever happened to me…'

It didn't matter that he was slightly off-key; everyone stood and broke into rapturous applause.

'Come and join us,' Eileen said, beckoning everyone.

Needing no second bidding Frances made a beeline for Luke who had no girlfriend with him.

'The older she gets the younger she likes 'em,' Dave observed as Penny pulled him to his feet.

'Good for her!' Penny retorted.

Michael took Natalie's hand.

'Do you mind, Eve? Can you keep an eye on Felicity?'

'I can do better than that!' Eve snapped out of her sentimental trance. She reached for her grand-daughter's hand.

'Want to dance with Grandma, Felicity?'

Nodding vigorously, Felicity jumped down from her chair and ran onto the floor. Eve had never seen her happier. And her heart swelled.

✦ ✦ ✦

EVE WAS JOGGING in the rain.

To say this was an unusual occurrence was a bit of an understatement. She couldn't remember the last time she jogged in any sort of weather let alone the deluge she was enduring now. Yet strangely enough she didn't seem to feel wet, so intent she was at reaching her destination. Looking down at her feet splashing through the ever-increasing puddles, she realised she was wearing the wrong trainers. In fact, she wasn't wearing her trainers but her gold flip-flops that were living up to their name making loud, farting, sploshing sounds, flipping and flopping with every step she took.

They sound like they're having a Bill and Ben conversation. Slobber lobber. Slobber lobber. Splish splosh. Flip flop.

Giggling out loud, she glanced at her watch and saw it was already five thirty. She was going to be late unless she hurried up. She would just have to run faster.

Run faster! Run faster! Run faster!

She repeated the mantra gradually getting faster, her steps increasing to match it. She could now see the lights of the airport off to her right, piercing the gloom caused by the dusk and the rain. Changing direction she veered off the road and across a wide stretch of grass but then too late she realised the grass ended abruptly in a large flight of steep, stone steps. Her ankle twisted and she jerked upright.

Startled, disorientated, she looked around blinking rapidly, her breath fast and shallow. Gradually her eyes focused and she took in the scene; the floral duvet cover, the white wardrobes and dressing table, the sepia paintings of a bygone Ibiza that adorned the walls and the child's head on the pillow. She was in the holiday villa.

What the hell was that all about?

She grinned to herself and slowly shook her head as details of the dream came back to her.

I worry myself sometimes.

A gentle thud drew her attention; *Peppa's Washing Day* slid to the floor. She picked it up and put it back on the bedside table on top of another four Peppa Pig books. Felicity would have brought her whole collection if she'd been allowed. Eve yawned and turned to look at the sleeping child lying beside her, smiling at the soft, rhythmic sighs coming from the rosebud lips whose sweet kisses she'd never tire of sharing. Reaching out her hand she brushed the glorious tight black halo of curls; she stroked a tiny upturned palm and offered her finger to chubby small ones that wrapped themselves tightly around it even in sleep.

'I love you so much,' she whispered, bending to place a slow kiss on the smooth brow.

Her whole body was consumed with love; she had never known such a love was possible but she knew she would lay down her life for this little one and would quite easily kill anyone who even thought about harming her in the slightest way.

She heard the sound of footsteps climbing the steps to the front porch and then the click of the door opening and an arc of bright light swept over the room. She kissed the child again, pulled the sheet up to her chin and tip-toed from the room into the lounge area of the house.

'Sorry we're a bit late. It went on longer than we thought,' Natalie said coming down the hallway while removing her fascinator and kicking off her shoes. 'You know what it's like. We kept on saying we were leaving and then got into conversation with someone else.'

'Or the DJ put on another song we liked,' Michael

added.

'I understand. Don't apologise. You were supposed to be enjoying yourselves.'

'Well we certainly did! It was a lovely evening and a really beautiful day. Especially meeting up with the others again. Just a shame I couldn't have a few vinos to toast the happy couple,' Natalie grumbled, only half seriously. 'Has she been okay?'

'As good as gold, Natalie. She had her milk and fell asleep just a few minutes into Peppa Pig.'

'Thanks for having her, Eve,' Michael said. 'You must be ready for bed yourself,' he added, noting she was in her pyjamas.

'I've already had a nap. I sent myself to sleep with the sound of my own voice. I was dreaming I was jogging to the airport in the rain with no luggage and just wearing my flip-flops.'

Natalie and Michael burst out laughing.

'I know! I worry myself, too, sometimes.'

'Do you want a cup of tea before bed?' Natalie asked, reaching for the kettle.

'I won't, thanks. I find it counter-productive. The camomile is supposed to make me sleep but if I drink it now I'll be up all night weeing and I need to try and get in a few hours at least. I'll try to go quietly in the morning. I'll have breakfast by seven and be on my way straight after that. The first flight lands at just after nine.'

'Blimey! That is early,' Natalie said. 'Long haul is so much more civilised!'

'Thanks so much for missing out to look after Felicity tonight, Eve.'

Michael pulled his mother into a tight embrace.

'It was no hardship, believe me. Every moment spent

with her is a sheer delight.'

There was a moment's silence; with Felicity Eve was making up for the time she hadn't been able to spend with Michael.

'And as soon as I'm back I'm coming along to watch her in her dance class again,' she added, turning to Natalie.

'You'll love it! It's amazing to see them all having the time of their lives. Felicity keeps up with the bigger ones. She's really come on since you saw her in the show.'

'I'm sure she's centre stage, after all it's in the genes,' Eve said, kissing her talented daughter-in-law on the cheek. 'And I think it's wonderful that children like Felicity can join in and have fun just like everyone else.'

'You'd be amazed at how many children with different abilities there are in the area. After the Gazette did that article about the inclusive classes and Felicity we were inundated with phone calls. We've got a waiting list now.'

'That's fantastic. I can't wait to see them all. But especially Felicity,' Eve added, smiling at the thought of her beautiful grand-daughter at dancing class. Natalie and Michael were so right to bring her up believing she could do, be and achieve anything. And judging by the evidence so far, Felicity agreed with them.

'Are you looking forward to this week, Eve?'

'Erm. I suppose so.'

'You don't sound very enthusiastic,' Michael said, chuckling.

'Well, it's wonderful to be back in Ibiza. It's been far too long. I'm just not sure about the tennis part of it, though.'

'I thought you loved your tennis.'

'I do, Natalie. But organising a week's tennis clinics and round robins is a bit different from cheering on Nadal and Murray on the TV or getting lucky in the Wimbledon Draw.'

'You're not planning on getting in touch with your inner Serena then?'

'Are you kidding? I think my playing days are behind me, although I might just be someone's hitting partner to make up the numbers if needed.' She sighed. 'Still, there's a resident pro taking daily clinics and organising the tournament. He even provides the paperwork. It's just a question of filling in who's won each match and keeping check of the scores, I suppose, so there's not that much to worry about.'

'And plenty of time left to party all night!' Michael teased.

'I don't know about that either,' Eve said. 'I think my dancing until dawn days are probably behind me, too.'

'I'll believe that when I see it.'

'And they're very lucky to have you, Eve,' Natalie said, hugging her again. 'You're the best tour manager Travel Together have ever had.'

DAY ONE

✦

*I*T'S A LONG *time since I've done this.*

Eve transferred her weight from one foot to the other and raised her flagging arms to lift her fluorescent orange T2G sign a little higher as she stood outside the Arrivals Hall in Ibiza Airport. It had been at least fifteen years since she'd worked a short-haul beach holiday for Travel Together. And she hoped it would be another fifteen before she did so again. Not that she didn't like Ibiza – quite the contrary – she loved it. But she was a long haul holidays and tours specialist, which were quite a different story. Her mind ran back three days to when she had set eyes on the island again for the first time in almost twenty years.

Looking out of the starboard window as the plane made its way along the East Coast of Ibiza, Eve was reminded why it had always been known as The White Island. Tiny white dolls houses were dotted among the almond, lemon and olive trees that covered the hills and cliffs in multi shades of green. And then along the coastline, hotels and apartment blocks of varying shapes and sizes but all painted white hugged the golden beaches and secluded coves that fringed the turquoise and cobalt Mediterranean. She was surprised to see how built-up the island looked compared to her last visit which had been almost twenty years earlier.

Twenty years?

She shuddered as she contemplated the rapid passing of time, which became even more evident as the plane flew low over Ibiza Town and then the resorts of Figueretes and Playa D'en Bossa, unrecognisable as the quiet, unspoilt, idyllic beaches she remembered from her very first visit in the 1980s, and now so built up they blended into one enormous resort. As the pilot gently placed the plane on the tarmac she yawned and stretched her legs. She'd been spoilt by years of long-haul, scheduled flights; she just wasn't used to budget airlines. Usually she'd take an aisle seat as she liked to get up and move around and hated disturbing anyone, but as the flight had only been just over two hours she'd chosen the window. And she'd been glad she had.

The doors to the Arrivals Hall opened ejecting another group of bewildered travellers and bringing her back to the present moment. Eve shifted her weight yet again. Yes, as beautiful as Ibiza was, she much preferred long-haul where she met the group in the Executive Lounge; all together, much more civilised.

She looked down and checked her list for the twentieth time in ten minutes.

Birmingham Flight: DA 2115 BHX 13:50 IBZ 17:25

Ambrose Leticia

Banks John

Cooke Michael

Fairhead Fiona

Jones Benjamin

Legg Adrian

Spicer James
Thomson Amy

The arrivals board was showing the flight had landed and *'passengers in baggage hall'*. She gave a half-smile of satisfaction as she knew they wouldn't be much longer. She was grateful that the flight had landed on-time. Only the Leeds-Bradford flight had been forty-five minutes late; everything else had behaved itself. It meant they'd all be able to meet up for pre-dinner drinks and a chat with Jesus the tennis pro at the Dunas Blancas.

Her eyes scanned the holidaymakers coming through the automatic doors and she lifted the sign up higher and took another step forward. She knew from experience that she could stand stark naked under an arch of neon lights waving her T2G sign for all she was worth yet there would still be those who walked past and would swear that she hadn't been there at all. Although her notes told her that this group all knew each other so they'd probably come through together. They'd been on four previous Travel Together tennis holidays. She gave an inward sigh; she hated it when there was a group within a group as any first-timer could feel left out. And although experience told her otherwise, she hoped they wouldn't be a clique.

'She's over here!'

A slim blond with a neat bob and huge bust wearing a jogging suit and very high espadrilles tottered over to Eve, pulling an industrial-sized suitcase behind her. A group which included three very dishevelled men followed her.

'Well done, Titty! You found her!'

'You're the man, Titty! You're the man!'

Oh, God! They're already drunk.

'We're with you,' the woman said. 'Eight of us.'

'You must be Ambrose, Banks, Cooke, Fairhead, Jones, Legg, Spicer and Thomson,' Eve said, ticking the names off as the blond nodded.

'You're a magician,' a stocky-built guy with a shaved head declared.

'You're older than most tour managers,' a reedy man said, scrutinising her with blood-shot eyes and breathing alcohol fumes in her face.

Eve took a step back resisting the temptation to wave the smell away from under her nose.

'How does someone like you get a job like this?'

'Just lucky, I guess,' Eve replied, realising it was useless in engaging him in conversation when he was bordering on the incoherent.

'Okay, so if you like to follow me to the minibus.'

'Woo hoo! Look out, Ibiza! The A-Team's coming to getcha!'

Eve walked outside slowly with the eight of them following behind her. She waited until they were all there and then crossed to where the minibus was parked. Miguel, the driver, jumped out smiling and opened up the rear door.

'Please leave your cases here. I will put in the bus,' he said, beaming at them.

'Your English is good,' the youngest of the three women said, handing him her case. 'Better than my Spanish anyway.'

'Thank you,'

'Muchos graciarses.'

The reedy man with bloodshot eyes let go of his case and it toppled over. He made two abortive attempts to pick it up. Miguel stepped forward and lifted it from the ground into the bus in one strong, fluid movement.

'Muchos graciarses,' he repeated before belching loudly.

'I'm sorry, Miguel,' Eve said once the clients were all inside the bus.

'No problem. I'm used to them. I only get angry if they vomit. I tell them if they vomit they pay twenty-five Euros for cleaning.'

'I don't blame you. I think they're okay. Just a bit loud.'

'Loud is no problem. I turn up the music even more loud.'

Eve chuckled. She'd only met Miguel that morning but she liked him already. She opened the minibus door at the front and climbed in next to him.

'How come you're the tour manager?' Bloodshot Eyes insisted. 'What happened to Jenny? She's always been the tour manager. We've come on loads of tennis holidays and we've always had Jenny.'

Eve knew what had happened to Jenny but she had no intention of sharing it with any of the clients, especially those who were drunk and knew her. The world of Travel Together was very small and tightly knit. She understood their curiosity but Eve's lips were sealed. Jenny had been fired for taking her boyfriend along on a Travel Together holiday to the Caribbean. Members of the group had felt it was wrong for the tour manager to be off with her partner every night leaving them on their own, when she was supposed to be the one leading the singles' holiday. And T2G had agreed with them so Jenny was a tour manager no more. Eve gave an inward sigh; it was incredible how stupid some people could be.

'We heard she got the sack,' the blonde said.

'I really don't know. I only met her a couple of times. We've only got a fairly short drive. About twenty minutes,' Eve said, changing the subject. 'And we'll have some fabulous views of Ibiza Town over on the right when we come out of these tunnels.'

'Is that the place they call Eivissa?' Eve thought the youngest woman was Amy.

'Yes, that's right.'

'What's it got two names for?'

'Ibiza is the Spanish name and Eivissa is the Ibicenco word.'

'Anyway, it looks nice,' Amy said, taking in the fortified city walls that surrounded the old town and trying to film them on her mobile.

'The high part within the walls is called D'Alt Vila,' Eve said, unsure if they were taking it in now as the men and the blonde woman were having a loud conversation about who would be last one standing at the bar that night and Amy then weighed in, so she was no longer listening, either.

I'm losing my ability to command people's attention.

Eve gave herself a wry grin and leaned back against the headrest, glad the journey to the Hotel Dunas Blancas was a short one. And even gladder that this was only a one-week holiday.

✦ ✦ ✦

ESTELLE HUNG HER last dress up in the wardrobe and slid the mirrored door closed, running her hand through her dishevelled, platinum hair when she saw her reflection.

Good thing it's short!

She put the suitcase between the double bed and the wall out of sight. She liked unpacking as soon as she arrived anywhere and couldn't understand people who lived out of their suitcase for their whole holiday. She looked at herself again, moving from side to side casting a critical eye over her thighs in their blue and yellow floral shorts. She'd managed to get down to a size fourteen again and she knew that playing tennis had helped with that. She'd gone up to an eighteen when she'd first found out about Joe. Comfort eating it was. And she'd only joined the tennis club in the first place because she'd found out that he took his new twin step-daughters there. Yet she'd surprised herself by discovering that she actually enjoyed playing. She'd come face-to-face with him just once and he had acted as if she was invisible. She'd smiled and gone to speak as he brushed past her his attention given fully to the two leggy teenagers striding beside him, their cheeks flushed from the recent exercise, long ponytails swinging behind them. They'd once called her Auntie Ess; now they barely acknowledged her.

Her legs went weak remembering the utter humiliation she'd suffered and she sank onto the bed. Even though he'd left her two years ago and married Marie, her replacement three months later, she still found it hard to accept they were no longer together, no longer a couple. Throughout the twelve inseparable years they'd spent together he'd always said he didn't want children. Then he left her for a woman with three. Three! Fifteen-year-old twins and a boy of eleven. A woman who'd been her business partner and closest friend. And six months after he walked out on Estelle, Marie had already given him a daughter of his own.

Estelle took a couple of deep breaths and told herself that she was in control of her life and that the past had gone and she had a great future ahead. She'd spent a lot of time and effort planning this holiday, not to mention her hard-earned cash; it wasn't a cheap week.

I'm buggered if I'm going to let him spoil it!

Taking one final deep breath she remembered that Nicole, the younger of the two women who had been on her flight from Gatwick, had said she'd be round the pool if either she or Sarah wanted to join her. Nicole was a good seven or eight years younger than Estelle but she seemed nice enough. And it had been kind of her to suggest it. She slipped her feet into her flip-flops and pulled back the curtain. She looked down to the pool and she could see Nicole, unmistakeable because of her fabulous figure and waist-length red hair neatly plaited over one shoulder, making herself comfortable on a sun-lounger.

Hmm. I'll look like a bloody whale next to her.

For a moment she hesitated.

Oh, sod it!

Grabbing her ready-prepared beach bag, Estelle set her shoulders determinedly and made her way down to the pool.

✦ ✦ ✦

'CAN I GET that for you?'

Liz glared at the older man who had sidled up and was standing next to her at the beach bar.

'Oh, it's not a chat-up line, love. I'm part of the Travel Together group, too. You're on the tennis holiday?'

'Well I am, actually. How did you know? Do I look like a tennis player? Or a typical single?'

'Course not! And after all, what's a typical single? We come in all shapes and sizes I reckon. No, I saw the porter taking you up to your room earlier and I noticed the label on your suitcase.'

'Hmm. Bright orange isn't really discreet, is it?'

'I'm Ron, by the way.' He held out his hand.

'Liz.' She shook it.

'So, can I get your drink?'

'A G and T, please.'

'Por favor!' Ron called down the bar. *'Una ginebra con tónica*

y una cerveza.'

'Oh, you speak Spanish.'

'Not really. Just food and drink. I've been coming to Spain for a long time and I've picked it up here and there.'

He signed the bill the barman offered him and then picked up both drinks.

'Shall we?'

He signalled a nearby table that had a large parasol over half of it.

'Which do you prefer, sun or shade?'

'Oh, sun! We don't get enough of it at home do we? And even after all the talk about it being the warmest summer in a long time, I'm still eager for more,' Liz said. 'Cheers!'

'Cheers!' Ron clinked his glass against hers.

'It looks like you're a sun-worshipper, too, Ron. You're very brown.'

'Oh, I spend all my time outside, me. I love my garden and when I'm not tending to it, you know, weeding and dead-heading and all that, like, then I'm sitting in it. I'm out there all day. And when I'm not there I'm down the tennis club.'

'So you're a good player then?'

'Not bad. I coach youngsters.'

'Really?'

'Yes. I took early retirement, like. I was in the fire brigade for thirty years. When there was all them cut backs a few years ago I was offered redundancy, well we all was, so I took it.'

'I don't blame you.'

'I'd had enough really. The pay-off wasn't bad. Enough for me to live on so I walked.'

'I take it you're from London?'

'I am a true Cockney. Born within the sound of Bow Bells. But I've lived most of me life in Essex. Rochford. You from up North?'

'Lincolnshire. Grantham.'

'Oh, blimey! Maggie Thatcher's town.' He creased his face in disapproval.

'Yep!' Liz wasn't going to get drawn on politics.

'So where'd you fly from then?'

'East Midlands. It's only just over thirty miles from me. Nice and handy.'

'Yes it good there's lots of local airports flying here now, in't there? I came from Southend. Five minutes in a taxi cos the roads was empty at that time of the morning. Beats having to go to Stansted. Or all the way to Gatwick. I bloody hate Gatwick.'

'Have you been on a Travel Together holiday before?'

'Yes. Five. Cuba, Thailand, Corfu, Marbella and Majorca. Corfu and Majorca was both tennis holidays.'

'Oh, you're a keen tennis player. I'm not really.'

'So what you doing 'ere then?'

'Well, what I mean is I'm keen but not that good,' she laughed. 'I am a member of our local club, more for the social side than anything else. One of my clients recommended I join and then someone at the club said they'd done a couple of single tennis holidays and they were good. So here I am.'

'What do you do for a living then?'

'I'm a mobile hairdresser and beautician.'

'Oh, that's nice.'

Ron thought that explained why she had so much make-up on in the sunshine.

'I like working for myself. And it was handy when my boys were all small.'

'They with their dad this week?'

'No!' Liz burst out laughing. 'They wouldn't know him if he stood in front of them. He walked out when they were five, three and six months. They're twenty-four, twenty-two and nineteen now.'

'You don't look old enough.' Ron knew it was a cliche but he couldn't help himself. She barely looked forty.

'Oh, thanks. And you?'

'Oh, I lost my wife a few years back.'

'I'm sorry to hear that. Can I get you another beer? What did you call it?'

'Cerveza. Una cerveza.'

'Una cerveza,' Liz repeated. '*Una cerveza* coming up, Ron!'

✦ ✦ ✦

AT HALF-PAST SEVEN Eve went into the bar to check the barman had remembered to lay out the drinks in the small lounge at the far end of the lounge area. She found him chatting to a tall, broad-shouldered, swarthy man in his early thirties.

'You must be Eve,' he said, stepping towards her and offering his hand.

Eve felt herself go momentarily weak as the dark brown eyes looked into hers and he flashed her a film-star smile.

'I am Jesus, the tennis pro.'

So that's how you say it, Hey-Zus.

She was glad she hadn't shown herself up and said Jesus with English pronunciation.

'And I am Juanca,' the barman said, also shaking her hand.

Did he say "wanker"?

The two men accompanied her into the small lounge

where chairs were set out and a large table at one end held ice buckets with beers and white wine. Jugs of orange juice and water and bottles of red stood next to them.

'Everything is here. I will stay to serve the drinks for you,' Juanca said laying out the glasses.

'Thank you.'

'So, I will tell them about the tennis clinics and the tournament set up I have arranged,' Jesus explained. 'Basically it will be clinics in the morning and tournament in the afternoons. Sometimes people prefer to play in the evening as it is cooler but other people like the evening for going out.'

'Well you've looked after lots of our groups so you know how it works. No rules. People can take part or not as they wish.'

'Yes, I have looked after nine Travel Together groups but always with Jenny. Why isn't she here this time?'

'She's left the company,' Eve said. 'Oh, hello! Come on in!'

She was pleased to see some of the group arriving cutting short Jesus's questions. She had no intention of spending the week discussing Jenny, although she understood why people would be curious as they were used to working with her.

'Please let our friend here know what you would like to drink and then take a seat.'

Eve hated not using people's names but she needed to ask the barman his name again when nobody else was around. She glanced over her list checking who the five people were who'd just come in.

The short, dark, slim woman was Jackie Nesbitt; the older, suntanned guy with the sparkling blue eyes was Ron Williams; the fair, freckly tall girl was Katrina Andrews; the bald, Asian guy was Charanjit Chaudray – although he'd told Eve at the airport that he'd always been called Charlie; and the mixed-race athletic type was Alex Chandler.

Jackie, Ron, Katrina, Charlie and Alex. Jackie, Ron, Katrina, Charlie and Alex.

She wasn't usually this nervous about names but that was because she was used to spending time with the group at Heathrow or Gatwick and then flying with them to the resort. Today she'd only met them for a couple of minutes before putting them into taxis as they'd come in from various UK regional airports.

Five women arrived together. A timid woman of about forty with long, straight brown hair who wore glasses and no make-up – Rosalind Maguire; a heavily made-up woman with short highlighted hair – Liz Wilkinson; a curvy thirty-year-old with a platinum blonde crop and heavy eyeliner – Estelle Oliver; the youngest member of the group, a lithe, leggy redhead with a plait that reached to her waist – Nicole Davies; and a confident woman in her mid-thirties wearing a short skirt and very high heeled mules – Sarah Woodford.

Rosalind, Liz, Estelle, Nicole and Sarah. Rosalind, Liz, Estelle, Nicole and Sarah.

'Well, this makes a change! The men usually outnumber the women on tennis holidays,' Charlie said.

'Not everyone's here yet. But you're right. We've got ten women and nine men.'

The five women joined the others and began chatting and introducing themselves.

'Good evening.'

A muscular redheaded guy strode into the room. No more than five-foot ten, but he exuded confidence and charisma which made him seem much taller.

Sean Bishop from the Stansted flight.

'Hello, Sean. Please take a drink.'

Heeding Eve's invitation Sean stopped and took a glass of red from Juanca.

'Well, hello, Sean,' Sarah said making a couple of the women grin in appreciation.

Eve glanced at her watch. It was ten to eight so the group of friends were already late. She wondered if they might not come. She'd give them a couple more minutes and then she'd start the meeting. Everyone else had managed to get there on time.

Suddenly there was loud laughter and shouting from the main bar and the missing eight tumbled in. Well, seven of them did. Bloodshot Eyes was missing.

'We're here! We're here! Couldn't find you. Oh nice one, mate!' James Spicer, who seemed to be the leader of the group within a group, turned and took a beer from the barman. 'Leggo's not coming,' he said to Eve. 'He's already wrecked. Couldn't get him outta his room.'

'Leggo?'

'Adrian Legg. Only we call him Leggo. We've all got nicknames.' He pointed round his group of friends as he spoke. 'I'm Spizz, Mike's Cookie, John's Banksy, Ben's Jonesy, Amy's Thommo, Fiona's Fee and Leticia's Titty for obvious reasons.' He leered at Leticia's very large bust. For a moment Eve did wonder how she managed to play tennis with such a magnificent bosom.

'How very grown up,' Sarah muttered to Jackie, loudly enough for almost everyone else to hear. She flicked her long brown hair with its expensive caramel highlights over her shoulder as she raised her eyebrows.

The seven late-comers took their seats and Eve began by introducing herself and Jesus.

'Jesus will take care off all things tennis and I'll do everything else. I've prepared a list of things to do outside of tennis, so, if you want to go on a boat trip or over to the West Coast to see the famous sunset and perhaps spend the evening in San Antonio then I can sort it out for you. A night trip into Ibiza Town is well worth doing, too. Or to Punta Arabi on Wednesday to the Hippy Market. Anyway, if you tick what you fancy and then I'll put a programme together so that nobody has to go anywhere on their own if they don't want to. Let me have the forms back at breakfast tomorrow, please.'

There was a momentary distraction as Juanca clanged two ice-buckets together as he gathered his stuff together.

'Sorry' he mouthed to Eve.

'You didn't tell us who he is,' Fee accused.

'Oh, she's eyeing up the local talent already!' Spizz said.

Shit! What am I going to say?

Eve gulped. Sensing her unease Jesus jumped in.

'This is Juanca, our barman.'

'Ha! Ha! Ha! The barman's a wanker!' Jonesy shouted.

'Oh, how droll! I bet he's never heard that before,' Sarah said.

'His name is Juan Carlos. We say Juanca for short but if you have a problem with pronouncing that just call him Juan,' Jesus continued.

'Ha ha! Wanker!' Jonesy repeated.

'God! It's like being back in the fourth-form,' Sarah muttered loudly. Several people rolled their eyes in agreement with her.

'Now, just a few general things before I let Jesus talk to you about the week's tennis,' Eve jumped back in not wanting to lose control of the meeting. 'Our holiday is breakfast only so we will be going out to eat in the evening. Breakfast is from seven o'clock until half-past ten in the main dining-room, which is on the left as you leave the bar area on the way to the terrace and the pool. Anyone who wants to come along with me to dinner should be in the bar at half-past seven or in reception at eight o'clock each evening. There are several good restaurants within walking distance and details about them is on the other side of the trips sheet I just gave you.'

'Erm, can I just ask about vegan options?' Katrina said.

'There'll be options for you everywhere I should imagine,' Eve said. 'Vegetarianism is hugely popular here.'

'But I'm a vegan…'

'That won't be a problem either,' Jesus interjected. 'Most restaurants offer vegan dishes. We even have some vegan restaurants.'

'Thanks,' Katrina beamed. 'Sorry to interrupt.'

'Not at all,' Eve said with a smile before turning back to address the whole group. 'Those of you who choose to play tennis in the evening can get a meal in the hotel dining-room until ten and the snack bar up until eleven o'clock. There's no pressure on anyone to do anything. It's your holiday so if you want to take part in the full tennis programme you can and if you want to have a break and come out with the group in the evening then you can choose to do that.'

'What about clubs? You haven't mentioned anything about clubbing?' Spizz interrupted.

'Come and talk to me about the type of club you want to go to and we'll sort something out for you,' Eve said. 'Perhaps if we go over to San An to Sunset Strip we can combine a music bar or club…'

'Oh! Groovy!' Spizz said, his sarcasm heavy. 'I was thinking more like *Es Paradis* or *Ushuaia*. They're supposed to be top places.'

'*Es Paradis* is a fairly young crowd but it depends very

much who's headlining. Let me make some enquiries and I'll get back to you.'

Eve chose to assume his raised eyebrows and eye rolls were a sign of consent.

'So, if we can just return to tonight, which is the exception because dinner is included as it's our first night in the hotel's restaurant and our table is booked for half-past eight. So, mindful that time's moving on I'm going to hand you over to Jesus to tell you all about the tennis.'

She gave an inward sigh of relief as she sat down and Jesus took over and talked to the group about the tennis programme he had arranged for them. He spoke clear, fluent, flawless English; only his slight accent gave him away as a non-native English speaker. It became clear, too, as he went on that he was highly experienced at running tennis holidays. Eve was pleased about that. It meant she could take her foot off the pedal a bit. Of course, she had to be around all day while they were playing, but it was good to be able to share some of the responsibility. She hoped some of the group would want to go out and about on the island as she was keen to see it again after such a long time.

Her first holiday to Ibiza had been in 1984 with her ex-husband. They had stayed in the Hotel Nautilus, a beautiful four-star hotel on San Antonio Bay and had had a wonderful time. It had been turned into an apartment block several years ago, which Eve thought was a shame. Her last trip to the island had been in 1999 with a Travel Together group and they'd stayed up in Portinatx. It hadn't been a roaring success as at that time Portinatx was a bit isolated. Now, of course, there were ring roads and underpasses and dual carriageways to almost every corner of the tiny island. Their hotel, the Dunas Blancas, was just outside Cala Llonga on the way to Santa Eulalia and it was easy to get everywhere from there.

No complaints of cabin fever this time!

Her thoughts strayed for a moment and she wondered how Michael and Natalie had spent the day. On the beach probably as Felicity was fascinated by sand and their holiday villa was beachside at Cala Tarida. She hoped she might get a few hours off to see them again before they left on Tuesday. And if she didn't, well, she'd be home at the end of the week. She smiled to herself; there was something to be said for a short-haul week away.

✦ ✦ ✦

ESTELLE WAS GLAD that Nicole was sitting next to her at dinner and that the ice had been broken when they had spent a little time together at the pool earlier. At least Estelle was friendly which was more than could be said for Leticia, Fiona and Amy, or Titty, Fee and Thommo as they seemed to be called. Estelle's attempts at conversation had been either ignored or given curt answers. And she'd noticed that every time any of the men had spoken to her or Nicole one of the women had jumped straight in and changed the subject. She was feeling decidedly uncomfortable as they shared in-jokes and reminisced about their previous tennis holidays and she had already made up her mind to give them a wide berth from now on.

'Is it me or are we being elbowed out?' Nicole whispered to her.

'No, it's not you. I think this is the first and the last time I sit with them,' Estelle whispered back.

'Me, too!'

The men on the table roared with laughter as Cookie reminded them of an incident in Rhodes involving Titty, a wet t-shirt and a thong. She retaliated by telling a story of his flatulence.

Estelle and Nicole rolled their eyes in unison and looked with envy at the other table where the rest of the group were enjoying each other's company, chatting animatedly.

'I bet they'll turn out to be teachers,' Charlie said indicating the loud laughter and much table banging going on beside them.

'It wouldn't surprise me,' Sarah shook her head. 'There were several on the other Travel Together holiday I did, to Mauritius. But what's with all the nicknames? Middle-aged men calling each other Jonesy and Spizz. And calling her Titty!' Her voice was full of derision. 'I suppose if you hang around all day with twelve-year-olds it's bound to rub off.'

'So how come you aren't working for Rafa in Manacor?' Sean asked Jesus referring to the academy the tennis star ran.

'Two reasons: one, I prefer not to coach children.'

'But there are adult sessions…'

'There are. That's true. But I think the coaches have to work with children, the summer schools and so on, as well as adults. And that isn't for me.' Jesus grinned and shook his head.

'And the second reason?'

'I'm very happy living and working here in Ibiza.'

'Have you been here long?'

'On the island for ten years and working as a coach for seven.'

'Do you only work here at the Dunas Blancas?'

'No. I coach at two tennis clubs and I also offer coaching through several concierge agencies.'

Eve grinned to herself. She was usually the one facing a barrage of personal questions on the first night. Having Jesus with them meant the heat was off her.

'Did you used to play tennis professionally?' Sarah asked Jesus.

'No. I always loved tennis but I lacked the dedication necessary to make a living as a player. And I suffered a knee injury playing football when I was thirteen; it left me with a dodgy kneecap.'

'Do you play any other sports?'

'I like kayaking and SUP.'

'What's that?'

'Stand up paddle. It's quite big here.'

'I'm surprised Travel Together haven't sorted out any tennis holidays to Nadal's Academy,' Sean said, bringing Eve into their conversation. 'I'd have thought you'd have had loads of people up for that.'

'Price would probably be a factor,' Eve said.

'Yes. It is expensive because you are getting top coaching,' Jesus agreed. 'And the hotel itself is five star.'

'And besides, it attracts lots of couples and youngsters. It might not suit a singles' group,' Eve added. 'I imagine the cost would be quite prohibitive, too.'

'The level of play is very high there,' Jesus continued. 'There are no beginners. Everyone can play reasonably well to start with. And they concentrate a lot on fitness training, too, not just improving technique. The gym facilities are state-of-the-art.'

'Manacor's miles from anywhere,' Charlie said, joining in. 'I went and had a look round last year. The Academy's got a museum and gift shop and you can go inside as a day visitor. But if you were staying there you'd need to get out and about.'

'Yes, it's a beautiful place but you're right about that,' Jesus said.

'Did you see Rafa?' Katrina asked.

'No. I saw Uncle Toni, though,' Charlie beamed.

'I just love Rafa,' Katrina said.

'Were you on the Travel Together tennis holiday in Majorca?' Ron asked Charlie.

'Yes. The September one.'

'I went in June. It was great, I thoroughly enjoyed myself. And we had an afternoon visiting the Academy, too. You can say what you like about Nadal, but he's got a good business head on his shoulders.' Ron nodded his head in approval.

'And he's opening up Academies worldwide,' Jesus told them. 'Mexico, Greece…'

'The world's his lobster,' Ron chuckled at his own joke.

'He's just so likeable,' Rosalind said. 'He's always generous in victory and humble in defeat.'

'I just wish he'd sort out his underpants,' Liz said, making them laugh. 'Get a pair that fits properly!'

'It's part of his OCD,' Sean said. 'He lines up his bottles…'

'Mansplaining!' Sarah called. 'She was actually joking, Sean'

A bright red flush quickly spread from Sean's neck to the roots of his hair.

'I do think he's a brilliant player but I get put off by all the preparation before every point,' Liz added, not wanting Sean to feel uncomfortable.

'So, how was dinner?' Eve asked changing the subject.

'That was pretty good!'

Ron licked his lips in appreciation at the *paella* he'd just finished.

'There's nowhere like Spain for a proper *paella*, I always say,' Ron agreed. 'I've tried it in lotsa Spanish restaurants in England but it's never the same, is it? No, when it comes to *paella* the Spanish know their onions!'

'I can't stand the ready meal ones. They always put bloody chorizo in it,' Sarah joined in. 'They put chorizo in everything vaguely Spanish,' she wailed. 'And I hate it.'

'In Spain we only put chorizo in dishes like *potaje:* chick-pea stew. Usually we eat it in small pieces as a tapa. Or sometimes in a sandwich,' Jesus said.

'I knew it!' Sarah grinned triumphantly.

'Don't you call it a *bocadillo*?' Ron asked him.

'Yes, we do. *Hablas español?*'

'I have a go,' Ron chuckled. 'With varying success! But I know what a *bocadillo* is. It's a roll, isn't it?'

'Yes. A bread roll with filling. Without filling it's a *panecillo.*'

'Can I ask you something, Jesus? What's the standard of tennis going to be like this week?'

'Good, I hope! This group is Improvers, so I think everyone has a good, basic game and wants to get better.'

'You don't look very convinced, Liz,' Alex said, smiling across the table at her.

'I just don't want to be shown up.'

'None of us do,' he agreed. 'Do you play much?'

'Well, I go to a local club. One of my clients recommended it. I only started last year but I enjoy it.'

'I used to go to a club but I found it a bit elitist and snobby to be honest. I usually just play with a few mates in the evenings now. During the summer months. Over the local park.'

'I find tennis clubs to be very competitive,' Charlie joined in. 'People play as if their lives depend on it. At least they do at mine.'

'Shouldn't sport be competitive?' Liz raised a thick, well-groomed eyebrow.

'Yes. But not to the exclusion of having fun and enjoying the game.'

'I think it can be both,' Katrina asserted. 'My club has a required standard of play for membership.'

'Well, I can understand that,' Alex said. 'But it's one of the reasons I prefer playing over the park! And what you're really saying is, you're going to so enjoy thrashing the rest of us. Probably me, at any rate.'

Katrina laughed.

'I'm really not that good,' she said.

'Where are you from?' Charlie asked her. 'I mean, I take it you're a Scot. From your accent.'

'Edinburgh. Born and bred. My mum runs a large nursing and residential home in the city and I work for her. You?'

'I live in Bradford. There's a surprise, eh? An Asian who lives in Bradford!'

'Well, I knew it was Yorkshire somewhere. From *your* accent. I take it Charlie isn't your actual name?'

'It's Charanjit. Charanjit Chaudray. My parents had a thing about alliteration.'

Katrina chuckled.

'But I've always answered to Charlie. We had an elderly neighbour who was deaf. Lovely old girl she was. When I was born she thought my dad said they'd named me Charlie Jim and that's what she always called me. Nobody liked to correct her and the name stuck,' he laughed.

'Where do you think everyone else is from?'

Charlie and Katrina looked round the table.

'I'd say Ron is a Londoner.'

'You taking my name in vain down there?' Ron asked overhearing them.

'We're just guessing you're from London,' Katrina

explained.

'And you guessed right! Born within the sound of Bow Bells,' he announced proudly.

'And I know Jackie's from near me because we came on the same flight,' Charlie continued.

'Yes. I'm from Pudsey,' Jackie smiled. 'Leeds. A Yorkshire lass.'

'Liz is from Maggie Thatcher's neck of the woods,' Ron volunteered.

'What? Finchley?' Alex asked, winking at her.

'No. Grantham,' Ron explained, Alex's humour going over his head.

'Where are you from, Rosalind?' Alex asked, bringing the softly-spoken woman who hadn't said much into the conversation.

'Dunstable.'

'Oh, where Jesus was born,' Sarah and Alex giggled together.

'What?'

Rosalind was confused.

'The Vicar of Dibley,' Sarah said, by way of explanation.

'You're not far from me, then,' Alex said. 'I live in Luton.'

'That's really close by,' Rosalind agreed.

'What about you, Sarah?' Charlie asked. 'You sound Southern to me.'

'Surrey. I live in Reigate and work in Dorking.'

'Nice and handy for Gatwick,' Eve said.

'Sean?'

'Not far from Ipswich.'

'Is that Norfolk?' Jackie asked.

'Suffolk.'

'And where are you from, Eve? Are you a Southerner,

too?' Charlie's questions continued around the table.

'I live in Essex but I'm not originally from there.'

'Essex? I live in Essex. Rochford,' Ron said, happy he'd found a bond with the tour manager. 'Been there thirty years.'

'Horndon-on-the-Hill.'

'That sounds posh,' Charlie said.

'And alliterative,' Sarah added, winking at him. He smiled.

'So, are you from somewhere else in the South?' Katrina asked.

'Yes.'

'Kent?'

'Surrey?'

'Further south.' Eve gave them a clue.

'Cornwall?'

Eve grinned and shook her head at the suggestions coming at her from all around the table.

'The Isle of Wight,'

'Nice try, Jackie. But still not right.'

'The Channel Islands?'

'Devon.'

'Somerset.'

'Nope.'

'There's nowhere else!' Liz said. 'Unless you're French.'

Eve's giggled.

'Getting warmer.'

'You're French?' Alex's eyes were wide in disbelief.

'Not French.'

'From Jersey?'

'We give in!' Liz said holding up her hands.

'I'm Greek.'

'Never!'

'Oh yes, I am. I was born and brought up on Corfu until I was almost eighteen.'

'You don't look Greek.'

'Because I'm not dark, Ron?'

'Well, yes. I always think of Greeks as being dark. Like the Spanish.'

'Not really. If we are dark it's because of the Turkish influence. In Greece, especially Corfu, you find many fair-headed people like me. And my skin is Mediterranean, isn't it?'

Everyone studied Eve's olive complexion and arms.

'Hmm. You just look suntanned.' Ron wasn't convinced.

'So, is your name really Eve? It doesn't sound very Greek,' Jackie said.

'My full name is Paraskevi. It's not terribly common. It was my father's godmother's name and that's how I was given it. It actually means Friday,' she said. 'My family shortened it to Evi and then once I was in England it became Eve. And I'm on my British passport as Eve.'

'But you've no accent at all.' Jackie insisted, still unwilling to believe it.

'I've spent more time out of Greece than in it, of course. And I think if you learn a foreign language before you're twenty then you have the best chance of losing your accent. Once you get into your twenties then its more difficult. Wouldn't you agree, Jesus?'

'Certainly. I learned English from my mother. She is Scottish, from Ayrshire.'

'I can't really hear a Scottish accent in your speech,' Katrina said. 'Although your English is perfect.'

'My mother's accent is not very pronounced. She moved around as a small child because her father was in the army so I was never really exposed to it.'

'I wonder where the others are from,' Liz said, looking at the other table where Estelle and Nicole were also sitting. 'They call themselves The A Team apparently.' Her sigh and shake of the head spoke volumes about her view on that.

'Somewhere in the Midlands, I'd say,' Charlie ventured. 'They sound like it at any rate.'

'They did come in on the Birmingham flight so you're probably right,' Eve said.

'Where are you all from?' Sean called across to them. 'The same place?'

'Birmingham. Rowley Regis. Well, that's where we all go to the same tennis club.'

'Imagine coming away on a singles' holiday with all your mates.' Sarah screwed up her nose. 'Where's the fun in that?'

'I suppose some people like the security of being with those they already know,' Katrina said.

'We're not!' Nicole said, wagging her finger from side to side indicating herself and Estelle who was sitting beside her. 'We're both from Surrey.'

'Are you mates as well?' Alex asked.

'No. We only met today.'

'Well, I bet Estelle and Nicole have felt out of it,' Sarah spoke to those in earshot.

'The three of you make up the Surrey Sisterhood,' Sean joked.

'I don't know them,' Sarah said. 'Never seen them before. Have you always lived in Ipswich?'

'Since I came out.'

'You're gay!'

'What? No! Out of prison.'

Sarah burst out laughing.

'Yeah! Right!'

'You all right, love?' Ron asked Liz who was sitting quietly beside him.

'Yes, I am. They're a nice group, aren't they?'

'I told you. It's always the same. Arrive as strangers, leave as friends,' he said, beaming at her. 'Anyone for pudding?' He raised his voice. 'Come on! We can eat what we like all week,' he said, standing up. 'We're gonna burn it off on the courts.'

Desserts were selected and eaten and Eve asked both tables if they wanted to walk down to the nearby bars or stay in the hotel for the rest of the evening. Rosalind, Katrina, Jackie and Sarah opted to stay in the hotel and the others decided to stretch their legs.

'I'll see you in the morning at nine-thirty sharp on the courts,' Jesus said to Eve as they reached reception. 'Enjoy your evening!'

'Thanks, Jesus. You, too! No sign of Leggo then,' she said turning to Fee, Spizz and Jonesy who were standing next to her. 'Are you sure he's okay? Should we check on him?'

'No need. He'll be fine. He always get shit-faced on the first day,' Fee giggled.

'Last year in Mallorca he missed most of the tennis for the first couple of days,' Jonesy said, grinning. 'Totally out of it until about four in the afternoon, then he was up and straight at the beers.'

'Well, if you're sure.'

'Christ! Who's overdone the aftershave?' Spizz screwed up his nose as Ron, resplendent in his Ralph Lauren college green polo shirt and olive chinos, strolled up to join them. 'People of Ibiza! Lock up your grandmas!'

His group of friends burst out laughing and even through his suntan Eve saw Ron colour up. She couldn't help feeling there was something unpleasant about Spizz and his cronies.

'Sauvage, isn't it?' Eve asked him inhaling deeply. 'Hmm! I love it, Ron. It's classy.'

'Yes, there's something about a man who smells good,' Liz joined in, smiling at him, lifting his spirits.

Checking that everyone who'd said they were coming was with them Eve guided the group out through the gardens of the Dunas Blancas and along a short road towards the neon lights of Bar Mar Blau and El Rincón de Magdalena. Mar Blau had a large terrace overlooking the sea with a couple of empty tables. El Rincón de Magdalena was full; heaving. The terrace was packed and groups of people stood holding drinks and swaying to the music being brought to them by DJ Tomeu.

Eve realised that keeping the group together was going to be impossible. She elbowed her way to the bar then turned to see Estelle, Nicole, Alex, Ron, Charlie, Liz and Sean were right behind her. They got their drinks but the music was so loud conversation was impossible. After much gesturing and head nodding and miming they made their way back out to the crowded terrace where the music was a couple of decibels lower. Eve could see the other seven standing together on the far side.

Everyone was swaying and bobbing to *Mi Gente* all agreeing they liked a bit of *reggaeton.* The volume was still a bit high, making conversation difficult but it didn't seem to matter. Eve looked round and smiled. It never failed to amaze her how a group of strangers could feel at ease in each other's company after such a short time. Ron's words at dinner came back to her: "Arrive as strangers, leave as friends." She certainly hoped that would be the case this week.

Suddenly there was a roar of approval as the opening note of *Despacito* rang out. Without exception all the Spanish-speakers sang loudly along, the English-speakers joining in at the language change. Eve's group upped the dancing ante; Ron giving it all he had.

'Way to go, Ron the Raver!' Liz shouted, dancing up next to him.

Eve felt her phone buzz. Taking it from her bag she saw Michael was calling. Stepping away from the group she walked off the terrace and back down the road a bit away from the noise of the music before she answered.

'Hello, Handsome!'

'Hi! How's it all going. It sounds like you're somewhere lively.'

'At a bar where there's a DJ.'

'Good group?'

'Yes. So far! Eight of them are mates from the same tennis club and they're sticking together but the rest seem fine.'

'Well, fingers crossed for you.'

'Thanks. How was your day?'

'Great! We were on the beach the whole day and the Princess didn't want to leave. She kicked and screamed and caused a right fuss. I had to bring sand in her bucket to put on the veranda as a bribe.'

'The maids are gonna love you!'

'Well, I'll just have to up their tip!'

'Is she asleep?'

'Sound asleep. She was so tired she hardly ate any dinner.'

'Oh bless, her. All that fresh, sea air. Still at least you two get some time together.'

'Natalie's snoring happily!' Michael laughed. 'So it's me

with my book. We're meeting Dave and Penny, Frances and Eileen and Murray for lunch on the beach tomorrow.'

'Oh that should be good. Give them my love.'

'I will. Shame you can't join us.'

'You know what it's like; first full day…'

'I know.' There was a moment's pause. 'Have you heard anything from Melv?'

'I told you yesterday, not for a couple of weeks. Why?'

'I just wondered. I spoke to him just before we came away.'

'How was he?'

'Hmm. I'm not sure. He sounded a bit preoccupied. But it's difficult to tell with him; you know what he's like. He said Radley is improving. Seems to understand more.'

Eve thought about Radley and a wave of sadness washed over her. Melv's strapping son who had been at University in the States on an athletic scholarship was involved in a road traffic accident which had resulted in the amputation of his lower right leg and brain damage which left him with very limited speech and little movement and control of the rest of his body. There was light in his eyes which changed to frustration with increasing frequency. Eve's heart wept whenever she thought of him. She had only seen him once during her visits to Antigua.

'He doesn't want people seeing him like that,' Melv had told her, his voice breaking.

Melv's house had been made totally accessible for Radley's wheelchair and his needs thanks to the compensation pay-out from the accident, which also meant Radley had full-time care. His two, strong, gentle male nurses, Rowan and Hugo, took turns with Melv to care for him around the clock. They bathed him, fed him, took him for walks, engaged him in conversation and encouraged him to do the limited physiotherapy he could manage. There was also a female companion, Rosetta, who spent time with Radley when Melv was working. Radley's mother visited him on Sundays for a couple of hours. Apparently it caused her too much pain to see her son as he now was.

'For her, it's as if he'd died in the accident,' Melv had said to her one night as they sat in the hammock on his veranda listening to the frogs croaking, his voice full of bitterness towards his ex-wife.

Having given their son Michael up for adoption at birth Eve kept her mouth shut feeling she had no room to criticise another mother's actions. She took Melv's hand and raised it to her lips.

'You're both mother and father to him.'

'I have to be.'

Melv spent every moment he wasn't working at the Mango Tree Resort with his son. His visits to see Eve in England had stopped and their plans of marrying and being together had been put well and truly onto the back burner.

'I can't help thinking he's clutching at straws.' Michael's voice interrupted her thoughts. 'He's searching so hard for improvements he's making himself see them where they don't exist.'

'I think you're right.'

'I mean, Melv tries to stay positive but reading between the lines Radley will never be able to do much more than he's doing now.' Michael's tone was full of sadness. 'When's your next trip to Antigua?'

'I'm down to do an Antigua next month. Although to be honest, I might give it a miss for a while.'

Michael sighed. He had held high hopes that his parents would finally get together but he accepted it looked like that wasn't going to happen. At least not for the foreseeable future.

'But you're Travel Together's Ms Antigua! I can't believe you'd let another tour manager get their feet under the table. You've worked hard to make it one of the company's most successful holidays.'

'Sometimes you have to know when to let go,' Eve said wistfully. 'Well, give my love to Natalie and Felicity and if I can work something out I'll come and see you before Tuesday.'

'Okay, Eve. Enjoy the rest of your evening. We love you.'

'And I love you all, too.'

As Eve rejoined her clients she could see they were all enjoying themselves, chatting, taking selfies; the ice was well and truly broken. She was glad; it meant she could probably make an exit fairly soon. She stifled a yawn.

I just could be getting too old for all this.

Now in her early-fifties, Eve never considered herself as even middle-aged. But it had been a long day. She gave her watch a surreptitious glance. It was half-past eleven. She'd done a sixteen-hour day so far.

'Can I get you a drink, Eve?'

'No, thanks, Alex. It's kind of you but I was just thinking about making my way back to the hotel. Paperwork to do.' She fell back on the tour manager's perennial excuse for leaving.

'I owe you one, then.'

'Definitely.'

'The music's good but I think I need to sit down,' Estelle said, coming off the dance floor. 'These sandals are cutting into my toes. It's the first time I've worn them.'

'Wanna go to the other bar?' Nicole said, nodding her head towards the Mar Blau.

'Yeah. Let's drink up and go.'

She emptied her glass and turned to the others.

'We're going to the other bar so that we can sit down. They've got music, too, but it's not quite as loud,' she told the others, who all decided to stay put as they liked the atmosphere and volume of the music.

'I'm off,' Eve told them. 'You remember the way back to the hotel?'

'Straight down the road!' Ron said as he mopped his forehead, sweating from his energetic dance session with Liz and Estelle.

'Enjoy the rest of the evening! See you at breakfast!'

She crossed to the far side of the terrace to tell the others she was leaving.

'Here she is! Our Great Leader!'

Spizz threw an arm around her neck and pulled her to his sweaty chest. Without the smile leaving her face, Eve expertly twirled free from his clutches.

'Can't stand the pace? Some tour manager! Jenny's always last man standing.'

Bully for Jenny!

Thommo and Fee were downing shots, encouraged by Cookie and Banksy. Jonesy's eyes were unfocused. Titty rubbed her body against Spizz's.

'Dance with me,' she whined.

Without acknowledging her Spizz embraced her, his hand fondling one of her bountiful breasts. She ground herself a little harder to him.

'I'll see you at breakfast. And don't forget, Tennis Clinic starts at half-past nine sharp.' Eve was glad it was time for her to go.

'We'll be there!'

Still smiling she turned on her heel and made her way

back to the Hotel Dunas Blancas.

✦ ✦ ✦

'SHIRLEY BALLAS! THAT'S who you look like!' Sarah told Jackie. 'Except you're much younger.'

'A couple of people have said that.'

'Who?' Katrina asked.

'She's a judge on Strictly.'

'I don't watch it.'

'You don't watch Strictly?' Rosalind's eyes became huge behind her glasses. 'I love it. Never miss it. It means Christmas is on the way once that comes on the telly.'

Sarah was amazed at how a couple of rum and cokes had brought Rosalind out of her shell.

'I go to a cinema club on a Saturday night,' Katrina explained. 'You know. Old films. Black and white. Nineteen fifties stuff mainly.'

'You can always watch it on catch up,' Rosalind insisted. She took a sip of her drink. 'Well, we're certainly a mixed bunch. All brought together by our love of tennis,' she added.

'Well, I have to confess I can't believe I'm on a tennis holiday,' Jackie confided. 'I don't play much.'

'So why are you here then?' Sarah raised an eyebrow.

'Someone told me tennis and golf holidays are a good way to meet men,' Jackie grinned.

'Well, I think we've blown that theory out of the water,' Sarah retorted making the others laugh.

'Well, I am here for the tennis, too. I want to learn as much as possible to improve my game. Especially now I've seen Jesus,' she added winking.

'I enjoy my tennis but I only plan to dip in and out,'

Sarah said.

'Do you belong to a club?'

'I do. I belong to a tennis club and a hiking group. I usually go on walking holidays but I thought I'd give the tennis a go this time. But I want to do some sunbathing and relaxing, too. Not all tennis.'

'To be honest… I've never played,'Jackie confessed.

'What are you doing here then?' Katrina asked, pulling a face.

'I want to give my boyfriend a surprise,' Jackie said, draining her glass of *sangría* and signalling to a passing waiter for another one. 'I wasn't going to mention him as I wasn't sure if it was allowed to come if you had a boyfriend.'

'And who's going to stop you?' Sarah laughed.

'Well, it'll be a surprise when he finds out you're on a singles' holiday!' Katrina quipped. 'I take it he doesn't know you're here?'

'No. He's in Dubai on a business trip. He's a right good player and I want to be able to play well so I can join his tennis club. There's a minimum standard for membership apparently and I fall way below that at the moment. So I'm going to improve all I can this week. I want to be able to share his hobby.'

'Well, good for you!' Rosalind said encouragingly, even though she thought Jackie would hardly get to elite club entry in a week.

'Are you a club player?' Katrina asked her.

'Yes, I am. I always played tennis as a teenager and then at university. It gets me out in the fresh air. I spend all day cooped up inside teaching piano.'

'I'd love to be able to play an instrument,' Jackie said. 'Play an instrument and speak a foreign language. Oh, *gracias*.' She smiled at the waiter who placed another large glass of sangría before her.

'Sounds like you're already on your way,' Sarah quipped.

She took another sip of her *Rioja*, then filled Katrina's glass and her own, emptying the bottle in the process.

'I willna make the clinic in the morning, never mind breakfast,' Katrina said, the drink strengthening her Edinburgh lilt. 'It's good stuff though! Cheers!'

'Cheers!'

'Salud!' Jackie couldn't resist.

'Oh! Poo! Gross!' Katrina waved a hand in front of her face. 'That must have been him!' She pointed at Leggo's disappearing back not knowing he was one of the Travel Together group.

'What a pig!' Sarah called loudly at the tall figure striding towards the foyer. 'I thought I heard him fart as he walked by.'

'Yeuk! God knows what he's eaten.' Jackie pinched her nostrils together. 'He looks like Mr Bean.'

'He smells like them, too!' Katrina said, making them laugh.

Sarah sat back in her chair, enjoying the company of the other three giggling women while marvelling at how diverse they were and how different from her usual companions. She considered herself a Man's Woman rather than a Woman's Woman. She could count on the fingers of one hand the close female friends she'd had during her almost forty-one years on Earth. Although, she didn't have that many close male friends either. Lots of lovers. But that wasn't the same thing.

A piano teacher, a carer and a veterinary nurse. Who would have thought it?

They were a pleasant enough band to spend the next seven days with; she didn't have to become life-long besties with them. Her thoughts drifted to the men in the group. She liked the look of Alex, the one from Luton. She couldn't remember what he did for a living. Perhaps he hadn't told her. She liked Charlie's sense of humour but at 5' 10" in her heels – she rarely wore flats – she'd tower over him by at least five inches. And then there was the hunky ginger one. Sean? She would't mind a quick fling with him if it was on the cards. He had a sense of humour and looked like he did something physical, too. She'd have to make it her business to find out what.

✦ ✦ ✦

'HE ENJOYS HIMSELF,' Charlie observed as he watched Ron giving it his all on the dance floor with Liz. 'He's got enough energy for all of us.'

'Yes, but what'll he be like in the morning?' Alex asked. 'Probably burn himself out and won't turn up for the tennis.'

'Nice to see an old fella enjoying himself, though. I hope I'll be like that when I'm his age.' Charlie took another sip of his beer.

'How old do you reckon he is?' Sean asked. 'He's gotta be over sixty, surely.'

'And the rest! I'd say he's probably late sixties.'

'Still, he's the only one of us who's got a woman on the dance floor,' Charlie laughed.

'Well, it's the first night. It takes a while to get to know people,' Sean said. 'You can't rush in.'

'Well, Ron has!'

'Yes, but with Liz.'

'What's wrong with Liz?' Charlie asked.

'Nothing if you like that sort of thing,' Sean said. 'She isn't that young, either. What do you reckon? Mid-forties?'

'Gotta be,' Alex agreed. 'I take it she's not on your shortlist then?' He grinned at Sean.

'Not my type really, mate. I mean, her body's not bad. But a bit too much makeup. It'll be interesting to see if she turns up to play tennis with all that caked on her face.'

'Who you eyeing up then?' Charlie asked them as he signalled to the barman for another round of drinks.

'I'm not eyeing up anyone!'

Charlie thought Sean was a bit defensive.

'The young redhead, the one with the long plait. She looks alright,' Sean admitted. 'Nicole, is it? Or Estelle's not bad. I like a blonde. That Titty…'

'Well, you've got no chance there, mate. She's obviously with Spizz.'

The three men looked across the dance floor to the far side of the terrace where Titty was draped around Spizz's neck.

'Sarah's a bit classy,' Alex said. 'She looks a bit aloof but she's alright.'

'And she's got a great figure,' Sean agreed.

'And you? Seen anyone you fancy?' Alex asked Charlie.

'Me? I'm here for the tennis, pal,' he chuckled. 'Cheers!'

✦ ✦ ✦

CLIMBING INTO BED Eve thought of Melv. He had been on the periphery of her thoughts since hearing *Their Song* at the wedding the previous day. It was a strange coincidence that Eileen and Murray had chosen it for their first dance. And Michael's earlier questions and chat about him had brought him once again centre stage in her thoughts.

Her mind, as it often did when she was tired, went into overdrive taking her back more than thirty years to their courtship and the hours they'd spent in each others' arms in Melv's tiny student bedsit with Gladys Knight on repeat. Just remembering the song gave her a thrill; it brought back a young Melv – handsome, strong, gentle and kind – and he was still all of those things. The touches of grey in his beard and hair just added to his attraction as far as she was concerned. And for a few moments she allowed herself to acknowledge that she missed him.

Her head whirled. Melv: the love of her life. Melv; divorced. Melv; more than four thousand miles away across the Atlantic Ocean in Antigua, caring for his disabled son. Melv; the man she'd lied to. For a second time.

Not lied exactly…

She missed him. She opened up her phone and scrolled through her photos. She studied his face, losing herself for a moment in the deep, dark pools that were his eyes. She knew every hair on his head and every inch of his body.

She thought about ringing him. Not so long ago they'd spoken every day they were apart regardless of where she was in the world. She longed to hear his voice but didn't know what she would say to him. Things had changed since Radley's accident and it had been on her last Travel Together trip to Antigua some five weeks earlier when she had realised just how much.

Eve hadn't gone to Melv's place; he came to her room on four nights but fell asleep in her arms within minutes on three of them, exhausted and drained by caring for his son and running the Mango Tree Resort. One day he had taken her out to Dickenson Bay for lunch. Conversation between them had been somewhat stilted and had petered out; the silences were awkward no longer the comfortable pauses of two people at ease in each others' company. She was unsure how much of that was down to her.

He'd said he'd take her out on the boat. On other visits they had shared some magical moments she had hoped they would go to their own special little spot at Five Islands and picnic again but they didn't. His beloved boat, the scene of so many happy hours spent together, bobbed in Jolly Harbour and their much-discussed plans for finally being together floated away on the tide.

Make plans and hear God laugh.

Her mother's words came into her head.

'You were so right, *Manamou*,' she said.

Feeling a sudden urge to hear Melv's voice she picked up her phone and WhatsApped him, her mind running on the time difference. It was 6pm in Antigua, a good time to get him. But all she heard was the solitary ring of his phone. Melv didn't pick up. Her disappointment surprised her. She hung up and threw the phone on the bedside cabinet in frustration. She gave a huge sigh. He could be anywhere, doing anything. He'd call back once he'd seen her missed call. Picking up the offending phone she checked her alarm was on before turning out the light.

✦ ✦ ✦

LIZ FINISHED HER rigorous, nightly cleansing routine and studied her reflection in the x8 magnifying mirror, tweezers at the ready to pluck out any stray hair that might have dared to pop its head through her skin in the last few hours.

Not bad for 42…

She knew people often pondered what she must look like without her make up on, but the answer was: Not very different at all! Her brows and lips were tattooed, as was her midnight-black eyeliner. All that changed was the tone of her blushed cheeks and her complexion and even that was remarkably blemish-free once her heavy foundation was off. She'd always kept her face out of the sun and a total absence of wrinkles was her reward.

She stretched her chin forward while smiling upwards and spent the next five minutes gurning and grinning doing her facial yoga. Then, with one final look through the curtains at the beautiful pool area and bright, starry sky above her, she climbed into bed. She'd decided to leave the curtains open so that she would wake up to this wonderful view as it got light. She didn't want to oversleep on her first morning.

She pondered on the fact she'd enjoyed her first day, and much of that had been down to Ron. He'd been good company; he'd made her laugh, was an accomplished dancer and he'd behaved like an absolute gentleman. He'd seen her right to her door but hadn't so much as tried to give her a peck on the cheek. She liked that.

'Night, night, love,' he'd said. 'See you bright and early for breakfast and tennis. Sleep well!'

And with that he'd strolled off down the corridor humming quietly to himself.

Yes, she liked that. And she liked Ron.

✦ ✦ ✦

I ENJOYED MYSELF!

Estelle smiled and wrapped her arms around the pillow as she snuggled down into the bed, getting comfortable. She liked Nicole and was glad she'd made the effort to go down to the pool with her that afternoon. The two of them had got on like a house on fire, probably because it was the first singles' holiday for both of them. Most of the group seemed nice but it felt good to have a mate. She hadn't told Nicole the full story of Joe and his treachery with Marie; she'd simply said she'd broken up with a long-term partner two years earlier. Nicole had been sympathetic. She'd started to say something about her boyfriend dying in a terrible accident but then she'd been interrupted. Still there was plenty of time to find out about Nicole and everyone else. She felt a little bit apprehensive about the tennis and hoped she wouldn't show herself up. She whispered a prayer that she'd done the right thing in coming on this holiday.

Oh well. Worse case scenario I can always be the ball girl!

✦ ✦ ✦

ROSALIND'S HEAD WAS slowly spinning. She kicked her sandals off and collapsed onto the bed, causing the spinning to speed up. The bedspread felt cool against her sweaty face and the air conditioning was wafting a welcome breeze over her limp body. Her glasses were digging into her temple but she couldn't bring herself to lift her hand up to take them off.

I'm pissed!

That surprised her because she hadn't had that much to drink. At least she didn't think she had. Her stomach lurched and for one awful minute she thought she might be sick. She rolled onto her back, arms outstretched, clutching the bed cover with her flexible pianist's fingers and breathed slowly and deeply. The nausea gradually subsided. In spite of not feeling too well, she thought she'd had an enjoyable evening all told. The other three women were great and she'd enjoyed their company. But something had happened or been said that had made her feel sad. In spite of not wanting anything to make her feel worse she couldn't stop herself re-running conversations. Her mind re-lived the latter part of the evening; her brain working overtime with erratic thoughts until she remembered what it was: Katrina ran a care home. Suddenly her body was shaking with sobs. From nowhere a wave of grief crashed down onto her and the anguish of her loss became a pain so acute that it cut her in two. She held her belly and curled up.

'Mother, I miss you,' she wailed.

✦ ✦ ✦

SEAN SAT ON his balcony enjoying a cigarette. He rarely smoked but tonight he just fancied one. A fag wasn't the only thing he fancied. The bulge in his boxers was getting bigger by the second. He thought about the women in the group again. Sarah, Estelle, Nicole… Any one of them would do. He also thought about the other men in the group, pondering their possible attraction to women. The group of eight would probably spend the whole week together.

Not much competition there.

And although that put Titty out of bounds, it also meant that five men would be out of the running.

Bunch of piss artists. They'd be rat-arsed most of the time. One of them hasn't even shown his face.

And although Alex and Charlie were nice enough blokes, he didn't really think they were competition for him where the women were concerned. Well, perhaps, Alex was. He was taller than Sean and just as athletic. He'd said he was a keen cyclist. And Sean conceded that his dark skin and height might be attractive to some women. But Charlie would struggle to get a woman.

His crotch gave a lurch, reminding him that so far he hadn't got one, either.

You've waited this long…

One more day wouldn't matter. He'd make sure that by this time tomorrow night his two year famine would be over. Except it hadn't been two years; his famine had been broken several times in the last three months by an escort. But that didn't count. Paying for it didn't count. He gave a sigh, followed by a groan. His frustration was getting the better of him. He stubbed out his cigarette and thrust his hand inside his boxers and indulged himself in some glorious relief that not even the drunken noise of Spizz and his group stumbling through the hotel gardens below could spoil or interrupt.

DAY TWO

✦

'YOU KNOW, YOU look everso familiar, Nicole,' Estelle said, sipping her coffee. 'I've been thinking that since I first saw you. I must have seen you around.'

'Well, as I said, I don't go to a tennis club. And I live and work in Brockham not Dorking itself.'

'And I live in Wotton. But perhaps I've seen you out and about when you're walking your dogs. I used to do quite a bit of driving.'

'Probably. Ah! My little babies! I wonder how they are without me.'

'How many do you walk?'

'Ten.'

'All at once?'

'No. First I take four gorgeous mongrels that belong to a couple with a smallish garden. Then an Alsatian and two cockerpoos that belong to an elderly lady who's riddled with arthritis and can't walk them herself. And finally three beagles, Benji, Bobby and Billy.'

'Imagine having four dogs when you haven't got much of a garden!'

'They're rescue dogs. All lovely. And so are Sybil and

Dennis their owners. They've got a lovely home with them. They just need a leg-stretch every morning and then Dennis takes them when he gets home from work at night.'

'So, not being rude, you make enough walking dogs to earn a living, then?'

'I get by. It's not marvellous money but I often get short-term jobs, you know, when people are going away for a weekend or a fortnight's holiday and don't want to put the dogs into kennels. I go round a couple of times a day, feed the dogs, clean up after them, play with them and take them out for a walk.'

'It's nice being your own boss, isn't it?'

'Yes. I love the freedom. And also I'm getting fresh air and regular exercise. I walk miles every day.'

'No wonder you look so good!'

'Aww. Thank you. What do you do?'

'I've got a flower stall. I used to have a proper shop but I split up with my business partner two years ago…'

'Morning, ladies.'

'Morning, Ron.'

'Well, this looks good.' Ron eyed his full English appreciatively. 'I usually have yeast and polish for breakfast.'

'Yeast and polish?' Nicole repeated.

'Yes, cos it helps me rise and shine,' he quipped, laughing loudly at his own joke while Nicole and Estelle groaned. 'But this'll do nicely. Set me up proper for the morning ahead!'

'You need all the calories you can get, Ron,' Eve said, joining them at the table. 'Can I have your form back please? You know, the one where you've marked what you want to do?'

'Oh, yeah. Course.'

Ron removed the form from his back pocket, smoothing it out before handing it to Eve.

'Two of the girls from the group are sitting over there,' Estelle said, indicating the far side of the restaurant. 'They've come in since you were here earlier.'

'Thanks. I'll go and see them. And I'll see you in twenty minutes on the courts.'

As she approached their table Eve could see Thommo and Fee were deep in conversation. She sighed. Everyone's holiday was everyone's holiday but she felt it was rude of people to come into a group where the others were trying hard to get to know each other with your ready-made friends and ignore the rest.

'Good morning. Sorry to interrupt your breakfast but I wanted to collect your trip forms.'

'Oh, I don't think we've decided yet,' Thommo said. 'We all want to go on a boat. I know that much. And go over to San An for Sunset Strip. But we might do other stuff on our own.'

'We need to confirm with the others,' Fee added.

'Well, if you can let me know this morning about the boat and Sunset because the price depends on how many we've got. I'll be with you on the courts.'

'Right-o. We'll talk to Spizz. Oh, here he is.'

'Morning, campers! Morning, Akela!' Spizz laughed at his own joke even though he looked a bit bleary-eyed.

'She's just asking about what we wanna do,' Fee said.

'We don't have to decide this minute, do we?'

'I need to know numbers by mid-morning because it's high season and boats will be booked up, if you want to do a boat trip that is,' Eve said.

'Alright, me duck. I'll round 'em up and let you know.'

'Thanks. Enjoy your breakfast!' Eve said and left them to it.

✦ ✦ ✦

EVE WAS FINDING watching Jesus put the group through their warm up and practice skills quite relaxing. It was a gorgeous morning; the digital thermometer by the pool had been showing 25C when she'd strolled past at twenty-five past nine. By now, ten-fifteen, it must surely be several degrees hotter, but she was in a beautiful shaded spot under the branches of a wide, spreading fig tree that stood up against the Club House – which the building housing the tennis courts bar, restaurant and changing rooms was called. She sipped her coffee and filled in her spreadsheet noting who wanted to go where. Fee had brought the group's lists to her; Leggo's was missing and Banksy and Jonesy had lost theirs so they'd added their names to Cookie's.

'We all want to go on a boat,' she said. 'And we wanna do Sunset Strip. But the rest of the time we'll probably just hang out on our own.'

'Thanks. Should I include Leggo in that? I haven't seen him…'

'Oh he turned up at the bar last night just as we were getting ready to leave. We had another one with him and then left him there. But he'll definitely wanna go on the boat. Definitely.'

'Great. Thanks. And you know the score – if you want to eat with the rest of us then we'll be in the bar at half past seven or in the reception area at eight o'clock. Tonight we're going to the tapas restaurant Jesus recommended. It's just a five minute walk up the road.'

'Well, if you see us, you see us.' And with that, Fee skipped down the crazy-paving steps to join the others on the courts.

Eve saw that everyone wanted to go out on the boat.

She'd discussed it with Jesus as the holiday included daily tennis tuition and Eve knew from experience how even missing half-an-hour's tuition would probably lead to someone complaining when they got home and wanting to claim compensation.

'Well, you could do an afternoon trip. The sun doesn't set until about nine and the sea is still warm until late so it's not much different from doing a day trip. And that way we can do tennis clinic in the morning and they will be free from lunchtime.'

'Good idea!'

Eve dialled the number of the boat charter company.

'Cruceros Poseidon, buenos días. Habla Anabel. En qué puedo asistirle?'

'Good morning. Do you speak English?'

'I do. Good morning. This is Poseidon Cruises. Anabel speaking.'

'Good morning, Anabel. My name's Eve from Travel Together. I'm with a group of people in the Hotel Dunas Blancas and I'd like to charter a boat one afternoon this week, please?'

'Oh, hi! Jenny isn't with the group?'

No she bloody isn't!

'Not this time. I've got a group of twenty, well that's including me and we'd like to take a trip on Thursday for the afternoon until sundown. Can you help?'

'Of course. We could offer you from two o'clock until approximately half past seven. That would be a tandem trip. So two boats as a motor boat is only licensed for twelve passengers. Unless you want a sailing boat?'

'No, two motor boats please.'

Five minutes later Eve hung up pleased with the deal she'd struck. The group would be picked up from Ibiza Port at two o'clock, have a great afternoon taking in a couple of beautiful beaches and coves with champagne and snacks included, have plenty of time for swimming and be returned for seven thirty. They had a complimentary coach to pick them up and return them to the Dunas Blancas. The price was reasonable and allowed for a commission for Eve herself. She ticked off Book Boat Trip on her list. She then checked her phone for the fortieth time but Melv still hadn't called her back. But then it was unlikely he would as it was half past four in the morning in Antigua and he would be sleeping soundly. She turned her attention for a moment to the tennis courts where the lesson was in full-swing.

✦ ✦ ✦

JESUS WAS STANDING just in front of the net and six of his students were on the opposite side, running towards the net and volleying the balls he was hitting to them. The rest were facing two ball-launching machines on the adjoining courts. Two boys aged about fifteen and dressed in immaculate tennis whites were running around gathering up the balls and returning them to the body of the launchers. Jesus had introduced them as Ivan and Daniel. They were all coping well so far, the ballboys and the players. It was obvious that some were better than others but that was to be expected. Jesus had got into a rhythm.

'Approach, plant feet, turn, racquet, contact. Approach, plant feet, turn, racquet, contact,' he chanted as they formed a continuous circle.

Well, this is all right. I haven't got much to do at all.

Even Leggo not turning up had worked in her favour because without him there were even numbers so she hadn't been required to partner anyone so far. And if her luck held she could be a spectator for the rest of the week.

'Okay. Let's have a short break,' Jesus called. 'Fifteen minutes for drinks and then we move on.'

'Enjoying it so far?' Eve asked Katrina, Sarah, Rosalind and Charlie who pulled out chairs to join her, each sucking on their water bottles as if they'd spent a whole day in the desert.

'So far, so good,' Katrina said. 'I expect it'll get harder as the week goes on, will it?'

'Probably.'

'The real fun will start this afternoon,' Charlie grinned. 'With the tournament. That's when the dick-measuring begins, if you'll pardon the phrase.'

'It's a bit like that on hiking holidays, too,' Sarah said as she joined them. 'If you say you walk ten miles every Sunday someone will walk twelve. It doesn't matter how many times the guide recommends pacing yourself, someone will always complain we're going too slow and forge ahead.' She shook her head.

'Yes, I can identify with that,' Eve said. 'The first trip I ever did with Travel Together was a walking weekend in Devon. It was a baptism of fire.'

'Oh, what happened? Tell us!' Sarah begged.

'Well, some of the group, about six men – sorry, Charlie, I'm not man-bashing just telling it as it was…'

'You think I don't know what prats men can be?'

'You'll get no argument from us, Charlie' Katrina quipped.

'Well, the guide had told us that the terrain would be a bit muddy and slippery so to take care and, of course, that they should all walk behind him and in front of me. I was bringing up the rear. At each rest point I arrived about ten minutes behind the others with the stragglers but I couldn't rush them along. Anyway, on the second day when we went to leave the first stop we realised that two walkers were missing. They were two men who'd been complaining all the time that the routes were too short and the pace was too slow.'

'Was it a beginners' group?' Sarah asked.

'Intermediate, as I remember,' Eve said.

'That's typical, that is. They are experienced hikers but they go on an intermediate group to make themselves look good and then complain.'

'A bit like here,' Rosalind muttered looking at the group within a group, before blushing furiously. 'Sorry. Didn't mean to say that out loud.'

'Oh yes, the Fourth Form are good!' Sarah said. 'Go on, Eve.'

'Well, we couldn't find them so we assumed they'd gone on ahead so we set off. After about fifteen minutes we saw the road we should have taken was quite wet and fearing it might be flooded the guide decided to take a slightly shorter route that would be safer. And it was a good job we did. A mile further on we went round a bend to find one of them lying in the road, clutching his ankle and grimacing in pain and the other slipping and sliding up a hill trying to get a signal on his mobile phone to call an ambulance. When he heard us approaching, he turned to call out, lost his footing and came tumbling down the hillside breaking his arm in the process.'

'You just can't tell some people,' Sarah said, shaking her head.

'Well, let's hope we don't have any broken bones this week!'

'From your mouth to God's ears, Charlie,' Eve said.

✦ ✦ ✦

OVER LUNCH, WHICH was a variety of toasted sandwiches, omelettes, salads or burgers, Eve consulted with the group about their planned evening in San Antonio.

'I was thinking Tuesday,' she said. 'As it'll probably be a late night Jesus said he's willing to start the clinic a bit later on Wednesday morning. And if you like, I can make a reservation on Sunset Strip for us. Somewhere like the Mint Lounge?'

'What's that?' Ron asked.

'It's a bar and restaurant on Sunset Strip.'

'We'd rather go to Mambo.' Spizz said as the other six nodded. 'My mate Darren's a DJ. He comes here every year. Reckons Mambo's the place to go.'

'There's a minimum spend there. Depending where you sit.'

'Well, that's not a problem, is it?'

'It might be for some of us,' Sarah said. 'How much is it, Eve?'

'I think it starts at about seventy-five euros. The Mint Lounge is just next door to Mambo and so the view of the sunset is the same. But I can book tables at both places, it isn't a problem.'

'Yes, that sounds good. Well, we all wanna go to Mambo,' Spizz said, the rest of his group nodding in agreement. 'No point in coming here and not visiting all the top places.'

'I'm happy to go to the Mint Lounge,' Sarah said, aware she might be the highest earner of them all but she refused to be dictated to by the Fourth Form, whom she already absolutely detested. An evening without them sounded like a very good idea.

'So how many for the Mint Lounge?' Eve asked.

The rest of the group put their hands up.

'Will Leggo join you?' Eve asked Spizz.

Spizz nodded. Eve made a note in her book. Spizz winked at her and strolled off back towards the courts with the rest of his group behind him.

'There's no point in spending a lot more money if we're watching the same sunset, is there?' Charlie said, finishing his tuna omelette.

'Exactly! And I'm happy to be anywhere away from the Fourth Form,' Sarah retorted.

'Oh, we're playing against Spizz and Titty,' Charlie said to Estelle, waving the Order of Play at her.

'I bet they're good,' Estelle said, pulling a face. 'Everyone looks good. Well, better than me, at any rate.'

'I've got Thommo in the singles,' Jackie said. 'And then Rosalind. They're both brilliant and I've realised this morning that I can't play for toffee.'

Overhearing them, Alex laughed.

'They all take it very seriously,' he said.

'Oh, don't!' Jackie said. 'I should have really gone on a beginners holiday. I was out of breath as soon as I started this morning.'

'Do you go to the gym?'

'No. Should I?'

'Well, it would help build your strength. The fitter you are the easier it will be to play tennis.'

'You look like you workout.'

'I do go to the gym. But I also cycle a lot.'

'I suppose that must help. I drive everywhere.'

'You need to get on your bike then! Come and see me I'll fix you up.'

'You sell bikes?'

'Yep! I've got a shop. That's why I do a lot of cycling.

I'm just outside Luton. Near Leagrave.'

'That's quite a hike for me. From Yorkshire. Or should I say a bike ride?'

Alex grinned at her joke.

'You're always welcome.'

'Now I feel really inadequate,' Jackie laughed. 'Rubbish at tennis and can't ride a bike! I'm only here to improve my tennis so that I can surprise my boyfriend by joining his tennis club. At the moment I don't meet the required standard for membership, as you probably all saw this morning! Scott's a brilliant player. He loves his tennis.'

'And was he all right with you coming away on your own?'

'He's in Dubai on business. He doesn't know I've come.'

'Okay.' Alex nodded.

'He'll be right at home in Dubai this week then,' Charlie said. 'There's a huge tennis tournament on. Biggest amateur one in the world. Lots of people from my club have gone.'

'Which club's that?' Jackie blurted out her question, already dreading the answer. Charlie lived in Bradford. Scott played tennis there.

'Golden Racquets. Do you know it?'

Jackie nodded, feeling as if she'd been thumped in the solar plexus. Alex and Charlie were talking but she no longer heard a word they were saying.

'I'll probably be bored stiff the whole week,' he'd told her. 'It'll be back-to-back meetings from breakfast until dinner. I wish you could come with me…'

And she'd believed him. She'd had a nagging doubt somewhere deep inside but she'd dismissed it as just being stupid and irrationally jealous. Just as Scott had accused her of being when she'd questioned him about Julie.

'She's one of the best women players at the club. Takes it seriously. Don't muck about,' he said. 'And you're being ridiculous if you think there's more to it than that. Crazy!'

And then he'd looked at her with his deep, grey eyes and gently pushed a stray strand of hair off her face.

'Don't spoil what we've got with silly, unfounded jealousies, Jackie. Me and Julie are only doubles partners. Honest.'

And although she'd wanted to believe him, she'd felt this little, niggle deep down in her belly, which was growing by the minute and was bubbling up to the surface.

'Jackie. Jackie!' Alex gently shook her shoulder. 'We're going back out to the courts.'

'Yes. Of course. Sorry.'

'Was I boring you?'

'No! Not at all. I just remembered something…'

✦ ✦ ✦

EVE HAD QUITE enjoyed her afternoon. She'd umpired two matches and nobody had argued with her decisions once. And she'd been particularly pleased to see that Ron had beaten both Jonesy and Cookie.

'Can I get you a drink, love?' Ron asked as he and Liz came into the Club House, fresh from their narrow defeat by Alex and Rosalind.

'I'm okay, thanks, Ron. I've just finished a coffee.'

'Don't you drink at all?'

'Not really, Liz. And especially not when I'm working. You never know when you're going to be needed and you need a clear head.'

'So you're tea-total?' Liz's eyes were wide in surprise.

'I do have the odd drink. You know, special occasions…'

'Well, as far as I'm concerned every day is a special occasion,' Ron said. 'Although my GP told me to watch my drinking so now I do most of it in front of a mirror,' he quipped picking up their drinks and heading for the terrace. 'See you later!'

Eve gave them a wave then checked the result sheets made a clean copy to put on the board in the Club House.

'Oh no! Does everyone have to see my shame?' Estelle said, putting her hands over her eyes trying to blot out the scores. 'I didn't win a point against Katrina never mind a game. And poor Charlie! We lost the doubles six-two, six-one.'

'Well, you can't win them all,' Charlie said, coming up behind her.

'Aww! That's nice of you, Charlie,' Estelle said.

Charlie smiled back at her even though he wasn't feeling very happy. He didn't expect everyone to be as good a player as he was, but he expected them to be able to hit the ball. Although Estelle could get herself around the court and when she made contact with the ball she hit it hard, her hand-eye co-ordination was lacking. She'd missed a couple of sitters!

'I'll see you all in the bar before dinner,' he said, taking himself off for a quiet beer.

'Yes, see you later for tapas,' Eve called after him. She collected her paperwork together and secured it on her clipboard. She thought she'd go back to her room and have a cup of tea on the balcony before getting ready for the evening session. She checked her watch. It was only half-past-five. She might even have a swim. Or a siesta…

✦ ✦ ✦

MOST OF THE group had gone to the main bar and pool area. Just Sarah and Jackie sat together on the far side of the Club House. As she passed them Eve could see by their body language that whatever they were discussing was private. Jackie was huddled over a drink, head down and Sarah's hand lay on her arm. Eve left without acknowledging them.

'It's supposed to be Improvers, not a fucking warm-up for Wimbledon,' Jackie gulped, tears running down her cheeks and plopping into her beer. 'I feel so stupid!'

'You won't be the only one who's finding it hard,' Sarah said, patting her forearm.

'But I'm the only one who lost six-love, six-love!' Jackie wailed.

'No, you're not! Estelle did against Katrina.'

'But I lost both my matches without winning a game! Rosalind was kind about it. But that bloody Thommo! She was smirking at her mates and they all burst out laughing as they walked away.'

Sarah let her cry for a few minutes; she felt sorry for Jackie. She'd umpired her match against Thommo and had seen first-hand how she had been completely thrashed. Thommo was a very good player and Sarah couldn't help but feel angry with her for not going on an advanced tennis course. She'd watched the Fourth Form and it had been clear even in that morning's clinic that they all played extremely well. But then, that was only to be expected; Jonesy had let slip they had all played at County level at one time and a couple of them were PE teachers.

'It couldn't have been any worse if I'd been playing against Johanna Konta,' Jackie sniffed. 'I'm not going to take part any more. I shouldn't have come! I've made an idiot of myself!'

'You looked to me as if you were having difficulty concentrating,' Sarah said. 'Is that it?'

Jackie sniffed twice and then nodded her head.

'Yes. I… I found something out today…'

'You don't have to tell me!' Sarah interrupted her. She wasn't used to girlie chats and confessions and wasn't sure how comfortable she felt listening to Jackie spill her heart out.

'I might as well.' She shrugged her shoulders and gave a huge sigh. 'I came here because I wanted to get to get my tennis up to a good enough standard to join my boyfriend's tennis club.'

'So you said last night,' Sarah nodded.

'But there's more to it than that… I've been suspicious he's been having an affair with Julie his doubles partner. Of course, he's denied it. Says I'm imagining it all. That they only play tennis together. That I'm being stupid… Anyway, he told me he had to be in Dubai on business this week. He said he didn't want to go; that it'd be boring, back-to-back meetings all day long and into the evening.' She took a swig of her beer, which was now lukewarm and grimaced.

'Anyway, earlier I was talking to Alex and Charlie and I mentioned that Scott was in Dubai and Charlie said there's the world's biggest amateur tennis tournament taking place there this week. He said lots of people from his club were there. It turns out he goes to Golden Racquets. And that's where Scott goes!'

'But that doesn't mean Scott's not in Dubai for business, or that he's there playing doubles with Julie. Have you spoken to him since he went?'

'Just for a few moments yesterday. He said he was busy but bored. The meetings went on for hours but weren't very interesting. He hasn't posted anything on Instagram, which isn't like him.'

'Well, call him again. Call him now!'

'I can't video call him because he'll see I'm not at home. They are together. They are. I just know it!' Jackie wailed again. 'I've known all along. There's just been something in the way he talks about her…'

'Well, there's only one way to find out,' Sarah said, fishing into her bag for her phone. 'Is she on Facebook?'

'Yes. I looked her up. When I first suspected. She's on Instagram, too, but her account's private.'

Sarah's thumbs flew across the screen.

'What's her surname?'

'Clithers.'

'Went to University of Exeter. Works at Yorkshire Bank. Lives in Leeds,' Sarah read from the screen.

'That's her,' Jackie nodded.

'Well, she's not in Leeds this week.'

Sarah passed her phone to Jackie, scrolling down the dozens of photos of Julie in tennis whites, her hair up in a neat bun and in a series of sexy dresses, her hair wild and loose, tumbling over her bare shoulders as she enjoyed the best that Dubai Night Life had to offer. Jackie's eyes scoured every photo seeking out Scott. Suddenly she let out a howl, which turned into a sob.

'The lying, cheating, bastard! Bastard!'

Sarah looked at the photo. Julie was pouting at the camera surrounded by several people who all looked half-cut.

'Him! That's him!' Jackie screeched pointing at a fair-haired man with bloodshot, blue eyes whose right arm was draped around Julie's bare shoulder, her dress strap having slipped down.

'Oh, dear…'

'And they are playing tennis!'

Sarah took the phone and studied the photos of the two of them in their tennis whites; he was holding her in his arms over the net in one, they were arm-in-arm with a couple in another and sharing what looked like a celebratory hug in another.

Jackie was sobbing uncontrollably; her mascara smudged her red, blotchy cheeks and her shoulders heaved. Sarah searched in her bag again, this time for a tissue to wipe the snotty streak that was slowly making its way from Jackie's right nostril. And then she sat holding Jackie's hand until her sobbing ceased and her shoulders stilled.

'You must think I'm right stupid,' Jackie finally said. 'Making all this fuss over him.'

'You've been badly let down by the sound of it,' Sarah said. She had never cried over anyone and didn't understand how or why anyone would let themselves be so dependant on another person.

When you love someone, always love them in such a way that you can leave them before they leave you.

Her first ever lover had told her that. She had been seventeen and he thirty-nine. He was preparing her for when their affair ended. And she had lived by those words ever since. She wished Jackie had a bit more backbone but now wasn't the moment for giving feedback.

'Even coming here thinking I could become a tennis player in a week… Talk about deluded!'

'Don't berate yourself! It's not your fault he's a lying cheat, is it?'

Jackie shook her head.

'But I don't want to make a fool of myself any longer. I'm going home.'

'Oh, don't!' Sarah said. 'You've paid your money, you're

in Ibiza, it's not all bad.'

'I can't face the humiliation of losing every game!'

'But you don't have to. Listen, I'm not too keen on the tournaments, either. Why don't we go to the morning clinics and then spend the afternoons round the pool or down on the beach? We're doing serves tomorrow apparently. What do you say?'

'But… you're good! Why wouldn't you want to play?'

'I never planned to be doing non-stop tennis for the whole week. This way, you get to improve your game by doing all the technical stuff so you can still join Golden Racquets when you get back if you want to…'

'Ugh! Just the thought of that makes me feel sick now!'

'Okay, well, not join then, but at least you'd have the satisfaction of knowing you've got something from the week and the two of us can have a couple of great afternoons together. Away from the group.'

'Hmm. It does sound tempting. I can see that being with the group all the time can be a bit claustrophobic.'

'Exactly! So, from tomorrow, it's tennis in the morning and chilling in the afternoon and evening.'

Jackie smiled and nodded her head.

'Come on then! Let's go to the pool bar and drink to our Plan B!'

✦ ✦ ✦

'DOS CERVEZAS, POR favor, Juanca,'

'En seguida, señor!'

'What does *in-say-gee-dar* mean?' Liz asked.

'Coming up or immediately,' Ron replied as they pulled up chairs to the table where Sean, Alex, Nicole, Estelle and Katrina were sitting.

'You speak Spanish, Ron?' Alex said.

'I get by. Just a few odd words and phrases.'

'Well, you sounded good to me,' Nicole said.

'Jackie's learning Spanish, too,' Katrina said. 'She was saying a few things last night.'

'She didn't look very happy just now,' Sean said. 'I think she was disappointed with her performance on court.'

'Well, she's no worse than me!' Estelle laughed. 'I love playing, but I'm just not very good.'

'That's why you're here, love,' Ron said. 'To improve.'

'I suppose so,' she sighed. 'You're such a nice man, Ron!'

'You're making him blush!' Sean said.

'Well, I think everyone did their best and after all, we're here to enjoy ourselves. It's not all about the winning.'

'Dick-measuring. That's what Charlie called it,' Nicole said as everyone laughed.

'Muchas gracias, Juanca,' Ron said as the waiter brought their beers.

'I can't believe his name,' Nicole giggled as Juanca walked away.

'He's a brave man working with English-speakers, I'll say that for him,' Alex said. 'He must get the mickey taken out of him.

'I wonder how you say wanker in Spanish,' Sean pondered. 'Do you know, Ron?'

'Not a clue, mate! I've never had cause to use it.'

'We'll have to ask Jesus,' Katrina said.

'What do we think of our tennis coach?' Nicole asked.

'Seems like a good bloke,' Alex said.

'Yes. I can't see anything not to like,' Liz agreed.

'I wonder if he's famous,' Nicole pondered. 'Anyone know?'

'Apparently he never played professionally. So he was telling us last night,' Alex said.

'Do you reckon he gets lots of women?' Ron asked. 'I mean, he's tall, dark and handsome.'

'Probably not as many as you, Ron,' Sean quipped.

'Well, you've either got it or you haven't!' Ron replied, running his hand over his thinning hair and smiling.

'Ha! Ha! You've certainly got it, Ron!' Nicole said laughing. 'How come you're single?'

'One of life's little mysteries,' Ron parried.

'Are you divorced?'

'I lost my wife.'

'Oh, I'm sorry,' Nicole said as the others murmured their condolences.

'How about you?' Alex asked Nicole.

'Never married!' She didn't want to tell everyone what had happened to Roland. 'You?'

'Ditto. A long-term relationship that ended last year so it's a bit like being divorced I suppose. Katrina?'

'I'm a member of the Never Married Club, too.'

'Ecstatically divorced!' Liz said, raising her glass. 'To singledom!'

'Estelle?'

'I was dumped two years ago by someone I'd lived with for twelve years. He went off with my best friend and business partner.'

Everyone looked at her; all unsure of what to say.

'I'm over him now. And it's because of him in a roundabout way that I'm on this holiday. So, no regrets. Onwards and upwards!'

'Good for you, girl! He must be a nutcase,' Ron said, sipping his beer.

'Aww, thank you, Ron!'

'What about you, Sean?'

'Divorced.' Sean finished his drink. 'Excuse me. I'm going for a shower. See you all later.'

'Something we said?' Sarah called after him as she and Jackie approached the table joining them.

'I think we touched a nerve,' Liz explained. 'We were talking about who's divorced or widowed.'

'Well, he has to be one or the other or he wouldn't be on the holiday!' Sarah retorted. 'Or never married. So what is he?'

'Divorced.'

'Perhaps it's recent and a bit raw,' Nicole said.

'Which category do you fall into?' Katrina asked Sarah.

'Me? Never married! I can't see the point,' Sarah said.

'It used to be the blokes that said, "Don't buy a cow when milk's cheap."' Ron quipped.

'Welcome to the twenty-first century!'

'There's a lot to be said for being single,' Alex said. 'Look at the Dalai Lama. Happiest man alive and he's been single for eighty years.'

Everyone laughed in appreciation of the point he was making.

'What are you having?' Sarah turned to Jackie hoping nobody would ask about her civil status and set her off again.

'I think I'll have a glass of dry white, please.'

Sarah signalled their drinks order to Juanca.

'Tapas tonight! I'm looking forward to that,' Ron said.

'I need to talk to Eve about the vegan options,' Katrina said. 'If not I'll have to find somewhere else.'

'Bound to be,' Ron replied. 'Jesus said you can find vegetarian restaurants all over.'

'Vegan,' Katrina corrected as Sarah raised her eyebrows.

'I just hope they can be trusted not to use animal fat or dairy to cook any of them,' Katrina said. 'Or palm oil! You can't be too careful.'

'Indeed you can't!' Sarah said.

✦ ✦ ✦

EVE HAD JUST taken off her dress in preparation for a short siesta when her phone rang. Seeing who the caller was brought a wide grin to her face.

'Melv!'

'What's up, baby?'

His deep chocolate tones still made her knees wobble even after all this time. His voice was sexy; everything about him was sexy. But the face that appeared on her screen looked strained and there were dark circles under his eyes.

'I'm fine. It's great to hear and see you. How are you?'

'I'm cool. I'm cool. Sorry I missed your call. I was in a meeting about the spa pool renovations, which are going to take a month longer than we thought and cost thirty percent more. And then… Well, you know how it is. There's always something going on here that needs my attention. And when I got home Radley had had a bit of a crisis…'

'What's happened to him?'

'He's depressed, you know. And I don't blame him. I mean, we're doing all we can for him, but he's frustrated at his own limitations, you know what I'm saying?'

'He must be. Poor Radley…'

'Anyhow, what you up to?'

'I've just come back to my room for a rest before getting ready for pre-dinner drinks.'

'Have you played any tennis?' She heard the laughter in his voice.

'I haven't. But I might surprise everyone before the week's out. I used to swing a racquet quite skilfully!'

'I'm sure you did. Did you enjoy the wedding?'

'It was beautiful. We had a lovely time.'

'Michael sent me some pictures. There was a great one of Felicity sitting on the sand.'

'She looked like a little fairy, didn't you think?' Eve shared his pride in their grand-daughter.

'She is so sweet. She's adorable. And Natalie's blooming.'

'She certainly is. I think she's got a boy this time.'

'Perhaps.'

'And our son is as handsome as ever!'

'He is. When are you home?' Melv asked.

'On Sunday. I leave here on Saturday but the flight's late in the evening.'

'Okay. Well, I'll call you on Sunday then. And we can talk. FaceTime.'

'We're talking now, aren't we?'

'When you're relaxed at home without your group. And I'll be home, too. You know what I mean.'

'Okay. Well, speak Sunday then.'

'Take care of yourself.'

'Love you!'

But he'd already gone. Eve hung up and shook her head. Melv didn't sound his usual self. But then if he was juggling issues at the Mango Tree Resort with problems and worries about Radley then it was to be expected. She wished she was there with him and could hug away all his problems. His calls usually lifted her spirits but this one had left her feeling down. And not just because he hadn't said he loved her. She re-ran their conversation in her head.

He didn't compliment me on how I looked in the photo.

✦ ✦ ✦

EVE ARRIVED IN the bar for pre-dinner drinks to find the Fourth Form were already there.

I have to stop calling them that! What if I said it out loud?

She cursed Sarah for coming up with it even though it was spot on.

They were occupying the far end of the bar with the three women sitting on stools and the five men, including Leggo, who had finally surfaced, standing around them. She smiled and waved at them but nobody seemed to have noticed her. She was relieved to see Rosalind, Ron and Charlie sitting at a table on the terrace. She strode across the bar to join them.

'Hello, love. 'Ere!' Ron pulled out a chair for her, his wonderful cologne wafting all around. Eve looked at him and smiled. He might be the oldest of the group by almost twenty years but he was one of the smartest, certainly the most well-groomed and probably the nicest of them all.

'What you gonna have?'

'A Diet Coke, please.'

'You're a cheap date,' he joked.

'How are you all?'

'Very well, thanks,' Rosalind said. 'I really enjoyed the tennis and then I went down to the beach and had a swim. The sea was gorgeous and there are lots of rocks at the far end. I might get a snorkel and take a closer look at what might be lurking around.'

'Would there be much to see?' Charlie asked Eve.

'I don't see why not. Probably the odd squid, sponges, starfish, eels…'

'Really?'

'Sounds good! I might join you,' Charlie said.

'You're welcome to,' Rosalind replied. 'I love the sea. I've never understood why people prefer a pool to the sea.'

'Neither have I,' Charlie said. 'I loved going to the seaside when I was growing up.'

'There's certainly something about it,'Eve said, looking beyond the hotel gardens to the sea in the distance.'

'I expect you've seen more seas than most people,' Rosalind said. 'With all your travelling.'

'I've been very fortunate. I've seen every ocean. And, of course, I grew up by the sea. My father used to take me fishing with him.'

For a moment she could almost smell the tang of the salt and the acrid tobacco of the Karelia cigarettes her father had smoked; the aromas that always hung around him. The two of them would go out at sunset and lay down the hooked lines and then return before sunrise to haul them in again, both shouting with glee at each fish that popped out of the water caught on their line. Sometimes the lines would be empty and others there would be dozens and dozens of fish. Eve pulled them off the hooks and threw them into the large buckets at her feet. When they got back home she would help her mother to gut them in preparation for the delicious dishes they would serve that night in the family taverna. They were happy days of simply-lived lives. It was sad to think how it had all turned out. Her father had died a few years earlier, three days before Michael's wedding. They had been estranged for many years, though. He had never understood why she had left her husband nor her need to get away from Corfu nor the part he'd played in that need. Her failure to go to his funeral had caused the rift to widen even further. Her brothers condemned her for putting her mixed-race, illegitimate son – one they hadn't known existed – before her family. Her real family. Her Greek family. She yearned to take Michael to Lefkimi, to the taverna to meet them all and to show him his roots, where he'd come from. But she knew their reception would not be warm and welcoming so she had made excuses not to take him whenever he had asked.

The arrival of her Diet Coke along with Katrina, Liz and Sean brought her out of her reverie.

'I need to talk to you about this tapas restaurant,' Katrina said, taking a seat next to Eve. 'Do they cater for vegans?'

'I would imagine so. Usually tapas include things like padron peppers, you know, the little green ones and Spanish omelette, spicy potatoes, roasted vegetables, various Spanish cheeses…'

'Hmm. Is it possible to check?'

Eve took out her phone and googled the restaurant bringing up its menu.

'Right. Spinach and chickpeas; vegan *fabada*…'

'What's that?'

'Erm… It's white bean stew,' Eve said, finding the menu in English. Vegan stuffed peppers; mixed vegetable omelette; Spanish omelette…'

'I don't eat eggs,' Katrina said.

'… aubergine fritters; ratatouille… There's quite a selection even if you exclude eggs.'

'What about palm oil? I never eat anything containing palm oil. I made sure Travel Together checked the hotel didn't use it before I booked.'

'Well, it doesn't say anything on the restaurant website about palm oil but I would imagine that everything is probably cooked in olive oil as we're in Spain.'

'It's not cooking in it, it's using it as an ingredient. Can you check, please? Give them a call? Because if not I'll have to go somewhere else.'

'Yes, of course,' Eve said, managing to smile politely as she dialled the restaurant.

'Blimey! She's fussy,' Ron whispered to Liz and Sean as Eve made her phone call. 'She should've been like me. One of twelve. You either ate what was put in front of you or you went hungry.'

'But palm oil is causing terrible deforestation,' Sean said.

'Oh, I know, and I admire her for having principles. But sometimes you just have to go with the flow. I was on holiday in Cuba two years ago. With Travel Together. Some of the group got right up my nose. Two women didn't stop complaining because we had rice and beans and pork chop three days running. Most Cubans are lucky if they have it once a week! Bloody people! They choose to go to a poor country and then complain all the time!'

'I can't bear people who preach vegetarianism,' Liz said. 'I mean, if you don't want to eat meat that's up to you, but don't tell the rest of us what to do.'

'I don't preach,' Katrina said. 'I deal with my own conscience not everyone else's'

'I didn't mean any offence,' Liz said, embarrassed that Katrina had overheard her and not wishing to be the cause of any upsets. 'It just gets me when these militant groups protest in the meat aisles in supermarkets.'

'Yes, that's not the way to get people to change their minds,' Sean agreed. 'All it does is piss people off.'

'No palm oil!' Eve declared, hanging up. 'They only use olive oil in the preparation of all their tapas.'

'How long have you been a vegetarian?' Charlie asked Katrina.

'A vegan,' she corrected him. 'About five years. Are you?'

'No. I grew up eating a lot of vegetables, like most

Indians. But I do like meat. And fish. Especially seafood, like prawns and squid and mussels.'

'I love cockles,' Ron said. 'They remind me of Sunday tea. We always used to have half a pint of shrimps and cockles. My wife used to do a lovely spread. You can't beat a cockle sandwich. Lots of black pepper on 'em. Squeeze of lemon. Bloody lovely!'

Seeing that everyone was now down Eve called the group to attention. She didn't want to raise her voice and disturb the other hotel guests who were on the terrace so she moved in closely to them. She confirmed she had booked their places at the Mint Lounge on Tuesday night and a 25-seater coach to take them over to the West Coast, to San Antonio. She suggested the return time should be one o'clock.

'Everyone okay with that? It gives us six hours.'

'Plenty of time I'd think,' Sarah said as the others nodded. 'And if anyone wants to stay later they can always take a taxi, can't they?'

'Yes, of course,' Eve said.

She then told them about the boat trip on Thursday, reassuring everyone it was going to be in the afternoon so they wouldn't miss the tennis clinic.

'What kind of boat is it?' Sean asked.

'There are two. Speed boats. We're doing a tandem cruise as each boat is only licensed to take twelve. We could have got a large catamaran, but that would have doubled the cost.'

'Tandem speed boats sound good to me,' Sean said.

'And the Fourth Form can be on their own,' Sarah muttered.

'And I thought of going into Ibiza Town for dinner tomorrow night. It's very lively around the port area and anyone that wants can go up into D'Alt Villa. We can get the bus. They run until midnight.'

'Brilliant!' Ron said.

'Right, I'll just go and tell the Forth… the others and then we can start to make our way to the restaurant,' Eve said, crossing the terrace and going back inside the bar area.

'It's our leader!'

Leggo had obviously already had quite a lot to drink.

'Good evening. How are you all?' Eve asked, smiling.

'All the better for seeing you!' Leggo said, throwing an arm around her shoulders, his foul, alcoholic breath right in her face, his eyes still bloodshot. 'Here! She's better looking than Jenny, in't she?'

'Put her down, Leggo!' Spizz said as Eve expertly disentangled herself. 'Sorry about him, love. He's still drunk from last night.'

Eve told them about the bookings she'd made.

'One o'clock's far too early to come back from San An,' Fee said. 'We wanna go round the pubs in the West End.'

'I might see if I can get two minibuses, then,' Eve said. 'Or you could go in two taxis and get cabs to come home in. There are always taxis in San Antonio. All through the night.'

'Yes, that sounds more like it,' Spizz said. 'That way we're not tied to a certain time.'

'Excellent!' Eve made a mental note to ring the coach company the following morning and change the booking. 'So, we're just off to the tapas restaurant if you're ready…'

'I'm fucking starving,' Leggo said. 'Last meal I had was yesterday.'

It looks like the last wash you had was yesterday, too.

Eve prayed she hadn't said that out loud.

✦ ✦ ✦

'GOD! I'M STUFFED!' Nicole threw her napkin down on her empty plate.

'It's hard to believe that little bits and pieces could be so filling, isn't it?' Alex agreed. 'I thought I was going to need a main course but I couldn't have been more wrong.'

'Haven't you had tapas before?'

'Not as good as these, I haven't. More wine?'

'Yes please!'

'How about you, Liz?' Alex asked turning to his other side.

'Oh go on then!' Liz giggled. 'I already feel a bit tipsy. It's lovely wine though.'

'It's a Rioja,' Ron piped up. 'Good stuff that!'

'Eve?'

Alex raised the bottle and his eyebrows towards the tour manager who was sitting opposite him.

'I'll stick to water, thanks.'

'I like the idea of Ibiza Town tomorrow night.'

'Oh, it's a great place, Alex. You'll enjoy it.'

'Do you know Ibiza well, Eve? You seem to.'

'I've been here a few times but not for quite a while. I was so surprised when I flew in to see how it's built up. Still beautiful, though.'

'Yes, it's a nice island. What I've seen of it, anyway. Got a bad reputation, though.'

'I think the worst time was the eighties and nineties, to be honest,' Eve said. 'And even then, you were really only talking about the centre of San Antonio for about six or seven weeks in the height of summer. I think they've cleaned up their act and there's something here for everyone.'

Their conversation was interrupted by a huge roar of laughter from Charlie, Rosalind, Sean, Jackie, Estelle and Sarah at the other end of the table. Eve smiled, pleased to see everyone was getting on.

'You're so funny, Charlie,' Jackie said, wiping her eyes. 'Oh, dear!'

'Working in local government's a laugh a minute!'

'You've made me cry!'

'Well at least you're crying with laughter now,' Sarah whispered to her.

'Thanks. You know. For earlier,' Jackie said, squeezing Sarah's arm.

'What do you do, Sarah?' Charlie asked, interrupting.

'I'm a solicitor.'

'Do you specialise in divorce? Are on this holiday touting for business?'

'Hardly! Everyone on this holiday is already free and single from what I can see,' Sarah retorted. 'No. I specialise in criminal law.'

Charlie's eyes widened in approval and admiration.

'Rosalind's a piano teacher, if I remember rightly.'

Rosalind nodded and smiled at him.

'Jackie?'

'I'm a veterinary nurse.'

'Aww!' The whole group liked that.

'Estelle?'

'I've got a flower stall.'

'Oh, that sounds beautiful,' Sarah said.

'I used to have a shop.'

'It must be very therapeutic working with flowers.'

'It can be. It's nice when you create something gorgeous and the recipient really appreciates it.'

'Not the case when you do wreaths, I suppose,' Charlie

observed before turning his attention to Sean.

'What do you do?'

'I'm a boat-builder.'

'That explains it,' Sarah said.

'What?'

'Your physique. It's obvious you do something physical.'

'Well, I row, too.'

Sean reddened and went quiet when he realised all eyes were on him.

'And you play tennis!' Sarah smiled at him.

'So you build boats and then you row them,' Jackie said.

'Not really,' Sean laughed. 'I build boats that are much larger than rowing boats. And a lot of my work is repairs.'

'Must be nice working in the open air,' Jackie said assuming that Sean did. 'I'm locked up inside all day.'

'Me, too,' Charlie said. 'What do the others do?'

'Ron's a retired fire-fighter, Sarah told them. 'Liz is a beautician. Katrina is a carer…'

'It's her mum's care home,' Jackie said. 'So she runs it really.'

'And what about Alex?'

'He's got a bike shop,' Estelle said. 'He told me earlier.'

'He looks like a cyclist,' Charlie said, with the slightest note of envy in his voice as he looked down the table at Alex who was chatting to Nicole.

'I bet he looks good in lycra,' Estelle said. 'What?' She looked round the table and laughed. 'It's what you're all thinking!'

I was thinking he'd look good naked!

Sarah grinned to herself at her thought. She wasn't sure if it was the three glasses of Rioja, but both Alex and Sean were beginning to look very attractive indeed.

'And the Fourth Form are all PE teachers,' she said.

'Not all of them. Leggo and one of the other men and Fee are. Thommo teaches English, I think,' Estelle said. 'But the rest aren't teachers. I can't remember what they do, to be honest. They told us that much when we sat with them last night.'

'Thommo and Titty. Thommo and Titty,' Charlie repeated. 'Now that sounds like a firm of solicitors if ever I've heard one,' he said, making the others roar with laughter again.

Sarah stood up to go to the Ladies. As she passed by Eve's chair she stopped and leaned in close enough to speak without being overheard.

'Just to let you know that Jackie and I are pulling out of the matches. We'll still attend the morning sessions but we aren't bothered about actually playing. We'd rather spend the afternoons sunbathing or doing our own thing.'

'That's absolutely fine. I'll make sure you're not on the lists,' Eve said, glad both of them had decided not to play. While there were even numbers she wouldn't have to join in. Although, now that Leggo had surfaced she might be needed. 'Is Jackie okay? She looked a bit upset earlier on.'

'She's had a romantic disappointment, which, when added to losing so emphatically this afternoon has sort of put her off playing. But don't worry. Auntie Sarah's taking care of her.'

Eve laughed.

'I'm sure she's in wonderful hands.'

'I'm not saying he's not a superb player, but for me he's not the Greatest Of All Time,' Katrina was saying. 'He's only won one French.'

'But he's still won Slams on all surfaces,' Charlie said.

'But he only won that French title because Rafa wasn't playing.'

'Rafa's only won one Australian…'

'But he's won three US Opens and they're played on hard court. It's not as if he can only play on clay.'

'But do you only measure a player's greatness by the Grand Slams they've won?' Rosalind asked. 'After all, Andy Murray's won Davis Cup, back-to-back Olympic Gold medals…'

'But he's not in the same class as Rafa and Federer, in my opinion,' Charlie said.

'What about Djokovic? He's untouchable,' Sean said.

'He might be at the moment but he's not consistent,' Charlie argued.

'I'm not sure I'd agree with that!'

'And I think there's an argument for Serena being the Greatest of all Time,' Katrina said.

'You're kidding me!' Charlie said.

'What?' Sean spluttered. 'She's good against other women over three sets but…'

'No man's ever won a Grand Slam while being pregnant!' Katrina retorted.

Estelle, Rosalind and Jackie all burst into a round of applause.

'I think that's game, set and match, Katrina! Shall we get another bottle or two?' Ron asked, waving the empty one in the air.

'Why not?' Alex called from down the table. 'Sounds good to me.'

There was general agreement from the others. The tapas bar was in a very pleasant spot down a picturesque side street overlooking several pretty houses and bars; the music was playing softly in the background; the company was amiable and the staff showed no signs of wanting to throw them out.

'Did you say you're a dog-walker?' Sean asked Nicole.

'Yes. I love them.'

'It must be nice being self-employed. No boss telling you what to do. Freedom.'

'It is. Although the dog owners are my bosses really. If I did anything to upset them and they took their business elsewhere then obviously my income would be hit, so I have to make sure they're all happy.'

'It certainly keeps you fit, too.'

'I walk a long way every day.' Nicole chose to ignore what else he might be saying.

They locked eyes and both blushed and then concentrated on the contents of their wine glasses.

'I've just realised who the Missing Link is,' Sarah said, returning to the table, nodding her head towards Leggo. 'He's the filthy pig who farted when he walked past us on the first night!'

Jackie, Rosalind and Katrina looked across at him and nodded.

'Yeuk! He was disgusting,' Katrina said. 'No apology. Just kept on walking.'

'And God knows what he'd eaten!' Jackie added. 'I'd never smelt anything like it.'

'Too much information!' Estelle said, wrinkling her nose at the thought.

'Some men are just pigs!' Jackie added.

'Oh so women don't fart then?' Charlie said.

'We merely get indigestion,' Katrina quipped.

'Do they do desserts here, Eve?' Liz asked.

'Indeed they do!'

'I just fancy an ice-cream or a sorbet.'

Eve asked the waitress to bring a dessert menu.

'I tell you,' she said. 'Ice-cream. Chocolate, coconut,

strawberry or pistachio. Lemon or orange sorbet. *Crema Catalana.* Or banana fritter.'

'What's *crema Catalana*?' Liz asked Ron.

'A sort of custard with burned sugar on the top. It's lovely!'

'I thought I was full, but the sound of the coconut ice-cream sounds tempting,' Nicole said.

'Hmm. I was thinking that,' Sean agreed. 'I love ice-cream.'

'Me, too.'

They smiled at each other without embarrassment this time.

'Is the ice-cream vegan, do you think?' Katrina asked Eve.

'I wouldn't have thought so. But let's ask.'

The waitress confirmed the ice-cream wasn't vegan, but on consulting with the Chef she announced that the sorbet was and the banana fritter could be as he could make one especially for her. Katrina beamed with delight. Desserts were ordered, everyone partaking except Ron and Sarah who decided to have an Irish coffee each instead.

'I once went out with a girl who made ice-cream and cakes,' Ron said.

'Did you?' Liz responded, wondering what he story he was going to tell.

'Yes. But she soon deserted me!'

'Oh, Ron!' The group laughed and groaned.

The mood was suddenly broken by a loud crash and the sound of splintering wood. Everyone turned to see Leggo and Fee thrashing around on the floor, their six mates screaming with laughter. Eve stood up.

'Is anyone hurt?'

'No. They're just messing. Leggo tried to sit on her lap

and the fucking chair broke,' Spizz said doubling over and clutching his stomach with laughter.

The waitress and the manager approached, helped them to their feet and checked they weren't injured.

'I've grazed my elbow,' Fee said, rubbing it. 'And my knee.' Blood was dripping down her shin.

'Want me to kiss it better?'

'Fuck off, Jonesy,' she said, pushing him aside. Eve dived into her handbag and pulled out some antiseptic wipes.

'Here. Use these. They don't sting.'

'Thank you.'

Fee took them and made her way to the Ladies. Eve wasn't sure whether Fee's unsteadiness was down to being shaken up or having a lot to drink. She'd keep an eye on Fee when she came back out, she decided, taking her seat again.

Then the manager examined the chair. Two of the legs had snapped, one of them splintering its full length.

'Sorry, mate. We was just messing,' Leggo said.'

'Yes, I see that,' the manager replied, visibly annoyed.

'You'd think you'd have metal chairs. Something a bit stronger.'

'Our chairs are strong enough for one person. Not for two.'

'Well, suppose you get a fat person. These chairs wouldn't hold them, would they?'

Titty, Thommo, Cookie and Banksy all roared out loud at their friend's comment. The manager felt they were laughing at him and he didn't like it.

'You have behaved in a very stupid way.'

'Who you calling stupid?' Leggo squared up to him.

'You are not children,' the manager said, refusing to be intimidated. 'You will pay for the damage.'

'You what?'

'Fifty euros. For breaking it.'

'You're having a fucking laugh, aren't you? I'm not paying for some fucking, substandard chair.' He swivelled round to the other table where everyone was watching the developing drama. 'Oi! You! Mrs Travel Together! This bloke's trying to rip me off here! Wants me to pay for the fucking chair.'

'Ignore him, love,' Ron said, putting his hand on Eve's arm as she stood up.

'Well, from what I've seen you did break his chair. And it's right you should pay for the damage, isn't it?'

'You having a fucking laugh?'

'No. I'm not. You broke the chair, didn't you?'

'You're supposed to be here sticking up for me!'

'I can't stick up for you if you're in the wrong. And I think you are,' Eve said, remaining perfectly calm. 'You were messing around, two of you sat on a chair built for one person and it broke.'

'And I could have broken my back falling on the floor like that!'

'But you didn't.'

Eve met his gaze. On both tables everyone sat in silence staring at them waiting to see what would happen next. Fee limped back to the table.

'He only fucking wants us to pay fifty euros for the chair,' Leggo whined.

'Us? It was you, not me,' she snapped at him. 'Course he wants paying for it. But you broke it so you can cough up!'

She picked up her wine glass and downed what was left then threw some euros on the table.

'I'm going back to the hotel,' she announced and with that hobbled from the restaurant as best she could.

'You pay for the chair or I call the police,' the manager threatened.

'All right, mate. No worries. We don't want no trouble,' Spizz told the manager. 'Just chuck the price of the chair onto our bill. We'll pay it from the kitty,' he told the others.

'Why should we?' Titty wasn't impressed. 'That's for our beer money.'

'Oops! The Fourth Form are all falling out,' Sarah said with a wry smile as she sipped her wine.

'Oh, for fuck's sake!' Leggo stuffed his hand into his pocket. 'Here! I'm paying for it. Okay?' He snarled at Titty. 'Okay?' He turned and snarled at the manager. 'And Travel Together will be hearing from me about you!' He pointed at Eve. 'You're a shit tour manager.'

'There's no need to take it out on Eve or speak to her like that.' Ron stood up as several others nodded in agreement with him.

'She's supposed to stick up for me. Jenny would of!'

'Have,' Sarah corrected him.

Eve refused to rise to the bait.

'I'm writing in about you as soon as I get home!'

'She'll be shaking in her boots,' Sarah was on a roll.

'You lot coming?'

Seeing she wasn't affected in the slightest by his threats Leggo turned his back on Eve and looked at his mates.

'Hang on, Leggo. We've gotta pay the bill and finish our drinks,' Spizz said.

Leggo threw himself onto his chair sulkily.

'Careful! You don't want to break another one,' Sarah said, loudly enough for everyone to hear.

There were a few grins.

'You got something to say to me?' Leggo snarled at her.

'Only that even you must realise you're behaving like an

oaf.'

Eve held her breath.

'Who the fuck do you think you're talking to?'

Leggo stood up and took a step towards her. Sarah shook her luxurious locks and looked at her nails, examining a non-existent chip. She spoke without looking at him.

'A petulant child by the looks of it. Now stop making a tit of yourself and piss off.'

'Come on, Leggo,' Spizz said. 'Let's find somewhere else.'

Thommo picked up their bill and a handful of notes and waved it towards the waitress as the other trooped out, Spizz nudging Leggo ahead of him.

'Sorry,' he mouthed at Eve as they left.

'You're terrible you are. A bit of a stirrer,' Alex said to Sarah.

'Stirrer? Moi? I don't know what you mean.'

'You okay, Eve?' Alex asked.

'I'm fine,' she replied. 'Oh, even better now,' she added as the waitress placed a large chocolate and coconut ice-cream in front of her.

'Sorry for the waiting,' the waitress said.

'And we're sorry. That you had to deal with such a prat,' Ron said. *'Imbecil. Idiota,'* he added when he saw she didn't understand prat.

'Ningún problema'

They tucked into their desserts and resumed their conversations, putting the uncomfortable incident behind them.

'You must meet all sorts, Eve,' Charlie said. 'I thought you kept your cool really well.'

'Yes! I'd lose my temper if I had to deal with people like him' Liz said. 'I get fussy customers sometimes but it's over quickly and I just don't book them again. I couldn't do your job. You get stuck with people for a week.'

'All in a day's work,' Eve said.

'I expect you've dealt with worse than that, haven't you?' Charlie asked.

'Much worse!'

'Have you ever had a really big problem to deal with? Like death?' Estelle's eyes grew wide.

'I've dealt with everything except a birth,' Eve said, making them laugh. 'Accidents, death, delays, illness, lost luggage, hurricanes, broken hearts… Just about everything.'

She saw no need to tell them that through a Travel Together holiday she'd been reunited with her son and his father. Although it wasn't a secret, some things she preferred to keep private.

'Do you get any proper romances?' Jackie asked, wistfully.

'Sometimes.'

'Don't you mean sex?' Sarah asked.

'Well, yes. You get both,' Eve said. 'I mean, you put a group of men and women together in a relaxing, holiday atmosphere, singles or otherwise, and things are bound to happen. But occasionally we have a real romance. The day before you all arrived I went to a wedding here on Ibiza of a lovely couple who met on a trip I accompanied to India four years ago.'

'Really?'

'And my son met his wife on a singles holiday, too,' she added, smiling at the thought.

'Well, you handle it all remarkably well,' Sarah said raising her glass. 'Well done, Eve!'

'Well done, Eve!'

'Ever thought about writing a book?' Katrina asked. 'You must have tons of material.'

'I've got enough for a series of books,' Eve said, only half jokingly.

'I bet they'd be brilliant,' Katrina said.

'I'd read 'em!' Ron agreed.

'And who's this Jenny they keep going on about?' Liz asked.

'She's a tour manager who does a lot of the tennis holidays because she plays herself. She's always been on the previous trips they've done so they know her quite well.'

'I've met her,' Ron said. 'She's not a patch on you. I heard she'd got the sack because she took her boyfriend along on one of the holidays.'

Blimey! News travels fast in the Travel Together Community!

'Not hot on discretion or empathy then,' Sarah said.

'Yes! Talk about rub it in. Parade your boyfriend in front of your single clients,' Jackie laughed, shaking her head.

'I don't know anything about that. Or her really,' Eve lied.

'Well, I think we're lucky to have you,' Katrina said, smiling.

'Thank you.'

'When you think about it singles' holidays are funny, aren't they?' Estelle pondered. 'I mean, we only met up yesterday yet you don't feel like strangers any more.'

'Ron said that yesterday,' Liz piped up. 'Meet as strangers, leave as friends.'

'It's true, though,' Ron agreed. 'It's always the same. I'm still in touch with quite a few people I've met on Travel Together holidays. And we're mates, you know. Proper mates.'

'Do people tell you things, Eve? Like confessions?' Katrina asked.

'Sometimes. But I think they tell each other things more than they do me,' she added knowing that wasn't totally true. So many times in her career she'd played the role of a Mother Confessor. So many nights she'd sat listening to people poor their hearts out, wiping their tears away. 'So, do you want to go on somewhere else?' Eve changed the subject away from herself.

'It might be nice just to stroll back to the hotel and sit on the terrace,' Charlie said. 'I'm not fussed about going out out tonight. Not if we're going into Ibiza tomorrow night.'

'And having to get up and be ready for tennis by half past nine kinda puts a lid on things,' Nicole said. 'Serves tomorrow! I'm looking forward to that.'

'You should be the first one to go out and have a good time,' Ron said. 'You're the youngest.'

'I am having a good time. Just being here with all of you. Sorry if that sounds a bit pathetic. I'm not trying to get up anyone's backside,' she added quickly. 'But I can't believe I've only known you all for two days. It's been a lovely meal tonight.'

'And that's the good thing about these holidays. Most people get on with each other. And most people are all right,' Ron said.

'Apart from the Fourth Form!' Sarah said, laughing.

'Well, at least we've got each other and don't have to worry about them,' Ron said.

Eve called for the bill. The waitress was very accommodating and had prepared separate bills just as Eve had requested when they'd first sat down. From experience she always asked how the group wanted to pay for meals as this was often a source of friction; those who were keen to split the bill were usually those who'd had the most expensive dishes on the menu and plenty of wine. Each paying their own always seemed to her the fairest way of doing things, unless the group were in agreement to split.

She smothered a yawn as she paid her own. She wouldn't need much rocking tonight.

✦ ✦ ✦

THE GROUP WANDERED back towards the hotel in twos and threes, chatting and joking as they went. Sean and Nicole found themselves walking together bringing up the rear, their pace becoming slower, the gap between them and the others getting wider.

'So how come you're on a singles' holiday?' Sean asked her.

'The same as you, probably. I decided about three weeks ago that I could juggle things and take some time off and that I could actually afford a break somewhere. None of my mates could take annual leave on such short notice so a singles' holiday seemed like the best solution.'

'And you play tennis at home?'

'Yes. I started at the club about eighteen months ago. I just thought a tennis holiday might be easier than being with a group and just lying on the beach or round the pool all day. At least this way the tennis sort of breaks up the day.'

'I know what you mean. There's less chance of getting stuck with any lame ducks. Most of the day you're busy.'

'Although most people seem all right, don't they? No lame ducks.'

'The Fourth Form are a bit odd,' Sean said.

'Still, they keep to themselves.'

'Yes. I don't think they have much in common with the rest of us.'

'I know what you mean.'

'Do you fancy having a drink here?'

Sean indicated a bar with a few tables outside that they were passing.

'Erm… yes. Okay.'

They went up the three steps leading to the small terrace of Bar Espardell as the others continued on their way back to the Hotel Dunas Blancas unaware their numbers were depleted.

✦ ✦ ✦

ROSALIND TOOK HER gin and tonic from the tray Ron was balancing and slipped into the chair next to Katrina who was chatting to Alex on her other side.

'I thought I'd bring them over,' Ron said. 'Juanca and co look a bit busy.'

'It's lively in here, tonight,' Sarah observed looking round. 'I expect there have been new arrivals today.'

'Yes. A large group of Spanish people,' Eve said, indicating some twenty people, couples in their fifties.

'Spanish people?' Estelle said. 'Here?'

'Why wouldn't Spanish people come here?' Charlie asked her, amused by her reaction.

'Just seems a bit odd.'

'No different from us going to Blackpool or Cleethorpes.'

'Just a tad more glamorous,' Sarah said.

'Oh, yes. Of course. I hadn't thought of it like that.' Estelle felt a bit foolish and took a large gulp of her drink to hide her embarrassment which went down the wrong hole bringing on a violent coughing spasm. Everyone was very attentive to her plight, which made her feel even worse.

'Cough up, chicken,' Liz said kindly, rubbing her back.

The lively group of Spanish People rose to their feet and took to the smallish dance floor at the far end of the bar area.

'Come on, Liz!' Ron grabbed her hand. 'Let's *paso doble*!'

The group looked on smiling as Ron and Liz joined in with gusto.

'It's not like the pasos they do on Strictly, is it?' Rosalind said, forgetting Katrina didn't watch it.

'They do the competitive ballroom version, I think,' Alex said. 'This is the basic Spanish paso.'

'Do you watch Strictly?'

'Occasionally. But my sisters used to do ballroom when they were younger so it kind of rubbed off.'

'Well, they're certainly enjoying themselves!' Katrina said, indicating Ron and Liz. 'Ron does have a raw energy for life.'

'Doesn't he just,' Alex agreed. 'It's nice to see.'

Eve smiled as she watched Liz and Ron dancing enthusiastically alongside the Spanish couples.

'Ole!'

Their shout was the loudest on the dance floor as all the couples changed direction. Eve loved to see people enjoying themselves. She'd dealt with more than her fair share of whiners and complainers over the years so watching her group having fun made her heart sing and the job worthwhile.

'Have you seen Nicole? I've just noticed she's not here.'

'I haven't, Estelle. The last time I saw her was as we were leaving the restaurant. Perhaps she's gone to bed.'

'Perhaps.' Estelle was a bit miffed to think Nicole might have gone to bed without saying anything to her.

Eve's practised eye immediately noticed that Sean was missing, too, so it wasn't hard to work out they'd probably gone off for a quiet drink together. Her two redheads. Well, that was nice. Both seemed like decent people from what she'd seen so far. She looked around the large table wondering if there'd be any more romances during the remainder of the holiday.

Sarah and Charlie? Not very likely.

Alex and Katrina? Could be…

Liz and Ron? Hmm. Quite possibly.

She watched as they made their way back to the table, both laughing, Ron's hand placed gently on Liz's back. They both seemed like decent people and in spite of the age gap were obviously getting on like a house on fire.

'Phew! That's taken it out of me!' Liz laughed as she flopped back into her chair. 'He'll have me doing flamenco next!'

'That sounds like it could be fun!' Sarah said. 'Here! Get that down you.' She pushed a glass of cava towards Liz. 'I topped you up.'

'Thanks. Dancing's thirsty work. What with the tennis! I'll be so fit by the time next Saturday comes round,' Liz said.

'Well, I must say they know how to enjoy themselves,' Charlie said, nodding towards the Spanish People who were now all singing loudly and waving their arms to a song that seemed to consist of lots of *"Aye! Aye! Aye!"*

'I think songs in foreign languages always sound so charming,' Estelle said.

'That's probably the equivalent of Three Lions. Or Opps Up Side Your Head,' Charlie said.

'You're such a romantic, Charlie!' Estelle grumbled. 'You've just ruined a beautiful moment!

'Sorry!'

'I like that song Once in a Meadow. I'm surprised I

haven't heard it yet.'

'Once in a Meadow? I don't think I know that one.'

'Yes, you do! You usually hear it all the time in Spain.'

Charlie shrugged. He had no idea what Estelle was talking about. He'd never heard Once in a Meadow.

Rosalind quietly sipped her drink, enjoying the music and the atmosphere of the hotel's lounge and the snippets of conversation from her new friends. She wanted to have a word with Katrina but this wasn't the moment. Katrina was still chatting animatedly to Alex. Rosalind thought Alex fancied Katrina. She studied them from behind her oval glasses and thought they made a handsome couple. Both were of athletic build; both had short, stylish haircuts, Katrina's a blondish pixie-cut, Alex's black, high top and geometric. He reminded her of Ashley Banjo. Yes, they made a good couple. She sighed to herself and wondered if there'd ever be anyone again for her. She'd hoped things might have developed into something with Matthew but they hadn't. And before him it had been several years since she'd had a boyfriend. She thought about Bradley. They'd been together for two years many moons ago. Her mother's words came to her: *"There's a lid for every pot,"* she used to say. And although Rosalind hadn't met her lid yet – she wasn't even sure if she was looking for one – here she was in Ibiza, six months down the line, realising that life truly did go on. Even after bereavement.

Out of the blue, her eyes filled with tears and a huge lump formed in her throat.

No! Not here! Not in front of everyone!

She gulped away the lump just as Ron and Liz stood up again and urged everyone to join them on the dance floor. Seeing some of the others get to their feet, Rosalind joined them, happy to lose herself and her thoughts in wild abandon to the music.

✦ ✦ ✦

ON THE TERRACE of Bar Espardell Sean was losing the will to live. He couldn't believe he had so misread her. From what he had seen thus far on the holiday Nicole had come across as being a bright, intelligent woman with a good sense of fun, as well as being stunningly beautiful, with her long, red hair and gorgeous figure. However, from the moment they'd taken their seats in a corner of the terrace under a gnarled and withered olive tree Nicole's whole conversation had been about her ex-boyfriend. At first he had been sympathetic to hear the guy had died.

'And the worst thing was I didn't hear about it until my friend Helga told me it was on the local TV news.'

'Nobody let you know? The Police? His family?'

'Nobody knew about me,' she said, shaking her head sadly. 'Not even Helga.'

'But she let you know…'

'In passing. Yes. She didn't phone me deliberately or anything.'

The penny dropped for Sean.

'You were his mistress?'

He coloured up as soon as he said it. He was kicking himself for sounding so judgemental and prejudiced; so bloody old-fashioned and twee.

'Well, at least you didn't say "bit on the side".'

'Sorry! I just… I assumed you were … like… a couple.'

'We were as far as we were both concerned. He treated me wonderfully well. Really took care of me. He was loving and thoughtful and kind. We'd often go down to the coast for the night and stay in a little boutique hotel. Or up to

London. See a show. Have a meal and stay in an apartment just off Sloan Square that belonged to a friend of his. He sent me flowers for every occasion. You know, Valentine's Day, my birthday…'

Her voice drifted to a halt and she sipped her drink. Sean thought it was almost as if she'd forgotten he was there. He coughed, desperately trying to think of something to say; a way of changing the subject.

'Sometimes he sent them just to show he cared and that he was thinking of me…'

'So how did you get involved with him?'

He mentally kicked himself for not thinking of something a bit more original. And for not changing the subject.

'Sorry. That's none of my business.'

Nicole seemed keen to tell him all about it, though.

'I met him when I was walking Benji, Bobby and Billy. They're the three beagles that belong to his mates, Lisa and Noel. That's where Helga works. She's their au pair and we became friends. And one day I was arriving back with the dogs as he was leaving. The dogs were all over him, which is always as good sign, you know, if a dog likes someone… And he didn't seem to mind their muddy footprints. He made a fuss of them and I liked that and so we got chatting. I can't even remember what we talked about now. Just that I thought he was handsome. And nice. And charismatic. Fifteen minutes later when I left the house to head home he was waiting at the top of the driveway for me. He invited me for a drink and we were together from then onwards. Until the accident.'

Her eyes welled up and Sean felt uncomfortable.

Oh God! No! Please don't let her cry!

Sean never could handle tearful women. His ex-wife had turned on the water taps at every opportunity. He gave his head a little shake. The last think he wanted was to think of *her*!

'So what happened to him?' The question exploded from his mouth before he could stop himself.

'His wife ran him over.'

Sean bit his bottom lip.

Please don't let me laugh! Please don't let me laugh!

'He was on the driveway bending over to pick up his keys that he'd dropped and she didn't see him and reversed right over him. She felt a bump and heard a noise and then drove forward again…'

'Christ!'

'And it made the local news because of who he was.'

'And who was he?'

'A very well-known solicitor. Everybody in and around Dorking knew him.'

'Perhaps Sarah knew him. She's a solicitor and she comes from your neck of the woods.'

Dismissing his suggestion Nicole had then spent the next fifteen minutes singing her late lover's praises. Sean couldn't help noticing that fidelity wasn't among his notable qualities. He began to feel uncomfortable; to listen to Nicole you'd think the guy had been the Pope. He smothered a yawn.

'Sorry. I'm boring you.'

Yes!

'No!'

'I'm just wilting a bit, that's all. It must be all the exercise and then the booze,' he said. 'Shall we go?'

He stood up before she could answer. As they made their way off the terrace he noticed two men looking at her, their admiration and envy showing on their faces. She was a stunner, there were no two ways about it. He chuckled to himself thinking he'd probably been as open-mouthed when he'd looked at her earlier.

Shame about the verbal diarrhoea!

He couldn't get back to the Dunas Blancas quickly enough.

✦ ✦ ✦

JACKIE HAD ENJOYED her evening but she was suddenly restless and needed to be away from these people. She.wanted some time to herself. She needed some time to herself. So she decided to go up to her room.

'Stay off Facebook!' Sarah had called a warning as Jackie had left the bar.

'Yes, of course!'

She willed the lift to move faster then she scurried down the corridor. She rushed inside, threw her bag on the floor, kicked off her shoes and jumped onto the bed, phone in hand, already scrolling down Julie Clithers's Facebook page. She rolled onto her side, her finger swiping, her anxious eyes frantically swivelling back and forth as they searched for more evidence of Scott's betrayal.

And there it was!

They had obviously had a busy night. Julie draped across the laps of three guys, one of them Scott. Julie and Scott sharing a large cocktail. Julie and Scott surrounded by drunken, smiling people. Julie had posted forty-seven photos half-an-hour ago. Jackie looked at her watch. It was twenty to twelve which meant it would be twenty to three in the morning in Dubai. Without thinking she decided to WhatsApp Scott. She'd pretend she'd got the time difference wrong if he complained it was late. And, of course, she'd also have to pretend she was still in Leeds so she switched her camera off. Scott's phone rang. And rang. And rang. He didn't pick up. Disheartened she hung up and sat there thinking.

He's probably fast asleep.

Sleeping alongside Julie Clithers.

Or still out and about and didn't hear it ring.

Out and about with Julie Clithers.

She started crying. Why hadn't she ignored Facebook and gone straight to bed? She knew the answer to that: she'd been itching to check Julie's page all night. And now she wished she hadn't! She lay down and closed her eyes, tears coursing down her face as she cried herself to sleep.

✦ ✦ ✦

'ERM, I'M JUST gonna have a quick word with Alex and Charlie,' Sean said, dismissing Nicole as they arrived back at the hotel.

'Okay,' she smiled sweetly at him and then raised her hand and smiled at Estelle who was waving at her from the other side of the bar.

Nicole headed towards Estelle, who was sitting with Katrina, Rosalind and Sarah. Sean went to the two men who were at the bar.

'We've had a fabulous time!' Estelle shrieked, throwing her arms around Nicole's neck. 'Those Spanish People are a right laugh.'

She pointed to the Spanish couples talking animatedly to Ron who was doing his best to follow the conversation and translate to Liz at the same time, whilst others were moving rhythmically and sensually to the *Sevillana* that was now being played.

'They've had us all dancing flamenco and all sorts.'

'What happened to you?' Sarah asked, the twinkle in her eye suggesting she already knew.

'Oh, I stopped and had a drink with Sean at one of the little bars we passed,' she said.

'Did you have a good time?'

'Yes. It was nice.'

✦ ✦ ✦

'CHRIST! I LOOKED round and the terrace was littered with two-legged donkeys!' Sean said, causing Alex to spit out his beer. 'She did not stop talking!'

'Isn't that better than someone with no conversation at all?' Charlie asked, playing Devil's Advocate.

'But it was all about her ex! Some top-drawer solicitor who was killed when his wife ran him over.'

'What on purpose? She ran him down?'

'No, it was an accident, apparently. Reversed over him as he was picking his keys up.'

Alex and Charlie laughed.

'You couldn't make it up!'

'Well, it looks like we both got it wrong tonight,' Alex said ruefully.

'Why? Did you bomb out, too?'

Alex nodded, took a sip of his beer and raised his eyebrows.

'With Katrina.'

'I wouldn't have thought she was your type,' Sean observed.

'Well, she's not as it happens. Turns out she bats for the other side.'

'Really?'

Alex nodded again.

'Well, yes, I suppose she does now you come to mention it,' Sean said, trying to pretend he wouldn't have made the same mistake. 'She is a bit female-athlete looking.'

'Well, that's a bit of a generalisation!' Charlie laughed.

'You know what I mean. Broad shoulders. Short hair. How did you find out?'

'We were chatting and I suggested we have dinner together somewhere in Ibiza Town tomorrow night. Just the two of us. You know, she's a vegan and I eat a lot of vegetarian food. She said she thought that would be a really good idea and then with the next fucking breath she's telling me about it was her girlfriend who'd converted her to veganism.'

'What's she doing on a singles' holiday if she's got a girlfriend?' Sean asked.

'Fuck knows.' Alex shrugged. 'Perhaps the girlfriend doesn't like travelling.'

'It's not on, though, is it? Singles' holidays should be for single people. And straight single people at that. I mean, there must be lesbian holiday groups she could've gone on.'

'Perhaps they don't do tennis holidays,' Alex suggested.

'Some you win, some you lose,' Charlie observed. 'And meanwhile Ron continues to be the only bloke who's getting a look in,' he added, raising his glass at Ron and Liz who were walking arm-in-arm towards the lifts.

'I wonder what's happened with the others. If Leggo's calmed down a bit.'

'He's a fucking nutter,' Sean said. 'He's trouble. Out of control. I've come across blokes like him…'

'The whole group of them are weird,' Charlie said. 'Funny set up that.'

'Shall we have another beer?' Alex asked.

'Best thing I've heard all night!' Charlie agreed.

✦ ✦ ✦

RON PRESSED THE button for the lift and smiled at Liz.

'We should be walking up the stairs really, shouldn't we?'

'I'm too whacked to walk up!'

'I usually walk, but my brother takes the lift. We were raised differently,' Ron said.

'Oh, Ron!' Liz giggled as the lift arrived.

Eve waited until the lift doors had closed on Liz and Ron before taking her leave of those who were left and made her way across the bar and into the foyer. She arrived at the lifts at the same time as Fee, who'd just come in.

'Hi! Everything okay?' Eve asked her, smiling.

'Fine!' Fee's reply was terse.

Eve was aware that Fee probably felt a bit embarrassed by what had gone on earlier. A lift arrived and both women got in.

'Which floor are you?' Eve asked.

'Three.'

Eve pressed three and four. The lift doors closed and the lift began to rise smoothly. She decided not to try and instigate any further conversation with Fee. The lift came to a halt on the third floor and the doors glided open. Fee stepped out.

'Good night, Fee,' Eve said.

'Look… I'm sorry about earlier…'

Eve put her foot in front of the lift door to stop it closing.

'…You know… Causing a scene.'

'You're fine. I understand.'

'Leggo's all right when he's sober. But he doesn't know when to stop when he's had a few drinks and he gets obnoxious. A right pain in the arse.'

'I was only concerned you might have hurt yourself. And I don't like to see anyone go off on their own.'

'I was okay. I found a quiet bar and had a few drinks with some people from Oldham. It made a nice change. New faces.'

'Why do you keep on going away with the same people?' Eve couldn't resist asking.

'I just sort of fell into it, really. I know it pisses the tour managers off sometimes. Don't get me wrong, they're an all right bunch. Just don't know when enough's enough sometimes. Especially Leggo.'

'Well, there are a whole bunch of people who I'm sure would love to get to know you.'

'Hmm.' Fee thought about it as if it was a novel idea. 'I might mingle a bit more in the morning.'

'I think you should give it a try. You might surprise yourself. They're all really nice. Worth getting to know'

'Yeah…well…we'll see. Sorry again. Goodnight.'

And with that she wandered down the corridor as the lift doors closed behind her and Eve, grinning to herself, continued to the fourth floor.

DAY THREE

✦

EVE WAITED UNTIL the coaching session was underway before calling Michael.

'Hello, darling!'

'Hi, Eve! How's it going?

'Erm… okay. Everyone's fine, although we had a bit of a falling out in the group of eight friends.'

'The Fourth Form?'

'Stop it! I'm trying hard not to call them that! But yes, one of the men behaved a bit stupidly last night and a chair got broken and he didn't want to pay for it but it's all sorted out now.'

She didn't tell her son how Leggo had behaved towards her as she knew he'd be tempted to jump into a taxi and come over to the Dunas Blancas and punch him on the nose.

'Unfortunately, I can't come to lunch today, though,' she said. 'I would really love to but if I do something's sure to happen here.'

'Oh, that's a shame.'

'So give them all my love. And to Natalie, too. How is she?'

'She's fine. She's managed the heat okay and with the excuse she's eating for two she's been tucking in and enjoying the Spanish food. Ouch! She's hitting me with a cushion!'

'No sympathy from me!' Eve joked. 'And give Felicity a great big kiss from Grandma.'

'I will.'

'Melv called last night. He said he was fine but he looked and sounded tired.'

'Probably nothing a visit from you wouldn't put right!'

'We'll see. As I said to you, I'm going to give him some space.'

'Is he okay with that?'

'We'll get around to discussing my next visit soon enough. We're going to talk again on Sunday.'

'And speaking of that, hopefully we'll see you next week.'

'Yes. I'll give you a ring on Sunday, too, and we can make plans. Enjoy your lunch!'

'We will. And you have a good day.'

'Love you!'

'Love you!'

Eve hung up and slipped her phone back into her bag with a big smile on her face. Her son made her so happy. Always. And his beautiful wife and delightful little daughter. She sighed acknowledging that she was blessed, so blessed at having them in her life. She wandered back and took her seat in the shade and watched the coaching sessions. Today they were working on first and second serves. Eve hadn't realised there was much difference between them. Jesus had invited her to join in any of the sessions she wanted to but she had declined. She was happy to sit in the shade, sipping coffee, watching the tennis enthusiasts run around in the heat.

She noticed that they were in three groups; the Fourth Form were together except Fee, who was with Charlie, Nicole, Alex, Estelle and Rosalind, while Sarah, Sean, Katrina, Jackie and Ron made up the third group. Jesus had got Ivan and Daniel to set up small cones which the group had to aim their serve at. The air was filled with the whoosh of the stroke closely followed by the shout of delight or disappointment from the server depending where it landed. Eve took out her phone again and started to look for restaurants in Ibiza Town for them to go to that evening. Given that it was the end of July the town would probably be heaving. But as Spaniards didn't eat until late – often after eleven o'clock – she didn't think it would be necessary to make a reservation anywhere. It was probably better to stroll through the port and Dalt Vila and let them decide where they wanted to stop and eat when they saw somewhere they fancied.

And I hope that won't be somewhere too expensive…

Eve liked her food and she liked to eat well but on trips where not all the meals were included she still had to remind herself after all the years of working for Travel Together that she wasn't on holiday. If she didn't she could end up out of pocket after a week's work. The Port of Ibiza wasn't the cheapest place in the world to eat and drink. She shrugged.

Worse case scenario I can always go to McDonald's.

She made a note of a couple of places and then settled back in her comfy chair letting the deep, intoxicating perfume of the nearby jasmine bush waft over her. She adored jasmine and had one at home. There was something luxurious yet comforting about its particular scent. She leant her head against the high back of the chair, inhaled deeply and closed her eyes.

She had barely begun to drift into a light sleep when she was rudely brought round.

'Fucking hell, Spizz! You twat!'

Eve jerked awake and stood up to see Leggo doubled over and clutching his face.

'Sorry, mate,' Spizz said, not looking very sorry.

Eve and Jesus went over to Leggo whose face had a livid red welt next to his left temple.

'The tosser aimed his serve right at me!' Leggo was indignant.

'Don't talk rubbish! Course I didn't. You weren't looking where you were going,' Spizz protested.

'Come over to the Club House. My first aid kit's on the table next to my bag,' Jesus said.

'Nah. I don't want a fuss.'

'You'll need to just disinfect the graze,' Jesus said. 'But then you'll know that as I'm sure it's what you'd say to one of your students.'

Reluctantly Leggo followed him, still clutching his face. Eve followed behind.

'Okay, everyone! Take a short break!' Jesus called to the rest of the group.

Eve was happy to leave the first aid to Jesus. She would have to complete an Accident Report Form for Travel Together which Leggo would need to sign but that could be done any time before they left on Saturday. She took her seat again outside the Club House and was soon joined by Estelle, Sean, Ron and Liz.

'Well, that couldn't have happened to a nicer person,' Ron observed.

'They do say Karma will always get you back,' Liz quipped. 'And I think Fee agrees with me,' she added, looking over to where Fee was standing talking animatedly to Titty and Thommo while looking rather smug.

Eve wouldn't admit to agreeing with Liz but she silently acknowledged that if anyone had to be hit in the face by a ball she wasn't sorry it was Leggo.

'How's it all going?' Eve asked them.

'I'm enjoying this morning more than I did yesterday,' Estelle said. 'My serve's so weak that all help is gladly received.'

'Well, that's why we're here, to improve,' Sean said giving her a smile. 'You looked like you were doing all right to me.'

Estelle annoyed herself by blushing at Sean's words.

Sarah and Jackie wandered over and joined them.

'Well, that was Karma in action,' Sarah said causing the others to laugh.

'That's just what I said,' Liz giggled.

On the other side of the terrace Jesus had applied disinfectant wipes to Leggo's face which now looked angrier than it had ten minutes earlier.

'It'll probably sting for a while,' Jesus said.

'I know!' Leggo snapped. 'I haven't been a PE teacher for eighteen years for nothing.'

'Then you'll also know you need to sit quietly for a few hours, take these,' he handed him some paracetamol, 'with lots of water and stay awake as you've had a head injury.'

Leggo tutted and stood up.

'It was only a slap with a tennis ball!'

'Sorry. My course my rules. I'm not letting you back on the court for the rest of the day.'

'You're having a fucking laugh! I've paid for this course…'

'Let me give you some advice,' Jesus said, standing up next to him and glaring into his eyes.

All round them conversation stopped as the group watched what was happening. Eve clutched the arms of the chair ready to launch herself towards the two men if things turned nasty. Although she couldn't hear what was being said it was obvious they were having a serious discussion from their stance.

'You think I need fucking advice from you?' Leggo raised his voice. Now everyone could hear him. 'I invented advice, mate.'

'Really? Well, here's a piece of advice you missed,' Jesus said, not giving an inch. 'Don't be a dickhead all your life. And if you can't manage the rest of your life, at least behave yourself for the rest of this week if you want to carry on being part of this course.'

'You can't stop me taking part!'

'I can and I will. So just calm down a bit.'

'Who the fuck do you think you're talking to?'

'That's an end of it, okay? Rest for today. Don't fall asleep and don't drink. If you feel drowsy let me or Eve know immediately. And come back tomorrow morning with a bit less attitude. Got that?'

Jesus gathered up his first aid kit and walked away from Leggo who stood open-mouthed and seething. His anger mounted when he saw everyone was looking at him.

'You can fuck off the lot of yous!'

He stomped into the Club House. Spizz and Titty looked at each other and then followed him inside.

'And how have you been getting on this morning?' Eve asked Jackie trying to bring a degree of normality back to the proceedings.

'It's been good. I really feel as if I've learned something.'

'Great! That's what we like to hear.'

'Do you want some feedback?' Sarah asked Eve. 'I think

there should be more than one coach,' she continued before Eve could reply. 'We're quite a large group and I think there should be one coach for every six of us.'

'All the tennis holidays I've been on with Travel Together have only had one coach,' Ron piped up. 'And Jesus is good...'

'It's no reflection on Jesus,' Sarah retorted. 'He's extremely good at his job and he's got Ivan and Daniel helping but they're not coaches. It's just an observation. For the price we've paid I think there should be at least one more coach.'

'I'll make a note of your comments and feedback to the company in my report,' Eve said, 'but you should have also been sent a questionnaire to fill in at the end of the holiday.'

'Yes, I did. I will complete that, too, of course.'

'Well, I think it's working well,' Ron told Eve as Sarah and Jackie made their way back to the courts out of earshot. 'There's always someone, isn't there?'

Eve smiled at him and made no comment. If that was the only negative comment about the holiday she was going to get she'd be happy.

'Okay, Everyone! Back to work!' Jesus jogged down to the courts and the stragglers followed him.

Spizz and Titty came out of the Club House.

'I think you'd better keep an eye on him,' Spizz said to Eve. 'I think he might start drinking.'

'He's already ordered a beer,' Titty said.

'I thought he was a PE teacher,' Eve said, knowing full-well that he was.

'He is.'

'Then he'll know more than anyone what he should and shouldn't do.'

'Well, I'm just letting you know,' Spizz said, sounding

put out. 'He's really pissed off he can't carry on playing today. He'll be entitled to a refund, won't, he?'

'He'll have to take that up with Travel Together when he gets home. I don't make decisions like that.'

Eve sighed. Stopping a forty-year-old man from going on a binge wasn't in her job description and if Leggo was bent on being stupid there wasn't much she could do. Certainly, he wouldn't appreciate her interference. She'd observe him from a far and if he appeared to be suffering from any of the symptoms of concussion she'd tell Jesus and they'd call a doctor or get him to a medical centre. It never failed to amaze her how daft people could be.

✦ ✦ ✦

'I'M SO GLAD we've opted out of the tournament,' Jackie said, energetically rubbing suntan lotion onto her face. 'This is more like being on holiday!'

'Well, it depends on the holiday you want,' Sarah said, sipping her glass of rose. She knew it was only early afternoon but she really didn't care.

'I'll certainly think twice before I book anything again! I don't know how I could have been so silly really. Although I did enjoy the stuff we did this morning. I felt as if I was serving much better at the end of the session.'

'Well, that's encouraging,' Sarah said, slipping in her earphones. 'Excuse me, I'm listening to an audio book.'

She settled back and closed her eyes. She could have left the audio book to one side and chatted to Jackie, but that hadn't occurred to her. As far as she was concerned she'd done more than enough to save Jackie from herself. She was certain Jackie was still stalking Julie and Scott through Facebook, though.

Why put yourself through it?

She didn't understand women who made themselves such victims. She had never wanted the full living-together relationship. She couldn't think of anything worse!

If you want sex have a one-night stand and if you want company get a dog.

She couldn't remember where she'd heard that but it certainly made sense to her. And the thought of wanting sex caused a sudden lurch between her thighs and she realised she hadn't had sex for more than a month. She'd got so used to having it almost on demand that she'd been spoilt. Things had certainly changed.

I'll have to find someone for tonight.

They were going to Ibiza Town which would widen the circle a bit. Surely she would find someone to scratch her itch; to satisfy her urge?

I bloody well hope so!

Jackie was suddenly startled by her phone ringing. She grabbed it from her bag and her heart lurched when she saw it was Scott calling her. She spun round guiltily and looked at Sarah, but with her earphones in she was oblivious to Jackie's call. A dozen thoughts ran through Jackie's head.

Should I answer?

She wanted to. She desperately wanted to. She wanted to hear Scott tell her he was having a miserable time in Dubai; that he was going to one boring meeting after another and was missing her like mad. And she knew that's exactly what he would say. And she knew he'd be lying to her again. The phone went quiet and lay still in her palm. A plethora of emotions swept over her – disappointment, sadness, regret but also relief. She was unsure she'd have been able to hide her anger when he lied to her and if he'd asked her where she was she was sure to have given herself away.

The phone buzzed again making her jump. He'd sent her a WhatsApp message.

> *Hi. I've just tried to get you. I saw you'd rung last night. Did you forget about the time difference? I was asleep. Just going for a shower and then another boring business dinner before bed. Will try you again later. Hope all's well. Are you missing me? Lyl.*

You fucking liar!

Her heart was racing and her stomach churned as she re-read the message several times.

What if I have got it wrong, though?

Checking Sarah's eyes were still tightly shut she scrolled through Julie Clither's Facebook page for the umpteenth time. She wasn't stupid. The evidence was there for all to see. She picked up her phone again and went onto WhatsApp.

> *Sorry I missed your call. I was in a meeting myself. Shame you're in such a great place as Dubai and having such a rotten time. Never mind! I've got an unforgettable weekend planned. Can't wait to see you!*

She laughed at what she'd written. She had no idea what to do yet, but she was determined to start plotting something. She'd have to talk to Sarah about it. She was certain she'd have lots of ideas.

✦ ✦ ✦

'NO SIGN OF our injured friend?' Jesus lifted his designer shades and placed them on top of his head to reveal his dark brown eyes with their fringe of long lashes. Eve and the group had returned to the Club House and crowded into the bar to quench their thirsts and enjoy their first alcohol of the day. Eve was pleased to note the atmosphere was happy and noisy. And once again, she'd enjoyed the match she'd umpired, even if Charlie had twice questioned her decision.

'Not since lunchtime. He hasn't been back.'

'Well, let's hope he's been sensible and taken himself back to his room to sit in the cool and rest.'

'And to sober up,' Eve grimaced. 'He was lurching as he left here.'

'I'll say to you what I always said to Jenny: I don't know how you do it! Sometimes adults behave worse than little children.'

'Yes, they do!' Eve agreed.

'You're all going into Ibiza Town tonight, yes?'

'Yes. I thought we could take a stroll through the Port and Dalt Vila and find somewhere for dinner on the way.'

'You'll be spoilt for choice. The port's very expensive, though. You might like to warn them.'

'Will do! Thanks.'

'I might see something of you. I live on Vara del Rey and usually go out for a stroll and a drink. In the port in the evenings.'

'I'd have thought you'd have had enough of us during the day,' Eve laughed. 'Especially after today.'

'It's always nice to see you, Eve.'

He gave her a beaming smile and squeezed her shoulder then made his departure from the Club House, waving to the others as he left.

If I wasn't old and cynical I'd take that as a come-on!

Eve giggled to herself and collected her paperwork together. She was going to have two hours to herself before drinks at seven-thirty.

✦ ✦ ✦

THE AFTERNOON'S TOURNAMENT had gone well. Estelle was beside herself with delight because she'd actually won three games against Liz in the singles and she and Charlie had been narrowly beaten 6-4 6-4 in the doubles by Liz and Ron.

'I really feel as if I've improved today,' she declared taking a large swig from her beer.

'You did well,' Charlie agreed, smiling. He certainly felt happier than yesterday and couldn't believe how much better Estelle had played.

'I'm really looking forward to going into Ibiza tonight,' Rosalind said, looking at her phone and scrolling. 'It looks great. Lots of people, lots of bars…'

'It should be fun,' Alex agreed.

'Can you Google vegan restaurants, please?' Katrina asked Rosalind. 'I left my phone in my room.'

Alex picked up his drink and headed towards the pool. Katrina's request had made him remember his suggestion the previous evening that they eat together in Ibiza tonight. Now he knew there was no chance of getting anywhere with her his enthusiasm had waned. He'd stick with the crowd. There's safety in numbers, he thought as he caught sight of Jackie and Sarah sunbathing side-by-side next to the pool. The area was fairly crowded but there was an empty sun lounger next to them.

'Mind if I join you?'

'Not at all,' Jackie said as he sat down.

'How was your afternoon?'

'Lovely! I think I've got a bit of a colour, although I have to be careful not to burn, but it's been ever so peaceful. How was the tennis?'

'Yes, good. I think everyone enjoyed the matches this afternoon.'

'No further incidents?' Sarah asked, removing her earphones and sitting up.

'All quiet and everyone behaving.'

'Well, that's encouraging. Let's hope tonight the Fourth Form just go off on their own.'

'I suppose that's the good thing about being in a larger group,' Jackie commented. 'There's always someone you can hang out with. Imagine if there was only two or three of us with them!'

'Did you win?' Sarah asked him.

'I did. I beat Jonesy 6-4 6-3 and then Rosalind and me beat Katrina and Sean 6-4 6-4.'

'Well done!'

'Thanks. Is the pool warm?'

'Gorgeous!' Both women chorused their reply.

Alex pulled his Fred Perry over his head, his dark, muscular back and then slipped out of his tennis shorts revealing plain blue swim shorts underneath. As he walked towards the pool the women exchanged a glance both realising they were drooling.

'Well, you wouldn't kick him out of bed for farting, would you?' Sarah said appreciatively as Alex executed a perfect dive into the deep end.

'You certainly wouldn't,' Jackie sighed. 'He's a hunk.'

'He comes across as a nice bloke, too, No edge to him from what I've seen.'

'He was chatting to Katrina a lot last night. I thought

they might be getting together.'

'I don't think she's interested in men.'

'Really? What makes you say that?'

'Something Sean said at breakfast. Apparently Alex had told him she's got a girlfriend.'

'But she's not butch or anything…'

'She doesn't have to be,' Sarah retorted, annoyed by Jackie's ignorance. 'My sister Rachel's gay and as feminine as they come.'

'Is she in a relationship?'

'Yes. She's been with her wife for seven years.'

'Oh, she's married?'

'Yes. It is legal, you know!' Sarah bit her lip. She hadn't meant to speak sharply to Jackie but comments and ignorance like hers were annoying. And they also served to remind Sarah how she hadn't always been as accepting of and loving towards her sister as she was now. She was ashamed when she thought about how she'd ribbed Rachel and called her names and made snide comments when she'd first come out. It was only as time went on and she'd seen how happy Rachel and Robyn were together that she'd realised how much courage it had taken for her sister to live life on her own terms. Their parents had been shocked and twelve years later still thought it was a phase she was going through. Rachel's coming out had rocked their little world.

One daughter gay and the other promiscuous!

She grinned to herself at the thought.

And why not? I'm not married, not in a relationship, I owe nothing to anyone.

With her shades hiding her eyes she watched Alex swimming strongly up and down the pool, his shoulders glistening as they came out of the water. When he reached the edge he stopped and flipped onto his back, floating, suspended. In one swift movement she got up from the sun lounger and waded down the steps until she was just inches from his face.

'Was it as gorgeous as I said?'

'Every bit as gorgeous,' he replied giving her a beaming smile. 'Are you always right about everything?'

'Usually,' she said as they trod water as close as they could possibly be without touching each other.

'So how come you're not playing in the tournaments? You looked like a good player to me.'

'Yeah, well, Jackie doesn't feel she's good enough for the tournaments. I'm happy to keep her company in the afternoons.'

'That's a shame you're missing out.'

'To be honest I can't be arsed with the competitiveness of it all, really. Everyone likes the frisson of competing and rivalry but some people seem to find the concept of playing for pleasure totally alien.'

'I know what you mean. That's why I stopped going to the tennis club.'

'So you don't play at home at all?'

'Yes. But I go over the local park with three mates.'

'Local park?'

She couldn't disguise the surprise and slight touch of distain in her voice.

'The courts are in good nick. We play for two hours solid and I save myself a fortune in membership fees, overpriced beers and all the bragging that goes on. What's wrong with that?'

'Nothing at all. You just don't look like a local park kind of man.'

The water-treading was becoming slower and closer. He studied her messy top-knot that still managed to look immaculate even though it was wet; her high, sculptured cheekbones supported her designer shades and below them her wide, sensuous lips. On any other woman he'd be convinced she'd had fillers and botox, but with Sarah he was certain she hadn't.'

'Well at the moment you don't exactly look like a solicitor,' he said, appreciation clear in his voice.

'You don't look like a boat-builder,' she retaliated.

'That's cos I'm not a boat-builder. I think you'll find that's Sean. I've got a cycle shop.'

'Well, whatever you do it keeps you fit,' she added, running her finger down his well-developed biceps.'

He smiled at her, liking what was happening.

'I'm finding it hard to imagine you wearing a wig and gown,' he said.

'The wigs are always itchy and the gowns archaic,' she said. 'But I'm not a barrister. Just a humble solicitor.'

'Hmm… I'm not sure humble's a word I'd use about you.'

'You have a problem with assertive women?'

'Not in the slightest. My mum was assertive.'

'Is she black? Or your dad?'

'My mum. She's Ghanaian. My dad's Welsh.'

'That's a bit of a combination! But you don't live in Wales, do you?'

'We never have. My dad met my mum in London. They were both nurses at the same hospital. And then after they got married and had my sister they moved to Dunstable.'

'Oh, yes. Where Jesus was born. I'd forgotten that,' Sarah laughed. 'So how come you've got a bike shop?'

'I've always liked cycling and it just seemed a logical step really when I decided I wanted to work for myself.'

'You don't seem like a typical cyclist.'

Alex laughed.

'What's a typical cyclist?'

'Oh, you know! Earnest. Smug. All think they're saving the planet.'

'Not that you're generalising!'

'And they hate motorists, yet they all jump traffic lights and ride on the pavements…'

'You forgot to mention the lycra. That's usually the first thing we hear about.'

'Oh, God! Yes. Lycra. The world's most unattractive material!'

Sarah gave a theatrical shudder.

'How come you're not wearing lycra?'

'Because I'm not cycling, that's why!'

'Thank goodness for that,' Sarah retorted. 'It's not the most flattering of fabrics, is it?'

'No, but it's not meant to flatter you. It's meant to be the most comfortable for riding.'

'I'm sure you look great in it.'

She gave him another appreciative look.

'Are you going into town tonight?'

'Yes. I'm looking forward to it. You?'

'Yes, me too.'

'Sarah! Do you want another drink?' Jackie's voice interrupted them.

'A fizzy water, please!'

'You're a cheap date,' Alex said.

'I so am not!' Sarah retorted, splashing him hard before swimming to the side and easily heaving herself out of the water leaving Alex alone in the middle of the pool.

She eased back onto her sun lounger, smiling to herself. Things were suddenly starting to look up.

✦ ✦ ✦

'THERE ARE LOADS of them,' Rosalind said, showing Katrina her phone. 'You'll be spoilt for choice.'

'Hmm, that's good.' Katrina studied the screen. 'Although I hope I won't be eating alone.'

She knew Alex probably wouldn't mention dinner together again. It saddened her to think that he'd obviously changed his mind. They had seemed to be getting along well and it had been his suggestion they should go to a vegan restaurant. But he hadn't referred to it again and she'd felt as if he was giving her a wide berth today. They'd played tennis together, or rather against each other. She'd partnered Sean and he'd partnered Rosalind. But as soon as the match was over he'd slipped away. It was almost an action replay of the previous evening when he'd been asking her about her vegetarianism; his face had suddenly frozen and less than two minutes later he'd excused himself and gone to stand with Charlie at the bar.

'I don't mind having some veggie stuff,' Charlie said.

'Nor do I,' Rosalind agreed.

'Great! Well, I'm off for a shower. I'll see you all in the bar at half seven.'

'See you later, Katrina!'

✦ ✦ ✦

LIZ LOOKED AT her reflection in the mirror and smiled. In spite of putting factor 50 and wearing her visor her face had caught the sun. She never understood how anyone would not put protection on their face. Nothing aged human beings more than sun damage. She knew from a lifetime in the beauty business that so many people were afraid they wouldn't get tanned at all if they wore a high factor cream. They were completely wrong, of course. They still got brown, they just didn't burn. She examined her face closely.

Yes! A nice, healthy glow!

She'd taken her time getting ready tonight and had decided on a pretty, lime-green dress with a low back. She was going to pair it with her Fit-flops. They were comfortable and dressy. She really liked wearing heels but remembered that Eve had said the streets of Ibiza Old Town were cobbled and the last thing she wanted was to stumble and break an ankle.

And besides, they'll make me a bit taller than Ron…

She looked at herself in the mirror in surprise.

Where had that come from?

She sat on the bed with a thump. She liked Ron, she really did. He'd been great company so far; he'd made the previous evening such a laugh. And he'd been a perfect gentleman. Again. He'd seen her to her room with a wave and a cheery "Goodnight, love!" And then he'd strolled off down the corridor to his own room.

Was I disappointed with that? Was I expecting more?

She told herself she wasn't but… She thought about Ron. He was a thoroughly nice man. He'd been kind and considerate towards her, the same as he'd been to everyone. He was older than her by… How much? She didn't know. She was forty-two and Ron was probably about sixty-five or sixty-six, perhaps. But he kept himself nice; he wore expensive clothes, was well-groomed and he always smelt wonderful.

Yes, I could do worse than Ron.

Except, of course, she wasn't doing anything with Ron! She laughed at herself.

You're getting ahead of yourself, Liz! Just go with the flow and enjoy his company.

She nodded at her own wise words. Then gave an extra squirt of Joy behind her ears and down her cleavage.

✦ ✦ ✦

EVE HAD HAD a busy couple of hours. She'd updated her tour report. She preferred to complete it daily to avoid forgetting things. It also meant that she could email it to Travel Together as soon as she got home. She'd objectively reported what had happened with Leggo and Fee the previous evening and that morning's incident of Spizz whacking Leggo with the ball and the action she and Jesus had taken, plus Leggo's reaction. She'd phoned Leggo's room to enquire how he was but there'd been no reply.

And now, at quarter to eight everyone was down in the bar, apart from the Fourth Form who were only represented by Spizz, Jonesy, Thommo, Fee and Banksy.

'It's all right. Don't wait for us, we'll find our own way into Ibiza,' Spizz told Eve. 'We wanna go onto Playa D'en Bossa anyway, so we probably won't see you until the morning.'

'Have you seen Leggo? I rang him earlier to check. he was okay but there was no reply.'

'No we haven't but he'll turn up,' Spizz said. 'As I told you on the first night, he likes to do his own thing.'

'Okay. Well, enjoy your evening!'

Eve wasn't sorry to hear they were going off on their own; if they were involved in any more aggro she wouldn't have to witness it or step in. She was slightly anxious about Leggo, though. Logic told her he was probably getting smashed in a bar somewhere; she just hoped he wasn't lying unconscious and concussed on the floor of his room.

'Just give me a minute, everyone,' she said, hurrying from the bar.

She went to the front desk and quickly explained why she needed to take a look inside Leggo's room. Luis the male receptionist came from behind the desk and accompanied her to the second floor where Leggo's room, 212, was located. He knocked on the door and called out but there was no reply so he swiped the passkey through the slot and the door clicked open. Eve stood aside to let him into the room first. As she followed behind she wrinkled her nose; the room stank of trainers, un-flushed toilet and beer. A pile of clothes sat on the chair next to Leggo's suitcase but there was no sign of him.

'Nobody here,' Luis said, joining in the nose-wrinkling.

'So I see. Thanks so much. I was just worried he might be unwell but he's probably out and about having a good time somewhere.'

'You're welcome, Eve. Always is better to check.'

Feeling relieved Eve hurried back down to the foyer where the others were waiting for her.

'Right! Let's get going. There should be a bus at the top of the road in three minutes,' she said as they all rushed out the main door.

✦ ✦ ✦

THE PORT OF Ibiza was heaving with a sea of people as they walked towards it. Music accompanied them most of the way along the Carrer Lluis Tur y Palau.

'Blimey! They like their dogs, don't they?' Nicole observed. 'I've never seen so many people walking dogs!'

'Now, there's dogs and there's dogs,' Ron said. 'That looks like a bloody rat being taken for a walk.' He pointed towards a very tall, thin man who had a tiny dog on a long lead.

'It's a Chihuahua, Ron,' Nicole said.

'A Chiwhata?'

'Oh, stop it!' Nicole giggled. 'You heard me.'

'I wouldn't like one of them!'

'I'd be frightened one of the bigger dog's would start on it,' Liz said.

'Or have it for dinner!'

Liz and Nicole laughed.

'The man at my local fruit shop's got a dog,' Ron said. 'But it always looks really sad to me. It's a melon collie.'

'Oh, Ron!'

Half the group laughed and half groaned.

'That's more like my kinda dog,' Ron said, indicating an Alsatian being walked by a glamorous woman in a pink lace dress that was split to the thigh. 'My kind of owner, too,' he added, laughing.

'Can you just gather round for a moment, please?'

Eve had stopped by a bench and waited for the group to come over to her.

'It's quite crowded here tonight and it'll be like this right through until the early hours. As I've said all along, we aren't joined at the hip so if any of you want to go off and explore by yourself or in small groups then please feel free to. The streets off to the left are well worth exploring. There are lots of shops and bars and restaurants. Great for people watching, too. The last bus is at half past eleven, so it'll mean taxis back to the hotel if you miss it.'

'What time do the shops close?' Estelle asked.

'Not until midnight-ish. And the restaurants are open much later because Spanish people don't have dinner until about eleven. It's probably best if you eat soon while you can still get a table.'

'I'd quite like to take a seat along here somewhere and have a drink and then find a place for dinner,' Ron said. 'You're all welcome to join me.'

There were a few nods from the group.

'Just bear in mind it's a bit on the pricey side in the port,' Eve said, remembering what Jesus had told her. 'And If you want to go up into Dalt Vila there are two ways in; either through the Portal de Ses Taules,' she pointed towards the left, 'Or through Portal Nou, just over there behind the Plaza del Parque.'

'Is it much of a climb?' Sarah asked. 'It looks it.'

'It's fairly high but you can take it slowly. And you don't have to go right to the top. There's a gentler slope if you go through Portal Nou, but it's cobbles all the way so if you're wearing heels you might struggle a bit.'

'Is it worth it?' Alex asked.

'Two thousand five hundred years of history,' Eve said. 'And the views from the top are amazing. It's a UNESCO World Heritage Site. And it's also got some fabulous little eating spots and bars, so yes, I think it's worth it.'

'Well, let's have a drink first, shall we?' Sarah said.

'Apparently, we're only a five minute walk from two vegan restaurants that come highly recommended on Trip Advisor,' Katrina told Rosalind and Charlie, consulting her phone.

'Shall we have dinner and then a little wander through the back streets afterwards?' Charlie suggested. 'That way we can get a table early and if everywhere's open until late we won't miss out.'

'Sounds good to me,' Katrina said and Rosalind nodded her approval.

'We're going to a vegan restaurant if anyone wants to

join us,' Charlie announced to the others.

'I'll pass on that,' Ron said. 'But thanks for the invite. I think a few of us are gonna have a drink over there,'. He pointed to a bar with very chic swing chairs and bucket seats.

'We might catch up with each other later then,' Eve called to Katrina, Rosalind and Charlie as they wandered off and the others settled themselves on the terrace of the bar.

'You see some sights here, don't you?' Ron said, to nobody in particular as his gaze followed the waitress who was wearing the tiniest denim shorts he'd ever seen which showed off her long legs and the bottom half of her bum cheeks. 'I'll have to have a word with Janice in the Cross Keys. See if she'll consider new uniforms for her barmaids,' he chuckled to himself.

'It's too cold in England to dress like that,' Liz said. 'Poor lasses would freeze to death.'

'Not in summer they wouldn't,' Ron insisted. 'We've had some really hot ones lately.'

'Waitresses or summers?'

'Both to be honest!' Ron and Liz giggled.

Eve sat back and smiled as she watched her little band of holidaymakers getting along. Her thoughts wandered to Michael and Natalie and, of course, gorgeous little Felicity. It saddened her that she hadn't been able to see them again before they left but she'd have time to make up for that when she got back to England. And right on cue she felt her phone vibrate in her handbag and when she looked at it the caller was Michael.

'Excuse me,' she said to her group as she walked a short way from the bar to where the music was less intrusive.

'Hi, Eve! What you up to?' Michael asked as she answered his call.

'I'm in Ibiza Town. In the port. We're just having a drink and people watching.'

'Sounds perfect,' he said. 'We're all packed and ready and have just had dinner. Now we're going to have a slow walk back to the apartment with one final ice-cream for Felicity and then bed. We've got a really early start. The taxi's coming at six o'clock.' She heard the grimace in his voice and sympathised.

'I feel your pain. I'm so sorry we weren't able to meet up again. Did you enjoy your lunch with the others?'

'We had a great time. It was so nice spending some time with them and Eileen and Murray seem really happy.'

'Who'd have thought?' Eve laughed.

'I know! Me and Dave were really ribbing him about what a misery he was until Eileen came into his life. But he took it well. He's mellowed. She's good for him. And they all made such a fuss of Felicity, who loved being the centre of attention, of course.'

'I'll bet she did. But she's so gorgeous, who could resist her?'

'So how's it going with you? Everyone happy?'

'More or less. The group within the group have gone off on their own tonight so that makes things a bit easier.'

'I don't know how you do it, Eve! I say that every time you tell me about a job or I see you in action.'

'Well, just be glad I do it, or you wouldn't be married to you beautiful wife,' she teased.

'I know! I still can't believe I pulled that off,' he said, remembering how he'd proposed to Natalie from the back of an elephant at the Taj Mahal. 'Anyway, I just wanted to say goodbye tonight as I thought you wouldn't appreciate an early morning call tomorrow.'

'It's always lovely to talk to you, you know that. But text

me when you've boarded…'

'And again when we've landed! Yes, I know the drill,' he laughed.

'Have a good journey and give my love to Natalie and Felicity. And I'll see you sometime next week.'

'Will do. Take care of yourself, Eve. Love you!'

'Love you, too.'

Eve couldn't help the huge grin that spread over her face as she walked back to join the others and took her seat.

'It's easy to see you've been talking to your boyfriend,' Ron said, winking at her. 'How does he feel about you travelling the world and leaving him at home?'

'It was my son, actually,' Eve said. 'He's here in Ibiza with his wife and daughter and they're leaving tomorrow.'

'Oh! You shoulda brought him over and introduced him.'

'He's been on the other side of the island.'

'Oh that's a shame,' Liz said. 'They've been here but you haven't been able to see them.'

'I did see them. The day before you all arrived. They were also guests at the wedding I went to. And besides, I'll see them next week.'

'How old is your grand-daughter?'

'Three. And there's another one on the way,' Eve beamed.

'You don't look old enough,' Sarah said. 'Seriously.'

'Thank you.'

Eve smiled at Sarah but said no more. Nobody needed to know how old she had been when she'd had Michael.

'Is there a Mr Eve?' Jackie asked, slowly moving her cocktail with the turquoise mermaid stirrer.

'No.'

'What? All the men you must've met on your trips and

you're still single?' Jackie was wide-eyed with disbelief.

'But when I meet them it's work for me. I don't see them as prospective partners or even as boyfriends. My job is to see they get the holiday they want and paid for. Not to chat them up!'

'I suppose there's a professional line you don't cross,' Alex said.

'There is,' Eve agreed.

'The trouble is,' Sarah joined in from across the table, 'that most of them will be intimidated by you.'

'Really?' Eve, Alex and Sean chorused.

'Yes, of course! Eve's attractive, articulate and doing a difficult job tremendously well,' Sarah explained. 'And, she's exceptionally well-travelled. I bet you get men trying to out-do you with places they've been to, don't you, Eve?'

'Erm, sometimes…'

'You do! I've seen it on some of the holidays I've been on,' Ron said. 'When I was in Malaga there was one bloke who reckoned he'd been on every holiday that Travel Together do. He kept trying to catch the tour manager out on things.'

'What a bore!' Sarah shook her head.

'But you probably get women who do that, too,' Sean said looking at Eve. 'Don't you?'

'Women can be as challenging as men,' Eve said deciding to be diplomatic. She was just glad she'd directed the questions away from her personal life.

'Look! There's Jesus!' Nicole said, pointing to a group of men who were just about to take their seats at a table across the other side of the terrace. 'Jesus! Jesus!'

Hearing his name Jesus looked round and broke into a smile when he saw them. He came over, leading a handsome King Charles spaniel on a pink rhinestone lead. Eve thought he looked different out of his tennis whites. And she realised the chat and the squeeze on the shoulder earlier had been nothing more than Jesus being nice.

'Good evening! I thought I might see you all,' he said, beaming around the table at them. 'Ibiza is such a small town. How are you enjoying yourselves?'

'We're having a grand time,' Ron said. 'Can I get you a drink?'

'No thanks. My friends will be getting me one. But thanks all the same.'

'And who's this?' Nicole had jumped up from her seat and was petting and talking to the dog who was ecstatic at the attention he was receiving.

'This is Lola,' Jesus said.

'Oh, my God! She's adorable!' Nicole buried her face in the dog's neck. 'She looks quite young.'

'She's eighteen months. And she's very naughty sometimes.'

'So, you out for dinner?' Eve asked him.

'Just for drinks. Most evenings we come here for drinks and to listen to the music. But I usually cook at home. Although many evenings I eat early. I am very un-Spanish in that,' he laughed. 'Are you going up to Dalt Vila? It's beautiful up there.'

'Possibly some will,' Eve said. 'We're just people watching for the moment.'

'And I see some of the group have gone off alone? There are lots of people missing.'

'Yes. The group of friends didn't join us, and Katrina, Rosalind and Charlie have gone off to a vegan restaurant,' Sarah told him.

'Well, whatever you do, enjoy your evening! And I'll see you all in the morning,' Jesus said. 'Come on, Lola! *Vamos!*

No seas mala…' he added as Lola dived under the table and started licking Sean's bare toes that he'd slipped out of his espadrilles.

Sean jolted his foot away as the dog's tongue tickled him, knocking his knee against the underside of the table and almost spilling the drinks.

'Oops! Steady!' Ron said grabbing his beer.

'Sorry about her,' Jesus said to Sean. 'I can't take her anywhere.'

'Sounds like my sister,' Sean said, smiling.

'I'll see you.'

'Well, I never saw that coming,' Ron said as Jesus went back to join his friends. 'I thought he was an 'unk who had no trouble pulling the women.'

'No, that's you, Ron,' Alex said and the others laughed. Liz blushed.

'Instead he's a hunk with no trouble pulling the men,' Sarah said looking at him. 'Yes. He is rather handsome.'

'Is it me or is it still hot considering the time of night?' Liz asked, frantically fanning herself.

'No, it is warm. Oh that's pretty,' Jackie said, admiring her fan.

'I got it in Lanzarote a couple of years ago. I always travel with it. It comes in handy. I even use it in England. Especially for swatting gnats. I bloody hate them.'

'Little bastards!' Jackie agreed.

'I never understood why Noah let gnats and mosquitoes back on the Arc,' Ron quipped.

'Or spiders!' Liz said. 'I don't like gnats but I am petrified of spiders.' She shuddered. 'Horrible, hairy things.'

'They can be beautiful, though,' Alex said. 'I've got two tarantulas.'

Liz leapt from her seat.

'Are you mad?'

'I haven't got them with me,' he said, grinning as Ron gently pulled her back onto her chair.

'But why? Why would you want to keep tarantulas?'

'Because I like them. Some people like cats and dogs or rabbits or guinea pigs. I just like big spiders.'

Liz was still trembling and she took a large swig of her gin and tonic.

'No wonder you're bloody single!'

'Oh, thank you, Liz,' Alex said, feigning hurt as a ripple of laughter went round the table.

'Everyone has something they don't like,' Eve said to several nods.

'My sister's terrified of clowns,' Sarah said.

'And I can't stand snakes!' Jackie trembled at the though.

'You don't come up against many snakes, do you?' Sean asked her. 'In Leeds?'

'No. And it's a good job I don't! Horrible things! They make my flesh crawl just thinking about them.'

'Are there any snakes here?' Ron asked Eve.

'I don't think so. I seem to remember being told there weren't any when I went on an Island Tour here years ago. And there are certainly no tarantulas.'

'Well, that's good!' Jackie said. 'Horrible things!'

✦ ✦ ✦

CHARLIE SHIFTED IN his chair and gave a long sigh. He was beginning to feel slightly peeved; slightly peeved and very left out.

I'm like the third fucking wheel!

Since they had left the others and wandered around

town in search of the vegan restaurant Katrina had fancied from its write up on Trip Advisor the two women had barely spoken to him. Rosalind had directed what he could only describe as a barrage of questions at Katrina about her work and her care home only bothering to speak to him when it came to ordering the wine. Katrina had demonstrated better manners, having tried to steer the conversation to include him on three occasions only for Rosalind to jump right back in.

'Well, that was most enjoyable,' Katrina said, putting her fork down on her empty plate. 'Did you enjoy your green curry, Charlie?'

'It's really good,' he said, taking the last mouthful. 'And so were the avocado rolls. I'm amazed at the amount of choice there was. I thought there would only be vegetarian lasagne and sweet potato fries,' he joked.

'I have to say, it's one of the best vegan restaurants I've ever seen. That jackfruit crispy duck was amazing.' Katrina beamed with satisfaction and took a sip of her mint and hibiscus lemonade. 'Did you like yours?' She turned to Rosalind.

'The falafel burger was nicer than the starter,' she said, unconvincingly.

'Well, shiitake meatballs with parsnip dressing are a bit of an acquired taste,' Charlie quipped.

'How was your meal?'

The Dutch waitress, whose name badge announced her as Eline, beamed at them.

'It was wonderful,' Katrina said. 'I was just saying that this is one of the best vegan restaurants I've ever been to. I'm quite surprised.'

'Maybe twenty years ago you wouldn't have found so many. One or two. But now you find them all over the island. We are very healthy in Ibiza!' She chuckled and began to take away their plates.

'Can I have another glass of wine, please?' Charlie asked.

'Of course! I will bring it now with the dessert menu.'

'I'm not sure I can manage a dessert,' Charlie said, patting his tummy.

'I'd like to see what there is,' Rosalind said.

Charlie suspected she was still hungry as she'd really only picked her main course and had left her started almost untouched.

'There you are!' Eline placed the glass of wine in front of Charlie.

'Is this a local wine?'

'Yes. From Cala San Vicente. It's organic and vegan.'

'Well, you'd never know,' Charlie quipped. 'It's really rather nice.'

'I like the sound of the lemon and coconut pie,' Rosalind said. 'Does it come with cream?'

'We can do it with ice-cream,' Eline said. 'Our ice-cream is, of course, vegan.'

'What's vegetarian cheese?' Charlie asked. 'Like paneer?'

'It's made from nuts, seeds and kimchi water.'

'What's that?' Rosalind asked.

'It's a Korean broth made from soaking radishes and cabbage in lightly salted water…'

'Yeuk!. I'll have the lemon and coconut pie with ice-cream, please.'

'And I'll have the cheesecake,' Katrina decided, closing the menu.

'Nothing for me thanks, I'll stick with the wine,' Charlie said.

There was a pleasant silence for a few moments as they all sipped their drinks.

'Have you got any more holidays planned this year?' Katrina asked them both.

'I'm going for a long weekend in Cork at the end of September,' Rosalind said. 'It's a weekend of Irish music.'

'That sounds good. Should be lively, like a ceilidh,' Katrina said.

'Sort of. It's more about Gaelic harping really. Music by O'Carolan…'

'I love the sound of the harp,' Katrina said.

'Oh, me, too.'

Charlie drifted off into his own thoughts again as Rosalind and Katrina waxed lyrical about the Harp and Irish music. He was thinking that he might invent a headache and leave them to it when Eline returned with the desserts.

'Here we go!'

She placed a mouth-watering cheesecake in front of Katrina and lemon and coconut pie with a huge topping of ice-cream before Rosalind. Charlie almost wished he hadn't been so petulant now.

'Enjoy!'

Eline sashayed off as the two women lifted their spoons and began to tuck in.

'Oh, my God! It's heavenly!' Katrina said, closing her eyes in delight. 'Want to try some?'

'Okay, thanks. And you can try some of my pie,' Rosalind replied.

Charlie watched as the two women spoon-fed each other, both pairs of eyes rolling in ecstasy; tongues sensually licking lips that has wrapped themselves around the exotic flavours offered from the other woman's spoon.

Then the penny dropped.

They've been chatting each other up! Coming on to each other! Rosalind's gay, too!

Charlie felt stupid. He downed the rest of his wine in one gulp then delved into his trouser pocket for some money.

'I'm suddenly not feeling very well. You'll have to excuse me,' he said throwing thirty euros on the table and hoping that would cover his part of the bill.

'Oh, dear. It's probably the food disagreed with you,' Rosalind said, looking and sounding concerned.

'Are you going to go back to the hotel?' Katrina asked.

'I think so.'

'Will you be all right? Do you want us to come with you incase you're ill on the way?'

'No! I'll be fine. Thanks. You just enjoy the rest of your evening.'

Charlie staggered out of the restaurant and hurried along the pavement, dodging the crowds of people strolling through the town until he reached the corner. He found himself in a large square edged with benches. He headed for an empty one and sat down. Then he burst out laughing.

Well done, Charlie! Spare part on a lesbian first date.

He chuckled and then looked at his watch. It was only twenty past nine. Too early to go back to the Dunas Blancas. He decided to head back towards the port and see if he could find any of the others. Just as he stood up his attention was drawn to a commotion kicking off on the far side of the square. He sat down again and watched the Fourth Form who were singing and dancing to music that was blaring from a nearby bar. Three burly security guards were remonstrating with them and trying to take their glasses from them. Charlie was too far to hear everything that was being said but it looked as if they'd walked out of a bar taking their drinks with them. One of the guards managed to wrestle Fee's and Titty's glasses from their hands but the men seemed to be fighting back. Spizz was remonstrating loudly with them while holding his glass high in the air over his head while going backwards in a circle keeping it out of reach of the security guard who was trying to snatch it. Charlie took out his phone; he had to capture this. He stood up and slowly walked nearer. He could hear them now.

'No! Just fuck off, mate! We paid ten euros each for these drinks!'

'You must stay in the bar and drink it,' the security guard said trying unsuccessfully to snatch the glass.

'Me cago en la puta!'

The third security guard hopped back in pain as Thommo kicked him sharply in the shins.

'That'll fucking teach you!' Thommo spat at him.

At that moment a large white minibus with *Policía Local* emblazoned on the sides and its blue lights flashing drove into the square and across the pedestrian precinct before pulling up next to the fracas. Before the driver had applied the handbrake four police officers leapt out and surrounded the group. A clipped conversation was shouted between the police and the security guards.

'It is against the law to walk in the streets with glasses in the hand,' the Sergeant said. The tone of his voice brooked no argument.

'Well nobody told us,' Jonesy whined.

'We are telling you this for ten minutes,' one of the security guards replied.

'Oh, sorry, mate! *No comprende! No comprende!*' Spizz said thinking he was speaking Spanish.

He downed the rest of his drink in one and handed the glass to the Sergeant. The others did the same.

'Sorry! Sorry, *amigos*!' Spizz continued raising his hands

and nodding deferentially at them.

'Enjoy yourselves but please behave respectfully,' the Sergeant replied.

'No problemo!'

The Fourth Form wandered away, crossing the square and laughing as they went. Charlie wished he could understand the comments the police officers and security guards were making to each other, although looking at their faces, he thought he could probably imagine them. He put his phone away and shook his head at the Fourth Form and their antics.

What a bunch of tossers!

He strolled off in the opposite direction, heading towards the port in search of some his Travel Together friends, clutching the phone containing the footage he couldn't wait to show them.

✦ ✦ ✦

'HOLA, RON!'

Ron had jumped at hearing his name. He and Liz had decided to have another drink before finding somewhere for dinner so the others had wandered off and the two of them had stayed on the terrace. Eyebrows had been raised when the bill had come.

'Bloody hell! Five euros for a Fanta?' Nicole's eyes had almost popped out of her head. 'I wish I'd had a proper drink now.'

'No you don't,' Estelle said. 'My gin and tonic was fourteen.'

Ron had shrugged the bill off.

'Well, we're in the posh part,' he'd said to Liz. 'It's a tourist area so you can't expect things to be cheap here, can you?'

'Well, I'm not flush, but I don't begrudge spending when I'm on holiday,' Liz replied. 'That's what you save up for, isn't it?'

'Exactly! I never mind paying if I'm enjoying myself. And I am enjoying myself.'

He reached out and patted Liz's hand and they'd sat there, comfortable in each other's company, chatting about everything and nothing for three more drinks. Ron was just beginning to feel nicely tipsy when he'd heard his name. He spun round and saw eight of The Spanish People he'd been chatting to in the hotel the previous evening.

'*Hola,*' he replied, jumping up and pumping their hands. '*Mi amiga, Liz,*' he said, dragging her forward for her round of handshakes.

'*Toma asiento,*' he said, pulling more chairs around the table for his new friends to make themselves comfortable. '*Quieren sangria?*'

They chatted away, commenting on the very diverse people who walked by with Ron translating for Liz as best he could and all joined in the music – getting up to dance on a make-shift dance floor between two tables to both Spanish and foreign songs.

'I'm amazed I can enjoy myself so much without speaking Spanish,' Liz said as she twirled back and forth with Domingo, balancing against his generous beer belly.

'You dancing very nice,' Domingo said.

'*Gracias!*' Liz replied giving one final twirl before flopping into her seat.

And that had been several large jugs of sangria ago. After an animated discussion The Spanish People had risen as one.

'*Nos vamos a cenar, Ron*' Domingo had said.

'They're going to have some dinner,' Ron told Liz as they started to clap rhythmically and two of them, Dolores and Rogelio, started singing with the rest of the group and several other people on surrounding tables all joined in.

'Cuando un amigo se va algo se muere en el alma, cuando un amigo se va,' they sang.

'It's something about a friend leaving but I can't get all of it,' Ron said.

'Never mind, it's lovely,' Liz said, finding the haunting melody was making her emotional. Or perhaps it was the sangria…

Many passers-by had stopped and joined in the singing, clapping and dancing. The atmosphere was electric as fifty or more people enjoyed themselves.

'It's like a flashmob,' Liz said, looking around in astonishment. 'I should have bloody filmed it!'

The song came to an end and a huge cheer went up, echoing along the port. The Spanish People smothered them in two-cheek kisses and handshakes and arm pumps before leaving them to go off and eat.

'We haven't had dinner,' Ron remembered.

'I'm not sure I want anything to eat,' Liz replied. 'I think I'm drunk. Nicely drunk, though. Like them. The Spanish People. They're nicely.'

'So shall we go back? Get a taxi?'

'Yep!'

It took Ron three attempts to get Liz out of the large cane armchair she was sitting in.

'It's not that my arse's too big. I'm not stuck,' she said to the group of Germans who had taken the seats The Spanish People had just vacated. 'These seats are too low.'

With a final effort, she shot from the chair into Ron's arms, sending him staggering backwards into a waiter, knocking his tray out of his hand. It hit the ground with an almighty crash.

'Sorry, mate. Sorry. *Lo siento mucho.*'

'Your Spanish is so good, Ron,' Liz said as they lurched along together arm-in-arm.

'I feel like it's getting better.'

'Like my tennis. I s'spose it's the same thing. If you practise you get better.'

'Yep!'

'Oh, look! McDonalds!'

Liz suddenly felt ravenous, her declaration of abstinence of five minutes earlier forgotten.

'I could just eat a juicy Big Mac!'

'Then your wish, *señora*, is my command.'

✦ ✦ ✦

IT WAS AFTER half past eleven before Eve, Sean, Alex, Sarah, Jackie, Nicole and Estelle finished their meal. They had found a small, reasonably-priced restaurant just inside Dalt Vila that specialised in fish and taken the last table on the terrace.

'This is glorious,' Sean said, looking up at the thick city walls rising high above them. 'They've really made the most of it.'

'Didn't you say it was a UNESCO World Heritage Site, Eve?' Sarah asked her.

'Yes, it is. Since the late nineteen nineties, I believe.'

'Since nineteen ninety-nine,' Jackie said, reading from her phone. 'But the walls were built in the sixteenth century by the Italian Calvi to protect the island from Turkish pirates…'

'But the city predates that by a lot. It was founded several hundred years BC,' Eve said. 'By the Carthaginians.'

'Who were they?' Nicole asked.

'North Africans. Carthage was where Tunisia is now, I believe.'

'Yes, they founded the city,' Jackie continued, 'And then the Romans came…'

'Those statues we saw as we came into Dalt Vila looked Roman,' Sarah joined in.

'And then the Vandals and the Byzantines and then the Moors.'

'Weren't the Moors North Africans, too?' Nicole asked. 'So what's the difference between them and the Carthaginians?'

'The Moors were Moroccans,' Alex said.

'Okay.'

'The Carthaginians called the city Ibossim, after the Egyptian God of music and dance,' Jackie added with a flourish.

'Well, that's very apt,' Eve quipped. 'The Club Capital of Europe!'

'I wanna go clubbing,' Nicole said to nobody in particular. Sean's ears pricked up.

If the music's loud she won't be able to keep on talking…

'Now, how are we going to settle the bill? Between us or each pay their own?' Eve asked as a waiter handed out very large menus.

'Pay our own?' Sarah suggested and the rest all nodded.

Eve gave a sigh of relief. That was always the best solution and certainly one that suited her when she heard Sarah add that she fancied the lobster.

'What's *bullit de peix*?' Jackie asked.

'Fish stew,' Alex said.

'Oh, do you speak Spanish?'

'No. It says what it is in English underneath the Spanish,' he replied.

'Oh, sorry. I didn't see that.'

'What on earth is seaman-style rape?' Estelle asked, reading from the menu as she burst out laughing.

'What?'

The rest of the group spluttered as they read the words.

'*A la marinera* means literally seaman-style,' Sarah said. 'It's a tomato and onion sauce.'

'So where does rape come in?' Estelle demanded to know.

'It's monkfish,' Alex said, consulting his phone. 'Also known as angler. It's pronounced *RA-pay*'

'Well, you'd think the restaurant would know that!' Sarah said.

'I'm sure they do,' Alex replied. 'Perhaps they've left it like that as a conversation starter. Or as a way of getting customers really involved in the menu. A bit of ropey translation gives them a bit of a laugh.'

'Rape's hardly a laughing matter,' Sarah retorted.

'Well, it's put me off!' Nicole declared. 'I'm going to have the sole.'

When the orders were taken Eve found she would be sharing her *bullit de peix* with Alex, Nicole and Jackie. When it arrived it was in a huge earthenware pot.

'Well, that looks wonderful,' Eve said. 'And it smells delicious.'

'Yeuk! I didn't know the fish'd come with the bloody heads on!'

Jackie recoiled in horror.

'You don't have to eat them,' Eve said. 'They're where all the flavour is. They're left on to add taste.'

Nicole took some photos of the pot and then asked

Sean to take a few more with her posing behind it before promptly posting them to her Instagram page.

'No head for me!' Jackie told the waiter who was dishing up for them.

'There's no answer to that,' Sean quipped and Alex laughed.

But by the end of the meal, even Jackie had to admit it had been wonderful. Everyone had enjoyed it.

'You see,' Sarah whispered to Jackie. 'New experiences. Move forward. Move on. No looking back'

Jackie's smile was unconvincing. She was trying so hard to enjoy herself – she WAS enjoying herself, but she couldn't stop her thoughts drifting to Scott. Even being at a fish restaurant in Ibiza Town reminded her of their holiday the previous year and the beautiful seafood they'd eaten in the Carihuela on the Costa del Sol. They'd been so happy then. She wondered if he was eating seafood with Julie tonight, or if he had been. And what were they doing now?

Sarah and Alex caught each other's eye for the umpteenth time over dinner. Each time they had smiled and Alex thought – hoped – he'd caught a glimpse of desire and promise in Sarah's look. He might have got it wrong with Katrina but there was no doubt that Sarah had been coming onto him in the pool that afternoon and was doing so again now. He jumped slightly as her bare toes caressed his ankle and slowly rose up the inside of his trouser leg. He looked at her again; her eyes penetrated his and she slowly licked her pouting, frosted lips before sipping her wine. His glance moved around the table wondering if anyone else might be aware of what was going on but they were all holding their own conversations.

But what IS going on?

He hoped Sarah wasn't going to turn out to be a time-waster; a cocktease. They were leaving on Saturday and it was already Monday night. He hadn't come on this holiday with the sole intention of pulling someone but if it happened it happened! And he could do a lot worse than Sarah. She looked as if she was probably a year or so older than him, but she was in great shape and took care of herself. Her long, caramel-tinted locks, her deep blue eyes, high cheekbones and wide, sensuous mouth made her very attractive. And so did her short skirts. But it was her confidence that rounded off her attraction and tipped it into sexy. She was nobody's fool and she was highly intelligent. He fancied her like mad and he could already feel himself swelling just looking at her and feeling her feet stroking his leg. He took a large swig of his beer and wondered how long it would be before they'd be going back to the hotel.

✦ ✦ ✦

'DO… DO YOU think people can be happy in a care home?' Rosalind finally bucked up the courage to ask Katrina as they wandered among the brightly lit stalls in the streets leading off La Marina.

'Most definitely,' Katrina said. 'Oh, look at these!'

She picked up the intricate silver and jade earrings and held them against her right ear.

'What do you reckon?'

'Yes. They're nice.'

Rosalind hoped she didn't sound petulant but she was a bit peeved that Katrina had dismissed her question to look at jewellery. Katrina twisted her head and looked at herself in the mirror the seller held in front of her.

'Do you make these yourself?'

'Yes. All the jewellery is made by me. Everything.'

'And how much are they?'

'Thirty-five euros. I also have them in turquoise and amethyst.'

'No, I like the jade. They'd match an outfit I've just bought for a wedding I'm going to in September.'

She jingled her head a bit more as Rosalind stood impatiently beside her.

'Do you take cards?'

'Yes. Debit card or credit card.'

'I'll take them!'

Feeling as pleased as punch with her purchase, Katrina dropped the earrings which had been gently wrapped in tissue paper before being put into a little gold velvet drawstring bag into the inside pocket of her bag, thanked the seller and turned towards Rosalind.

'Aren't you going to buy anything?'

'I don't think so. There's nothing I want really.'

'Ooh! I like that!'

Katrina zoomed across the street to a pink, linen top that was hanging beside a matching, layered skirt.

'It's got a real seventies look, don't you think? Sort of hippy…'

'That's our Moda Adlib.'

Katrina turned to see an older woman, who was wearing the same outfit she'd admired but in a cool, peppermint green. The woman scooped back her pure white hair and secured it with a large comb.

'It's very famous. For almost fifty years,' she explained, her black eyes smiling.

Katrina thought she was one of the most attractive women she'd ever seen.

'Well, it looks great on you!'

'Would you like to try it on?'

'I'm not sure… What do you think?' She turned to Rosalind who shrugged.

'It's up to you. It's nice. But will you wear it in Edinburgh?'

'Oh, aye. I could wear it anywhere in summer, couldn't I? Although I'm not sure about pink now that I look at it…'

'I have white, black, orange, lemon, red, this green I am wearing…'

'Actually, I quite like the black.'

'You can always put on a bright necklace or a scarf to make it not so serious. Or with a coloured bag.'

'That's true.

'Come inside. Nobody can see,' the woman said, standing aside to let Katrina step into the space at the back of the stall.

She pulled a curtain across and Katrina found herself inside a little changing cubicle.

'What do you think?'

She asked two minutes later pulling the curtain open and looking at herself in the full-length mirror, liking what she saw.

'It does look nice on you,' Rosalind said, a tad begrudgingly.

Katrina looked at the price tag on the blouse and winced inwardly. She'd hoped to get both pieces for that price.

'I give you ten percent discount,' the woman said, noticing. 'And this to make it brighter.'

She held up an eye-catching orange, green and yellow paisley scarf against the black top.

'I'll take them!'

'Wasn't she attractive?' Katrina said as they walked away from the stall. 'Those black eyes and the white hair. I wonder how old she was…'

'She told me while you were getting changed she's been selling clothes in Ibiza since nineteen seventy-two. Apparently she came from mainland Spain.'

'She was probably one of the original hippies. How fantastic! So she must be late sixties! Hell! I hope I look as good when I'm that age. If I'm not kicking up the daisies, that is.'

They walked on another few yards when Katrina suddenly realised that Rosalind was crying.

'What on earth's the matter?'

'Sorry. I'm just being silly.'

'What's upset you?'

Rosalind didn't answer. She took off her glasses and wiped her eyes with a tissue she'd taken from her bag.

'Is it something I've said?'

'Yyyy…yes,' Rosalind stammered.

'Dear God in Heaven! How have I upset you?'

Rosalind shook her head and continued to cry.

'Come and have a drink and we can sort this out.'

Katrina grabbed her arm and almost frog-marched her to a table on a terrace, that in spite of being almost full, was reasonably quiet.

'Two brandies, please,' she said as soon as they'd sat down. 'Now, please, tell me what's going on.'

'You said "kicking up the daisies" and I lost my mother at the beginning of the year. Stupid, isn't it?'

'Oh, Rosalind, I'm so sorry. And no, it isn't stupid.'

Katrina put her hand over Rosalind's prompting another flow of tears.

'But it's not just that… I wanted to talk to you because I'd put her in a home for the last two years of her life. And I did it because she was getting to be a bit of a handful so I put her away and I lost two precious years with her and I know she was unhappy and I just can't forgive myself…'

'Woah! Woah! Just stop right there! Here, drink this.'

Katrina passed her one of the brandies and Rosalind downed most of it in one swig, Katrina following suit.

'Now, just slow down and tell me the whole story.'

Rosalind sniffed deeply, wiped her cheeks with the back of her hand and started her story.

'I was always very close to my mum. I've got a brother, Robert. He's three years older than me and he lives in Cornwall. He buys and resells stuff on eBay and spends the rest of his time writing music and painting. Dad died when I was sixteen and Rob was already away at university. So it was just me and Mum. When I started teaching she let me use our dining-room for my private piano pupils. Mum was so good about it. She said she loved me teaching from home. I was company for her and she enjoyed hearing the music and the coming and going of young people and their parents.'

She paused and took another gulp of her brandy and then gave a little smile.

'She'd always ply them with homemade cakes and cups of tea. I used to joke that she spent more housekeeping on my students than she did on us. Then when she was only fifty-nine she was diagnosed with early-onset vascular dementia.'

Katrina nodded her understanding; she'd seen far too many people with that during her career. She knew exactly what it meant.

'She lost her energy. She stopped making cakes and one day when she had offered to make one of my adult students a coffee she'd taken so long I went to see what had happened to her and she was standing staring at the kettle. I asked her what was wrong and she said she didn't know how to make a cup of coffee.'

Katrina grabbed a wad of paper napkins from the dispenser on the neighbouring table and gave them to Rosalind who was sobbing.

'Things got steadily worse. She sometimes had trouble understanding what I was saying to her and she couldn't follow what was going on if we watched a soap or a film. In the end I took her to see our doctor and they did some tests and said it was vascular dementia. She hadn't had a stroke or anything; it had simply developed by itself. I wanted to be with her and take care of her myself. It meant I had to cut back on some of my teaching but I didn't care. I rang Rob and explained the situation to him. He came up a couple of days later and sod's law, she was fine. Seeing him sort of gave her a boost so he said we should hang on for a bit longer before we asked for care assistance. But as soon as he went back to Cornwall she got worse rather quickly. She couldn't even go to our local parade of shops without getting lost and I couldn't leave her in case she started a fire or did something to cause damage or if she fell or had an accident.'

'It must have been very hard for you.'

'It was, but she'd done so much for me. And then I met Matthew… His son Oliver was a piano pupil and at Easter when he'd gone away with his Mum, Matthew asked me out for lunch. I got our neighbour Betty to sit with Mum. Matthew was quite ordinary, really. Not handsome or anything. Looking back, I don't understand why I took notice of him. Perhaps because he was the first man to show any interest in me for years. And he was a paramedic so I thought he'd understand more than I did… He was sympathetic, but he said that Mum wouldn't get any better, only worse. He said the kindest thing for her and for me would be to get her into a home before she really deteriorated. I couldn't imagine her being any worse than she was. She was already asking me the same thing twenty times in the space of five minutes… Oh, God! The questions…'

'I know what that can be like,' Katrina said, signalling the waitress to bring two more brandies. 'It can wear you down.'

'Not only that. Matthew seemed really interested in me but I knew it could never come to anything between us because I was tied down looking after Mum. Oh, God! That sounds so shallow and selfish!'

'You're entitled to a life, Rosalind.'

'I know… But…'

She gave a deep sigh and blew out her cheeks.

'Anyway, Matthew rang me one night and said he'd had a call out to a care home that day but the person had died when they'd got to hospital. He said it was the sort of place that usually had a waiting list but he'd spoken to the manager and explained about me and she was willing to hold the place for a couple of days if I wanted to go and see her. So I did and within a week Mum was living in the Golden Road Care Home.'

She stopped to take a breath and another sip of her brandy. Katrina didn't say anything but she knew there was more to come.

'And then the dementia got even worse. She couldn't do anything for herself.'

'So, it was a blessing she was in the home and had twenty-four hour care. You couldn't have done that, could you?'

'But she wasn't happy! She hated it. She fought the carers and nurses with what little strength she had. She called me terrible things. She used language I'd never imagined she even knew. Even though she didn't recognise me most of the time she knew I'd done something terrible to her. I should have left her at home. At least she would have had all her own things around her. She died not knowing where she was or who was with her.'

'Listen to me, Rosalind,' Katrina said, taking her hands and holding them tightly. 'You've just said, she died without knowing where she was. So even if she'd been in her own home, she wouldn't have known that. And you'd have had two years of hell. I've seen people struggle on out of a misguided sense of duty to care for a loved one, until their own health is put at risk. They become exhausted, worn out and end up hospitalised themselves. Your mum was in the best place. It was a nice home?'

'Yes.' Rosalind nodded. 'It was. I know some can be pretty grim but it was a beautiful place. It was bright and cheerful and the staff were loving and kind towards her.'

'Oh, aye. One terrible home gets us all a bad name. And I know there are some that I'd be reluctant to leave my dog in but there are also many, many more that are grand places.'

Katrina smiled at her and the two women sat in silence for a few moments. Katrina felt that there was more Rosalind wanted to say. And she was right.

'But moving Mum into the home didn't make way for my relationship with Matthew. I spent every minute I didn't have a pupil visiting her; just sitting with her and holding her hand, hoping she wouldn't suddenly leap into one of her mood swings.'

She gave a hollow laugh.

'Be careful what you wish for! Her mood swings became fewer and fewer until she just sat or lay there gazing into space or with her eyes closed. And I became afraid to leave her in case she died while I wasn't there. So eventually I only ever saw Matthew when he dropped Oliver off for his lesson.'

'That's a shame. I know she was your mum and I understand how you felt. But couldn't you have found an hour a week for him?'

'To be honest, he never asked me! We went out to dinner a few times but I wonder if I saw more into the relationship than there ever was,' she gave a wry smile through her tears. 'Perhaps when he helped me he was just being kind…'

'But he asked you out to dinner…'

'Yes and it's a wonder he ever asked me out again.'

'That's a shame because you're a lovely woman.'

'Thanks.'

Rosalind took another brandy pause.

'So… Do you… You know, as a professional… Do you think Mum was happy, then?'

Katrina exhaled slowly and deeply.

'I think happy is the wrong word for you to use, because we can only think of it in terms of ourselves, or people who are able to communicate with us and tell us they're happy or unhappy. From what I've seen of elderly people who have suffered strokes and have all kinds of dementia it's not a question of happiness, rather of giving them love, kindness and their dignity, as far as that's possible. Your mum's violent outbursts weren't because you'd put her into a home. She possibly didn't even realise that or know where she was. Violent mood and behavioural changes are part and parcel of the disease. She'd probably have struck out at you if you'd been looking after her in her own bedroom or lounge.'

'Really?'

'Yes. Especially in the late afternoon. For some reason dementia sufferers become agitated as the day goes on.

Sundowning, or late day confusion it's called. I've been on the receiving end of many a black eye at tea-time,' Katrina said.

Rosalind began to feel a little reassured.

'You did your best for your mum until you couldn't care for her by yourself any longer. And then you visited her every single day. So you have nothing to reproach yourself for. There are people in our home that are lucky if a family member calls by once a fortnight,' she added. 'Some are just left for us to take care of completely. You didn't do that. And up until her condition reached Stage Seven, your mum knew you were by her side, loving her and taking care of her. Believe me. Deep inside, she knew.'

'Oh thank you!'

Rosalind threw her arms around Katrina's neck and sobbed into her shoulder. Katrina returned the hug, patting the back of her head and making soothing noises as if Rosalind was a small child.

Charlie came strolling along and caught sight of the two of them. He stopped in his tracks open-mouthed. He whisked out his phone and took a volley of photos of their embrace. And afterwards, if you'd asked him why, he wouldn't have been able to tell you.

✦ ✦ ✦

EVE STIFLED A yawn as the group meandered back down to the Marina. She had decided she wanted to go back to the hotel.

'Are we going to have a drink?' Sean asked as they looked around. 'I can't believe it's busier now than it was two hours ago.'

'Ibiza people are night owls,' Nicole said.

'I think I'm going to make my way back to the hotel,' Eve said. 'It's almost midnight and that's when tour managers turn into pumpkins.'

'I'll come, too,' Jackie said. 'I'll never get up for tennis in the morning if not.'

Everyone else nodded and murmured their agreement and so they strolled along the Marina towards the taxi rank by the Hotel Montesol.

'Oh, hello, Charlie,' Eve said as he crossed their path. 'We're just going for taxis. Have you had a good evening.'

'Not bad. The meal was great but I left the two girls to it. I'm going back myself so I'll join you.'

Charlie fell into step beside Eve.

'I saw the Fourth Form. They were already pissed and getting into trouble and that was a couple of hours ago.'

'Really? What were they doing?'

Charlie took his phone from his pocket and scrolled until he found the video. The whole group crowded around him and Eve to have a look.

'What a bunch of idiots! Absolute twats!' Sarah left nobody in any doubt as to her feelings about them.

'Let's hope they calmed down a bit,' Eve said, not really believing they would.

They got into the first two taxis on the rank and sped off towards Cala Llonga.

'What happened with the girls then?' Estelle asked Charlie after a couple of moments. 'Did they go back to the hotel earlier?'

'No. I left them in the restaurant. They were getting on well and I decided to go for a walk round.'

'When you say "Getting on well" are you saying what I think you're saying?' Sean asked grinning.

'What do you mean?' Estelle asked.

'Oh, just something Alex said.'

'And?'

'Apparently Katrina's got a girlfriend.'

'What? So you think she's off with Rosalind?' Nicole scoffed.

'I'm only telling you what I saw,' Charlie replied. 'Spoon-feeding each other desserts… I was the gooseberry. And then I saw them a bit later at another bar. Having a snog.'

'You're kidding!' Sean said.

Charlie whipped out his phone again, scrolled through the photos and then passed it over his shoulder to the other three on the back seat.

'They are all over each other,' Sean said looking at the photo of the two women in each other's arms.

'Well, so what?' Nicole said. 'They're grown women. They're not doing anyone any harm. It's only Charlie's ego that's taken a bit of a bash.'

'No, it hasn't!'

'Methinks the lady doth protest too much.'

'What?'

'It's Shakespeare.'

'What's he got to do with anything? Alex was the one that was put out. He was chatting her up last night and she knocked him back cos she's gay.'

'You men should behave yourselves and not chat about the women,' Nicole admonished him.

'We weren't! Alex just mentioned it in passing.'

Sean was glad it was night-time and Nicole couldn't see him blushing. He kept very quiet and hoped Charlie would, too, and not mention what he'd said about Nicole and drop him in it. They'd been getting on better tonight and although they'd both decided to give the club a miss he reckoned he was in with a chance when they got back to the hotel. He just hoped she wouldn't get verbal diarrhoea again about her late boyfriend.

✦ ✦ ✦

IN THE OTHER taxi Alex had helped Eve into the front seat next to the driver and then climbed into the back next to Sarah who had Jackie on her other side. His arm was resting on the top of the seat behind her. He could feel the full length of Sarah's thigh pressing against his and then she leant back so that the nape of her neck was against his arm. His thigh gave an involuntary jerk as her hand rested on it. He covered it with his own hand and gently caressed her wrist as her fingers crept in slow circles further up his leg. He tuned out as Jackie and Eve held some banal conversation about Travel Together holiday destinations and just enjoyed the moment. He wished the driver would put his foot down a bit.

✦ ✦ ✦

RON AND LIZ had both had a skinful. After their burgers they'd found a small bar in a side street and shared another jug of *sangria*. Strangely enough, Liz now though she was more sober than Ron, whose head had fallen onto his chest as they sat on a bench waiting for a taxi.

'Here's one!'

She jumped up as she saw the green light and waved frantically at the taxi.

'Ron! Ron! I've got us a taxi!'

Ron's head shot up and he bounced off the bench and scrambled into the car behind her. He struggled with his seatbelt.

'If you drunk I no take you,' the driver said.

'Oh, we're not drunk!'

Liz reached round Ron and gave a sigh of relief as she felt the belt finally click into place after two attempts. A heavy, sickly artificial perfume permeated the taxi from an air freshener that was dangling from the hand strap next to her. It was turning her stomach. Ron's head had immediately fallen onto his chest again and she thought she could hear faint snoring.

Blimey! How does he do that?

'Yes? Where you go?'

The taxi-driver looked at her in the mirror.

'Erm… Hotel Bonkas Donkas.'

'Dónde?'

'Hotel Bonkas Donkas?'

She could see his blank stare in the mirror. She tried again.

'Boonas Doonas.'

The taxi-driver tutted. She was aware he was losing patience and started to panic.

'Oonas Bloomers. Donkas Onkas. Oh it's something like that!'

'Where is? San Antonio?'

'No. Not San Antonio.'

Her head was spinning and she felt a bit nauseous.

Try to think! Try to think! And don't be sick!

'Near Cala Llonga.'

'Near Cala Llonga is big place.'

'I'm sure it's the Bonkas Donkas.'

'Please. You leave from my taxi.'

The taxi-driver leaned over and opened the rear door on Ron's side. Panicking, Liz shook Ron with all her might.

'Ron! Ron! Wake up!'

'Whaa?'

Ron raised his head slightly.

'Ron! What's the name of our hotel?'

'Dunas Blancas.'

'Yes! That's it! Hotel Dunas Blancas,' she announced to the taxi-driver as she pulled the car door closed again.

'Dunas Blancas,' the taxi-driver repeated.

'Yes.'

He shook his head and muttered to himself as he put the car into gear and pulled away.

'And fucking hurry up,' Liz whispered under her breath. 'Before I throw up all over your nice, clean cab!'

✦ ✦ ✦

EVE MADE STRAIGHT for reception as soon as she got inside the Hotel Dunas Blancas.

'Any sign of Mr Legg? Room two one two? Nobody's seen him since this morning.'

'Luis told me to look out for him when we did the shift change, but I haven't seen him come in,' the night manager said.

'Okay. Thanks. Good night.'

'Good night! See you at breakfast,' she called to the others as she walked towards the lifts. Jackie and Estelle followed.

'Oh, where did Nicole go?' Estelle asked, surprised to see the others weren't behind them.

'I think they might have gone towards the bar,' Eve said.

'I'm too tired to join them,' Jackie said. 'I've had enough to drink, too.'

She didn't add that she was itching to be on her own so

that in spite of everything she'd promised Sarah, she could check Julie Clithers's Facebook page again.

'It would have been nice to have been asked if we wanted a nightcap with them,' Estelle muttered.

She was feeling a bit peeved with Nicole. This was the second night running she'd disappeared without saying anything yet the previous evening she just said she and Sean had a chat over a drink. She sighed as she left Jackie and Eve.

Perhaps all they had done was have a drink! Why doesn't anyone want to have a drink with me?

Her mind ran over the men in the group as she kicked off her shoes and thumped down onto the bed. None of them was her type, really and besides, she'd come away to improve her tennis not snare a bloke. It just suddenly felt as if everyone was getting it except her!

✦ ✦ ✦

CHARLIE WAS AS cheesed off as Estelle. He nursed a cocktail alone at the bar and felt a bit sorry for himself. He knew he wasn't the handsomest man in the world and being short didn't exactly help. But he usually did all right with the women on singles' holidays. And it wasn't as if he hadn't had a few girlfriends over the years. He'd never met one he'd wanted to spend his life with and thanked his lucky stars that his parents had never tried to arrange for him to marry any of their friends' daughters. But it would have been nice to have had some decent female company on the holiday. Or even just for tonight. The others seemed to be pairing up.

Sean and Nicole. Alex and Sarah. Katrina and Rosalind.

He glanced at the glass in his hand.

And me and Margarita.

✦ ✦ ✦

SARAH AND ALEX hung back until Eve, Jackie and Estelle had gone up in one of the lifts and then they moved towards the others.

'Mine,' Sarah said, pressing 4. The door closed silently behind them and the lift swiftly rose.

She preferred her own room; she could roll over and go to sleep as soon as it was over without having to collect up her clothes and creep back down the corridor. And going to Sarah's room suited Alex, too. He wasn't the tidiest of men and he knew she wouldn't be impressed by seeing the pile of worn clothes accumulating on the chair. Alex reached for her as soon as they were inside.

'Wow! Easy, tiger,' she said, twirling out of his reach.

He stopped in his tracks, wondering if he'd made a mistake yet sure he hadn't misread the signs.

'Don't look so glum! Let's start by taking a nice, steamy shower together,' Sarah said, stepping effortlessly out of her dress, her underwear following it.

Alex blinked several times then gave a broad grin as he watched her shapely backside shimmy into the bathroom. Before she'd had time to turn the taps on he stepped into the shower behind her. He poured some of her expensive shower gel into his palms, the sexy aroma seducing his senses, the silky foam giving him an electric thrill as he began to smooth it across her shoulders. She leaned her body against him and he enveloped her with his arms, his hands caressing her breasts as the water pounded down onto them. He knew this was going to be a night to remember.

✦ ✦ ✦

DOWN ON THE beach Nicole and Sean were making unfettered, passionate love with great abandon. Nicole was loud; gasping and groaning and edging him on like no woman he'd ever been with and he found it such a turn on. He didn't care if anyone could hear or see them. He just wanted this to carry on all night – or even better, for ever. He studied her as he thrust forward with all his might. Her eyes were closed, her lips parted and her tongue showed between her teeth. Her long, red hair had spilled out of its knot and draped across her shoulders and chest, her breasts poking through it. He leaned forward and began kissing and nibbling them. She let out a shriek followed by a long moan. And he couldn't control himself any longer. With a rasp of his own he collapsed on top of her as she wrapped her legs around his waist pulling him tighter to her.

He was so emotional he thought he might burst into tears. He'd spent three long years waiting for this moment and it had been everything he'd dreamed of and more. The relief had been exquisite and he didn't think he'd ever be able to move again.

✦ ✦ ✦

'RON! RON! WE'RE here!'

Liz shook Ron hard as the taxi pulled into the Hotel Dunas Blancas driveway. When Liz saw the name blazoned over the door she giggled to herself thinking she'd never ever forget it again.

Ron opened his eyes and sat up.

'We here? That was quick,' he said, looking round somewhat startled.

'Twenty euros,' the taxi-driver said, putting on the light.

Ron blinked as it shone into his eyes. He shut them tight as if it were a laser and reached into his pocket.

'I've got it,' Liz said.

'Bugger off! You're not paying the taxi! I've got money here,' he protested pulling out a fist full of euros. He studied them for several moments without moving or reacting.

'Twenty. Twenty euros,' the taxi driver repeated.

'Here!'

Liz dipped into her bag then leant forward and gave him the money.

'Put that back in your pocket,' she said to Ron as he stumbled from the taxi. She took hold of his hands and placed the money into them, wrapping his fingers tightly around the notes. Then, holding his arm the two of them lurched into the foyer and over to the lifts. They stumbled inside and Liz successfully pressed 2 at the second attempt.

When they spilled out of the lift on the second floor they continued arm-in-arm to Liz's door.

'Night, night,' Ron said, beaming in her direction, his eyes unfocused. 'See you at breakfast.'

He tottered off down the corridor.

'Ron!'

He stopped and turned.

'Your room's the other way.'

'Oops!'

He manoeuvred himself around and swayed past her.

'Ron!'

He stopped again. This time when he turned round Liz was standing right behind him. She leant forward, took his face in her hands and planted a long, lingering kiss on his lips.

'Night, night, Ron.'

And she disappeared into her room without a backwards glance. Ron stood motionless for a minute or so. He didn't even blink. Then he gave a deep sigh and, clutching the wall to steady himself, continued along the corridor to the sanctuary of his own room.

✦ ✦ ✦

ROSALIND CLOSED THE door to her room and walked over to the patio doors and pushed them open wide. She stepped outside and slowly lowered herself onto one of the chairs and sat very still. She could hear faint music, which she assumed was coming from the bar and the occasional sound of voices and laughter floated up and mingled with the sounds of the sea gently breaking against the beach. She looked down and saw the elegant palm trees that lined the pathway through the hotel gardens and the colourful shrubs lit up by cleverly camouflaged lights that lead to the sapphire pool.

'It's beautiful,' she whispered as if she were seeing it for the first time.

And then she looked up and saw the whole sky full of stars shining down on her. She gave a sigh of satisfaction and contentment.

Now I understand. I understand, Mum. And I know you do, too.

She slipped into timelessness, staring at the stars and the trees, listening to the hypnotic sound of the sea. And much later, she had no idea how long it had been, she stood up, gave a smile and blew a kiss skywards.

'Goodnight, Mum. God bless.'

Then she went inside, slipped into bed and enjoyed the deepest, most peaceful sleep she'd had in many months.

DAY FOUR

✦

EVE WAS SURPRISED to be woken up the following morning by the sound of heavy rain splattering on the balcony and against the windows. She pulled back the curtains startled by the ferocity of the rain and took a step back as a zig-zag of lightning flashed in front of her. From habit Eve started counting. Twenty seconds later the thunder rumbled.

Four miles away.

Her husband Brian had taught her that if you counted the seconds between the lightning and thunder and divided it by five you could work out how many miles away the storm was. It was all to do with the speed of light being five times faster than the speed of sound, he'd said. She smiled as she remembered asking him for the formula for working out how far the storm was in kilometres and he'd said he hadn't gone metric. Brian had been a decent man, one her family had approved of. But he simply hadn't been Melv.

She pulled the curtain wide open and watched the rain, mesmerised as always. For Eve, a child of Southern Europe, there was nothing like a storm over the Mediterranean. The big, fat raindrops plopped against the terracotta tiles before running in rivulets into the small drain in the corner of the balcony. More lightning lit up the gloomy morning followed by a loud volley of thunder fifteen seconds later.

It's getting nearer. Only three miles away now.

As she stood hypnotised by the storm Eve's thoughts wandered back six years to another storm on another island more than four thousand miles away from Ibiza to Tropical Storm Charlotte on Antigua. Charlotte had been ferocious and wild. She had totally flooded the areas surrounding the Mango Tree Resort leaving them cut off for several hours. And she had provided an awesome Sound and Lights Spectacular; a dramatic background for Eve and Melv to rekindle the passionate love affair of their youth. A huge wave of longing, lust and love for him swept over her, its strength and depth taking her by surprise so that she clutched the curtain to steady herself. She knew there never had and never would be any man who could come close to the place Melv had held in her heart since she was seventeen.

The jangling of the room phone jarred her back into the present.

'Eve, it's Jesus. *Buenos días,'*

'Hi, Jesus. Are you ringing to tell me the tennis is going to be cancelled because of the rain?'

'No. Not really. The forecast says the rain will stop in half an hour or so, which means the courts will be dry enough for us by ten o'clock. Ten thirty the latest.'

'They won't be slippery? It's just that I can see lots of Accident Report Forms flashing before my eyes here!'

'Trust me, they will be dry,' Jesus said, laughing at her. 'That's the good thing about clay courts. They aren't usually as slippery as hard courts or grass and they also dry out very quickly.'

'Oh, dear. I get the feeling I should have known that. I'm sure Jenny would have done!'

'Perhaps she would, but then again she is a tennis specialist and you aren't so she should know. And don't be hard on yourself. You're a ten times better tour manager than her. You don't act as if you're on holiday.'

'Why, thank you, sir!' Eve felt ridiculously pleased by the compliment. 'So, I'll get myself down to breakfast now and tell them half-past ten, shall I?'

'Yes. And we'll finish an hour later to make up the time.'

She had barely hung up on Jesus when the phone rang again.

'*Buenos días,* Eve. This is Luis on the front desk. Your client Mr Legg has checked out.'

'When?'

'About ten minutes ago. I was calling you to tell you but your phone was engaged.'

'Did he say where he was going?'

'I did not ask. But he asked for a taxi to take him to San Miguel.'

'Thanks, Luis.'

Eve sank onto the bed.

Well, the good news is he's alive and well. The bad news is I don't know where in San Miguel he is or why he's gone there.

Eve gave a shrug. Her clients were adults who could choose where they went and what they did. She grabbed her iPad and rattled off an e-mail to the Customer Services Department of Travel Together informing them what had happened so they would be forewarned if – more likely when – Leggo got in touch to complain and ask for a refund. Just then her mobile beeped.

Boarding now. We love you xxx

She typed her message back to Michael.

I love you all more. Safe flight! Xxxx

She threw her phone into her bag, snapped the iPad shut and headed for the shower, thinking that if she didn't hurry up she'd be the last one down to breakfast.

✦ ✦ ✦

'I THINK I'M a bit hung over,' Liz said as she slid into a chair next to Sarah and Charlie. 'Thank God it's raining. I'm assuming that means the tennis will be cancelled this morning.'

'Probably not,' Charlie replied. 'It looks like it's clearing up already.'

'Did you have a skinful?' Sarah asked.

'Did I! I don't know why I do it. My boys are always telling me off about it. *"Mum, don't get legless. Mum watch what you're drinking. Mum, a bit of moderation."* We have a sort of role-reversal,' she joked. 'I got so bloody drunk I couldn't remember the name of the hotel! I was calling it Bonkas Donkas at one point. The taxi driver thought I was mad,' she roared.

'So, where was Ron? He speaks Spanish,' Sarah protested.

'He was asleep. He got into the cab and it was like he'd fallen under hypnosis. You know what I mean: Counting backwards from five. Well, not even five,' she corrected herself. 'More like three. He won't be surfacing this morning.'

'He's already been and gone,' Charlie said.

'What? He's had his breakfast?'

'When I came down at a quarter to eight he was just finishing off a full-English. He said he was going for a walk down to the supermarket to see if he could get a Spanish newspaper.'

'I can't keep up with him,' Liz wailed.

'Nobody can. He's been among the last to bed and the first one up ever since we got here,' Sarah said, finishing her bowl of fruit salad and yoghurt and breaking open a Danish pastry.

The long, satisfying sex-session with Alex had meant she'd woken up ravenous. There was no sign of him yet. She didn't know what time it was when he'd crept from her room but she was glad he had. She liked her room to herself in the morning. But she was more than willing to share it with him again that night. And every night for the rest of the holiday.

'Good morning!'

Eve hurried over to the table with some scrambled egg, bacon and toast on a plate. She sat down and poured herself a long, black coffee from the steaming pot that sat in front of her.

'There will be tennis this morning. Jesus says it'll have stopped raining and the courts will be dry by half-past ten.'

'I thought as much,' Charlie said, looking a bit smug. 'Have you let the others know?'

'I thought I'd catch everyone at breakfast.'

'People could have had a lie-in if you'd rung their rooms, though.'

Eve decided not to answer Charlie's criticism and tucked into her breakfast.

'Perhaps some will lie in. They'll guess we'll be starting later because of the rain,' Sarah said.

'It looks like most people are up,' Liz said as Sean, Alex,

Rosalind, Estelle and Katrina all arrived together. 'You did the right thing, Eve.'

As she greeted them, Eve saw the Fourth Form had also come into the dining-room and were settling on the round table next to theirs. She went over to them, noting they all looked a bit bleary-eyed.

'Hi. Good morning.'

There were a couple of mumbled responses.

'Just to let you know that we'll be starting tennis a bit later this morning. At half-past ten. So that the courts have time to dry out. And also, reception told me that Leggo checked out.'

'When?' Spizz seemed shocked and the others were all looking at her in surprise.

'About half-past seven this morning.'

'Where's he gone?' Titty asked.

'Apparently he took a taxi to San Miguel.'

A soprano chorus greeted her news.

'San Miguel?'

'Who does he know in San Miguel?' Jonesy asked.

'Where the fuck is San Miguel?' Spizz joined in.

'That's all I can tell you, I'm afraid. He left me no message. I only know he was going to San Miguel because he asked Luis to call him a taxi and you have to tell the driver your destination when you ring.'

They all looked at Eve in disbelief, as if she was spinning them a tale.

'He's gone off on his own before. On other holidays,' Thommo said. 'But he's never checked out. You must have really pissed him off yesterday, Spizz.'

'Don't blame me! Hitting him with the ball was an accident and he knows that. It was Fee who got nasty with him.'

'Too fucking right, I did! He never knows when to stop. I'm not sorry he's gone. He's behaved like an idiot since we got here.'

'Well, you've changed your tune,' Banksy said. 'You usually laugh at his antics. You love a bit of banter with him. Give as good as you get, you do.'

'Erm, well, I'll see you on the courts at half-past ten,' Eve said, not wanting to witness any more of their childishness. 'And I'll cancel his place at Cafe Mambo. If I don't you might be charged for him.'

'Trouble in Paradise?' Sarah asked her as she walked back to her breakfast.

'Leggo's checked out,' Eve said. 'I've no idea why or where he's gone,' she added, not seeing any reason why she should tell the rest of them that he'd taken a taxi to San Miguel. She could do without the cross-examination that would inevitably follow.

'How childish!'

Eve shrugged and made no comment. Although she considered Leggo to be a bit of a prat she wasn't in the habit of running down one client to the others.

'Morning! Am I the last?'

Nicole burst into the dining-room, her long, red plait swinging, her shades covering her eyes, even though the sun still wasn't properly out after the rain.

'I don't think you are,' Eve said, looking round the table.

'If it's Ron you're looking for, he's been and gone. Up with the lark,' Liz said, laughing.

'I don't know where he gets his energy from,' Alex said, shaking his head, then wishing he hadn't. His eyes hurt from lack of sleep and his head gave the dull throb of hangover.

He caught Sarah's eye and they exchanged a knowing smile, as scenes of last night came back to both of them.

Further down the table Sean looked at Nicole who seemed to be concentrating on her bowl of muesli. She hadn't so much as glanced his way since she'd joined them and while he didn't want a needy woman clinging onto him for the rest of the holiday, he was banking on having a couple of action replays of last night's little session down at the beach. He couldn't believe how she'd totally gone for it and how much that had turned him on. And apart from her sighs and groans and squeals of encouragement she'd hardly said a word. That was an added bonus! Sexy and silent. An end to the wittering. The answer to his prayers!

'Did you sleep well?' Katrina asked Rosalind as she bashed her boiled egg sharply with her spoon.

'I did, thank you. The best night's sleep in ages.'

'Good.'

'I can't thank you enough,' Rosalind gushed.

'Och, I didn't do anything at all.'

'You listened and you understood and you made me feel better about myself.'

'I only helped you see what you already knew.'

Rosalind gave Katrina a huge smile. Studying them from the other end of the table, Charlie pursed his lips. He loved it when he was right about something and the others would see that he was. After Nicole's reaction last night he wondered if he'd done the wrong thing showing them the photos but he noted that both Jackie and Sean were surreptitiously watching the two women, too. Charlie didn't have a problem with lesbians, or with gay men. So he couldn't quite work out why he was fixated upon Rosalind and Katrina. It never occurred to him that his pride had taken a childish knock when he'd felt edged out by them.

✦ ✦ ✦

THE GROUP SAT on the terrace of the Club House drinking coffee to pass the time until ten thirty. To Eve's surprise, the Fourth Form had joined them. They hadn't exactly integrated but rather sat around the edge of the others. Spizz found himself next to Estelle.

'Is it Surrey you said you come from?'

'Yes. A place called Wootton.'

'And what do you do there?'

'I've got a flower stall.'

'Oh, right. Think you might get a shop one day?'

'I had my own shop for years.'

'What did you do, downsize?'

'Something like that.'

Estelle had no desire to explain what had happened when she'd found out her fella and her business partner had been having an affair for ages. It was nobody's business and even though she'd moved on and was making something of her life again, she always felt like an abject failure whenever she told anyone about it. She must have been stupid and blind not to have seen what was going on right under her nose. Or was she only guilty of having been trusting and good-hearted? Either way, she wasn't going to discuss it with Spizz.

'You're a PE teacher, aren't you?'

'Me? No. I'm a butcher.'

'Really?' Estelle was taken by surprise. She was sure the Fourth Form had all been teachers.

'Yep! I work in a proper butchers. None of this pre-packed supermarket stuff in our shop.'

'You'd better not tell Katrina, then,' Estelle said, 'She's a vegan.'

'Wash your mouth out!' Spizz quipped and she laughed.

'You're from Birmingham, aren't you?'

'Just outside. A place called Rowley Regis. Born and bred. You enjoying your tennis?'

'Yes. I think I am.'

'You sound surprised and unsure.'

'I've only been playing a little while and I'm not very good. But I really do feel as if I'm improving.'

'Well, that's what it's all about, isn't it? Can I get you another coffee?'

'Oh. Yes. Thank you very much.'

As Spizz got up to go for the coffees Nicole looked at Estelle and raised her eyebrows. Estelle pretended she hadn't seen her do it. He'd only offered her a coffee. And besides, Estelle was still a bit miffed at Nicole for going off with Sean yet again. At least, that's what she'd assumed had happened. She decided she wouldn't mention a thing to Nicole about it. And she certainly wouldn't ask her outright about Sean. Really it wasn't any of her business.

Behind her shades, Nicole wasn't sure how she felt about Sean or last night. She'd enjoyed herself, which had surprised her. She hadn't thought any man would ever match up to Roland, but Sean had. Although she had to admit that the setting had been a bit of a turn on. She and Roland had never made love on a beach under a huge blanket of stars and a bright moon with the hypnotic whispering of the sea beside them. And they never would, of course, not now. A little knot formed in her throat when she considered that. She missed Roland. And she felt a tad guilty for being with Sean. She knew Roland wouldn't have liked that. He wasn't the type to have wanted her to be happy without him. He'd have been more than a little put out that she wasn't draped and veiled in black and still crying with grief every day.

Still, he'd have loved knowing that when she and Sean

were screwing each other's brains out down on the beach last night, that she was thinking it was him that she was with. That would have soothed his ego.

Eve handed out the tournament sheet for the afternoon session, reminding everyone that they would be leaving at 7pm sharp for San Antonio and Sunset Strip.

'Only doubles this afternoon?' Charlie queried.

'Yes. We're starting the clinic late which means we'll start the afternoon session late, too and the sunset won't wait for us, so we have to be there on time. And anyway, if we aren't we'll probably lose our tables.'

'Let's hope there's no more rain,' Alex said. 'That'll put the kibosh on any sunset.'

'Don't even joke about more rain!' Jackie said. 'I'd ordered glorious sunshine for this week.'

'It's showing sun for the rest of the day,' Estelle said, consulting her phone. 'And for most of the rest of the week. Apart from tomorrow. That looks a bit iffy.'

'Let's all think positively! The weather is going to be fantastic from now on,' Jesus agreed, joining them on the terrace. 'Perhaps just an odd shower. We often get bad storms at the end of August.'

'I'd have thought the weather in August would've been good,' Estelle said.

'We have storms because the heat of summer builds up. Next week there are more storms forecast.'

'We'll be back home by then,' Estelle said, wistfully.

'Anyway, good morning, everyone! Sorry about the hold up. But the courts are now dry enough for us to start the clinic, so I'll see you there as soon as possible, please.'

Everyone stood up and began to make their way to the courts as Eve took Jesus to one side.

'Just to let you know that Leggo checked out of the hotel this morning.'

'Really?'

'Yes. He's gone to San Miguel, apparently. That's all we know.'

'Oh, well, that's a good thing. At least he is no longer here being stupid and spoiling things for the others. And us!'

As Jesus jogged down the steps to join his class Eve's phone beeped.

Just landed! Enjoy the rest of your stay. Xxx

Her face broke into a smile as she read the happy news that her little family had landed safely.

I'll try. Love to you all xxx

As she sent it she noticed mail in her inbox. She gave a sigh when she read the email from a Travel Together colleague, Shona, whom she didn't know asking her if Leggo had filled in a Holiday Curtailment Form.

Did you read my bloody email properly? How could I get him to fill in a form if I only found out he'd checked out after he'd gone?

She thought she had better moderate her tone before replying to Shona. She took a deep breath and composed herself.

Dear Shona,

Can I refer you to my earlier email? Mr Legg left the hotel without informing me. I heard he had checked out from the receptionist ten minutes after he had gone off in a taxi. He didn't contact me in any way to tell me. So it has not been possible to get his Holiday Curtailment Form completed.

Regards

She hesitated wondering if she should have written *Kind regards* but decided if Shona didn't have the intelligence to work out why there was no signed Holiday Curtailment Form then she didn't deserve Eve's regards to be kind. Her attention was attracted to the courts by a lot of noise. Looking over she saw Charlie and Spizz were having a volley rally as the others counted each stroke loudly.

Thirty-two! Thirty-three! Thirty-four!

They all shouted the tally loudly, encouraging the two men to carry on their bout of tennis's version of keepy-uppy. Back and forth, back and forth the ball went over the net, from forehand to backhand, the shots getting shorter and the shouts louder. Eve went to the edge of the courts and joined in the counting.

Forty-eight! Forty-nine! Fifty!

All the others were now surrounding them and clapping along every time the ball hit the racquet. Eve noticed that both men were sweating profusely and she wondered how much male pride was the cause of that rather than physical exertion. Whoever lost this would doubtless take some ribbing.

Sixty-four! Sixty-five! Sixty-six!

The noise of the shouts was deafening so Eve didn't hear her phone ring but she felt it vibrate in her hand. Looking down she was thrilled to see Melv was calling her again. She rang back up the steps to take his call in the relative quiet of the Club House.

'You're up early!'

'I couldn't sleep. So I thought I'd give you a call. You know, while it's quiet. Before all the madness of the day begins.'

'You sound weary.'

'A bit tired. The resort's full what with it being Carnival.'

'Of course! Lots going on, huh?'

'You know how it is. They're having a gala dinner for one of the beauty pageants here. More than five hundred people. And a few VIPs staying. I won't be sorry when it's over.'

'Aren't you going to watch the parades?'

'Possibly. It depends if Radley wants to. You know he doesn't like people seeing him so probably not. Anyway, when are you coming back? We've got a Travel Together group in a few weeks. I guess you'll be with them but I wondered if you'd be coming before then?'

'I'm pencilled in to do the group so I probably won't come out before.'

A couple of years ago she'd have jumped at the chance of going to spend time with him, but gradually and unconsciously their relationship had changed. And Eve knew the part she'd played in that even if Melv didn't.

'Okay. Well, maybe we can have a long FaceTime one day next week, huh? It's a while since we've chatted. Chatted properly I mean.'

'Of course. I thought we'd agreed on Sunday?'

'Did we? Okay.' He paused. 'I do miss you, babe.'

There was a beat's silence.

'I miss you, too,' she whispered.

'I kinda thought you and me'd be together by now…'

'Make plans and God laughs.'

'Yep! That's what they say.'

'I've got to go, Melv. Thanks for the call.'

'You don't have to thank me, Eve. I'm just sorry we don't talk daily the way we used to. Take care of yourself. I love you, babe.'

'Love you, too.'

And she did love him. Whatever happened, whatever

she'd done, the one truth that ran through the threads of her life was that she loved Melv.

She heard a huge cheer go up from the courts where Charlie had just played shot two hundred and ninety-one as a drop-shot. Spizz had slid towards it but was unable to flip it back over the net before it bounced low.

'Yay! Go, Charlie!'

The group were going wild; thumping Charlie on the back, cheering him and commiserating with Spizz, who although competitive was taking defeat with good humour.

'Well, the court was wet, of course, that's what made me slip,' he said as he shook Charlie's hand. 'But that's no excuse! Well done, mate! All credit to you.'

'And the beers are on you, Spizz!' Cookie said. 'Loser pays.'

'Yeah, I pay for Charlie not for you bunch of tossers!'

'Charming!' Sarah said.

'I didn't mean you. I meant them,' Spizz said, pointing at members of the Fourth Form.

'That must be some sort of record, mustn't it?' Estelle asked Jesus as they climbed the steps back to the Club House for a break.

'Probably not. The record is thousands.'

'Thousands? Really?'

'Yes. I think it's two brothers who did it. Did you see that, Eve?' Jesus asked.

'Most of it. Well done!'

'Well, you've got a long way to go before you match any records.' Estelle said consulting her phone. 'According to Google, the record in a match is held by two women! Six hundred and forty-three strokes.'

'Let's hear it for women's tennis!' Katrina shouted, punching the air.

'But they didn't have to contend with a wet court,' Spizz quipped.

'But the Guinness Book of Records says the volley record is held by the Rossetti Brothers, so you were right, Jesus. And how many do you think they did?'

'A thousand?' Ron suggested.

'Nope!'

'Two?' Jackie offered.

'It's a lot more than that,' Jesus told them.

'Twenty thousand,' Katrina said.

'More!'

'Twenty-five thousand,' Liz said.

'Oh, just bloody tell us,' Sean said.

'Thirty thousand, five hundred and seventy-six,' Estelle announced.

'Well that makes you two look a bit pathetic,' Cookie said.

'Ignore him, Charlie! He's just miffed because I didn't buy him a beer,' Spizz said.

Eve breathed a sigh of relief as they all made their way back to the courts. She happily registered the camaraderie that seemed to now include the Fourth Form. Perhaps Leggo had been a negative influence and now that he'd gone the group dynamics might improve. She certainly hoped so.

✦ ✦ ✦

'SO, HOW ARE you?' Alex asked Sarah as he slipped onto the chair beside her at lunch.

'Fine. You?'

'Fine.'

He was unsure how to continue. Sarah seemed aloof, almost stand-offish. He felt uncomfortable. He didn't like women who played games, it didn't matter how attractive or good they were in bed. He decided he'd finish his tuna salad and go and sit somewhere else.

Next to him, Sarah was lost in thought. She'd overheard him and Sean talking earlier and she was puzzled. They seemed to know what had happened, yet she knew that was surely impossible. She wanted to ask Alex outright, yet she felt curiously tongue-tied, an unusual situation she rarely found herself in. She decided to bide her time and wait for a better moment, after all, sitting eating lunch in front of everyone else certainly wasn't good time to talk about something so personal. She turned to Alex and smiled.

'Looking forward to Sunset Strip?'

✦ ✦ ✦

'ESTELLE! ESTELLE!'

Startled at hearing her name, Estelle turned round to see who was calling her just as the lift doors opened. Spizz hurried towards her and stepped into the lift beside her.

'I was just wondering if you're going to San An tonight?'

'Everybody's going, aren't they?'

'Well, I wasn't sure.'

'Why?'

'Erm, do you want to come to Cafe Mambo with us?'

Estelle was taken aback by the surprising offer. She liked the idea of going to Cafe Mambo. She'd heard people talking about it seemed out of her financial league.

'I've already booked my place for the Mint Lounge with the others,' she said. 'But they're side by side, aren't they?'

'Apparently, yes. So, why don't we have a drink together then. In one place or the other once we've had dinner?'

He could see she was still hesitating.

'I mean just you and me. Not with all the other knobs. They wanna go to Es Paradis but I'm not sure I fancy it. From what Eve said it's a young crowd and who wants to be with a bunch of twenty-year-olds, eh?'

He was aware he was gabbling. The lift stopped, the doors opened and he realised it was his floor. He held his breath.

'Yes. Okay. That'll be nice,' Estelle said.

'See you later then.'

The doors whooshed close. Spizz did a little dance down the corridor to his room, smiling to himself. And inside the lift Estelle hoped she'd done the right thing in accepting his invitation. He seemed so different from Joe.

And that's no bad thing! Lighten up! He's asked you to meet him for a drink, not to marry him!

✦ ✦ ✦

'AND THEY'RE HAVING a fling then?'

Sarah and Jackie were lying on their usual sun-loungers by the pool watching Katrina and Rosalind who were disappearing down the path to the beach.

'That's what Charlie said. And he showed us some photos he'd taken of them.'

'Why was he spying on them?'

'I don't think he was spying on them. Just came across them as he was wandering through the town.'

'And what were they doing in these photos.'

'Cuddling from what I could see. It was dark in the taxi. I only got a quick look because Sean and Nicole were holding Charlie's phone. They were holding each other and Rosalind's head was pressed into Katrina's neck.'

'People are always going to get off with each other on a

singles' holiday,' Sarah said.

'I think Nicole and Sean have paired up.'

'What makes you say that?'

'Just the way they were with each other last night. Sitting very close in the taxi and then they walked off together as soon as we arrived back.'

'They might have just been heading in the same direction.'

'What? Towards the beach? And besides, this morning they seem a bit awkward with each other.'

'I didn't notice anything.'

'Because you weren't looking! And anyway, you've got someone yourself, haven't you?'

'Have I?'

Sarah gave her a sharp look.

'You and Alex.'

'What about me and Alex?'

'You got together last night, didn't you?'

Sarah didn't care that Jackie knew, she was just curious as to how she'd found out.

'What makes you say that?'

'I could hear you! Your bathroom backs onto mine and sound travels through open ventilation shafts.'

Jackie was pleased to see that for a few seconds she'd rendered Sarah speechless.

'It sounded like you were having a right old time!'

'Did you deliberately listen to us?' Sarah spluttered.

'I couldn't be off it. I had to use the toilet. And don't forget the headboards are up against the adjoining wall.'

Sarah recalled the headboard had made a bit of a racket. Surprisingly she felt herself blush.

'So, tell me, was he as good as you made him appear?' Jackie wanted to know.

Sarah looked at her square in the eyes.

'Jackie, he was even better!'

Jackie screeched loudly and clapped her hands with glee.

'Eeeh! I'm right pleased for you!'

'Thank you. And I hope you didn't waste the night stalking that worthless boyfriend of yours, did you?'

'I did have a look on her Facebook page. She hadn't posted any new photos. But I've been thinking. I want to plot my revenge. Got any ideas?'

'What sort of revenge did you have in mind?'

'I'm not sure, I thought you'd probably come up with something.'

'To be perfectly honest with you, I don't believe in getting revenge.'

'That's strange coming from a lawyer.'

'I believe in justice not revenge. I think the best revenge is to live well. I honestly do. When you get back just finish with him. Don't get angry just get rid. That'll wind him up because you won't be giving him the opportunity to lie even more or try to convince you you're wrong. And then get on with your life and let Karma take care of him. And she will, because she's a bitch with a very long memory.'

Jackie was a bit disappointed. She'd be expecting Sarah to come up with a fabulous plan to get her own back. But perhaps Sarah was right.

'But if Karma's a bit too slow for your liking, you might find a huge dose of laxative in the last ever dinner you cook for him does the trick.'

Jackie roared so loudly that the people on the sun loungers on the other side of the pool looked over at them. Sarah joined in and soon they were both laughing hysterically.

'And the best way to get on with your life is to take a

new lover. Anyone in the group you can throw yourself at?' Sarah asked as the two of them calmed down.

'I don't really fancy any of them. Alex and Sean are taken. Charlie's a laugh but he's not my type. And I absolutely love Ron but he's a bit old for me. And besides, I think he might be with Liz.'

'What about the Fourth Form? Or is that a silly question?'

'Oh, per-lease! No. I'll pass on sex this holiday. It's no big deal and I am enjoying myself. Really. I am.'

Neither of them was totally convinced that she was.

✦ ✦ ✦

'YOU'RE A BIT quiet today? Are you still hungover?'

Ron looked up from reading the copy of Diario de Ibiza that he'd bought in the supermarket earlier that morning to see Liz hovering beside him.

'No, I'm fine, love. I rarely get hangovers. I'm lucky like that. Drink lots of water before I go out and again before I get into bed,' he said. 'I'm just getting in a bit of Spanish reading practice until it's our turn in the doubles.'

'I felt rough this morning,' Liz said, taking the seat next to him. 'I try to keep hydrated, too, but obviously I didn't drink enough. Still, good night, wasn't it? The Spanish People know how to enjoy themselves, don't they?'

'Oh, they're lovely people. Smashing bunch. I think they said they're leaving tonight. I must find them to say goodbye.'

'I'm looking forward to Sunset Strip later. And the boat trip on Thursday,' Liz said, sipping her coffee. 'It'll make a nice change from the tennis.'

'I love a boat trip,' Ron agreed.

He couldn't remember a lot of what had happened the previous night. But he did remember kissing Liz. He didn't know how it happened or what had lead up to it; he simply remembered the feel of her hands on his face and her lips on his lips. It was the first thing he thought of when he'd woken up that morning lying fully dressed on top of the bed. He was relieved to see he was in his own room. He really liked Liz. She was a thoroughly decent woman whose company he had enjoyed and there was no way he wanted her to think he was leading her on or even had dishonourable intentions towards her. They were friends and he wanted to keep her as a friend. He looked at her for clues as to what had gone on, but she simply seemed to be the same as always.

Perhaps you dreamt it all, you silly old sod!

He decided to take his cue from Liz and act as if nothing at all had happened.

✦ ✦ ✦

ESTELLE HAD CHANGED her outfit three times and still wasn't convinced by the fourth one as she studied her appearance in the mirror. She turned from side to side and then faced the other way and threw a critical look over her shoulder at her back view in the mini-skirt and long shirt.

No! It looks wrong!

She pulled the shirt over her head without undoing the buttons and stepped out of the skirt throwing both onto the bed to join the heap of other outfits. She gave a huge sigh, blowing out her lips and grabbed the linen, floral maxi-dress again. It was her favourite, bought especially for the holiday. She really liked it; the long slits at both sides showed off her legs that were beginning to look nicely tanned, without revealing too much. And the cut favoured her curvy size sixteen figure.

Is it too dressy, though?

She repeated the side to side then face the other way and look over shoulder routine.

Oh, this'll do!

She slipped her feet into her Carvela espadrilles and gave herself one final inspection, tugging at her platinum cropped hair to make the spikes stand up a bit more. She touched up her eye-liner; she'd always liked to wear plenty of eye-liner since she was in her teens. It gave her confidence. She looked at her watch and grabbed her bag. She didn't want to be the last one down.

✦ ✦ ✦

THE TWO MINIBUSES pulled up behind Sunset Strip in Calle Balanzat and the group spilled out. Eve agreed the time and place for the pick up for the bus that was coming back and confirmed with the Fourth Form that they'd be making their own way with taxis.

'Wow! What an atmosphere!' Nicole looked around stunned as they took their seats at their reserved table on the Mint Lounge terrace. It was heaving with people.

Eve accompanied the Fourth Form to Cafe Mambo and stayed until they'd been shown to their table.

'Enjoy your evening,' she said.

'We always do,' Titty said. 'It's a fabulous place, isn't it?'

'Amazing!' Eve agreed.

She gave them a wave and made her way back to join the others. There was little conversation going on; everyone was looking around taking in their surroundings. There were people everywhere. Not only was every table taken on every bar's terrace, the wooden steps between the bars were filled with people sitting clutching their drinks and looking out over the Bay of San Antonio towards Conejera, the huge rock that dominated it, soaking up the atmosphere, swaying to the music and waiting for the sunset. And in front of the terraces, hundreds more people sat on the rocks, a sweet-smelling cloud floating above them as they smoked, drank, laughed, chatted and sang.

'I'm going to have a cocktail first,' Sarah declared.

'Good idea!' Everyone agreed with her as they studied the cocktail list.

'They all sound amazing, I can't make my mind up,' Jackie protested.

'The Watermelon Sunset sounds good, I think I'll have that,' Nicole declared.

An attentive waitress hovered as they decided what they wanted then weaved her way through the pedestrians, skaters and a large stag-party on segways who were using the coastal pathway that lay between the bar and its terrace on her way to get their drinks.

'I don't think they'll do separate bills in here, so you'll just have to keep a tab on what you've had,' Eve explained.

'We're all grown ups, that shouldn't be a problem,' Alex said.

The waitress braved the pathway again, this time skilfully balancing a huge tray with a colourful rainbow of cocktails and drinks.

Sarah looked at Jackie and was pleased to see she was holding an enormous glass with a fruit cocktail on a stick dipped into it and was beaming from ear to ear as she gazed out to sea. Sarah thought it was the most relaxed she'd seen her all week.

'Penny for them,' she said.

'I'm just thinking how brilliant it is to be here. On Sunset Strip. In Ibiza.'

'You're winning at life!' Sarah quipped. 'Why don't you let me take a pic and you can put it on your Facebook?'

'But Scott doesn't know I'm here…'

'Are you really not going to finish with him after all the lies he's told you?'

'Of course I am!'

'So why are you unwilling to let him know where you are? He started it.'

Jackie thought about it for a moment, biting her lip.

'You're right! Here!' She tossed her mobile across the table to Sarah and then struck a pose in profile, against the sea, with her glass raised high.

'That's brilliant! I love it,' Sarah studied the photo. 'Alex! Sean! Get in the photo with Jackie,' she ordered the two men who were on either side of her.

Each of them obliged, putting an arm around Jackie's shoulder, their heads against hers and gave a sexy smile to the camera.

'Blimey! Get me!' Jackie said when she saw the shots.

'Upload them before you lose your nerve.'

Jackie did just that. As she pressed *Share* she felt such a thrill of joy; a surge of power she'd never experienced before. She was taking control of her life back. She didn't need a bloke and certainly not a lying cheating one. Julie Clithers was welcome to him. She grinned again and emboldened by the cocktail turned and gave Alex and Sean a peck on the cheek.

'Thanks, guys.'

'My pleasure,' Alex said, winking at her.

And then she turned her phone off. She didn't care if Scott saw the post or not. She'd already worked it out that she'd be home several hours before him on Saturday. She was going to contact a local locksmith to change the locks in the afternoon and then she was going to put all Scott's stuff in bin liners and leave them at the front gate.

Julie Clithers can take him in.

She downed the rest of her cocktail in one and turned her attention to the menu. Suddenly she was ravenous.

✦ ✦ ✦

SUNSET WAS APPROACHING. The sky was clear and turning pink as the sun at the end of her day's journey dipped down to rest and gently touched the sea. Everyone's eyes were turned towards the west; an ocean of heads, shoulders and arms were swaying gently to the haunting melody with its underlying staccato beat washing over them.

'Oh, yes! Brilliant choice, Mr DJ,' Charlie said, his eyes half closed and his head moving from side to side.

'What is it?' Liz whispered, afraid of breaking the spell.

'Doldrums. Ame,' he said.

Liz nodded. She was unsure which was the artist and which the title of the song, but she agreed with Charlie. The music was hypnotic, chilled and totally fitting. The DJ timed it perfectly so that the final notes rang out as the sun slipped below the horizon. Time was suspended and then a huge cheer went up and a wave of applause rippled from the bars, across the pathway and terraces and over the wooden steps and the rocks towards the sea.

They couldn't explain how sharing such an experience with hundreds of others could still be such an intimate moment, and yet that's exactly what it had been. They all knew they had shared something that was extra special.

✦ ✦ ✦

'DO YOU KNOW where the pathway leads, Eve?' Katrina asked.

'If you turn left it takes you into San Antonio, along the seafront and then it continues around the bay over to the Hotel Hawaii and beyond,' she said, pointing to the hotel across the water. 'Perhaps even right round the Bay. I know there was talk of extending it.'

'And the other way?'

'Down to Cala Gracio.'

'Fancy a leg stretch, anyone?' Katrina looked round the table of happy people.

'I'm okay here, thanks,' Charlie said, not wishing to play gooseberry again.

'I'll come,' Rosalind said. 'It'll be nice to see the town at night.'

'We'll see you back on the bus,' Katrina said as the two of them left their bill money with Eve and set off on their stroll unaware of the eyes that followed them and the looks that passed from some members of the group to the other.

'There was a frog on a bus I took last week,' Ron announced.

One or two people looked at him unsure whether it was another of his jokes.

'He had to get the bus cos he'd had his car toad,' he declared, laughing as he delivered the punchline.

'Oh, Ron!' the groan went up.

'I'm loving the music,' Charlie said.

'Yes, me, too,' Sean agreed. 'The DJ knows his stuff. The beat's kicked in now.'

'Walking With Elephants,' Charlie said. 'Ten Walls. Top stuff.'

'Is this house?' Eve asked.

'Yep.'

She smiled, proud of herself.

'The way it's gone from chill out to this. Like the transition between day and night. Magic,' Sean said.

'You're poetic!' Nicole teased him. 'But you're right,' she conceded, looking around at the hundreds of people who had now gathered on the walkway all moving to the beat. She raised her arms in the air and joined in.

'I might go for a walk in a while,' Ron said. 'Be nice to see a bit of the place while we're here. After all, we didn't see that much of Ibiza Town, did we, Liz?'

'We went to McDonald's!' Liz roared, making the others laugh. 'And there must be hundreds of bars here.'

'Thousands,' Ron agreed.

'Millions,' Liz added and they both burst out laughing.

Charlie was glad he could lose himself in the music. He was starting to feel like the third wheel again.

✦ ✦ ✦

'HOW WAS YOUR meal?'

Estelle looked up to see Spizz standing next to her. He'd squeezed his way between the tables and had taken the seat that Katrina had just vacated.

'Bloody lovely. It's all been fantastic. The food, the music, the atmosphere…'

'I know. It's a blinding place.'

'How was Mambo?'

'Awesome. We only had our table until ten so the others have gone down into town.'

'You not joining them?'

'I said I'd follow on and meet up with them. Titty said

she'd text me to let me know where they are. I'd rather spend some time with you. If that's all right, that is?'

Estelle beamed at him.

'Course it is.'

'Want another drink? Or do you wanna go somewhere else?'

'I'd like a gin and tonic, please. It's nice here. Some of the others have taken the pathway into town. But it seems a shame to leave when the atmosphere's so good.'

'Too right! A gin and tonic and a San Miguel, please,' he asked a passing waiter. 'Everyone all right? You look like you're having a good time.'

He looked around the table at the others and smiled. All chilled out and mellowed by the food, the drink, the atmosphere and the music, they smiled at him and nodded their agreement. Sean's arm was around Nicole's waist and she leaned back against him; Liz, Ron and Charlie chatted amiably with Eve; Sarah and Alex flirted with each other and Jackie sat smiling broadly, head nodding in time to the music, thinking about her future, happily tipsy.

Eve, her mood mellow, was enjoying her evening. It had turned out to be rather wonderful and she'd soaked up the atmosphere reminding herself that Ibiza really was a special kind of place. She'd broken her self-imposed *No Drinks On Duty* rule and had ended the meal with an Irish coffee that had just hit the spot and gone down wonderfully well. She watched Estelle and Spizz and liked the fact that he'd joined them.

Leggo's disappeared, Spizz has crossed over. Perhaps the Fourth Form will have totally disintegrated by the time the holiday's over.

She loved seeing how everybody mixed with everybody; she didn't like cliques or sub-groups in her groups. And on the whole this was a pleasant one. Certainly she was enjoying their company, especially her chat with Charlie, Liz and Ron.'

'Well, they might be grown up and tower over me, but they're not too old to get a clip round the ear,' Liz was saying. 'It's just that I have to get the kitchen steps to deliver it,' she added, laughing. 'It's a problem when you're so tall!'

'Tell me about it!' Charlie quipped.

'Well, your lack of height hasn't hampered your tennis playing, has it?' Ron said. 'You're the best player here!'

'Think how good I'd've been if I'd been six inches taller.'

'Ferrer wasn't tall and he did all right, like. Agassi as well. Look at all he won.'

'Yes. And he wooed Steffi Graff! Although I think he was taller than me, though.'

'I used to love Andre Agassi,' Liz said.

'Lleyton Hewitt won a lot, too,' Ron continued. 'And players like Rod Laver. Blimey! You don't get better than Rod Laver, do you?'

'Now you're making me feel good,' Charlie said.

'It's only in recent years tennis players seem to have got taller. The women as well,' Eve observed. 'Billie-Jean King, Chris Evert, even Martina Navratilova you wouldn't call tall.'

'I think the very tall players look awkward,' Liz said.

'Yep,' Ron agreed. 'Some of the men who are like, six seven, six eight. They might have a good reach but they ain't as flexible as the little ones.'

'So perhaps there's still time for me to get to Wimbledon, do you reckon?' Charlie asked.

'Definitely!' Liz and Eve echoed, raising their empty glasses to him.

✦ ✦ ✦

'OH, LOOK! A funfair!'

Rosalind pointed over to the far left beyond the main square.

'Shall we go and have a look? I like a fair, do you?'

'Yes. Okay. If you like.'

Katrina tried to sound enthusiastic. She was indifferent as far as fairs were concerned but Rosalind seemed keen. They paid for their drinks and walked the length of the square, past the ornate fountains and crossed over in front of the famous Egg Statue, onto the pathway next to the sea which led to Avenida Dr Fleming and the fair.

'Oh, it's next to Es Paradis. Isn't that the place the Fourth Form were going on about?' Katrina asked as they drew near.

'Possibly. I wasn't paying much attention to be honest. And besides I prefer the fair to a club any day.'

They crossed the road and found themselves in Slingshot Amusement Park.

'Oh, yes! We have to do this!' Rosalind squealed. 'Zero to one hundred and sixty kilometres an hour in one point three seconds' she read. 'Come on!'

She rushed forward to join a small queue. Katrina hesitantly joined her.

'I'm not sure about this…'

'Don't you like heights?'

'It's not that. We've just eaten…'

'That was two hours ago. We'll be fine.'

'Erm… I'm…'

'It'll be fun!' Rosalind insisted. 'But I don't mind going on by myself if you're not keen.'

Rosalind's face was lit up. Katrina felt like a real spoilsport. It was nice to see Rosalind happy after her upset and guilty sobbing of the previous night. Reluctantly she agreed.

'Okay. I'll come!'

'Great!'

Rosalind took her arm and squeezed it and the two of them moved forward in the queue, watching others get into the capsules and hearing their screams of terror as they were catapulted into the sky. Before long it was their turn. Katrina's stomach churned as the safety harness closed over and around her. She clutched it with sweaty palms wondering what the hell she was doing and why she'd let herself be talked into riding the slingshot.

'Oh my God! I'm so excited! I can't believe we're doing this!' Rosalind's voice was an octave higher and full of elation.

'SHIT! SHIT! SHIT!'

Katrina didn't know what hit her. She thought she probably had shit herself as she was suddenly hurtled heavenward, her stomach left far behind at ground level and struggling to catch up, the wind whistling past her head, the whole of San Antonio somersaulting below.

'Wow! Fantastic!' Beside her Rosalind was ecstatic. 'Yes!'

Then they lunged downwards.

'NOOOOOOOO!'

Then they rebounded towards infinity and beyond again.

'Oh, look at the view!'

Shut up, Ros! Just shut the fuck up!

'It's brilliant! Isn't it brilliant?'

Katrina, a lapsed Catholic, found herself reciting the Rosary.

'Did you like it?' Rosalind insisted as they were slowly, finally, lowered back to earth.

'I think perhaps it's an acquired taste,' Katrina replied finally opening her eyes.

She turned to look at Rosalind and then she burst out laughing.

'I think I just discovered that adrenaline is brown,' she quipped. 'I can't believe I did it. Jesus! That was scary!'

'Wanna go again?'

'No! Once was enough. Let's nae spoil a good thing,' she said, taking the hand of the young worker who helped her step from the capsule.

'Let's go and get the video,' Rosalind said.

'I'm not sure I want to see it.'

'Oh, come on! Then we'll have a drink.'

'Now that's the best thing you've said for a wee while.'

✦ ✦ ✦

'SHALL WE GO and find another bar?' Ron asked Charlie, Liz and Eve. 'I quite fancy walking through the West End. Heard it's good and it seems a shame to be here and not see it.'

'I'm up for it,' Liz said.

'Perhaps some of the others will join us,' Eve suggested.

'You up for a walk round the West End?' Ron called down the table.

Jackie, Estelle and Spizz said they were so the seven of them set off up Calle San Antonio which lead them into the heart of the West End.

'It's lively, isn't it?' Liz said, dodging around a group of young girls, tottering on incredibly high heeled sandals, giggling loudly.

'It certainly is,' Eve agreed, grinning to herself. 'It's been years since I've been here. But basically it hasn't changed.'

As she meandered through the packed streets, full of noise and life and colour, she marvelled at how the centre of this tiny, fishing village had become the good-time capital of Europe. Possibly the world!

'Oh, we've gotta go in here,' Spizz said, pointing down a small street on their right.

They followed him along the road, the strains of *With Or Without You* being sung by dozens of voices rising up to greet them as they came to Joe Spoons Irish Bar.

'This looks good,' Charlie said. 'Let's have one in here, shall we?'

Spizz and Charlie took their orders and went inside while the others stood on the neat little terrace.

'They're going!' Jackie said, seeing two older couples standing up ready to leave.

She scurried over to secure the table for them as Estelle, Liz, Eve and Charlie followed her. The music changed to something slightly more upbeat. They all smiled as they recognised *Uptown Girl.* They looked through the open windows to the packed interior where mostly young people were having a great time, swaying, waving their arms and singing along to the guitar-playing duo who were having the best time playing their music for all to enjoy. Eve thought back to earlier visits to the bar.

Thirty years ago!

She remembered Joe Spoons himself. The wild-looking Irishman with his ear-ring, his unruly black curls and his sparkling blue eyes had entertained tourists and visitors for so many years with his spoon playing and the rousing renditions of his Neil Diamond melody. She'd sat on this terrace and inside the bar with Brian and they'd had a great time. And here she was years later, back again.

And enjoying myself again!

'I usually only like going to local places when I'm abroad,' Ron said, cutting into her train of thought. 'But this is good, innit?

'Got to be done, Ron,' Eve said. 'Got to be done.'

✦ ✦ ✦

NICOLE AND SEAN had decided to take the costal pathway to the right, away from the town. The atmosphere at the Mint Lounge was brilliant and it was now heaving with people, but their mood was mellow and neither was up for a wild night of bars and drinking.

'Shall we go for a stroll when this one finishes?' Sean asked her as his head bobbed along to the Man With The Red Face.

'That sounds good. But let's find somewhere quiet and peaceful, shall we?'

And after a slow, amiable stroll with their arms around each other's waists they had arrived at the Golden Buddha. The bar was busy with lots of local people, many of whom were still eating dinner. They found a table on the terrace with a very low-slung sofa beside it and made themselves comfortable. They held hands and leaned back, reclining side-by-side looking up at the vast, cloudless, dark sky above them which provided a navy, velvet backcloth for thousands of stars and a flirty half-moon that smiled down on them.

'I used to long to see the sky,' Sean said after the waiter had served their drinks and left them alone.

'What do you mean? Were you stuck inside somewhere?'

'You could say that.'

Nicole sipped her drink waiting for him to continue. He bit his lip, half wishing he'd kept quiet. But he needed to talk about what had happened to him. He wanted to unburden himself and Nicole seemed like the right person to hear his confession. He kept his eyes skyward.

'Not being able to see the night sky was the worse thing about being inside. In prison.'

Nicole gulped. She wasn't expecting confessions out of the blue but her curiosity was piqued and she wanted to hear what Sean had to say.

'What were you in for?'

'Manslaughter. I killed my wife's lover in a fight.'

'Blimey!' Nicole coughed as she choked on her drink. She put her glass on the table and sat up staring at him. He continued to look at the sky.

'I hadn't meant to kill him. Just mess him up a bit. Give him a hiding. I confronted him outside his house as he arrived home to his wife and three kids after spending the afternoon shagging my wife in a hotel room. I'd followed her and taken pictures of the two of them. Not in bed, of course, but I'd got shots of them snogging in the bar and getting in the lift together. He couldn't deny it. And he made no attempt to deny it. He gave a cocky grin, a smirk. He got right in my face. Said someone had to give her what I obviously couldn't. Then he told me not to bother saying anything to his wife cos she wouldn't believe me. He'd cheated throughout their marriage and she'd never believed any of the accusations. My wife had been just one of the many. She'd thrown away all we had together on a bastard who treated her as just another notch on the bedpost.'

He gulped. His mouth had gone dry but he couldn't bring himself to sit up and reach for his glass. That would break his momentum and then he'd never be able to bring himself to mention it again.

'I just saw red. I was in so much pain, my whole life destroyed and he seemed to find that amusing. I lashed out and punched that smug, taunting smile from his face as hard as I could. I felt his nose crunch against my fist. He staggered from the blow and tripped backwards up the kerb. He sprawled onto his back and smashed his head on the pavement. And he was dead. Just like that.'

Sean was breathing heavily and beads of sweat had broken out on his forehead. Nicole felt his pain. She reached out and grabbed his hand and his fingers curled around hers like a baby's.

'How long did you get?'

He slowly turned his gaze from the stars to Nicole's face. She was staring at him intently her face full of sympathy for him.

'Five years but I only served three. The judge took into account my previous clean record and he believed that I had only intended to teach him a lesson but he said even though I'd been provoked I shouldn't have taken the law into my own hands and attacked him. And I suppose I can't argue with that.'

He sat up and swigged his drink. He suddenly felt light-headed; almost as if he were drunk. They faced each other on the sofa.

'I'm sorry. I didn't want to burden you with that. I don't know why I did… I just felt like I needed to talk to someone about it.'

'I understand. And I'm flattered you chose me.'

She bent forward and planted a kiss on his forehead.

'It must have been terrible for you. Inside.'

'It wasn't a picnic. You know, you've got blokes who think they've got something to prove. I was fortunate they mainly left me alone. I volunteered for the library. It was quiet and I could sit and read in peace. I spent most of the rest of my time in the gym.'

'That explains your physique.'

There was a moment's silence.

'What happened to your wife? Your marriage?'

'She filed for divorce while I was inside. Said she'd planned to divorce me anyway before I'd murdered the love of her life. She'd truly believed she was going to start a new life with him.'

He gave a bitter laugh and Nicole shook her head in disbelief, the irony of her own situation going right past her.

'When I got out I went back to Ipswich. Why shouldn't I? I had nothing to hide. I'd done my time. I had enough from the sale of our house to buy a little flat and I got a job back at my old company. My boss stood by me. She fucked off and now lives somewhere in Lincolnshire.'

'Well, you seem to have got your life back together again.'

'Yes. But once you've been in prison you're never the same person. Something in you changes.' He was surprised to realise he was crying. 'Sorry. Thanks for listening.'

'Thanks for telling me. And you know it won't go any further than me. I won't tell anyone.'

'Thank you.'

✦ ✦ ✦

ESTELLE WAS ENJOYING having a snog with Spizz on the minibus going back to the Dunas Blancas. She'd enjoyed the whole evening, especially the latter part when she'd been in his company. She couldn't remember the last time she'd had such a great time. Of course, it hadn't been just Spizz; the whole evening had been top notch and she'd had a ball with the others in the Irish bar, too. They came out of a long kiss and she gave a little giggle before snuggling her head against his shoulder, his arm wrapped around her waist.

'Can I ask you something?'

'Ask away!'

She moved closer to his ear so that nobody else could hear their conversation, although if she'd bothered to look around she'd have seen everyone was either deep in conversations of their own or being gently lulled to sleep by the sway of the bus.

'I'm not treading on Titty's toes, am I? By being with you?'

'Course not! She's not my girlfriend.'

'Only you seemed quite close at the beginning of the holiday…'

'That's because she was pissed. She always gets like that when she's had too much to drink. All over the men. Last Saturday night it was me. On last year's holiday she made a play for Jonesy.'

'So, you don't see each other in England or anything?'

'We see each other at the tennis club. We all see each other. But there's nothing going on with her. Nothing at all.'

He gently placed his hand under her chin and gazed into her eyes and planted a long, lingering kiss on his lips just as the coach jolted to a halt.

'Hotel Dunas Blancas,' Miguel announced.

'Not Bonkas Donkas?' Ron quipped, nudging Liz in the ribs and making her laugh.

'I'm never gonna bloody live that down, am I?'

Everyone headed for the lifts.

'I still cannot believe you got me on that bloody cannon ball,' Katrina said to Rosalind.

'I don't know how you had the nerve,' Sarah said. 'You wouldn't get me up there!'

'I thought you enjoyed living dangerously,' Alex said, giving her a sly grin.

'I don't like heights.'

'It's nae just the height!' Katrina protested. 'It's the fucking speed! And the bouncing back up again. Jeez! What was I thinking?'

'Still, you did it. Something you can tick off your bucket list.'

'It was never on there, Eve. More like on my Fuck It List. Still, as you say, I've done it now.'

She chuckled at herself as they all piled into the two lifts calling their good nights to each other. Spizz took Estelle's hand as the lift doors opened on the third floor and pulled her out with him. They walked along the corridor a little way before Estelle stopped.

'What's wrong?' Spizz asked.

'I'm not…'

'Not ready to spend the night with me?'

'No.'

'That's okay. I understand.'

He pulled her closer to him and planted a kiss on her forehead.

'I like you. I really do. But I'm not sure if I'm ready for a holiday romance. And I don't want you to think I'm leading you on…'

'I don't think that,' he said smiling. 'I like you, too. And we can take this as slowly as you want.'

They shared another kiss, caressing each other's backs and then pulled apart as the lift opened again discharging two couples who looked at them and smiled as they walked past.

'I'll see you in the morning then,' Estelle said.

'See you in the morning. And thanks for a great night.'

They began to walk away from each other holding hands until the last possible second, their fingers caressing and then they went their separate, each with a huge grin on their face.

✦ ✦ ✦

IF SEAN HAD been unsure as to whether Nicole might want to continue their relationship after knowing what he'd done, he soon found out his uncertainty was unfounded. If anything, Nicole seemed keener and wilder than before. He pitied the people in the room below as they wouldn't be getting much sleep. The bed twanged a loud crescendo and an increasingly frantic rhythm as she pulled him to her and clawed his back and then pushed him away as she flayed from side to side, clutching her boobs and stroking her belly, her gorgeous red hair an exotic fan across the pillows.

Three years of celibacy have all been worth it!

And not only was the sex amazing, he actually liked her.

✦ ✦ ✦

RON AND LIZ had got out of the lift on the second floor and stood awkwardly facing each other. Liz had gone to make her way down the corridor when she realised Ron wasn't following as he had on previous nights to accompany her to her door.

'Everything all right, Ron?'

'Yes. Well, no. I feel a bit stupid. I know we kissed last night. At least I think we did?'

'Yes.' Liz nodded.

'Well, I'm sorry if I came across as rude or a bit of an oaf.'

'But you didn't!'

'Are you sure?'

'Ron, it was me. I kissed you.'

'And did I kiss you back?'

Liz chortled; Ron was a funny man.

'Sort of.'

'I'm sorry. I'd had a few…'

'So you'd only give me a kiss if you've had a few?'

She was joking but saw that he was serious.

'I don't mean it like that, Liz. You're a lovely woman. You're attractive, you've got a good heart and you're fun to be with.'

'I feel a great big but coming on here. And it doesn't matter. Really it doesn't because I've already worked it out.'

'You have?'

'You're still in love with your wife, aren't you?'

Ron slowly nodded his head.

'With Veronica.'

He let out a long sigh.

'It's hard when you've only ever had one woman in your life. We met in Ilford Palais on her sixteenth birthday…'

His voice trailed off as he got momentarily lost in his memories.

'They called it puppy love when I met her. I remember out first kiss. Her nose was cold and slightly damp.'

Liz had got to know him enough to see that cracking one of his terrible jokes was his way of dealing with the situation.

'I understand and I think that's lovely. You've been a good mate so far this holiday and I'm happy for us to just be friends. And don't worry! It was only a kiss. And as you said, we'd both had a few. Night, night, Ron.'

She squeezed his arm and made her way down the corridor to her room. Ron watched her go with sadness etched on his face. She opened her door and gave him a little wave with her fingers. He nodded his head towards her and gave her his best smile. Then he gave a deep sigh and went in the opposite direction to his own room.

DAY FIVE

✦

WEDNESDAY MORNING DAWNED with the whole island covered in dark clouds and rain lashing down. Eve consulted her iPad and saw that it was quarter past seven and going to be wet for the whole morning, brightening up after midday. That meant there would be no tennis until the afternoon. She knew the company only gave refunds for full day wash-outs. Hopefully they'd be playing again by lunchtime. Just then Jesus rang.

'Good morning, Eve. No tennis until after twelve, I'm afraid. But I'm going to do a strength-building workshop in the hotel gym for those who want to attend. And at least that way the morning won't be completely wasted.'

'That's a good idea! I'm sure some of them will want to go along.'

'Tell them to meet me at the gym at half past nine. And then we'll pencil in playing this afternoon from half past one. We'll do some clinic and some matches. How does that sound? *Bien?*'

'Perfect! I'll get down to breakfast early and spread the word.'

Twenty minutes later she was pouring herself a coffee,

alone at the Travel Together tables, apart from Ron, who was tucking into his usual Full English.

'Don't you ever sleep, Ron?'

'What me? Nah! Too afraid I'm missing something,' he joked. 'Why stay in bed when you can be up and about and doing stuff? Life's for living.'

'I love your attitude.'

'I've known so many people who don't seem to know they're alive,' he said, dipping a sausage in his egg yolk. 'My neighbour's never been abroad! Can you imagine that? Never been further than Great Yarmouth. He sits indoors watching telly, even when it's a beautiful day. He gets the car out the garage on a Saturday morning and goes to Lidl then gives it a wash and puts it away for the week and on Sunday he walks up to the newsagents and gets the paper and spends the rest of the day reading it.'

'Still, perhaps he's happy.'

'It just don't seem right, though. I know we can't all be explorers or astronauts but there's more to life than just sitting at home watching the box. There's other people who'd give anything to have a shot at life who can't.'

'Morning!'

Liz, Estelle, Jackie, Nicole and Katrina all arrived together. They sorted out their food and drinks, Eve told them about Jesus's plans for the morning and then they tucked into their breakfasts.

'You seemed to be getting on all right with Spizz,' Nicole whispered to Estelle. 'Do you like him?'

'I do,' Estelle nodded. 'He's nice when you get to know him a bit. And he's a butcher not a teacher.'

'That's interesting.'

'Is it?'

'And did you? You know?' Nicole raised her eyebrows

at Estelle.

'No. I didn't want to. Oh, we had a bit of a kiss and cuddle, but I didn't feel ready to go the whole hog with him.'

'And he's all right with that?'

'He's going to have to be! Actually, he is. And I spoke to him about Titty. He said there's nothing going on between them. They're just friends. She gets a bit frisky when she's had a few.'

'Who doesn't?' Nicole quipped, making Estelle laugh.

By nine o'clock everyone was down except Fee, Thommo, Cookie, Banksy and Jonesy. Titty had made a point of sitting next to Spizz.

'What happened to you? I sent you a text every time we changed bar.'

'Oh, we went to Joe Spoons. The Irish bar. It was a good night.'

'We went in there but we didn't see you. About half past two.'

'We'd left long before that. What time did you get back?'

'About four, I think.'

'Jesus is doing a strength workshop in the gym from half past nine,' Eve told her. 'And then there'll be tennis on the courts from half past one.'

'I'll let the others know,' she said. 'Although I doubt they'll surface much before lunchtime. Except Banksy,' she added seeing him heading towards them.

'Can I have a word, please, Eve?'

Banksy's head was down and his hand was over the lower part of his face.

'Of course,'

Eve stood up and went to walk away from the others so they could speak in private.

'Oh, fuck! I'd forgotten about that!' Titty roared out

laughing. 'He lost his teeth on the slingshot!'

Banksy went scarlet as everyone turned to look at him.

'You mouthy cow,' he lisped, giving Titty daggers.

'What? They can all see what's happened to you.'

Eve took Banksy's elbow and guided him towards an empty table where she proceeded to talk to him about dentistry and Travel Together's insurance policy. Eve thought he probably wouldn't be covered as he'd lost his denture on a ride that wasn't an official part of the holiday.

'I couldn't believe it. We shot forward and it shot out. I didn't realise at first. It was only as we was being lowered to the ground I realised I didn't have it. Some poor bastard strolling along the pathway probably got hit in the face with it,' he said, grinning and making Eve laugh, in spite of herself. 'I've only had it a few months. Lost my two front teeth playing rugby in the winter.'

'I can ring a local dentist for you if you like and see if they can do something temporarily…'

'Nah. Thanks all the same but it'll probably be at least tomorrow and we're going on the boat then. And it'll probably cost an arm and a leg and if I'm not gonna get it back on the insurance, I'd rather wait and get myself sorted out at home. It's only three days, in't it?'

'Well, if you're sure.'

✦ ✦ ✦

ALEX, SEAN, CHARLIE, Ron, Spizz, Katrina, Rosalind and Sarah decided to join Jesus in the gym. Nicole, Estelle, Jackie and Liz joined Eve in the bar for coffee and chat. They sat by the ceiling to floor windows, pulled across to stop the rain from blowing in and watched the deluge fall gradually slower until it stopped completely and the clouds turned from grey to white and the sun popped up between them.

'Do you know what? I don't think I can be arsed to play tennis this afternoon,' Estelle said. 'I think I might go down to the beach.'

'Why don't you join me and Sarah round the pool?' Jackie asked.

'To be honest, I want to go topless and I think it's in poor taste to do that by the pool. On the beach it seems different somehow.'

'Is topless sunbathing not allowed round the pool then, Eve?' Jackie asked.

'I think it's allowed if you're lying down on a sun lounger, but they ask you to cover up if you go to the bar or inside the hotel.'

'That sounds fair enough.'

'Well, that's where I'll be,' Estelle said. 'I just feel like relaxing today. It's after all that sunset chilling out last night.'

Liz thought the idea of a couple of hours topless sunbathing sounded tempting. But she'd paid her money for tennis tuition and that was what she was going to take part in. Perhaps she'd go topless on the boat trip…

She hadn't seen him coming towards her or what was in his hand. She just felt the brush of it as it came over her shoulder and fell into her lap, touching her arm. She looked down and froze. Her heart stopped for a few seconds; time stood still.

And then her body jolted as if ten thousand volts had shot through it. She let out a primordial scream and leapt to her feet knocking the table and its contents flying. Eve, Estelle, Jackie and Nicole stood up staring at her, not knowing what had happened. Liz fled from the bar, out onto the terrace where she stood in the pouring rain, crying hysterically.

'What did you do?' Eve asked Jonesy who had crept up behind Liz and now stood in front of them grinning foolishly.

'I was just having a bit of a laugh. A joke,' he said, bending down to pick up a huge, black and brown rubber spider. 'I bought it off some street seller last night.'

'She's petrified of them,' Estelle said. 'She was telling us the other night.'

'Well, I didn't know, did I? It was just a joke.'

'Didn't it occur to you she might be scared of them?' Eve asked.

'No.'

He looked at Eve as if she was mad.

'You can see it's not real. Christ! They don't even come that big in the Amazon!'

Jonesy stuffed the spider into his shorts pocket and walked out of the bar. Liz screamed and ran to the other side of the terrace to get out of his way.

'Sorry! Just having a laugh,' he called to her, patting his pocket as he went.

Liz's legs buckled underneath her and she stumbled, sitting down in a large puddle. Eve and Nicole rushed outside to help her in. She was shaking, crying and soaking wet.

'I fff… feel such a fool,' she sobbed.

'Don't! It's him that should feel bad. Stupid arsehole!' Nicole shouted at Jonesy's retreating figure.

'Here!' Estelle took her towel from inside her beach bag and wrapped it around Liz's shoulders.

Two waiters had righted the table and collected the coffee cups, some of which had broken.

'Would you like more coffee?'

'Yes please,' Eve said. 'You need a hot drink, Liz.'

'Can I have a hot chocolate, please? And I'll pay for any damage,' she blubbed.

'No problem, madam. We have things breaking all the time.'

'What a fucking idiot!' Nicole shook her head again in disbelief at what Jonesy had just done.

Jackie rubbed the towel up and down Liz's arms in an attempt to dry them and warm her up.

'He might have stopped to think that other people don't like them,' Estelle said.

'You need half a brain to work that out,' Nicole said. 'And he obviously hasn't got even that!'

'He needs to realise that scaring someone witless might be a joke to him but not everyone finds it funny,' Eve said. 'Drink your hot chocolate and then go and get yourself sorted out.'

'I'm gonna be on edge now in case he brings it near me again,' she whispered.

'He won't,' Eve said.

✦ ✦ ✦

THE FOURTH FORM had gradually found each other just after noon, each of them looking the worse for wear. They shared a large table at the Club House dressed ready for the afternoon's tennis. They sipped water and coffee. Cookie was eating a toasted sandwich. Banksy looked at him with envy.

'Reckon I'll be on a liquid diet for the rest of the holiday,' he said, wistfully. 'Good job I like soup!'

Although he was sitting with them after his morning in the gym Spizz was keeping an eye out for Estelle and he was surprised to see her heading towards the beach, obviously ready for a serious sunbathing session. He wondered if she wanted some company.

'Given you the elbow has she?'

Titty followed his gaze and curled her lip.

'Oh shut the fuck up, will you? Christ! We're on a singles' holiday. I'm mixing with the other punters. Being friendly. What's wrong with that?'

'Mix away! I'm not stopping you. But you're the one that's usually all for us sticking together,' she retorted.

'Can I have a word?' Eve asked Jonesy as she came up to the table.

'I know what this is about. You're gonna tell me off.'

'What about?' Titty asked.

'I put my spider on someone's arm. Liz, is it? And she screamed blue murder. Knocked the table over, broke the crockery the lot,'

He chuckled as he said it and looked around at his mates waiting for their approval. Eve, a pacifist at heart, wished she could wipe the smug grin off his face with the back of her hand. Cookie and Banksy laughed.

'You might find it hilariously funny, but Liz is petrified of spiders. Now, I appreciate you couldn't have known that, but now you do, I'm sure there's no way you'd want to cause her any more upset or fear.'

'You knob-head, Jonesy,' Fee said. 'That's not funny.'

'So please make sure the spider stays in your room. And please lock it away in your suitcase. The maid might have a phobia, too.'

'Why should I?'

Eve felt that Jonesy was actually squaring up to her.

'Because I am asking you to. After all, why would a grown man want to bully and torment a woman? And that's what you'd be doing if you deliberately went anywhere near her with it now you know she's afraid.'

Jonesy curled his lip. He didn't like being told off in front of his mates.

'Oh, for fuck's sake!' Fee began to lose her temper with him. 'Grow up, Jonesy! She was scared stiff. You've had a laugh. So put the fucking thing away.'

Much to Jonesy's surprise – and Eve's – the others nodded in agreement with Fee.

'Alright, Akela,' he said, using the nick-name to have a dig at Eve. 'It's in my room and when I go back I promise I'll put it in my suitcase. Scout's honour.'

'Good! Thank you.'

Eve turned and walked away. Jonesy pulled a face but none of them laughed.

'Just don't!' Titty said, turning her back on him.

'We're being waved at,' Fee said, indicating Jesus who was calling everyone down to the courts.

They got up to leave. Spizz stayed where he was.

'Not coming, mate? Banksy asked.

'Nah. I knackered myself in the gym this morning. Might take a few hours off.'

The others wandered off. Titty looked back towards the terrace and saw Spizz head along the path towards the main hotel building. She snarled and gritted her teeth.

✦ ✦ ✦

THE BEACH WAS busy as tourists emerged from the morning curfew imposed by the rain, but it wasn't overly crowded and Estelle easily managed to find a sun lounger down on the water's edge. She lay back and undid her bikini top, enjoying the freedom of feeling the sea breeze and the sun on her breasts. She'd made sure she'd put on plenty of sun cream in her room. The last thing she wanted was sore, sunburnt boobs! The sea looked inviting but she liked to wait until she was really warm before she took a dip to cool off. She still felt a bit tired from the late night and decided not to read but to have a little siesta. She was just drifting off when she heard a sun lounger being pulled very close to hers and then a shadow fell over her. She opened her eyes and immediately crossed her arms over her chest.

'Fancy meeting you here.'

'Not playing this afternoon?'

'No. I wore myself out in the gym this morning. Christ! Jesus really put us through it. So I thought I'd give myself the afternoon off. You?'

'I lost momentum with not doing anything this morning. I couldn't be bothered to play. I thought I'd have a couple of hours here. It's turned out beautiful.'

'It has.'

Spizz made himself comfortable next to her, his eyes flitting over her body. Estelle continued to lie stiff and unmoving beside him, with her arms covering her modesty.

I feel like I've been laid out.

The thought made her giggle and taking a deep breath she slid her arms back down by her sides. Her face was scarlet and it wasn't down to the sun, but she'd come down here to sunbathe topless and sunbathe topless was what she was going to do.

And if Spizz wants an eyeful I hope he likes what he sees.

Spizz did like what he saw. Very much so. He grinned. He was enjoying himself. The two of them lay side by side, sharing an easy, unhurried conversation. After half an hour or so Estelle thought she should top up the suntan cream on her boobs but she didn't want to do it in front of Spizz and she certainly wasn't going to ask him to help.

'I really fancy a drink,' she said, ignoring the bottle of water that was sticking out of the top of her beach bag.

'What a proper drink you mean?'

'Well… yes. A beer or something.'

'I'll go and get us a couple.'

She waited until Spizz was halfway to the beach bar and quickly massaged a large dollop of cream all over her chest and stomach. She rubbed a bit more into her nose, too, which always went red. She finished just in time to see him coming back with the beers. Just behind him she saw Fee and Titty waving and calling him. He waved back but carried on walking towards her. They were making themselves comfortable on loungers, both topless. One look at Titty made Estelle feel totally inadequate.

'She must be an HH cup at least!'

Estelle looked down at her own C cups and winced. In spite of battling her weight over the last couple of years her boobs had never really got any bigger. She sighed. There was nothing she could do about it.

'Here you are! Nice and cold. Cheers!'

Spizz clinked his bottle against hers. And they settled down for what turned out to be a very pleasant couple of hours.

✦ ✦ ✦

WHEN EVE MET up with the group as they came off the courts, they all seemed to agree that they didn't want to venture too far for dinner that night.

'I'm up for eating here, to be honest,' Alex said. 'That meal we had on the first night was good enough for me.'

'Yes, I'm happy to eat here,' Sarah agreed. She didn't want to have to get too dressed up to go out to dinner. 'I don't want to have to rush anywhere.'

'Shall I book a couple of tables here then?' Eve asked. 'I think it's twenty euros for the buffet.'

'That's reasonable,' Alex nodded in agreement.

'Jackie will eat with us I think,' Sarah said. She'd decided to play tennis and Jackie had been happy to go to the pool by herself. 'I'll go via the pool now and let her know.'

'The vegan option was good,' Katrina conceded.

'Well, they know about you,' Eve said. 'So if I tell them you're among our number tonight there'll be a selection for you.'

'Good!'

'I'm not sure about us,' Thommo said, looking at Cookie, Banksy and Jonesy. 'The others might want to go out.'

'Then let them,' Banksy said. 'I'm happy to eat here. Well, to eat as best I can,' he grinned his toothless grin at Eve.

'Me, too,' Jonesy and Cookie echoed.

'So that leaves four,' Eve said.

'Estelle's on the beach,' Nicole said. 'I'll let her know.'

'I'll book for everyone and if there are a couple of no-shows, it's not the end of the world,' Eve said. 'So, I'll see you all in the bar at eight?'

'See you then, Eve,' Ron said, speaking for them all.

'Erm, I just wanted to say sorry,' Jonesy said, approaching Liz.

She froze on the spot then took a couple of steps backwards, away from him. Seeing what was happening both Nicole and Ron stepped between them. Jonesy raised his hands palms up towards Liz.

'I haven't got it on me. I'm sorry I scared you. I didn't realise you'd be so frightened of it. And I promise I won't come near you with it again,' he said.

Liz stared at him, trying to take in what he'd said. She slowly nodded her head.

'Thank you,' she whispered.

'Sorry.' He turned to the others who had stopped what they were doing and were watching him. 'Sorry,' he said to all of them. 'I was out of order.'

One or two of them nodded and Jonesy scuttled off.

✦ ✦ ✦

'ONCE IN A Meadow!' Estelle declared as the band struck up their next number. 'See! I knew we'd hear it sooner or later. My favourite Spanish song!'

'I think this one's called *Guantanamera*,' Eve said.

'Really? Well, anyway I love it! Come on!' She grabbed Spizz's hand and the two of them took to the floor followed by several others.

'Once in a meadow,' they all sang at the top of their voices when the chorus came round, making Estelle laugh and giggle.

'Well, that's what I thought it was,' she said to Spizz as he held her tightly.

'I reckon you're right and Eve's got it wrong. After all, everyone else seems to know the words,' he joked. 'Just listen to them.'

'Once in a mea-dow. Oh oh oh! Once in mea-dow!'

The whole lounge was singing along now and Estelle felt a huge surge of happiness. Her first singles' holiday was turning out to be such fun. She was having a great time and much of that was down to the lovely people in the group, and Spizz, of course. As if he felt he happiness, he squeezed her hand tightly just at that moment and pulled her a little closer.

Eve was happy to see the group enjoying themselves. They had eaten in the hotel and the meal had been a huge success with everyone agreeing that the buffet had been good value for money with loads of choice, even for Katrina. Rain had started falling again as dinner ended so instead of going out they'd all come through to the hotel lounge where a band was playing middle of the road dance music for all ages. The sangria and beer were flowing and the atmosphere was great. Even Liz seemed to be her usual smiling self and several of the group, especially Ron, had closed ranks around her. Eve raised a mental eyebrow as she thought about Jonesy. He'd thought he was being such a Jack-the-Lad when all he'd achieved had been to alienate almost everyone. She'd really felt for Liz. Rarely had she seen anyone show such fear.

The band brought the song to an end with a flourish and the dancers made their way from the dance floor, smiling and chatting to each other as they caught their breath, most heading for the bar. Spizz put his arm on Estelle's elbow and guided her towards the table where they'd left their drinks.

'I won't be a minute. Gotta go to the gents,' Spizz said, smiling at her and going towards the foyer. Estelle returned the smile; she was having a wonderful time.

The wine came out of nowhere, giving her a sharp slap and causing her to stop in her tracks.

'What you doing with my man?' Titty screeched blocking her pathway.

With wine running from her hair into her eyes and down her chin and dripping into her cleavage, Estelle grabbed the remains of a beer on the table next to her and threw it into Titty's face.

'Oi!' Charlie wasn't very happy at seeing his drink disappear in such a fashion.

Titty growled, stepped forward and delivered a stinging blow to Estelle's face, turning her head to one side. Estelle slapped her back good and hard.

'You fucking bitch!'

A crowd had started to gather to watch the undignified scene being played out before their eyes. Titty reached for Estelle's hair, her fingers unable to get a good grip on the short strands so she snatched at her top and used it to swing her around. Estelle grabbed Titty's jaw-length bob and pulled as hard as she possibly could. The crowd moved sharply out of their way. Eve turned round at the bar where she was assuring Katrina there would be vegan snacks on the boat to see what the commotion was and her mouth dropped open at the sight of the two women brawling. In two leaping steps she was beside them as they lurched from side to side, pulling each other back and forth in an inelegant, syncopated tango.

'I'll teach you to flaunt your tits in his face!' Titty was screaming.

'That's enough! Pack it in!'

Eve fought her way between the two of them forcing them apart and to back away from each other. Ron and Sean had joined her, each clutching onto a woman's arm.

'She's been asking for it!' Titty yelled lunging towards Estelle again. 'Get off me!'

She turned to Sean and tried to kick him. Cookie, Banksy, Jonesy and Thommo arrived on the scene, closing ranks around Titty. Thommo put a protective arm around her.

'Now just calm down and behave yourself!' Eve said to Titty. 'Both of you,' she added, wishing to appear impartial.

'She started it!' Estelle said, a livid red mark on her

cheek.

'You did by coming onto Spizz!'

'How old are you? Twelve?' Ron asked, contempt written all over his face.

'Just stop it! You're both being pathetic. You're lucky the bar staff haven't called security,' Eve said.

'What's going on?' Spizz asked arriving back from the gents and looking at the scene before him with bewilderment.

'I've just had wine thrown over me and been slapped because I've taken her man, apparently,' Estelle said, looking daggers at Titty who suddenly burst into tears.

'What?'

'Well, let's all just calm down and walk away, shall we?' Eve said. 'I'll need to speak to both of you tomorrow but in the meantime I think it's best if no more's said. Just try and act like grown ups and stay away from each other.'

Titty, who by now was giving an Oscar-winning performance, crying and claiming she'd been the wronged party, was lead off by the Fourth Form to their table on the far side of the lounge and Spizz and Ron walked Estelle back to join the others.

'Want a brandy, love?' Ron asked her. 'I think you need one.'

'No, thanks, Ron. I just want to go to my room and get cleaned up.'

She turned on her heel and fled from the lounge. Spizz made to go after her, but Eve stopped him.

'She's said she's going to get cleaned up. Probably best to leave her to it.'

'Eve, I swear I don't know what Titty's playing at…'

'Let's not talk about it now. Let's all just get on with enjoying what's left of the evening.'

Spizz sat down and looked round the group, feeling a bit foolish.

'What the fuck happened?'

'You've got them fighting over you, mate,' Sean said. 'Estelle was coming back to the table and Titty came across and threw a glass of wine in her face. Estelle retaliated…'

'As you would! And I don't blame her!' Sarah cut in.

'…Then Titty slapped her and it all kicked off.'

'I heard her say, "What you doing with my man?"' Nicole added.

'Well, you did appear to be together at the beginning of the holiday,' Sarah reasoned.

Spizz went scarlet. While he might have welcomed the idea of two women fighting over him, even boasted about it over a beer in the tennis club bar or with the lads in the shop, he felt embarrassed that it had actually happened.

What the fuck was Titty thinking?

He picked up his beer and downed it in one swig. Everyone was looking at him making him feel he was to blame for the fracas. He glanced across the lounge to where the Fourth Form were sitting; the hostility coming from them towards him was almost tangible. Without saying a word he stood up and strode from the lounge.

'Is it a common occurrence? People fighting on your holidays?' Nicole asked Eve.

'No, I'm pleased to say it isn't.'

'But you must have had some trouble,' Charlie insisted. 'Didn't you say you'd been with Travel Together for eighteen years?'

'As I said the other night, I've dealt with everything except a birth,' Eve quipped.

'You should definitely write a book,' Sarah said, grinning. 'You must have so much material for one. Eighteen years of singles' holidays!'

'I don't kiss and tell,' Eve quipped.

'Didn't one of your tour managers do that? Write a book?' Ron asked. 'And she got the sack for it…'

'Yes, she did,' Eve said, remembering the tour manager in question who had been popular and she'd personally liked and got on with.

'I heard Travel Together knew all about it but dropped her like a hot brick when someone complained,' Charlie said.

'Then I'll let that be a lesson to me!' Eve replied not wanting to have to defend the company against the indefensible. They had known about the tour manager's book; they'd actually encouraged her to write it and then they sacked her when one woman had complained. 'I'll keep all my stories to myself until after I've retired.'

Although after today's little episodes I think my retirement's looming ever nearer!

'How undignified!' Sarah sniffed. 'Two women scrapping like that over a bloke like him!'

'I quite like the idea of two women scrapping,' Alex quipped.

'You're the type of man who boasts he likes lesbians,' she shot back, 'when what you mean is you like watching girl-on-girl porn.'

Everyone's eyes swivelled towards Katrina and Rosalind who were deep in conversation about what had just happened and were completely oblivious to the sideways glances.

'Hey! Steady on!' Alex was stunned by Sarah's comment. 'That's a bit of an assumption.'

Sarah gave him a wink, which she seemed to think took the sting out of her words. Alex ignored it. One thing was enjoying great sex, which he certainly was with Sarah, but it didn't mean he had to put up with her comments and insults in front of everyone.

'Shall we have another drink?' Ron asked.

Some agreed, some waved away his offer, insisting they'd had enough. The band leader announced they were about to start their final medley of the night so now was the time to return to the dance floor for one last dance. Only Ron and Liz took him up on his suggestion. The others sat and watched, sipping their drinks, somewhat subdued by what they'd witnessed. Eve was aware her presence was probably adding to that; they were waiting for her to leave so they could talk freely about the goings on. She decided she'd had enough for one night. She was tired. It didn't look as if Estelle was coming back down so it probably wouldn't kick off again. And even if it did, she wasn't a referee. Picking up her bag, she smiled round the table.

'I'm going to love and leave you,' she announced. 'Enjoy the rest of the evening. I'll see you in the morning. And don't forget, we've got the boat trip tomorrow afternoon!'

'Did you say you'd checked the food?' Katrina asked. 'We got interrupted…'

Yes! Because that's my job!

'I have, Katrina. They know you're on board and they'll cater for you accordingly,' she said with a bright smile.

She crossed the lounge to the Fourth Form. She'd had less hostile receptions in her time. They were all glaring at her so she gave them her best smile.

'I'm just off. Don't forget it's the boat trip tomorrow afternoon…'

'I'm not getting on a boat with her! Or him!' Titty spat.

'You won't have to. I thought I'd already explained that we've got tandem boats as the maximum each one can take is twelve. That way you'll be able to keep away from each other.'

'Good!'

'But I can't separate the tennis programme. So you'll just have to get on with it and act like grown ups,' Eve said, her anger rising at Titty's attitude. 'Assaulting people isn't acceptable behaviour in any way, shape or form. And tomorrow I'll need to see you to fill in an incident report.'

'I'm not filling in anything!'

'Okay. That's up to you. I can't force you. I'll speak to Estelle and it's up to her if she wants to press charges.'

'What? Are you having a laugh?'

'Not at all. But from what I've heard from several independent witnesses you attacked her first. Totally unprovoked. That's assault. And it would be a police matter. Good night.'

She got a childish and most unprofessional kick at the row of dropped jaws before she turned on her heel and sashayed from the lounge.

✦ ✦ ✦

ESTELLE WAS SHAKING as she sat on the bed. She'd stepped straight into the shower to wash the wine from her hair and body and now, wrapped in two towels the drama of what had just happened finally hit her. She looked down at her beautiful top, which lay in a crumpled heap on the floor. She picked it up and tearfully studied it, logic telling her it would all come out in the wash and that it wasn't ruined. In her minds eye she reran the events several times, as if they were on a loop in her brain, becoming more and more upset each time she relived the the wine smacking against her head. What hurt most were Titty's words.

That'll teach you to flaunt your tits in his face! That'll teach you to flaunt your tits in his face! That'll teach you to flaunt your tits in his face!

She gave a stifled sob.

I wasn't flaunting my tits at him! We're in Ibiza for Christ's sake! Everyone goes topless here. Even Titty! She was topless and hers are three times the size of mine!

She leaned back against the headboard and drew her knees up to her chest, hugging them. She turned her head and placed her face on her knees. She felt thoroughly miserable. Yet she'd been having such a nice time.

Why does everything always go wrong for me?

✦ ✦ ✦

'WELL, THAT LIVENED up the evening,' Charlie said as soon as Eve had left.

'I think it's bloody disgraceful. Two women fighting,' Ron said. 'Or even two men! Nobody should behave like that.'

'Haven't you ever seen any fighting on any of your other Travel Together holidays?' Liz asked.

'No! I mean, there's been a couple of disagreements…'

'There's bound to be,' Sean said. 'Not everyone gets on with everyone, do they?'

'Yeah, but then you just give 'em a wide berth, don't you? You don't chuck your wine over them or give 'em a smack in the gob!'

'I'd think Estelle's got a good case for assault.' Sarah gave her legal take on the situation.

'What, even though she hit her back?' Nicole asked, finishing her drink and giving a hiccough.

'Titty started it. Estelle would argue she was only defending herself.'

'She won't get the police involved, will she?' Nicole looked around anxiously.

'What are you getting worked up about?' Sean asked her.

'I'm not! I just think that would really spoil the holiday for everyone…'

'You're right, Nicole,' Katrina chimed in.

'Yes. Least said soonest mended,' Ron agreed.

'Well, tomorrow's going to be fun,' Charlie continued. 'All together for tennis and then on the boat. They don't look very happy, do they?' He looked over at the Fourth Form.

'Eve said we're on two boats,' Jackie told him.

'That's good!'

'And for tennis clinic people are just going to have to grow up and get along with each other,' Sarah said.

'You can't blame Estelle if she doesn't want to be in her company,' Jackie said, glancing across the lounge to where the Fourth Form were still sitting in a tight group and Titty was talking animatedly, her hands and arms waving around. 'I wouldn't want her anywhere near me!'

'Well I blame him. Spizz,' Liz said. 'He was definitely with Titty to start with, wasn't he? I mean, they were all over each other in that bar on the first night. And then he's made a play for Estelle.'

'Oh, here we go! Blame the man!' Charlie said. 'She shouldn't have got together with him if he was with Titty.'

'Yeah. Right. Because men always tell the truth, don't they?' Sarah argued back. 'He shouldn't have gone after Estelle if he was with Titty!'

'And you don't know what lies he might have told her,' Jackie added, warming to the theme. 'He probably said he was just friends with Titty and that she fancied him but he didn't fancy her and even if they had got together there was nothing in it!'

'But we don't know all of that, do we?' Charlie said. 'We're just speculating because none of us has heard what he said.'

'She told me she'd asked him about Titty and he'd said there was nothing going on with her. He told Estelle he really liked her.' The drink had loosened Nicole's tongue. 'Men do tell lies. My ex told me he was unhappily married but I'm not sure he was.'

'Well, happily married men don't get murdered by their wives, do they?' Alex blurted out.

'How do you know about that?' Nicole asked, staring at him, wide-eyed and open mouthed.

Sean went scarlet and grimaced.

'Thanks, mate,' he muttered to Alex.

'Erm, didn't you tell us?' Alex said.

'How was your ex murdered?' Jackie jumped in and asked.

'He wasn't! His wife ran him over,' Nicole said.

The women in the group and Ron looked at her stunned.

'Blimey!' Ron said. 'On purpose?'

'No, it was an accident. But why am I telling you this?' Nicole had a lucid moment through her tipsy haze. 'I didn't tell anyone about Roland. Except you!'

She turned on Sean.

'You're a bastard!'

'You didn't tell me it was a secret…'

'And I didn't tell you to spread it round the group, either!'

'I didn't! I only told Alex and Charlie…'

'Oh, well that's all right then! You only told two people and one of them has just told everyone else.'

'You've just told us what Estelle told you that Spizz had said to her! That's gossiping,' Sean retaliated.

'It's not the same! You told me stuff about you last night that I wouldn't dream of telling everyone else.'

Everyone else looked at the sparring couple expectantly, waiting to hear what the private stuff about Sean was. But Nicole had nothing more to say. She burst into tears.

'Come on, Nicole,' Katrina said, standing up and coming over to her. 'Let's go and get some air, shall we?'

Nicole stood up and let Katrina start to lead her away from the table.

'I thought you were my friend! My friends! You're just a bunch of gossips' she shouted over her shoulder as tears ran down her face.

'Nice one, Alex,' Sean said. 'You dropped me right in it.'

'No point in blaming him. You've all obviously been talking about her,' Jackie said, indignant on Nicole's behalf.

'I just mentioned that she hadn't stopped rabbiting on when we were having a drink on Sunday night. After tapas. I couldn't get a word in edgeways. All she could talk about was her ex and their affair and how his wife, who hadn't understood him, had run him over! I made a silly joke about two-legged donkeys…'

'Yes, he didn't tell us maliciously,' Charlie said. 'We were just having a bit of a laugh, You know. Banter. We joked that the only one who'd pulled was Ron…'

'I ain't pulled!' Ron glared at Charlie as Liz blushed.

'And Sean said he'd got Nicole on her own but she didn't stop talking. And even Alex joked about making a mistake and trying to get off with a lesbian!'

'What?'

There was silence around the table as everyone looked at Charlie and then at Alex.

'He'd been chatting up Katrina…' Charlie started to explain.

'Katrina's not a lesbian,' Rosalind protested.

'Well, you would say that,' Charlie said.

'What do you mean?'

A second awkward silence fell over the table as Rosalind and Charlie stared at each other. Alex looked at his feet. Everyone watched them, waiting with baited breath. A deep pink flush crept up Rosalind's face and her jaw dropped.

'Do you think that me and Katrina are lesbians?'

'No! Well, yes… I thought you were after the other night in the vegan restaurant. You seemed to be getting on well… and… I saw you afterwards.'

Charlie didn't think it was necessary to mention he'd taken photos of the two of them sharing an embrace and had shared them with other members of the group.

'You're unbelievable!' Rosalind stared at him, then stood up and grabbed her bag. 'Katrina has been very supportive to me in the last few days. She's answered questions and has helped me understand what happened with my mother. Who died in a care home. Where I'd shoved her. And I felt terrible about it. Okay? She was being kind. She was being a friend, not shagging me. So now you know. You're like a bunch of kids!'

She stomped her way out of the lounge.

'Well, all in all, it's been a very successful evening!' Ron said, downing his drink and standing up. 'Good night!'

He made his way from the lounge without looking back. Liz followed him with her eyes, disappointment welling up inside her. She noticed several of the group were looking at her and she suddenly felt angry.

'I don't know what you're all looking at me for!'

She snatched her handbag and made her own exit. Her

night had been spoilt; the lovely time she'd been having with her mate Ron had been completely ruined yet she hadn't done anything wrong. She went hot at the thought that she and Ron had been the subject of gossip and speculation within the group and that it had now tainted her friendship with him. It had somehow made it feel grubby and nasty. And that made her very upset.

✦ ✦ ✦

SITTING AT A table on the deserted terrace of the Club House, Nicole was grateful they were in the shadows and that Katrina couldn't see her face properly. She was certain it was blotchy and her eyes were puffy.

'I feel such a fool.'

'You've no reason to. You told Sean something in confidence. It wasn't nice of him to break that confidence.'

'But even so, I've just showed myself right up by over-reacting to it.'

'I don't think you over-reacted at all. People can be cruel, even if they don't mean to.'

'But he's right. I didn't tell him not to tell anybody.'

'Even so. He shouldn't have told the others. Och, they'll try and fob you off saying it was just a bit of lads' banter. But it's time they were pulled up on it.'

'The sad thing is, I like Sean,' Nicole sniffed. 'Oh, God! That sounds pathetic, doesn't it?'

'More disappointed than pathetic.'

They sat in silence as Nicole searched in her bag for a tissue.

'I dread facing everyone in the morning,' she said. 'They're going to think I'm an idiot. A right snowflake.'

'They won't. And if any of them does, they'd be wise to

keep quiet about it,' Katrina said, oblivious that she had also been the subject of gossip and speculation.

'I don't want there to be an atmosphere because of me.'

'If there's an atmosphere it's more likely to be because of Estelle and Titty, don't you think?'

'Possibly.'

'Look, if I were you, I'd go and get a good night's sleep and tomorrow just act as if nothing's happened. If you like, I'll come and collect you for breakfast. How about that?'

'Would you?'

'Of course! And here. Put a few drops of this under your tongue.'

She produced a small bottle from her bag and undid the stopper.

'It's Rescue Remedy. You need it. You've had a shock.'

Nicole obediently opened her mouth as Katrina squirted a few drops into it.

'And now try and forget all about it. You haven't done anything wrong, after all.'

✦ ✦ ✦

SARAH WASN'T STUPID. She had seen how much her remark about him liking girl-on-girl porn had pissed Alex off, even though that hadn't been her intention. He had responded by hardly looking at her and going into a sulk, although undoubtedly that also had quite a lot to do with the embarrassment he must have felt after blurting it out to everyone about Nicole's ex.

Nicole's ex. Who was called Roland. And was run over by his wife.

She thought about it, running several possibilities through her head. But each time she came back to the only scenario possible. And what she thought she'd overheard – Sean and Alex talking about her – hadn't been about her at all.

'You're quiet, Sarah,' Jackie said, breaking into her thoughts.

'Speechless after all that's gone on,' Sarah replied.

She and Jackie were the only two left at the table. Sean, Alex and Charlie were standing together drinking at the bar. And there was no sign of the Fourth Form either.

'It looks like everyone's opted for an early night,' she said, unable to hide a wry grin. 'And I'm going to turn in, too.'

'No hanky panky tonight then?'

'I'm not in the mood.'

✦ ✦ ✦

EVE SAVED THE completed Incident Report Form, switched off her iPad and yawned loudly. Both women would have the opportunity to add their own versions, their own truth, to it tomorrow and then she would email it back to Head Office. She was still shaking her head at disbelief at the evening's events, especially coming hot on the tail of Spidergate.

Just when you think you've seen it all…

Of course, she was unaware of what had taken place once she'd left and that there were several more very unhappy Travel Together clients dotted around the hotel. She stretched, switched off the air conditioning and then slipped under the sheet, hoping that tomorrow with the excitement of the boat trip things would calm down and go back to normal. She reached for the light switch above the bedside table just as her phone sprang into life.

Oh, now what?

Her irritability melted instantly when she saw her caller was Melv.

'Darling! Hello. This is a pleasant surprise. How are things?'

There was silence on the line.

'Melv? Melv? Can you hear me?'

'I hear you.'

The agony in his deep, warm voice rolled down the connection and hit her full on.

'Melv?'

'Radley died an hour ago.'

DAY SIX

✦

EVE HAD WATCHED the dawn's slow progress, from dark, total silence, through the birdsong to the muted clinks, noises and voices announcing the awaking of the resort around her and the gradual change from black to blue to grey to cream to yellow that heralded the new day breaking. The sun rose and sparkled over the Mediterranean at Cala Llonga and so Thursday appeared, promising to blossom into a beautiful summer's day.

This is the first day that Radley will never see.

This better truth stabbed at her and brought yet another lump to her throat and tears to her eyes. She'd been sitting there on the balcony, wrapped in the bed cover for hours. Melv had asked her to tell Michael and she planned to call him in a while. There was little to be gained by ringing him in the middle of the night. His half-brother had gone. There was nothing he could do. But he had to know. Eve ran through what she was going to say to him for the hundredth time before replaying her conversation with Melv.

She had sat down with a bump when she'd heard his words.

'He went into the pool.'

Eve couldn't quite understand what Melv was telling her. His house had been converted to accommodate Radley's needs, putting everything on one level so that his wheelchair could access the whole house and yard. That included the pool area where either Hugo or Rowan exercised with him daily. There was a hoist they used to lift him from is chair into the water.

'Did the hoist break?'

'No. He drove himself into the pool. In his chair.'

'What?'

'Hugo had left him on the patio while he went for lemonade. All he had to do was grab the tray so he was gone probably less than a minute. As he was coming out he saw the chair hit the water. Rowan was still around even though his shift had ended and between them they managed to undo the belt and drag Radley up the ramp and out of the pool and give him CPR until the paramedics got there.'

Melv's voice shook.

'They called me and I got there as they were still working on him. He was taken to Mount St John's but I knew there was nothing…'. His voice faltered. 'Nothing could be done to save him.'

Eve's heart bled for him; nobody should have to watch their child die.

'But… How did it happen? Did Hugo leave the brake off?'

'He swears he didn't. And I believe him. I think Radley drove himself forward deliberately.'

'Oh, God! No!'

Eve shuddered. That didn't bear thinking about.

'How's Mary?' Eve asked about Melv's ex-wife, Radley's mother.

'She's devastated, naturally. But, you know what she's

like. She's never been able to handle his accident and his injuries. She barely saw him. But that's between her and her conscience…'

Eve just didn't know what to say. Any words would sound like empty, hollow platitudes. So she just let him talk.

'It wasn't just drowning,' Melv continued. 'His heart gave out, the doctors are saying. Although Hugo and. Rowan got to him fast. It wasn't enough. Like, it's not as if he was strong to start with… They did all they could at Mount St. John's. Maybe if we'd been able to get him airlifted somewhere else…'

'But from what you say he'd died before he got there.'

'Yes. I'm going round in circles. I don't even know what I'm saying. A whole load of ifs and maybes might have saved him. But the bottom line in all of this is he just didn't want to live as the person he'd become. He'd had enough. At twenty-three he'd had enough of life. Of his life…'

She thought her heart would break at the anguish in his words. Radley had been through so much, more than anyone should have had to handle with the unspeakably dreadful accident that cost him a leg and given him a very restricted life in a wheelchair.

'Melv, he's at peace.'

'I know. He's at peace and the rest of us face a lifetime of hell without him. And pondering on how he went…'

She had no words of comfort, of anything. So they had shared a few moments of uneasy silence until he suddenly broke it.

'Will you come, Eve?'

'Of course I will. For as long as you want me to. And I'll tell Michael,' she added, wanting to spare Melv the additional agony of telling his son that the brother he'd known for such a short time had died in the most awful of circumstances.

As the call disconnected tears coursed down Eve's cheeks. Hearing Melv's pain was more than she could bear. She imagined the scenario and series of events. Hugo's shock as he saw the wheelchair going into the water; he and Rowan fighting to free Radley from the chair and from the water; the paramedics; Melv's arrival. And the terrible realisation that Radley, who just a couple of years earlier had been a promising athlete with his whole life ahead of him, had ended his own life because it was worthless. The cruelty of the blows he'd been dealt cut her like a knife.

What did he do to deserve this? Eh, God? What did he do?

She railed against a deity she didn't believe in; against the Universe; against whoever it was that had given Radley such a raw deal in life.

At half-past two, still wide-awake, the images and words going round and round in her head she'd got out of bed and booked her flight for the following Tuesday. That would only give her two days at home but it didn't matter. She had left the return open. She would wait and see how things panned out in Antigua. And she knew Melv would need her support more than ever once the funeral was over. And she'd rattled off an email to Travel Together telling them she was going to be unavailable for work until further notice.

If ever again…

The shrill beep of her alarm going off inside her room made her jump and brought her back to the present. She shuffled inside trying hard not to trip over the bed cover, wrapped round her like a cloak and silenced the jarring sound that had set her nerves on edge. Then the brawl between Titty and Estelle came back to her causing her heart to sink at what might be awaiting her when she met the group. She just hoped and prayed that everyone would act like a grown up and there'd be no more nastiness, fights, squabbles and scaring each other. She yawned loudly and looked at her bed, which was now beckoning to her temptingly. Knowing that she dare not lie down even for a second she stood up and headed for the bathroom.

✦ ✦ ✦

AS SHE STEPPED out of the shower Katrina heard a rap on her door.

'Just a moment!'

She grabbed the thick, white, fluffy towel from the rack and wrapped it around her tall, lithe frame. She opened the door and Rosalind tumbled into the room.

'Oh, Katrina! I haven't slept a wink…'

'What on earth's wrong?'

'You're never going to believe it!'

'Believe what?'

'What Charlie said. In front of everyone, too. I was absolutely mortified. Mortified! I don't know how or why he thought it or why the others believed him…'

'Ros, will you just stop blathering on and tell me what the fuck you're talking about?'

Suddenly deflated by Katrina's words Rosalind sank onto the bed like a three-day-old balloon.

'After you'd gone, there was a bit of chat about what had happened and what had been said about Nicole. Sean was trying to defend himself and said that it had all been innocent, a bit of a joke between him, Alex and Charlie.'

'What had?' Katrina asked through gritted teeth. 'Spit it out!'

'They had been joking that Ron had been the only one to pull – except that he hadn't! Apparently there's nothing going on between him and Liz and he seemed annoyed that people thought there was and Liz looked embarrassed…'

'AND?' Katrina raised her voice.

'And one of them said that Alex had quipped he'd made a mistake and tried to get off with you but you're a lesbian. And Charlie said we both were!'

Katrina stared at her.

'Are you?' Rosalind was suddenly unsure. 'Not that there's a problem if you are but I told them all you weren't. That I didn't think you were. And I'm not,' she babbled.

'No, I'm not,' Katrina said, feeling slightly bewildered.

'And then Charlie said he thought we'd got together in the vegan restaurant and then he'd seen us afterwards…'

'Well, they've certainly got hold of the wrong end of the stick, haven't they? I bloody hate gossip,' she added with a vengeance.

✦ ✦ ✦

'WHERE IS EVERYONE?'

Jesus looked around the Club House terrace and noted several people were missing.

'I'm not sure how many will come along this morning,' Eve said. 'We were thin on the ground at breakfast. There was… erm… an incident last night.'

'You're kidding me!' Jesus said, shaking his head after Eve had told him what had gone on. 'How childish, no?'

'But, apparently, after I'd left there was a further bust up with Nicole and Sean over him gossiping about her and Rosalind got upset because people thought she and Katrina were having an affair!'

'What?'

'I heard all this at breakfast from Jackie and Liz. So I'm

not sure who's coming along this morning and who isn't,' she said, looking around.

The Fourth Form were spread round two tables; Spizz was sitting with Alex, Sean and Charlie; Sarah, Jackie and Liz were together on the far side and Ron was sitting a little apart from everyone else.

'Estelle isn't here and neither's Titty. Nicole's missing. And I can't see Rosalind or Katrina, either.'

'We're going to be a little male-heavy,' Jesus said just as Katrina appeared.

'Sorry I'm late,' she trilled. 'I overslept. Having slept alone, I hasten to add.'

She raised her voice and deliberately stared over at Sean, Charlie and Alex. Alex looked as if he wanted the earth to swallow him up.

'I'm so sorry…'

Then Katrina burst out laughing.

'Easy mistake to make, Alex. I said my girlfriend had introduced me to veganism and she had. But that's all she was. A girl who's a friend. You misinterpreted my words. Sorry to disappoint you. But, I am tall and muscular I suppose, so it's an easy mistake to make,' she added.

'Katrina, I'm sorry,' Alex said, standing up.

'So you've said.'

She looked at him sternly then her face twitched and broke into another smile.

'I expect the gossip mill went into overtime. But there's no harm done. After all, being thought a lesbian is hardly an insult, is it?'

The relief on Alex's face was plain for all to see.

'And Rosalind's okay about it. She's just gone to the ladies,' she said to Jesus and Eve, by way of explanation for Rosalind's absence.

'Well, that's good to hear,' Eve said, giving a sigh of relief that not everyone was feeling bellicose towards everyone else.

As soon as Rosalind appeared Jesus lead the group down to the courts where Ivan and Daniel had everything set up. Today they were working on improving the accuracy of placing their shots.

So that just leaves Titty, Estelle and Nicole.

She decided to have another coffee, to make sure she stayed awake before going in search of the missing women. And then she'd ring Michael. But she wasn't halfway through her decaf americano when Estelle appeared. She was wearing her swimsuit and sarong. Large, black sunglasses totally hid her eyes.

'I wanted to apologise for my behaviour last night,' she started saying before her backside had even hit the chair. 'She was in the wrong for starting it, but I shouldn't have retaliated. I abhor violence and I behaved like a fishwife. Sorry, Eve.'

Her voice broke and a fat tear rolled from under her shades and crept slowly down her cheek. She flicked it away with her forefinger.

'Apology accepted, Estelle,' Eve said, feeling sorry for her. 'I don't blame you for hitting back, I think most people would have done in your situation.'

She opened up her iPad and brought the Incident Report Form up onto the screen, turning it for Estelle to read.

'I've had to fill this out. Take a look at it and then you can add your statement if you want to.'

Estelle's eyes flew across the screen, her lips silently mouthing the words, her face colouring with embarrassment at what she was reading.

'Can I just add that I agree with what you've written.

She did start it and she provoked me. I'm not making excuses for myself but that's how it was and as I said, I want to apologise to you and the others. But not her.'

'Do you want to take it further? Make a police report?'

'No. I know that technically she assaulted me, but I don't want to get involved with the Spanish police.' She shuddered at the thought.

'I understand. And I think that's good of you. I hope Titty realises how lucky she is.'

'I just want to have some time on my own. I'm going to spend this morning down on the beach. I've had enough tennis, I think.'

'That sounds good. I'll print off the report and get you to sign it and you get to keep a copy,' Eve said. 'And don't forget, we've got the coach at half past one for the boat trip.'

'I'll be there. I'm looking forward to it. As long as I'm not on the same boat as Titty and her cronies.'

'I'll make sure you're not.'

As Estelle left for the beach Eve reached into her bag for a couple of paracetamols. Her head was thumping through lack of sleep and her eyes itched. She decided to go in search of Titty to see if she wanted to discuss the report and also, although Eve had very little sympathy for her, she did want to check that she was okay. Then she'd look for a spot in the shade and see if she could sneak a short nap before getting ready for the boat trip.

✦ ✦ ✦

'MIND IF I join you? Unless, you'd rather be on your own,' Nicole added quickly as Estelle gave her a sharp look.

'No, I'd like some company. You just made me jump, that's all.'

Nicole smoothed out her towel on the sun lounger and made herself comfortable. Seeing that Estelle was topless, she decided to join her.

'Aren't you putting on any sun tan lotion?' Estelle asked, rigorously topping up her own.

'I'm wearing that stuff you only put on once a day. In the morning. It's supposed to give you protection all day.'

'Any good?'

'Dunno. This is the first time I've properly tried it out. Although it seems to have done the job on my face. Usually by now I'd be a mass of freckles.'

There was a moment's silence as they both intensely studied the beautiful sea and the happy holidaymakers frolicking in it.

'You ok, hun?' Nicole asked, turning to look at her.

'I'll live. I felt humiliated last night and a bit disappointed in myself that I went down to her level.'

'I don't bloody blame you, though! What a cow!'

'I just felt a bit stupid, really. Brawling over a bloke isn't really me. I mean, when I found out about Joe and Marie I never resorted to blows.'

'Who's Joe and Marie?'

'Joe's my ex-boyfriend of thirteen years, who's now married to Marie, my ex-business partner. The friend I ran my florist's shop with.'

'No! Really?'

'Yep! It'd been going on right under my nose and I hadn't seen it. That's why I've got a stall now. I had to give up the shop, I couldn't run it or even afford to run it on my own. I often thought about giving her a good slapping but I didn't…'

'Yes, but, Titty started it, didn't she?'

'It just came out of the blue. One minute I was walking

back to the table happy as Larry singing Once in a Meadow at the top of my voice and the next I was covered in wine. And I just lashed out.'

'Good for you!'

'But I'd already spoken to Spizz about her.'

'Yes, you told me yesterday.'

'I'd said I didn't want to tread on anyone's toes. And he said nothing was going on. They're just friends he reckons.'

'Well, men aren't always totally trustworthy, are they?' Nicole said with a touch of bitterness.

'Why do you say that? You sound a bit off…'

'Bloody Sean!'

'What's Sean done?'

'I told him something the other night when we were having a drink about my boyfriend being run over and killed by his wife and he told Alex who blurted it out in front of everyone. It was after you left.'

'No!'

'I could've smacked him one, I tell you.'

Estelle's mind was whirring at Nicole's words. Images flashed and then fell into place.

'Was he a solicitor who lived in a big house? Roland something?'

'How did you know that?'

'It was on BBC Radio Surrey and the local TV News. Everyone was talking about it. I delivered flowers for him. To his wife.'

Estelle remembered turning into the crescent-shaped driveway that led to the imposing, immaculate house with its sumptuous flowerbeds a riot of colour in spring and summer and a tasteful display of winter climbing roses the rest of the year. The shingle had crunched under her feet as she'd unloaded the various extravagant, expensive floral displays and then rung the bell on the ornate, black front door. And she remembered the gaunt, blonde woman who'd opened the door, in her designer clothes, her haunted air and the inevitable dark glasses she usually wore.

'And that's why I've been thinking I knew you ever since we first me. I delivered a red rose heart box to you on Valentine's Day a couple of years back. Right?'

'Jesus! Yes. Red roses with a red, silk thong in the centre.'

Nicole had a flashback to the selfies she'd sent to him wearing only the thong. He'd been distraught they couldn't spend Valentine's Day together because he'd had to go up north on business. So he'd asked to see some photos of her wearing his present. Two weeks later he was dead.

'How do you remember that? You must deliver hundreds of bouquets on Valentine's Day.'

'Because it was one of the biggest flower orders we'd ever had. We danced around the shop when Marie took the order over the phone. Over four hundred quid's worth of flowers.'

'What? For a dozen roses and a thong?'

'Erm… No.'

Estelle hesitated, unsure of how much she should say. But obviously Nicole knew that her late fella had had a wife so she ploughed on.

'He placed four different orders. Yours, an exotic tropical plant for an elderly woman in a nursing home who was probably his mum cos she had the same surname and two enormous displays of roses. I can't remember how many now, but the wife's alone cost two hundred. And the three lots of flowers all had the same message on the card…'

'Weak at the knees and two kisses,' Nicole interrupted. 'That's how he always said I made him feel. That he'd gone weak at the knees when he'd first seen me.'

Estelle bit her lip. She could see Nicole was visibly shaken and she was kicking herself for adding to her anguish. She slid off the lounger and put her arms around her.

'I'm so sorry, Nicole. But when we heard his wife had run him over just after we'd delivered the flowers, well… of course we knew who he was. I didn't mean to upset you…'

'I know he could be a bit of a bastard. And people don't understand why I was happy to share him with his wife. But I believed what he told me about their relationship,' she said, her tears wetting Estelle's arm.

'You're not the only woman to be guilty of believing a married man.'

'But it looks like I wasn't the only one he had on the go. Who was the other one? The one who got the enormous display of roses alongside the wife.'

'I never met her. I delivered them to an office block. It was where he worked, too, if I remember rightly.'

'Bastard! Bastard!'

Nicole pulled away from Estelle and dried her face with her towel.

'Sorry!' She wiped the towel down Estelle's wet arm.

'It hurts to think how naive I bloody was.'

'You're a nice person. You trusted him. Just like me with Joe.'

Nicole blotted her face again and then put the towel back on the lounger.

'Do you think she did it on purpose? Running him over?'

Nicole thought for a moment before replying.

'I like to think she didn't. Apparently the police did take her in for questioning but she managed to convince them it was a tragic accident. Certainly there wasn't enough evidence to charge her. I did wonder. I wondered if she'd found out about me and they'd had a row. That he'd died because of me. But, the Coroner recorded a verdict of Accidental Death.'

Estelle thought the poor woman had probably been running away from him. She'd always got the feeling that she was imprisoned in that house; a prisoner in her own home. She was so jittery, so on edge and afraid.

'Do you know what? I'm not going to spend another second even thinking about him and his wife and his other girlfriend,' Nicole suddenly declared, shaking her head and making her plait dance. 'Let's have a cocktail!'

She waved at a passing waiter.

'But it's only half past eleven.'

'Who cares? He's dead and I'm alive and in Ibiza. And I intend to feel alive for every single second of the rest of my holiday. So what do you fancy?'

'A mojito, if you insist,' Estelle said, beaming.

✦ ✦ ✦

EVE HAD FOUND Titty sitting alone nursing a *cafe con leche* and looking very sorry for herself. She bristled defensively when she saw Eve approaching.

'If you've come to lecture me you can fuck off.'

'Please don't speak to me like that.'

I am so not in the mood!

'Well, I expect you're here to tell me off for being a naughty girl.'

'It's not my place to tell anyone off. We've all got a conscience and you're the only person who's got to live with yours. I'm just here to do my job and that's to show you the

Incident Report Form I've completed. You can add whatever you like to it or you can add nothing. Either way, before we leave I will give you a copy and file a copy to the company. Got that?'

Titty nodded begrudgingly as Eve took a seat opposite her and opened her iPad, scrolling until she found the report. She turned it round so that Titty could read it, which she did, sullenly.

'At least you've put my proper name and not Titty.'

Eve looked at her for a moment and then both women gave each other a wary grin.

'Why do you let them call you that?'

'It just sort of happened really. After the first holiday. Leggo started saying it and it stuck.'

'But if you don't like it…'

'You go along with things, though, don't you? And we've all got a nickname, it's not as if I've been singled out.'

'Although yours is the only one that refers to a physical characteristic.'

'That's true.'

'What are you usually called?'

'Tisha.'

She gave a sigh and her eyes filled.

'Then let's start by calling you that, shall we, Tisha?'

'Thank you.'

She sat staring at her hands for a moment then she turned to Eve.

'Look, I know we pissed you off cos we're in a group. People always ask why we don't just go away on our own and I honestly don't know why we don't. I suppose everyone likes to be in their own group. Their own tribe…'

'But that's why people come on Travel Together holidays, because they haven't got their own group and it can be off-putting to arrive and find a group within the group. And often that group becomes a clique.'

'I think this'll be the last time we come away all together. For me, anyway. It's not as much fun as it used to be. And to be honest, I'm not sure I've got much in common with them any more.'

'You must spend quite a lot of time together if you all belong to the same tennis club.'

'We only see each other once a week or so. Sometimes twice if we go to the Club barbecue on Sunday afternoons. It's not as if we're all best mates. To be honest, I can't stand Leggo, Jonesy's a twat and Fee thinks she's better than everyone else.'

Eve shook her head in amazement that someone would go on holiday with people she couldn't stand and thought were twats.

'So, you and Spizz aren't together, then?'

'Not really. We sort of get together on and off on these holidays. The odd shag,' she said, her face reddening, before blurting out, 'I don't know what happened last night!'

In spite of the aggro she'd caused Eve actually started to feel sorry for Tisha.

'What you doing with my man?' She mimicked her own words of the previous evening. 'God! I sounded like the fucking Tammy Wynette songs my dad used to play. How bloody pathetic. And over Spizz!'

She shook her head in disbelief at her own stupidity and wiped a tear away with the back of her hand.

'Do you think Estelle would accept my apology?'

'We can only ask her,' Eve said, hoping she would. 'She seems like a pleasant enough woman. I'm sure she won't want an awkward atmosphere to mar what's left of the holiday. And whether she does or she doesn't at least you'll have been the bigger person and offered the olive branch. And after that, it's probably best to keep away from each other.'

'I suppose I'm lucky she didn't want to involve the police.'

'Yep!'

'Is she on the courts?'

'No. She said she was going to the beach. Do you want me to come with you while you speak to her?'

'Yes, please,' Tisha nodded gratefully.

✦ ✦ ✦

ESTELLE AND NICOLE were on their second mojito when Eve and Tisha approached them.

'Good morning, erm, afternoon, ladies,' Eve said, looking at her watch and seeing it was already just after twelve. Her hopes for a short nap had totally evaporated as the coach for the boat trip was leaving at half past one and she still had to find a moment to ring Michael. Her stomach flipped again at the thought.

The two women turned to her and smiled, the smiles evaporating when they saw Tisha standing next to Eve.

'Tisha would like to speak to you for a moment, Estelle,' Eve said.

'Who? Oh!'

It took her a moment to realise that Tisha was Titty.

Estelle looked at both women and then slowly nodded her head.

'Erm, in private,' Eve said, when a wide-eyed Nicole showed no sign of moving.

Estelle stood up, wrapped her sarong around her body and walked a few yards down the beach and after a glance at

Eve, Tisha followed.

'I just wanted to apologise for my behaviour last night,' Tisha said, plunging straight in as she came alongside Estelle. 'I behaved like a pathetic idiot and I'm truly sorry. If the wine damaged your clothes please let me pay for the cleaning or a replacement.'

Estelle looked at the woman standing before her. She wore no make up, her eyes were puffy from crying and lack of sleep. Her usual chic bob was pulled back in a scrunchy and anxiety was stamped all over her face. Last night she'd have gladly told her to fuck off and stick her apology where the sun don't shine. But two mojitos had mellowed her mood and having heard about Nicole's little incident, she thought that somehow her embarrassment in front of the group had been diluted. And even if it hadn't, as she stood there with the sun beating down on her shoulders and face, a mojito in her hand, the soft squish of sand between her toes, the Mediterranean sparkling in front of her and the thought of a wonderful boat-trip, the events of the previous evening paled into insignificance.

'There's no need. I washed my top out in the sink and it seems to be all right. Don't worry. And apology accepted,' she added, noting the smile of relief that spread across Tisha's face. 'We all do daft stuff at some time.'

'Thanks. Thanks very much. I am truly, truly sorry.'

'I know you are. Let's just forget it.'

Eve gave an involuntary sigh of relief as she saw the two women speaking civilly to each other and then walk back towards her and Nicole, both smiling.

Another problem solved!

She hurried back to her room and added a paragraph to the Incident Report Form informing the company that Ms Ambrose had apologised to Ms Oliver and that the apology had been accepted so *No Further Action* was needed and emailed it off with a sense of relief. Now all she had to do was ring Michael. Although she rarely drank alcohol, she was tempted to go down and have a large brandy before she made the call, but she didn't. She needed a clear head for what she was about to do.

She decided to FaceTime him. He deserved to be able to see her as he heard the news that she knew would devastate him. She hoped he would be working from home today. He was.

'Hello, Eve. This is a nice surprise.'

He took off his glasses and ran his hand over his eyes and his handsome face filled her screen.

'First day back at the coal face and I'm struggling,' he said, laughing. 'I'm just glad I said I wouldn't go into the office until tomorrow.'

'Michael, I'm afraid I've got something very sad to tell you…'

The waves of shock were etched on Michael's face as Eve gave him the news and circumstances of his half-brother's death.

'He must have been in a terrible place. So alone… hopeless… I wish I'd spent more time with him' he blurted out.

'Everybody does now. But who was to know? Melv often said that he was depressed, but then, who wouldn't be with all he'd been through and the disabilities he was living with. You just never know what's going on inside anyone's head, do you?'

'How is Melv? Stupid question, I know.' He immediately corrected himself.

'Numb. Stunned. Beating himself up for not being there but he couldn't have got him out of the water any quicker than Hugo and Rowan did.'

'It must have been a terrible shock for them, too.'

They shared a moment's reflective silence.

'Are you going to him?'

'Of course. I've already told Travel Together not to roster me for anything for a few weeks. I've booked a ticket for Tuesday. That means I'll miss Felicity's dance class but I hope you and Natalie will understand.'

'Of course. There'll be loads more dance classes. I'll ring Melv in a while,' he added. 'Perhaps I'll message him first. He's probably overwhelmed with things at the moment and sick of talking about it and telling everyone what's happened.'

'He'll always have time for you,' she said.

Especially now you're his only son…

'And he needs your support.'

'You're right.'

'Okay, well, I'll leave you to it, then. And take care of yourself,' she added, aware that the grief of losing his brother would probably hit him harder in the days to come when the reality of what had actually happened had caused the initial shock and numbness of the news to dissolve.

✦ ✦ ✦

NICOLE CAME OUT of her room to find Sean lurking in the corridor.

'I owe you an apology,' he said plunging straight in. 'I was bang out of order telling Alex and Charlie what you'd told me. I've got no excuse. None at all. I was just trying to be the big bloke…'

He paused and took a big gulp. Nicole was looking at him, her mouth slightly open.

'And I'm really, really sorry. I wouldn't upset you for the

world. Honest.'

Nicole was taken aback to find him outside her room and also by the honesty and sincerity of his apology. He hadn't made any excuses; hadn't blamed being inside.

'I understand if you want me to keep my distance for the rest of the holiday. If you tell me to piss off I will and I won't bother you again. But I hope you won't,' he added.

'Last night I could've murdered you. But do you know what? Worst stuff happened to other people last night; I've had a couple of mojitos and none of it really matters. At least you didn't throw a spider at me,' she said trying to lighten the mood.

'Or frighten you with my snake,' he quipped. 'Oh, sor-ry!'

He squirmed, thinking he'd blown it again. But Nicole burst out laughing. She took his arm.

'Come on!'

✦ ✦ ✦

IT WAS JUST before two when the group tumbled from the coach and gathered next to the Corsairs Obelisk in Ibiza Marina.

'It looks so different in the daytime, doesn't it?' Liz said.

'Still lovely, though,' Ron said, zapping the scene before them with his phone.

'Good afternoon, I'm Carmen.'

A dark-haired woman wearing a turquoise blue uniform came smiling towards them.

'You must be Eve,' she said, holding out her hand.

'Lovely to meet you, Carmen,' Eve replied. 'We're one missing so it's nineteen instead of twenty.'

'No problem. This way please, ladies and gentlemen.'

Eve and Carmen exchanged pleasantries as the made their way along the marina to where the two *Cruceros Poseidon* boats were moored.

'Do they look any good?' Alex asked Sean.

'They certainly do. Sunseeker Camargues. Pair of beauties.'

Carmen introduced the two captains to the group, Pedro and Jordi and told them again it was a maximum of twelve on each boat. Eve stood back and let the group board ahead of her. The Fourth Form, minus Spizz boarded first. They took the boat moored furthest from the group. The others got onto the other one. Eve then joined the Fourth Form, making it eight on their boat, *Dolores*, and eleven on *Milagros*.

Sean took the seat next to Jordi, asking him technical questions about the vessel.

'I see you understand boats,' Jordi said.

'I work in a boat-building yard.'

'Then probably you can tell me more than I can tell to you!' Jordi roared.

Expertly the two captains manoeuvred the vessels and within no time at all they were headed out of the port. On both boats all eyes were on Dalt Vila and phones recorded footage like crazy as they admired the timeless majesty of the high city walls from the sea.

'Wow! It's amazing,' Katrina said, 'The whole town is so beautiful. Magnificent.'

'And aren't we lucky to be seeing it from the water,' Jackie agreed, beaming. 'I bloody love this island!'

She'd seen a plethora of WhatsApp messages and missed calls from Scott when she'd turned her phone on so that she could use the camera. But she hadn't read even one. And as soon as she'd finished filming she was going to turn it off again. She felt so pleased with herself. Panning her phone round to film the other boat and some of her Travel Together friends she beamed broadly and realised that this wonderful feeling that was bubbling inside her and sending a tingle all through her body was happiness.

The boats moved forward slowly and their passengers were spoilt for choice, not knowing whether to look to port or starboard for the best views. Once outside the port, the captains opened up the throttles and the powerful speed-boats lurched forward.

'Jesus! It's like the bloody Slingshot all over again!' Katrina declared, clutching hold of the rail as Rosalind roared with laughter at her.

'What does *Milagros* mean, Ron?' Liz asked, smiling at him.

He'd given her a wide berth for most of the day and it pained her. They had been having such a good time together and now it felt as if they were strangers.

'I don't know. Ask the captain.'

Ron winced at the sharpness of his own words which had come out much brusquer than he'd intended. He'd been embarrassed by what had happened last night. He was an old-fashioned man at heart and he hated to think Liz had been the subject of gossip and speculation among the group as to whether the two of them had been sleeping together. He felt himself blush at the thought. She was a lovely woman and they'd become friends and now it had been spoilt.

Stung by his rebuke, Liz looked out to sea. She no longer cared what bloody *Milagros* meant. She glanced towards Ron from the side of her eye and saw he, too, was staring at the horizon. She'd been pissed off last night when she thought the group had been gossiping about them, wrongly thinking they were having an affair. But in the cold light of day, she'd laughed it off. People had thought far worse of her than that over the years. She sighed. She liked Ron, but she wasn't going to let a sulky man spoil her holiday. She'd paid hard-earned money to come here and she was going to have a great time. She turned and started chatting to Jackie, who looked like she was having a ball.

✦ ✦ ✦

ON BOARD *DOLORES* Pedro was pointing out places of interest to his passengers.

'That's *Las Salinas* a very famous beach. Salt flats. Lots of nudists.'

'Can't we go a bit closer to the shore?' Jonesy asked as the boat swept past the long, wide crescent-shaped beach that lay before a back drop of sand dunes and pine trees.

'Wow! It's something else,' Fee said, smiling at Pedro.

Eve glanced across at Tisha and was glad to see she was leaning back, her face towards the sun looking at ease and peace with herself. She was also glad to be with the Fourth Form who were quite happy to talk among themselves as if she wasn't there. It meant she could sit quietly and tune out. She still felt numb at the news from Antigua but she didn't want to dwell on it any longer this afternoon. A few hours at sea was the medicine she needed to get her through until Saturday evening when she'd finally be back in her own home. Meanwhile, there was nothing she could do for Melv and by going over their conversation again and again was just driving herself crazy. She leaned back, took a deep breath of the sea air, felt the sun on her face and turned to enjoy the beauty of the passing shoreline.

'And this is *Cap de Ses Portes*. Most southerly point of

Ibiza,' Pedro said, pointing to the headland. 'Now we go to *Espalmador.*'

'What's that?' Fee asked.

'Paradise,' he replied.

They left Cap de Ses Portes behind them and headed south towards the chain of islets that led from the south of Ibiza to the north of Formentera, the area known as *Es Freus.*

'Some of these are seriously beautiful,' Sean said, looking in admiration at two yachts that passed them.

'Wait until we get to *Espalmador* then you will see some beautiful boats. Really beautiful,' Jordi said. 'Look! Over there!'

Everyone turned to look at a sleek, blue, yacht that was passing them in the distance and at speed.

'You are tennis players, yes?'

'Yes,' Sean said.

'Rafael Nadal,' Jordi announced.

'What?'

Everyone jumped up, wide-eyed and open-mouthed. They all waved frantically at the yacht, too far away to see if anyone was waving back.

'Oh, bugger! By the time I got my phone out he'd gone.' Jackie grumbled.

'Looks like a nice boat,' Ron observed.

'Is a Monte Carlo Yacht 76,' Jordi said. 'But when we reach *Espalmador* we might see even more important people.'

'What, like Eve and the Fourth Form?' Charlie quipped. Everyone laughed except Jordi, who had no idea what the joke was.

Soon their mouths were gaping again as the boats stopped alongside each other and dropped their anchors in the clearest turquoise water ever seen.

'*Playa s'Alga,*' both Pedro and Jordi announced to their passengers.

'They're all starkers!' Spizz said, looking at the people who were sunbathing or strolling along the waters edge or cooling off in the crystal water.

'You don't worry. You can keep on your swim trunks,' Jordi said.

'Oh, I plan to, don't you worry!'

The captains opened large coolers and began serving cold beers, wine and soft drinks to their passengers. Everyone took a drink and then got into the water to drink it.

'This is what I imagine the Caribbean to be like. Is it?'

'Parts of it are, Rosalind,' Eve said. 'There are lots of deserted silver beaches and water this colour blue.'

'Oh, it's perfect. I love it.'

'Jordi said that yacht used to belong to the King of Spain,' Sean told Nicole and Estelle, pointing at a large, sleek silver-white vessel, that bobbed and glistened just off-shore. 'Not the present King, the other one. His dad. Who abdicated.'

'Who are you? The Royal Archivist?' Nicole teased him.

'No. I'm just interested.'

'Who does it belong to now?' Nicole asked.

'I dunno. I'm not sure he said…'

'Oh. Gorgeous or what?' Alex said, joining them and sinking into the water while keeping his beer held high. 'What a fantastic place.'

'Anyone want to come to the mud pool?' Eve called.

'Is it far? I can't be arsed to walk,' Alex said.

'Just a couple of minutes. It's supposed to be very therapeutic and good for your skin. Then we can come back here and have a dip to wash it all off.'

'Oh, blimey, yes!' Ron was very keen. 'When you gonna have another opportunity to do this?'

Everyone agreed with him and they finished their drinks and set off with Eve along a narrow pathway through scrubland at the back of the beach. Fee, Thommo and Tisha were all topless. Everyone tried to avert their gaze from Tisha's bosom which swung and bounced ahead of her, some with more success than others. Within no time at all they arrived at a wide salt plain with liquid mud at its centre.

'It's supposed to be a therapeutical experience,' Eve warned, trying hard not to look at the Fourth Form. 'So mucking about and throwing mud at each other isn't allowed.'

Heeding her words they all slipped into the smooth, thick mud.

'Oh, it's lovely and cool,' Katrina said, lying back in it.

'It feels funny, doesn't it?' Jackie observed. 'Odd, funny. Not what I was expecting.'

'It don't smell all that, but it'll wash off. And it's doing us good. Makes you look young, apparently. We'll be able to go on an 18-30's holiday once we get outta this.'

'Perish the thought, Ron,' Sarah said. 'I couldn't think of anything worse!'

They languished in the mud, relaxing and completely immersing themselves. All except Rosalind and Fee.

'I can't bring myself to put my face in it,' Fee said, screwing up her nose.

'I know what you mean. I can't either,' Rosalind said sitting up to her neck. 'Everyone's telling me how great it is but I just can't.'

Dripping in mud it was hard to recognise each other and Spizz only realised he was lying next to Tisha when he heard her speak.

'Enjoying yourself?' he asked.

'Shouldn't you be somewhere, wanking?' Tisha's retort stung him.

'There's no need for that, Titty.'

'Don't call me that! My name's Tisha.'

'What you being like this for? It was you made an idiot of yourself not me.'

'Oh, fuck off, Spizz!' Tisha stood up. 'I'm going to go back to the beach.'

'We should probably all go now,' Eve said, as reluctant as she was to leave. She felt wonderfully relaxed, cocooned in the cool, mud womb.

'It'll be brilliant getting in the sea now to wash it all off,' Ron said, striding ahead with Tisha and heading back towards the beach.

The next two hours were spent in sheer and utter bliss. Jordi and Pedro provided some wonderful tapas-style snacks and drinks before offering snorkels to those who wanted to take a look at the fine array of fish and sea creatures that *Espalmador* had to offer while the rest of the group floated in the clear water, strolled up and down along the water's edge or lay on the deck making the most of the sun, deepening their tans. All the women had taken the plunge and gone topless now, except Eve, who always kept her swimsuit on, even more so in this age of social media. She thought the Managing Director of Travel Together, the most conservative of men, would probably have a touch of the vapours if a photo of a topless tour manager ever appeared on Facebook. He was more than a bit of a stuffed shirt.

Then they reluctantly bid farewell to *Espalmador* as the two speedboats whisked them westward on an unforgettable trip around the magical rock that is *Es Vedra.*

'You just can't beat a boat trip, can you?' Sean observed

to nobody in particular.

'Do you sail a lot?' Nicole asked him.

'I've started to,' he said looking at her. 'Now that I can.'

She smiled at him, thinking how awful it must be to find yourself locked away. She leant towards him so they couldn't be overheard.

'Was hearing the doors clang behind you the worse part?'

'It was all the worst part. Doors clanging, men shouting and screaming, fights, loss of freedom to do even the most basic things. And as I told you, not being able to see the night sky.'

Nicole planted a kiss on his forehead and he put his arm around her, pulling her close. He gave a deep sigh and offered up a prayer of thanks. Just a couple of months ago he never imagined he'd be sitting on the deck of a Sunseeker Camarague with one arm around a beautiful girl, holding a glass of champagne, the sun warming his back and breathing in the clean, fresh sea air. And he was glad she'd forgiven him for blabbing to Alex and Charlie.

For her part, Nicole didn't believe in bearing a grudge. Life was far too short and Sean had already told her how sorry he was and she believed him.

Sarah was observing them.

They've obviously made it up.

They made a nice couple even though at the start of the holiday she'd thought for a moment she might end up with him. She'd backed the wrong horse with Alex. They'd had two very pleasant nights together but she'd pissed him right off with her light-hearted comment about him liking to watch girl-on-girl porn. He'd really got on his high horse about that and had snubbed her ever since.

Oh well! If he can't take a joke…

There were only two nights to go now, anyway. She wasn't bothered that she'd probably spend them alone. She grinned to herself thinking that she'd had more than her fair share of sex over the years. She looked around at the other women and thought it possible she'd had more sex than the rest of them put together so if she faced celibacy until the weekend she could live with that. On Sunday she'd been invited to a barbecue by one of the new junior partners who'd been giving her the eye. She hadn't intended to go as it was the day after she arrived back from holiday but now the thought of turning up, suntanned and sexy and flirting with him to see how the land lay suddenly seemed very appealing.

✦ ✦ ✦

IT WAS AFTER eight o'clock by the time they climbed back onto the coach, having taken their leave of Jordi and Pedro and given them both a very generous tip. Eve counted heads, noting red noses, salty, sun-bleached hair and a general glow of contentment that every member of the group wore as a badge of holiday pride. She sat next to Miguel and picked up the microphone.

'Did you all enjoy that?'

'Yes!' The reply roared down the coach at her.

'Now it's going to be half past eight before we get back tonight, so I don't know what you want to do for dinner…'

'I think we're gonna pass,' Jonesy said as the rest of the Fourth Form nodded in agreement.

'And me!'

'And me!'

'And me!'

Agreement echoed round the coach.

'I might go for some tapas. That place we went the other night,' Ron said. 'It's close by and we ain't gotta dress up or nothing, have we?'

'I can't be arsed, though,' Sarah said. 'I think I'm going to have a shower and room service.'

'Yes, I'm shattered,' Jackie said. 'I've had such a good time but I really am going to get an early night. Especially as tomorrow's our last day of tennis clinic.'

'Well, let's say if you want to go to tapas, meet in the lobby at half past nine,' Eve said. 'And if not, you can have room service, or a bar snack, or eat at the hotel's buffet again.'

Everyone nodded in agreement. Eve hoped Ron would have company going to the tapas restaurant then perhaps she could order a sandwich in her own room. She was so relaxed that all she really wanted to do was sleep.

Her prayers were answered when Alex, Sean, Nicole, Liz, Charlie and Katrina all turned up to join Ron to go for tapas. Liz had been the last to join them, running from the lift at exactly half past nine.

'Sorry! I thought you might have gone without me. It took me ages getting clean in the shower. That mud gets in all your special little places, doesn't it?'

Katrina and Nicole roared with laughing at her while the men actually blushed.

'We'll have clogged up the hotel's drains, I reckon,' Ron said, smiling at her.

She was glad to see he was back to his old self and she returned the smile.

The six of them set off and Eve went back to her room. She thought about ringing Melv, but dismissed the idea.

What will I say to him? What can we talk about that isn't going over and over what happened to Radley?

She didn't feel at all hungry. In fact, suddenly, she didn't feel very well. She felt faint. She staggered across the room and collapsed onto the bed. She began to sweat, even though the air conditioning was on. Her mouth was very dry, she was nauseous and there was a ringing in her ears that was getting louder and louder. Her heart was pounding, her pulse racing and her breathing became laboured as she realised she had pins and needles in her legs and feet.

Please don't let me be having a heart attack! Breathe, Eve, breathe!

She began to control her breathing. She breathed in through her nose to a slow count of five and then out through her mouth for the same. Logic told her she was suffering from anxiety and not cardiac arrest. She continued to breathe slowly and rhythmically: in – two three four, out – two three four. And again, two three four, and out two three four. After a couple of minutes her pulse seemed to slow. The ringing in her ears quietened down; she could feel her legs and feet again and she stopped sweating. After ten minutes she had recovered enough to sit up and sip some water. She still felt queasy and was glad she'd decided not to eat.

What the hell was that all about?

She knew that what she'd had was an anxiety attack and it had surprised her. She wasn't the anxiety attack type – no tour manager was; they couldn't do their job if they were. She went through to the bathroom and soaked her flannel in cold water and put it onto her forehead and sat down on the bed again leaning against the headboard. She thought about the holiday.

Tennis, so I'm out of my comfort zone, but it's nothing like some of the holidays I've been on.

She'd done climbing and zip-lining, golf and even cycling holidays. That had been torture compared to this one, which had been quite a doddle in many ways.

The women got into a fight.

But I've dealt with worse than that. Her mind went back over the deaths she'd witnessed and the accidents and the earthquake in China. There had never been anything she hadn't been able to handle, and handle well.

Probably a touch of sunstroke or dehydration from the boat…

She thought it possible. But she was used to the sun; she always wore a high factor protector, a sun hat and drank plenty of water.

But Radley's died…

She knew that the shock of hearing the news, combined with the events of the last couple of days had shaken her and it was anxiety that had caused her little interlude tonight.

I've had a panic attack.

The thought left her disconcerted; perhaps she was getting too old to do the job? She shook her head dismissing the idea. She was fit and well and fifty-four was no age.

But eighteen years has been a long time…

Yes, eighteen years as a tour manager had taken its toll but in her heart of hearts she knew that Melv and their relationship was what was truly at the bottom of all this.

'What's to become of us?'

She whispered the words out loud in the hope that she might get a reply. None came. But she knew that the biggest challenge she faced – they faced – was sorting out whether or not they could have a life together.

'We can't! We just can't,' she said as her stomach lurched and the tears once again began to flow.

DAY SEVEN

✦

FRIDAY DAWNED BRIGHT and beautiful. The sky was a huge, eternal expanse of cobalt blue with not a cloud in sight.

'Smashing day,' Ron observed as Eve joined him for breakfast. 'We're gonna get a load of tennis in if it stays like this all day.'

'The weather forecast is good, so fingers crossed. I must say, Ron, I don't know how you do it,' Eve said, pouring herself a coffee from the steaming pot. 'You're always the first one down to breakfast. Yet I bet you didn't have an early night, did you?'

'About midnight, I think.'

'I'd been snoring happily for an hour by then,' Eve said.

She'd surprised herself by going straight off after her panic attack and then having more than eight hours uninterrupted sleep. She chided herself for thinking of the panic attack; she'd promised herself she'd forget all about it.

'We only went for tapas but it was a nice evening. We didn't go out until half past nine, did we? We had a couple of beers and chatted and then we come back here. We was all tired after the boat trip. What with the sea air and the mud! That mud bath was brilliant. I loved it!'

'So, you've enjoyed yourself, then?'

'I always do, love. I always do.'

Eve liked Ron. She loved his attitude to life and his positivity. She'd done a double take when she'd seen in the paperwork that he was seventy-one. She felt twenty years older than him at the moment.

Be more Ron!

She decided that was going to be her mantra.

'Oh, I can't believe it's our last day,' Katrina complained as she, Charlie, Jackie and Rosalind joined them at the table. 'This week has flown by!'

'And what a glorious last day it's going to be,' Ron said. 'Look at that sky!'

'You're right, Ron, but a week at home goes by at half the rate of a week on holiday,' Charlie complained. 'Another seventy-two hours and I'll be back in the Council offices. Rock and roll!'

'*Buenos días a todos,*' Jesus said, pulling up a chair.

'*Buenos días,*' they chorused back at him.

'I just wanted to say that I have a little farewell reception arranged at the end of the afternoon. When we finish playing. At six o'clock in the Club House.'

'Oh, that's nice of you.'

'It's nothing really, Eve. I always do it. Everyone gets their diploma to say they have taken part and I have a couple of presentations. And we drink *cava* and have some *Manchego* cheese and *Serrano* ham to go with it and lots of bread and *ali oli*.'

'Sounds wonderful,' Eve said.

Her stomach had settled now and she was enjoying her breakfast of yoghurt and fruit. Soon everyone was down and tucking in and the atmosphere was cordial. That was what she wanted. A bit of harmony for the last day.

'Can I ask you something, Jesus?' Ron said, lowering his voice. 'Yesterday the speedboats were called *Dolores* and *Milagros*. I know *Dolores* is a woman's name, but what does *Milagros* mean?'

'That also is a woman's name. It literally means miracles.'

'Miracles? You have women in Spain called Miracles?'

'Yes. *Dolores* actually means Pains.'

'What?' Ron spat out his tea in disbelief.

'Both are named after saints. *La Virgen de los Dolores,* the Virgin of the Pains and *La Virgen de los Milagros,* the Virgin of the Miracles. But *Dolores* and *Milagros* for short. They were the names of the two grandmothers of Jaime who owns *Cruceros Poseidon.*'

'That's really interesting.'

Ron thought about what he'd just learned. He'd tell Liz later. Not because he wanted to show off but because he wanted to make it up to her for being off with her the day before. They'd had a very pleasant evening at tapas with the others but they hadn't sought each other out or been alone together. She hadn't been off with him, not at all; just a little distant. They'd walked back to the hotel with the others and had gone up to their rooms in separate lifts. That saddened him. He'd make sure he and Liz were friends before they left.

✦ ✦ ✦

EVE WAS SITTING on the veranda of the Club House watching the tennis clinic in progress and listening to the hypnotic whack of balls. She was wondering why she hadn't had a reply from Melv to the message she'd left him about her flight when she became aware of someone coming up beside her. She turned to see Leggo with a woman in tow.

'I want a word with you,' he said as he reached her.

'Good morning,' Eve said, smiling at him.

He ignored her greeting and ploughed on.

'This fucking hotel's only let my room go. I've paid for it up until tomorrow. And now they're saying I have to pay if I want to use it.'

'As I understood it you checked out.'

'Yeah. But I've still paid for the room.'

'But once you check out, you're ending your contract with the hotel.'

'My contract with the hotel was through your poxy company. So you're responsible. And my contract was for a week and that week's not up. So you can get off your arse and go and sort it out for me!'

'Taking an attitude with me won't get you checked back into the hotel.'

'They're making money twice. That's illegal.'

'You checked out. The hotel was expecting the room to be occupied for a full week. They're entitled to keep the money for the whole week and besides, the room could still be empty which would mean they're not making money twice.'

'It is empty. I asked to go back into my own room and they said it's available but they want a hundred and forty fucking euros for it.'

'And that's their right. If you get on a train from Birmingham to London but then decide to get off before the train reaches Euston you can't expect the train company to give you any money back. Or for nobody else to sit in the seat,' she added.

It was then Eve realised the woman with Leggo was

filming their conversation.

'Yeah, that's right, she's making sure you can't wheedle your way out of this when I take you to Court over this.'

Leggo took a step nearer to Eve, who turned to the woman.

'Please, put the phone down,' Eve said.

'Keep filming, Miriana,' Leggo ordered her. Then he turned back to Eve and spoke loudly and clearly, looking occasionally into the camera. 'So, you, the Travel Together tour manager are refusing to help me then, are you?'

'What is it that you want me to help you with? I am at a loss as to what has gone on. The last time I saw you was four days ago when you took off after injuring another member of the group by hitting them in the face with a tennis ball. Prior to that, you'd pulled an unwilling female member of the group onto your lap in a restaurant, resulting in the chair collapsing from beneath the two of you and leaving the woman in question with scratches and lacerations to her arm and leg.'

'Don't you start on at me! That's got nothing to do with this…'

'Oh, but it has. Because after you injured the group member with the ball you completely disappeared. I was unable to find you, I heard nothing from you and then the following morning the hotel management told me you'd checked out. So as far as we are concerned, you terminated your holiday and therefore your contract with the hotel and us.'

Eve wasn't sure exactly how true that was, especially as Leggo hadn't signed a Holiday Curtailment Form, but she'd delivered it in such a confident manner she could see he was wavering, in spite of his earlier bravado.

'And now, will you please take that camera off me?'

'Don't Miriana! So you're absolutely refusing to help me?'

'I can't make the hotel give you a room free of charge.'

'But we've got nowhere to sleep tonight.'

'Leggo! What you doing here?'

Jonesy, Cookie and Banksy came bounding over when they saw their friend.

'Trying to get my fucking room back. Apparently I can't have it unless I'm prepared to fork out a fortune.'

'Where you been, mate?' Banksy asked. 'And who's this?'

'Christ! What happened to your teeth?'

'Long story. Who's she?'

'This is Miriana. She's from Romania. She lives here.'

'Bulgaria,' Miriana muttered.

'So you been with her since Tuesday?'

'Yes. She looks after a villa in San Miguel for some French people and I've been staying there with her. Fucking amazing place! Huge! Gorgeous grounds, pool, everything. But they're arriving back on the island today. So I've come back here to my room back but they're refusing to let me have it.'

'Well, I suppose if you checked out, mate…'

'Whose fucking side you on, Cookie?'

Eve shook her head. Even Cookie could see that Leggo wasn't entitled to have his room back. Leggo seemed to have forgotten she was there. The rest of the group made their way to the Club House for their break, all looking surprised to see Leggo back among them. Fee and Thommo ran up the steps to join them, both eyeing Miriana up and down. Eve noticed that both Spizz and Tisha kept their distance. Spizz sat at a table with Estelle, Liz, Charlie and Alex, while Tisha was chatting to Sarah. It was strange how things turned around sometimes.

'Well, there's a spare bed in my room,' Banksy was saying. 'I've got a twin.'

'Well, we can't both sleep in with you, can we? Unless you wanna give us your room and you can bunk in with one of the others.'

'Erm… no thanks.'

'Where does she live when she's not looking after the villa?' Thommo asked, nodding towards Miriana.

'With a couple of her mates in Figueretes.'

'Well, can't you go there?'

'It's only small, apparently. And she shares a room with another girl.'

'It looks like you're either gonna have to fork out then, or have a cosy little threesome,' Fee giggled.

'Can't you go in with Thommo and let us have yours?'

'Piss off! You shouldn't have checked out, Leggo. You behaved like a twat and now it's come back to bite you on the bum,' Thommo said, laughing.

She and Fee went inside to the bar to get themselves a drink.

'She looks rough,' Fee said. 'Miriana. Even for him.'

'Well, he's never gonna pull anyone decent is he? She probably barely speaks English. That's the only way he can get someone to put up with him, if she can't understand the rubbish he spouts and what he's going on about.'

'You know Leggo. Once a prat always a prat,' Fee said.

The two friends laughed together as they ordered their coffees and waters. Eve, who'd overheard them, gave a wry smile. Miriana had stopped filming and was standing next to Leggo twisting a long, section of over-dyed, dry, blonde hair around her boney finger. Eve thought she didn't look very healthy for someone who lived on a Mediterranean island.

Jesus called everyone back onto the courts. Cookie, Banksy and Jonesy took their leave of Leggo, who then muttered something to Miriana and the two of them marched off together. Eve made a note of what had happened on her iPad to add to her report. There was nothing she could do; she'd never felt more disinclined to help anyone in her life. Where Leggo decided to spend his last night on Ibiza was really nothing to do with her any more.

✦ ✦ ✦

'YAY! I DID it! I got through a week of tennis clinics!'

Jackie was buzzing at the thought as she tackled her chicken salad.

'I know I'm never gonna be very good but I feel as if I've actually achieved something.'

'You have achieved something,' Alex said. 'Well done!'

'Thanks. I'm going to have a drink to celebrate.'

'Here! Let me get it for you. What would you like?'

'I think it calls for a glass of *cava*.'

'I think we all deserve one,' Sarah said, coming up to join them with Ron and Katrina.

'Shall we get a couple of bottles?' Ron suggested.

Alex blanched at the suggestion, fearing he might be footing the bill, but Ron soon made it very clear that he was paying.

'You can't do that, Ron,' Katrina protested.

'I can do what I like, love,' he said, smiling at her. 'I'm old and I'm on my holidays.'

He disappeared inside the Club House and came out a few moments later followed by a waiter carrying champagne flutes. A couple of ice-buckets soon appeared with four bottles of *cava* wedged inside them.

'Here's to all of you!' Ron said, raising his glass. 'But specially to Jackie who's realised she's not a tennis player, but she's done the clinics. Well done, Jackie!'

Everyone raised their glasses and toasted Jackie, who was beaming at being the centre of attention, and then each other.

'Do you know what I've liked most about this holiday?' Ron asked nobody in particular.

'No, what?' Eve asked.

'The fact that I've called some of the women *love* and nobody's snapped my head off.'

There were a few chuckles at his words.

'I know I'm old and I'm old-fashioned. There's not much that's PC about me but I was brought up different. In the old ways. And although I'm not PC, I don't mean no offence either. When I was in Cuba I called a woman *love* one day and she bit my bloody head off! *"I'm not your love!"* Bloody hell! She wasn't kidding. Told me off for saying *ladies* as well. How can that be wrong?'

He looked round the group, genuinely mystified and misunderstood.

'The term is *women*, Ron,' Sarah said.

'Well how come? You don't say *Women and Gentlemen* when you're addressing people, do you?'

'Let's not fall out on our last day,' Sarah said, clinking her glass against his. 'Cheers!'

'Are we going anywhere special for dinner tonight, Eve? As it's our last night,' Charlie asked.

'Is there somewhere special you'd like to go?'

'I'm not fussed. But it would be nice to end up with a really nice last supper, wouldn't it? Somewhere that caters for vegans, too,' he added hastily smiling at Katrina.

'Jesus is having a little reception for us at six o'clock when tennis finishes. There'll be food there, so do you want to eat a bit later tonight? Say meet for pre-dinner drinks at eight?'

'That sounds good,' Charlie said.

'There's a beachside restaurant in Santa Eulalia we could go to called *C'an Catalina*,' Eve suggested. 'It has brilliant fish and meat and it does vegan dishes, too. I checked earlier while you were playing tennis,' she added to appease Katrina.

'Sounds good to me,' Alex said and the others nodded.

'So, how many am I booking for?'

Everyone put their hand up except Fee, Thommo, Banksy, Jonesy and Cookie.

'We thought we'd go back into Ibiza Town,' Cookie said, looking at Spizz and Tisha. 'You coming?'

'Nah. I'm gonna give Santa Eulalia a go,' Spizz said.

'Me, too,' Tisha piped up, to everyone's surprise.

'Ding! Ding! Round Two!' Charlie announced in a stage whisper.

'We're going to go off exploring on a girlie night after dinner,' Sarah said, giving him a look. 'Me and Tisha.'

Eve booked a table for fourteen in *Casa Catalina* for nine o'clock and everyone was happy. She found herself wishing the day away. She just wanted it to be tomorrow night so that she could be home and alone with her thoughts. She'd had a couple of text messages from Michael but nothing from Melv. She'd sent him a WhatsApp message asking how he was and telling him how much she was looking forward to seeing him on Tuesday, in spite of the terrible circumstances of their reunion. He hadn't replied. She gave a sigh and told herself to concentrate on her job and her group for the time that was left.

✦ ✦ ✦

'AND THE MEN'S Singles Winner is Spizz!' Jesus announced as everyone clapped and Jonesy whistled.

Spizz stepped forward and took his certificate and shook hands with Jesus while Estelle took photos with his phone and her own.

'And the Women's Singles Winner is Katrina!'

There was more loud applause and cheering as a blushing Katrina accepted a kiss on both cheeks from Jesus and gave a beaming smile while Rosalind took some photos for her.

'But, I have added another certificate that I want to give to someone who fought so hard. To lose six-seven six-seven in the final and ten-twelve in the tie-break is disappointing. So here's my special Sporting Award which goes to Thommo!'

Thommo gave a loud *whoop* and dropped a deep curtsey before taking her certificate and kiss from Jesus. The applause the group gave her was heart-felt and genuine.

'That was a cracking match,' Sarah said as everyone nodded their agreement. They'd all been mesmerised by it. 'It really could have gone either way.'

They stood and sat around chatting to each other and Jesus, Daniel and Ivan, thanking them for all they'd done and on the group's behalf Eve gave them each a tip envelope. Nobody had moaned about contributing and she'd found that refreshing. Perhaps those who went on tennis holidays appreciated the etiquette of tipping.

'*Milagros* means Miracles.'

'What?'

Liz was taken by surprise as Ron appeared beside her. She looked at him somewhat bewildered.

'The name of the boat we was on. *Milagros.* It means Miracles.'

'Oh, right. Did you look it up?'

'Yes.'

'Thanks.'

There was a moment's silence between them. He gave a half-hearted cough. Liz didn't seem very impressed with what he was telling her.

'Named after the boat owner's granny, apparently. It's a woman's name.'

'That's a funny sort of name for someone. Miracles. Hmm. Not something I would've chosen.'

'What're your boys called?'

'David, Stephen and Daniel.'

'Oh that's nice. You can't go wrong with good old names I don't think. I'm not too keen on some of these modern ones.'

'I know what you mean,' Liz chuckled.

'So, are we mates then?'

'Why? Haven't we been mates all along?'

'Yes, I suppose so. Sorry if I was a bit off…'

'What was that all about?'

'Just… I didn't like people thinking we'd been having some 'anky panky when we hadn't, like. It's a shame, innit? You know, when people think you can't just be friends with someone?'

'It is a shame. And a shame you took it out on me,'

'Oh, Liz…'

'It's all right. No harm done. I've brought up three sons, so I know how odd men can be,' she said.

'I'm not sure if that's a compliment,' Ron quipped making her laugh.

Liz was glad they were friends again even though she

still wasn't sure what she'd done wrong. She wasn't going to lose any sleep over it. By lunch time tomorrow she'd never see Ron again. She'd be back home getting ready for a full work diary starting with two mani-pedis, three leg waxes, two sets of eyelashes and five eyebrow shapings. She smiled at the thought. She'd enjoyed her tennis holiday but she'd be just as happy to get back to work.

✦ ✦ ✦

'DO YOU WORK at Harding, Tweedie and Walsh?'

Sarah was surprised by Estelle's question, which had seemed to come out of the blue and caught her off-guard.

'Why? Do you want some free legal advice?'

'No, not at all,' Estelle laughed. 'I'm just asking.'

'Well, as a matter of fact, I do.'

'So you knew Roland? The guy whose wife ran him over a couple of years back?'

Sarah took a swig of her drink, unsure where Estelle might be going with this line of questioning.

'I knew who he was and we'd say "Good morning" to each other or exchange pleasantries. But we worked in different departments. Why do you ask?'

'Well, I'm not gossiping… Well, perhaps I am… But I wondered if you knew he was having an affair with someone at the practice?'

'Why would I know that? And how do you know he was?'

'I'm a florist. And my shop used to deliver flowers for him so we knew he had a couple of women on the go beside his wife, that is. And, of course, when we saw on the news he'd died the way he did we recognised him because two weeks earlier on Valentine's Day I'd delivered a huge bouquet to his wife, another one to a woman at your offices and the other one was to Nicole!'

'I'd gathered it was him when Sean blurted it out the other night.'

'Didn't you say anything to Nicole?'

'Why would I? It's not really my business. It was two years ago and Nicole probably felt bad enough without me firing questions at her.'

Estelle blushed at Sarah's barbed comment, wishing she'd kept her mouth shut yet also rather pleased with herself that she'd worked it all out.

Sarah looked around the room until her eyes found Nicole who was standing at the bar laughing and chatting with Sean, Charlie and Jesus.

'Yes! Small world, eh?'

'Hmm…'

'So you didn't know her? The woman he was having an affair with?'

'No idea! As I said, I barely knew him.'

'I'm not surprised his wife ran him over. I'd've mowed the bastard down, too!' Estelle said laughing.

'Another drink?' Spizz asked coming over to them.

'Oh, yes please!'

'Not for me, thanks.' Sarah said, moving outside to the terrace.

So, Roland. It wasn't just me and your down-trodden wife then?

She'd always seen Roland for what he was; a womaniser and a bully. She had been quite happy to have an affair with him because it was always on her terms. Sex, good sex, had always happened at the office, usually while everyone else was there. They got away with it because they collaborated on a lot of cases so being together didn't raise any eyebrows. She'd lock her door and close the blinds and tell her secretary she wasn't to be disturbed. And then they'd enjoy wild sex on the floor, on the desk, on the sofa while the world of Harding, Tweedie and Walsh carried on regardless on the other side of the door and window. She refused to let him go to her place, leading him to believe she had a partner. The truth was Sarah was very good at compartmentalising her life. Roland belonged at work and there he would remain. She was very protective of her private life; her home was her private castle and she wanted no man coming over the drawbridge interfering and telling her what to do. She'd never met a man who didn't want to tell her what to do. And she knew Roland wouldn't be the exception. She'd seen his wife a couple of times at the company Christmas Party. The poor woman was like a shadow. She was impeccably dressed in classy outfits without a hair out of place and her makeup was worthy of a Red Carpet. Yet she looked fragile and nervous; as if she would break in two or burst into tears if you made her jump. Sarah had often wondered if she'd suddenly snapped and had deliberately run him over. She wouldn't have been surprised and now, knowing that Roland had someone else on the go besides her, she'd be even less surprised.

She'd never had any illusions about Roland; she'd known she hadn't been his first lover and probably wouldn't be his last. She glanced at Nicole again and gave a wry smile.

Well, he certainly liked variety. We're nothing alike!

Sarah herself was a caramel brunette, Nicole a redhead and the wife a Scandi-blonde.

'You okay, Sarah?' Eve called to her.

'I'm fine, thanks, Eve. Just pondering on variety being the spice of life!'

She laughed at her own joke as Eve raised her eyebrows, not understanding what Sarah meant at all.

✦ ✦ ✦

'CAN I ASK you something, Eve?'

'Ask away, Spizz'

'I wanna take Estelle somewhere nice for a drink after dinner. Just the two of us. Any suggestions?'

'Do you want somewhere classy? Local? Secluded? Lively?'

'Oh, somewhere classy. She's been good company and I want to, you know, thank her.'

'There's a beautiful rooftop bar at *Aguas de Ibiza*. It's a five star hotel and spa but you can go in and have a drink. The views are spectacular.'

Eve had never been there, but the hotel had come up on Google when she'd been looking for information on the resort and it certainly looked amazing and had excellent reviews.

'I think Estelle will be impressed,' she said.

✦ ✦ ✦

IT WAS A sad moment when Jesus, Daniel and Ivan left them for the last time.

'Sorry if Leggo behaved like a prat,' Spizz said to Jesus as they shook hands.

'You cannot be responsible for your friend's behaviour,' Jesus replied. 'And besides, it was an accident.'

'Thank you.'

Spizz smiled as Jesus moved on to take his leave of Alex.

An accident! Yeah, right!

There'd been nothing accidental about the whack that Spizz had given the ball. Leggo had been winding him up.

All the boasting he did seeming to think that because he was a PE teacher it made him better than Spizz the Butcher. And the way he showed off and bragged about staying out all night drinking yet still playing tennis and winning. He'd started to think Leggo was a bit dangerous. The whack in the face had got rid of him. Spizz had expected him to go off sulking for a while but learning he'd checked out had been an added bonus. And now he'd disappeared again after surfacing this morning.

And let's hope that's the last we see of him until the airport.

Jesus gave Eve a hug, one that was full of affection. And she hugged him right back.

'You've been brilliant, Jesus. You really know your stuff and you gave them some fantastic tips and advice. They all loved you.'

'And so have you! You're a great tour manager. You're professional yet you're fun and your people have a great time. Travel Together are lucky to have you and I shall tell them so in my feedback.'

'Thanks so much.'

'And I know you don't usually do tennis holidays but I hope our paths cross again.'

'So do I, Jesus.'

'And here's a little thank-you gift.'

He reached into his bag and pulled out a bottle of *Hierbas Ibicencas*, a local drink with an anisette base infused with many of the varied herbs that grow in the wild on Ibiza. Eve thought it an acquired taste but she was grateful and touched by his gesture.

'Oh, Jesus! Thank so much. That's really kind of you.'

'De nada, mujer. De nada.'

'You take care of yourself. And thanks again.'

✦ ✦ ✦

THE MEAL AT *C'an Catalina* was a huge success. The venue, which was shabby-chic on the beach, illuminated with fairy lights and candles was a delight and the exquisite food reasonably priced.

'It's a good job this was a tennis holiday or I'd be going home a stone heavier,' Liz muttered as she put the last spoonful of strawberry cheesecake into her mouth and gave a groan of delight. 'That was bloody delicious.'

'I'll be in that gym on Monday!' Estelle said. 'I've enjoyed this week and I want to keep the momentum going.'

'Good for you,' Spizz said, smiling at her.

'Have you enjoyed your week, Eve?' Katrina asked her.

'Yes, I have, thanks. I know I haven't done much as far as the tennis goes but I enjoyed watching you all in the clinics and playing your matches. And I enjoyed the bit of umpiring that I did.'

'And you've done a great job with the social stuff,' Charlie said. 'Everywhere you took us was excellent.'

'Thank you.'

'Erm, can we ask for the bill, Eve? Spizz asked. 'We're gonna give that place you suggested a try.'

Eve called for the bill and then Spizz and Estelle set off on the fifteen minute walk to *Aguas de Ibiza.*

'We're off, too,' Sarah announced as she and Tisha stood up.

She caught Alex's eye for a second and then they both looked away.

'We'll see you at breakfast. Don't wait up!'

'Where are you off to?' Alex asked Tisha.

'Es Cana. Apparently there are some great bars there.'

Sarah grabbed Tisha's arm and shoved her towards the

exit. She didn't want Alex tagging along. He'd had his chance with her and he'd blown it by getting all high-and-mighty over a joke. As they stepped outside the restaurant Sarah saw the green light of a taxi heading towards them.

'Taxi!' She waved her arm and shouted.

The taxi came to a halt and the pair of them tumbled into the back. It was their last night in Ibiza and they were going to have the best last night ever!

Alex watched them go with mixed feelings. He'd liked to have gone along but it was obvious that Sarah didn't want to include him. He thought she could be a right bitch if she wanted.

So what if I do like to watch a bit of porn? What bloke doesn't?

He reckoned she must have had a look at his phone while he was in her bathroom after their second session together. She must have seen the teenage lesbian stuff he'd downloaded. He hadn't liked the way she'd thrown it at him in front of everyone.

She said it as if she was joking. But mud sticks.

The irony of that went right over his own head. Part of him wished he'd cleared up the matter of Katrina's sexuality before jumping to conclusions, but it was too late to do anything about that now. He gave a sigh.

I can't complain. I had two wild nights. Two out of seven. Not bad.

'You coming, Alex?'

Charlie broke into his thoughts.

'We're going for a wander to find a lively bar.'

Alex looked at the others and nodded his head.

'I'm coming,' he said.

✦ ✦ ✦

THE TAXI HAD dropped Sarah and Tisha outside a waterfront bar with a large, crowded terrace. They got a bottle of wine and two glasses and went onto the terrace to see if they could find a little corner.

'Here y'are, love! There's two seats here!'

A dark-haired woman in her late fifties was waving at them and pointing to two empty chairs at the table she was sharing with another woman, who looked so much like her she had to be her sister, and two men, one hefty with a bald head and the other short and slight with a full head of grey hair and goatee.

Sarah shuddered. Her first instinct was to run a mile from these people. But Tisha had already strode across and parked herself on one of the chairs, turning to Sarah and indicating she sit on the other one. Reluctantly Sarah joined her.

'That was lucky, wasn't it? It's always full in here but specially on the nights Chelmsford Cliff is on,' the woman said. 'Have you seen him?'

'We haven't had the pleasure,' Sarah said wondering who the hell the woman was talking about.

'Oh, we come here every time he's on,' she continued. 'He makes our holiday really, doesn't he?'

She turned to the other three who all nodded in agreement.

'We wouldn't miss him,' the hefty bloke said. 'You're in for a treat.'

Tisha and Sarah looked at each other and giggled.

'Where you staying?'

'At the Dunas Blancas.'

'Oh, I've not heard of that one? Is it apartments?'

'No, it's a hotel. Near Cala Llonga.'

'So you've come quite some distance to see Cliff then.

I'm not surprised. People come from all over the island,' the sister said.

'We're in an apartment. At *Ricardo's*. It's like home from home, isn't it?'

Once again the other three all nodded their agreement at what she was saying.

'Spotlessly clean. Cos that's important,' she continued. 'I couldn't stay anywhere dirty, could you? But it's comfortable and we've got a beautiful view. We cook our own dinner then we come down here afterwards to see the tribute acts. Smashing! What more could you ask for?'

'Indeed!' Sarah said, concentrating on her drink, knowing that if she looked at Tisha she'd burst out laughing.

'I'm Pat, by the way,' the woman continued. 'And that's my husband Bob,' she said indicating the hefty man. 'And my sister Jill and her husband Les.'

'I'm Tisha and this is Sarah.'

'Les used to look like Cliff when I first met him. That's what attracted me to him,' Jill said, beaming at Les.

Tisha and Sarah smiled politely. Sarah assumed the Cliff being discussed was Cliff Richard but apart from his size, she couldn't see Les bore any resemblance to him what so ever.

I think we've just slipped into some sort of parallel Universe.

She was just about to suggest to Tisha that they drink up and find another bar when the lights on the terrace dimmed and strobe lighting took its place, flicking into every nook and cranny. Loud intro music she didn't recognise started up.

'And now, ladies and gentlemen, the act you've all come here to see tonight. All the way from Chelmsford, Essex, that's in *Inglaterra* for those that don't know, bringing the world's most famous, the only, the best, Cliff Richard tribute act to all you *Living Dolls* in the audience, please welcome, the Chelmsford Cliff, aka John White, *Batchelor Boy*!'

The opening chords of *Summer Holiday* rang out as a man in his sixties sprang onto the stage. He wore a silver suit; his hair was dyed black and worn in a quiff. He started to sing, the entire public apart from Tisha and Sarah joining in. His voice wasn't bad. He wasn't Cliff, but at least he was in the right key and hitting the notes. Tisha emptied the wine into their two glasses.

'I think we're gonna need another bottle,' she said waving at a waiter.

'We're going where the sun shines brightly. We're going where the sea is blue.'

Sarah was surprised she actually knew the words. She seemed to remember her mum being a bit of a Cliff fan and sitting with her as a child watching a film where a group of young people went abroad on a bus. The second bottle of wine arrived and Tisha poured her a generous glass.

'We're winning at life, Sarah!'

Tisha clinked her glass against Sarah's and they both took huge swigs of their drinks. Sarah relaxed back into the chair, singing along loudly. She was beginning to enjoy herself.

✦ ✦ ✦

ESTELLE AND SPIZZ couldn't believe how beautiful the *Aguas de Ibiza* was. Although Eve had told him non-residents could go up to the terrace for a drink, Spizz was a tad nervous as they stepped inside the foyer. He was hoping a big, burly bouncer wasn't going to throw them out. He wouldn't care if he was on his own, but he didn't want that to happen while he was with Estelle. She'd gone through enough this week with Titty making an idiot of herself.

Making a tit of herself, more like.

He grinned at his own witticism as he strode forward with an air of purpose, his hand against Estelle's back, gently guiding her towards the lifts.

'Good evening. The roof garden?'

A uniformed hall porter smiled at them and pressed the lift call button.

'Thank you very much.'

Spizz nodded his thanks at the porter as they stepped into the lift, looking to all the world as if he had drinks on the roof terrace of five star hotels every night of his life.

'It's beautiful, isn't it?' Estelle whispered as the lift rose. They felt it stop and for a few seconds nothing happened. Then they realised the doors behind them had opened. Giggling they stepped outside onto an amazing terrace bar and lounge with discreet lighting and music playing at just the right volume. The bar itself was covered by a pergola that was made of boat rope. It was classy and modern. There were several levels to the area, each joined by a couple of steps up or down. There was also a pool. Small groups of people and couples lay on loungers around it or sat on low, comfortable sofas or modern bucket chairs.

'Oh, look at the view!'

Estelle was open-mouthed as they went to a table that overlooked the hotel's ground-floor pool and garden area, with the Santa Eulalia Marina and town in the background.

'Oops!'

Estelle clutched the rail as she gingerly lowered herself into the bucket chair, which was surprisingly comfortable once you were in it.

'I thought I was going over the rail,' she giggled. 'What a beautiful spot, Spizz.'

'It's magic, innit? Look at the church over there.'

He pointed to Puig de Missa, Santa Eulalia's sixteenth century church set high up on a hill over to their right.

'And I think that's the part they call *La Siesta* or *La Fiesta* or something,' he said, indicating the white one and two-storey buildings that peppered the hillside to their left.

A waiter appeared to take their order.

'What you gonna have?' Spizz asked her.

'A gin and tonic, please,' Estelle said.

'Would you like Gordon's, Hendricks, Larios, Alkkemist, Tanqueray…?' the waiter enquired.

'Hendricks.'

'And I'll have a rum and coke.'

'Black rum or white rum, sir?'

'Bacardi,' Spizz said, naming the only white rum he knew.

Their drinks were served and they sat sipping them in a pleasant silence, broken only by the soft music and Estelle crunching the cucumber that accompanied her drink as delicately as she could.

'I don't want to go home tomorrow,' Spizz said. 'I'm usually keen to be off when it comes to the end but meeting you… I just wish we had a few more days together.'

'Aww, that's nice of you to say that,' Estelle said. 'Perhaps if you'd joined in the group from the beginning and not just hung out with the Fourth Form we would've had.'

'The Fourth Form.'

'Sorry, but you know that's been your nickname since the beginning. Someone, I think it was Sarah, was convinced you were all teachers or something and it just led from there.'

Spizz gave a self-deprecating laugh.

'We probably should consider ourselves lucky you didn't

call us *The Bunch of Prats* or something.'

'Everyone makes mistakes,' Estelle said, giving him a smile that melted his heart.

'Can I have your number before we leave. I'd like to keep in touch.'

He blurted it out before his courage failed him and he also thought if he said it quickly enough she'd have to agree. As it was, she did.

'That'd be nice. What you mean, like WhatsApp each other?'

'Yeah. You know, speak regularly. Meet up.'

'Meet up?'

'Well, we're not that far apart, are we?'

'I could probably drive to yours in a couple of hours. Straight down the M1 then round the M25…'

Estelle looked at him and smiled. Now that he'd said it she realised that she would like to stay friends with him and see him again. She liked the thought of him coming to see her, perhaps even staying for the weekend. For more than one weekend.

'I'd like that.'

'Good. I would, too,' he said, reaching forward and taking her hand.

He pulled it towards his lips wanting to kiss her fingers, but she was leaning back in the bucket chair which meant he had to veer forward at an awkward angle and before he knew it he found himself on his knees with the seat on his back. Estelle couldn't help herself; she roared with laughter.

'You look like a tortoise!'

'I'm okay! I'm okay!' Spizz told the concerned waiter who'd rushed over, unsure whether he was drunk or had been taken ill.

The waiter removed the chair from his back and help lift

Spizz onto to his feet.

'Thank you,' he said, as he embarrassedly brushed the knees of his trousers. 'No harm done.'

'I'm sorry! I didn't mean to laugh, but you looked so funny!'

Tears were running down Estelle's face. Several times she tried to compose herself but started laughing again. In the end Spizz found himself joining in. They sat together roaring with laughter, totally at ease with each other.

✦ ✦ ✦

EVE HAD ENJOYED her evening. They had wandered along the costal path back towards the centre of the town and had found a pleasant bar with a good vibe, mainly filled with people who looked like foreign residents. Eve loved the way they dressed; it reminded her of ex-pats on Corfu who also adopted the layered, boho look. She gave a rueful sigh that she hadn't bought herself any clothes during her time here. Not that she needed them, but it was a style that she loved and which suited her and which would come in handy with the beach holidays she accompanied. The thought made her laugh to herself.

One minute you're leaving the company and the next you're planning your wardrobe for your next trip!

'I'm getting yours, Eve,' Ron said. 'What you having? And please don't say a Diet Coke.'

'I'm gonna have an Irish coffee,' Liz said. 'I'm getting a taste for them. Why don't you have one?'

'Actually, I think I will,' Eve said, surprising herself.

And why not? It's the last night and all I've got to do is get into a taxi for the short ride back to the hotel.

'And you deserve it, Eve,' Ron said. 'You've been lovely.

Been a pleasure to meet you.'

'Hear! Hear!' Liz said and the others all nodded their approval.

'I went to the doctor's about my hearing,' Ron said. 'He said, "You sure you've got a problem with your left ear?" And I said, "I'm definite."'

He beamed round at everyone waiting for them to get the punchline.

'Don't give up the day job, Ron,' Alex said, as the others groaned and giggled.

'I'm happily retired. No day job. I used to be a fireman but everyone kept on sending me to blazes,' he quipped, causing an even louder groan and more giggling.

Eve grinned at what he said; Blazes was the name of the nightclub in Windsor where she'd met Melv all those years ago. It was a small, dark place with a tiny dance floor, but to her it was just the best place ever. In Corfu she hadn't been allowed to go out to clubs and so she'd made the most of the new-found freedom she'd experienced when she'd arrived in England. She was still smiling as her Irish coffee arrived and it looked amazing.

'Oh, I wish I'd had one of those now,' Jackie grumbled eyeing the Irish coffees.

'I'll get you one,' Ron said, jumping up.

'No, I'd better not. Thanks, Ron, but it's a long day tomorrow what with going home and that and I need my wits about me. The red wine will do nicely.'

She thought about the day ahead of her and prayed yet again that her flight would be on time and that Scott's would be delayed for a couple of hours, just so she'd have time to carry out all her plans.

The future's bright!

She turned to Eve who was sitting further down the

table between Alex and Charlie.

'I've had a lovely time, Eve. Thanks.'

'That's good to hear.'

'Yep! Sorry for messing up the tennis bit by being so rubbish. No, I did!' She put her hand up to silence Eve and those who were jumping in to say she hadn't been rubbish. 'I know I was. I should've gone to a beginners' group. Well, actually, I shouldn't've come on a tennis holiday at all, but there we are. Hindsight and all that. And Sarah was brilliant, and you've all been nice about it. But I've had a great time.'

She suddenly blushed realising all eyes were on her and took a sip of her wine. It had been a bit of a roller coaster week for her, especially at the beginning. But now she was back on an even keel and raring to go.

✦ ✦ ✦

SEAN AND NICOLE had hung back from the others as they'd left *C'an Catalina* and now they were in Nicole's room enjoying their final session of the holiday. As Sean pounded away for all he was worth and Nicole ran her nails up and down his back sending him wild while surrendering herself to the thrill and ecstasy of the orgasms that awaited her, they would have been surprised to realise they were both thinking the same thoughts.

It's been great but it's just been a holiday fling.

They had enjoyed each other – and how! But tomorrow it would be home time and neither had any desire to keep in touch with the other. Nicole had buried the ghost of Roland and was happy to move forward and get on with her life and to look for a future with a man who was available; one with no strings attached. Sean was as happy as Larry. With Nicole he'd enjoyed the sort of sex he'd spent three years dreaming about. It had been wild, free and uncomplicated. Nicole hadn't been clingy or needy and she was happy to have a no-strings-attached affair. She'd forgiven him for shouting his mouth off to Alex and Charlie and she hadn't said a word about his being inside, or the reasons for it. None of it had seemed to put her off. And now the ice of his celibacy had been well and truly broken and he was going back to Ipswich with a feeling of positivity he hadn't felt in years. He thought he'd try a few dating apps. That was the way forward!

✦ ✦ ✦

IN ANOTHER PART of the hotel Spizz and Estelle were letting themselves into her room. On the beautiful rooftop terrace, and having moved to one of the low sofas, they had continued talking about seeing each other and keeping in touch. They held hands and suddenly found themselves kissing, first of all gently and then with more intensity. When they'd broken apart it had been Estelle who'd taken the lead.

'Come on, let's go back to the hotel,' she'd said, reaching for her bag.

'I'll get the bill,' he said.

He was glad she'd gone to the Ladies when the bill arrived. He'd done a double and then a triple take.

Eighteen euros for a gin and tonic?

He broke out in a sweat. He only had twenty euros left in his wallet and they were going to have to get a taxi back to the hotel. He couldn't ask Estelle to pay. It'd look bad now that she was willing to sleep with him.

That is what she was suggesting, wasn't it?

The bill had left him so flustered he began to doubt himself and hoped he hadn't misunderstood her.

Shit! That would be really embarrassing.

'Do you take cards, mate?'

'Of course, sir.'

The waiter handed him the card reader. It asked him if he wanted to add a gratuity. He hated it when that happened.

No, I fucking don't!

He was just putting his card back into his wallet when Estelle came back to join him.

'I'm happy for us to go Dutch,' she said.

Too bloody late!

'I wouldn't hear of it,' he said, taking her hand and leading her towards the lift, with a cheery wave at the waiter.

And here in her room Spizz gently took her into his arms and started to kiss her lips, her eyes, her nose, her forehead and her neck. She caressed his head, mussing up his hair, pushing his face further down. He slipped the thin straps of her pretty dress down over her shoulders exposing her bra, which he pulled away, leaving two luscious breasts on display. He studied them for a moment. He'd lusted after them since their afternoon at the beach. And now, here they were; before him, nipples erect, waiting for his mouth to envelop them. They both gave a groan of delight as his lips fondled the first nipple.

They had the best night.

✦ ✦ ✦

SARAH AND TISHA were also having a great night. Sarah couldn't believe she was having such a good time watching *Bachelor Boy the Essex Cliff*, with Pat and Bob and Jill and Les. She couldn't remember the last time she'd enjoyed herself so much. She knew nobody in the whole place, except Tisha, so she couldn't have cared less who saw her or what they thought of her.

I will never see these people again!

The thing was, every single person in the whole bar and terrace thought she and Tisha were amazing. Looking through the wine-induced haze she saw Tisha jiving with a man who must have been seventy to a song she'd never heard of.

Grandad might be old but he's certainly got the moves!

He spun Tisha round and then back again and then for a third time, but she staggered to the left and he missed her hand leaving her to totter, giddily into the arms of a slightly younger partner who took over where Grandad had left off, leading her in a sort of syncopated shuffle. Sarah beamed at them. The song ended and *Devil Woman* came on for the third time that night.

'Come on, Sarah!'

A man she vaguely recognised from earlier – Gerry? – pulled her to her feet again. They shimmied against each other in time to the music. At least Sarah thought she was in time to the music. But if she wasn't, she didn't care! The song ended and the MC announced that it was time for the music to be switched off to comply with local bye-laws.

'Boo! Boo!' Sarah shouted, giving a big thumbs down with both hands.

'Boo! Boo!' Tisha joined in, throwing her arms around her new best friend's neck.

'We're going now,' Pat said as the two of them staggered back to the table. 'It's half-past one and we've to be up early in the morning. We're going to Formentera.'

'No! Stay for one more!' Sarah said, clinging onto her arm.

Pat gently disentangled herself.

'It's such a shame you didn't find us until your last night,' Jill said. 'You'd've love the Take That Tribute that was here on Thursday.'

They shared hugs and kisses and swore to keep in touch, although they hadn't actually exchanged any contact details. Alone, the two women sank down onto their chairs.

'I don't want anything else to drink,' Tisha announced. 'Think we'd better go home?'

'Already?' Sarah belched loudly. 'What time is it?'

'I dunno. I think it's probably about eleven.'

Tisha giggled. She was looking at her phone but her eyes couldn't focus.

'It's quarter to two, love,' a woman on a nearby table called out to her.

'My taxi for the airport is at half-past eight,' Sarah said, surprising herself she'd actually remembered. 'P'raps we oughta be going.'

They both stood up, wobbled, grabbed each other, steadied themselves and then slowly made their way towards the road, calling farewell greetings to everyone else as they went. They lurched down the road.

'Can you see a taxi?' Tisha asked.

'Nope!'

Tisha walked ahead vaguely aware there was a taxi rank in the centre of the village that she'd seen as they arrived. A hundred yards further down the road and she was rewarded by the sight of a couple of green lights.

'Taxis! Sarah! Taxis!'

Squealing with delight, Tisha weaved her way forward, tottering on heeled sandals that she thought might have to be surgically removed, so deeply were they cutting into her toes. She was grateful for the numbing effect of the wine. She reached the taxi and managed to open the door on the second attempt. She turned to tell Sarah to hurry up. She had disappeared.

'Sarah? SARAH!'

Tisha bellowed at the empty street. A couple of young lads who were walking past looked at her and grinned.

'I'll be Sarah if you want,' one of them said.

'Piss off!'

Her drink-addled brain was working slowly. All she was aware of was that Sarah was nowhere to be seen.

'Momento,' she said to the taxi-driver, surprised that the alcohol had unleashed her linguistic skills. He tutted and raised his eyebrows as she almost took the door off its hinges when she slammed it and staggered back down the road.

'SaaaaaRAH! SaaaaaRAH!'

She soon found herself back at the bar, which had emptied out and she could see there was no sign of Sarah.

Where the fuck is she?

She leaned over and attempted to take off her shoes, but the catches on the straps evaded her. Standing upright again, she steadied herself against a chair and made her way back towards the taxi rank. Each step stabbed pain into her toes, along her feet and up her legs. She tried dragging her feet along but that didn't really help and she suddenly shot forward having tripped over an uneven paving stone.

'Fuck's sake!'

'Help!'

She thought she heard someone calling for help. A woman's voice. She looked round her but couldn't see anyone. She spun a full three hundred and sixty degrees on her heels so that her toes wouldn't hurt and then back again.

'Help!'

'Sarah? Is that you Sarah?'

The silence of the night played tricks on her, and the wine joined in so she couldn't work out where the voice was coming from.

'*Señora?* Everything is okay?'

She hadn't realised a car had pulled up beside her. She peered at it, unable to make out through the glass who was talking to her. The driver opened the window. Now she could see two policemen looking at her. They didn't look very happy to see her.

'I've lost my friend,' she started.

'You left her in a bar?'

'No. Just now. Just a few minutes ago. She was here and now she's not here. Pff! Gone! Just like that.' She clicked her fingers to explain what she was saying.

'Help!'

The voice came again but this time the police officers had also heard it. They got out of their vehicle and joined Tisha on the pavement.

'I think that's her.'

Whether it was Sarah or not, the policemen heard the cry for help and started looking around to find who was calling out.

'*Por aquí*,' one of them said, turning towards a long, low hedge that separated a garden bar from the pavement.

'Help!'

The cries continued but the two police officers looked at each other puzzled as there was nobody to be seen. Then one of them stepped forward and took out his torch. He shone it along the hedge, then holding one end, he parted the interwoven branches of the bush with it to reveal Sarah's bum with its red flash of thong stuck up in the air, her head and shoulders buried deep within the prickly, green foliage.

'*Ay, caramba*,' the other policeman said.

Slowly and carefully they lifted Sarah out of the bush and back up onto her feet. She protested at every inch of progress as the sharp, spiteful leaves scratched her entire body. Once she was upright they could see trickles of blood on her face, neck, chest and arms. Bits of foliage were stuck all over her clothes and in her hair making her look like a bedraggled, forgotten Christmas tree, long after Twelfth Night.

'You have insurance? We take you to 'ospital?'

'No. I'm okay,' she said. 'No hospital. I have a plane to catch.'

DAY EIGHT

EVE ARRIVED AT the door of the hotel dining room at half past seven just as the head waiter was opening up. Her own flight wasn't until six o'clock that evening, but she wanted to make sure that everyone was up and ready on time for their taxi or minibus and that nobody missed their flight. She sat down and ran her eyes over her transfer list one more time.

First off at half-past eight would be Nicole, Estelle and Sarah who were on the Gatwick flight and they were sharing the transfer minibus with Charlie and Jackie whose flight to Leeds/Bradford took off thirty-five minutes later. Then it was Rosalind and Alex to Luton and Liz to East Midlands at half-past nine in a taxi. Sean to Stansted, Ron to Southend and Katrina to Edinburgh would be in a second taxi at eleven o'clock and finally the minibus again for the Fourth Form to Birmingham at twelve o'clock. Then she would have a peaceful lunch by herself and a sit by the pool reading her book before her own taxi at half-past three.

'I expect you'll be pleased to see the back of us,' Ron said, coming to sit beside her. She'd known it was him before he spoke or she looked up because of his wonderful cologne.

'Why would I? You've mainly behaved yourselves,' she joked.

'I s'pose it's five o'clock on a Friday for you this morning, isn't it?'

'That's it exactly, Ron.'

'Here's a little something from me just to say "Thank you",' he said, taking her hand and pressing something into the palm. 'I've had a smashing week and you've done a great job.'

'Thank you, Ron. That's very kind of you.'

'Not at all. And don't forget to write them books. You're a clever woman. And I'll buy them all,' he said, giving her a wink before wandering over to the hot buffet table.

She pocketed the generous tip, poured herself a coffee and looked up to see Estelle and Nicole coming over closely followed by Spizz.

'I hate the last day!' Nicole said. 'I know I'm happy to go home because I know I have to go home and besides, I've missed the doggies, but even so…'

'At least we haven't got any hanging around,' Estelle said. 'Thank God we haven't got one of those flights where you have to get out your room at lunchtime and hang around for a midnight flight.'

'Oh, yes. I couldn't be arsed with all that. Is the flight on time, Eve?'

'I haven't looked yet. I usually wait until just before the transport's due then I check the inbound leg has taken off from the UK airport. There shouldn't be any problems with early morning flights,' she said, mentally crossing her fingers for luck.

'What time are you leaving, Ron?' Nicole asked him as he sat down to tuck into his full English.

'Eleven o'clock from here. My flight's at quarter to two.'

He didn't add that he was going to hang around and see Liz off at half-past nine. Charlie and Jackie had now joined them and both were tucking into a hearty breakfast. Eve looked at her watch and saw it was ten past eight.

'Anyone seen Sarah?'

Nobody had. She felt a bit uneasy as Sarah had been a good time-keeper throughout the week. Excusing herself she went out to the foyer to ring Sarah's room. Just as she was crossing to the front desk the lift doors opened and Sarah stepped out. At least Eve thought it was Sarah.

'What on earth has happened to you?'

Sarah's face and hands were covered in angry-looking scratches. In spite of the high temperature, she wore a high-neck, long-sleeve blouse and trousers, making Eve wonder what injuries might be hiding beneath them.

'You look like you lost a fight with a tiger.'

'I tripped up last night on a wonky paving stone and fell against a prickly bush.'

'Good heavens! Did you get any medical treatment? Disinfectant…'

'Yes, yes, I'm fine. No need to fuss,' she snapped as a porter came and took her suitcase, giving her a numbered ticket in return.

'It's for the eight-thirty transfer,' Eve told him.

'I don't want any breakfast. Do you think you could get me a coffee?'

Eve gave her a sharp look.

'Please, Eve! I don't want everyone to see me like this and start asking questions. It'll be bad enough when Nicole and Estelle see me. And besides, I haven't really got time for breakfast, have I?'

'White no sugar?' Eve asked.

Sarah nodded.

'I'll be right back'

Eve hurried back inside the dining-room and Sarah delved into her bag and gulped down half a bottle of water and two paracetamols.

I feel like shit.

Not only did she have a hangover and a half, her body was sore and throbbing from the myriad of tiny cuts caused by the frigging bushes. She had no idea what type of bushes they were but she wished them drought and a painful, prolonged death. She hoped every drunken tourist would wee on them and poison them and cause them to shrivel up. Her whole upper body including her arms felt as if it was on fire. The slightest movement send hundreds of stabbing pains jarring through her flesh.

I'm lucky I didn't poke an eye out.

Tisha had said that to her several times on their way back to the hotel in the back of the police car. She shuddered at the recollection. Eve reappeared with a coffee for her, which she accepted gratefully. She had only taken a couple of sips when Nicole, Estelle and Spizz came into the foyer with Jackie and Charlie following closely behind.

'Christ! What happened to you?' Jackie squealed.

'I tripped on a paving stone and found myself head-first in a bush.'

'Well, we've all been there,' Charlie quipped causing Spizz give a loud guffaw.

Sarah tutted and ignored them.

'Have you put some disinfectant on it?' Ron asked, coming up to join them. 'I've got some Germolene if you need it. Good stuff that. I swear by it…'

'Yes, I've put something on it,' Sarah snapped and then felt mean because Ron was only trying to help. 'Sorry, Ron.

Thanks for offering but I'm okay.'

Sarah was willing the transfer bus to turn up early. She hadn't realised that Jackie and Charlie would be going with them and she supposed Spizz had turned up to say a fond farewell to Estelle. While she was pleased to get the chance to say goodbye to Jackie, whose company she'd enjoyed throughout the week, she'd been hoping to avoid as many people as she could. She wished she had the panache to pull off wearing a veil.

'Here's the minibus,' Eve announced as Miguel pulled to a halt in front of the main doors and the porter took everyone's luggage receipt and then pulled the correct cases outside to be loaded.

Jackie gave Ron a hug.

'You've been great company, Ron the Raver,' she said. 'And thanks very much, Eve. I've enjoyed myself.'

Charlie shook Ron and Eve's hands and clambered aboard.

'No Sean?' Sarah couldn't resist asking Nicole.

'No.'

She saw no reason to tell Sarah that they'd said their goodbyes finally and unsentimentally the night before. She gave Ron and Eve a hug before boarding. Sarah didn't get near anyone in case they tried to hug her in which case she thought she'd probably scream so loudly they'd hear her in Barcelona.

'Thanks, Eve. Bye, Ron.'

Eve turned to see what was delaying Estelle and she saw it was Spizz. The two of them were locked in a tight embrace. She gave them another ten seconds or so but when they showed no signs of letting each other go she gave a cough.

'The bus is ready to leave, Estelle.'

With fat tears rolling down her cheeks Estelle pulled herself away from Spizz's arms and got into the minibus.

'Hasta luego, Eve,' Miguel said, slamming the door shut. 'I come back at twelve o'clock.

Eve, Ron and Spizz waved at the occupants as the minibus pulled off, made its way down the hotel driveway, turned onto the main road and disappeared out of sight.

'You all right, mate?' Ron asked Spizz.

'I'll live. She's a nice girl, though. I've enjoyed her company.'

'Nice you sorted things out. After the little misunderstanding.'

'It's been a funny old week,' Spizz said. 'Two women having a fight; a mud bath; a magic sunset; the best ever boat trip…'

'Liz scared shitless by a spider and Once in a Meadow!' Ron declared.

'Not to mention Leggo breaking a chair, me whacking him with the ball and two lesbians that wasn't'

The two men laughed and patted each other on the back.

'You gonna stay in touch with Estelle?'

'I hope so.'

'Where there's a will there's a way,' Ron said. 'Fancy a beer?'

'Fuck's sake, Ron! It's only half past eight.'

'Old habits die hard,' Ron quipped.

✦ ✦ ✦

SEAN, KATRINA AND Ron joined Eve to wave off Alex, Rosalind and Liz at half past nine.

'Thanks again, Katrina,' Rosalind said, giving her a hug.

'I hope I didn't spoil your holiday by bothering you…'

'Och, don't be silly. I'm glad I was able to reassure you. You did your very best in rotten circumstances. Now, just go back home and get on with the rest of your life.'

'I will.'

'Have a safe journey, love,' Ron said to Liz, taking both her hands in his. 'It was a real pleasure meeting you and I've enjoyed your company.'

'And I've enjoyed yours. What was it you said? Meet as strangers and leave as friends?'

'That's it! Should be the Travel Together tagline. Got your book to read on the plane?'

'I usually do puzzles.'

'I hope nobody interrupts you cos you'll give 'em a crossword.'

Liz giggled at his silly joke.

'You're a lovely man, Ron. And I hope one day you'll be able to let go of Veronica enough to enjoy the rest of your days with a woman who deserves you.'

'Bless you.' He placed the tenderest of kisses on her forehead and tears sprang into her eyes. Without looking up at him she got onto the bus.

'Take care of yourselves,' Alex said, shaking Ron's hand and giving Eve a hug. Then he turned to Katrina. 'And I'm sorry again for what I said.'

'You're becoming a bore now with so much apologising,' she said, giving him a peck on the cheek. 'Have a good flight!'

Eve ticked the names off her list and went back inside to wait for the next departure at eleven o'clock. She decided to join Sean, Ron, Katrina and Spizz down at the Club House for a coffee. They'd just got settled in when Tisha came rushing over looking a little worse for wear. Her hair was pulled back in a band and she had her sunglasses on, even though it was overcast. And she was wearing her beach flip flops with plasters in every toe.

'Has Sarah gone?'

'Yes. She left on the half-past eight transfer.'

'Are you sure?'

'Of course I am.'

'So she made it then?'

'Yes.'

Tisha gave a huge sigh of relief and collapsed onto a chair.

'What happened to her?' Spizz voiced the question on everyone's lips.

'She fell into a bush. She was absolutely rat-arsed. Well, we both were, really. We'd been dancing all night to a Cliff Richard tribute act.'

Everyone's jaw dropped open.

'Blimey! I thought you was gonna say you'd been to some posh club or other,' Ron said.

'Nope. 'Fraid not. It was all a bit surreal really. And we shared a table with some nice people. Two couples. Sisters and their husbands.'

She couldn't remember any of their names for the life of her.

'And we downed a couple of bottles of red. Well, I think it might have been four. Anyway, we had a fabulous night and then going to get a taxi I lost her. I turned round and she wasn't there. I went back to the bar, but she wasn't there either. And then two policemen turned up and we could hear someone calling out 'Help!' But we still couldn't see her. And then one of the coppers started separating the bushes with his torch and we could see her arse sticking up in the air.'

Tisha started to giggle loudly as she recalled what had happened and in spite of themselves the others found their lips twitching.

'The coppers couldn't believe their eyes! Her skirt was round her waist and all she had on was a thong. They tried to help her up without looking at her and I was trying to pull her skirt down and she was shouting at them not to pull her cos the prickles were digging into her. Ha ha ha! And when they finally got her to stand up she was covered from head to foot in blood and leaves!' Tisha roared with laughter. 'I know it's not funny cos she hurt herself. Ha ha ha! But if you'd seen her! Ha ha ha! And I couldn't find her! And neither could the policemen! Ha ha ha!'

Everyone was laughing along with Tisha now, even Eve.

'Christ! I bet that was a sight for sore eyes!' Ron said, wiping his own eyes with the back of his hand. 'Mind you, she looked in a right state this morning.'

'Did she get any medical treatment?' Eve asked. 'She said she had.'

'The policemen took us to some first aid place and they wiped her all over with disinfectant swabs and gave her some pain-killers. I think they gave her a supply of the swabs to use this morning. I'm just glad she got up in time for the flight, though. It must have been after four when we got back here. The police gave us a lift. They were brilliant, I have to say.'

'Oh dear, poor girl,' Ron said, still chuckling to himself at the thought of Sarah's arse sticking up out of the hedge.

It occurred to Eve that she hadn't filled in an Accident Report Form. She shrugged it off.

'Shame I was too drunk to film her,' Tisha said starting to laugh again. 'I couldn't find her. Ha ha ha! She was so far in the bush. And her arse was in the air! Ha ha ha!'

✦ ✦ ✦

THE PLANES HAD all been more or less on time, with just Ron on the Southend flight suffering half an hour delay and Alex and Rosalind on the Luton forty-five minutes. Hopeful that her own flight would be just as punctual Eve went into the Club House and ordered a mushroom omelette with a mixed salad. She was just waiting for it to be delivered when her phone rang. It was a UK mobile number she didn't recognise. For a moment she was tempted to ignore it, thinking it might be someone trying to get her to claim for an accident she'd never had, but she thought she'd better answer.

'Eve? It's Spizz.'

'Hi, Spizz. What's up?'

'It's Leggo. There's no sign of him at the gate and the flight's closing any minute. They won't tell me if he's checked in. He's gonna miss it.'

'There's nothing we can do, Spizz. If he isn't there in time he misses it.'

'For fuck's sake! He's like a little kid…'

'He could be anywhere. Sorry, but it's his responsibility to get to the airport. There was a place in the minibus from here for him but he didn't show up. There's nothing to be done.'

Spizz gave a long sigh and there was a few seconds silence.

'I know you're right, Eve. I just thought I'd ring you cos you might have some magic answer. Thanks anyway. I've gotta go as they're waving at me. The flight's closing now.'

'Make sure you don't miss it, too. Safe journey!'

But Spizz had already hung up. Eve shook her head in disbelief as she dropped her phone into her bag.

Some people just never grow up!

She tucked into her lunch and had almost finished when a porter came looking for her.

'Excuse me, Eve, the police is on the phone. He wants to talk to you.'

Indicating she'd take the call inside the Club House, Eve shoved the last forkful of food into her mouth and headed for the phone. After establishing that she didn't speak Spanish but the officer did speak English she listened to what was being said with disbelief.

'Mr Adrian Legg has told us you are his representative. Is that correct?'

'I was his tour manager but he checked himself out of the hotel earlier in the week.'

'Well, we are holding him here at Ibiza Airport because he assaulted a member of airline staff. He broke her nose…'

'A woman? He hit a woman?'

'Yes. She told him the check-in for his flight was closed because he was too late. He started to argue and was very aggressive. A lot of witnesses saw him because other flights were also checking in. He became angry, jumped over the desk and hit her.'

'Well, I am absolutely appalled by that,' Eve said. 'But I, too, am on my way to the airport as my contract ends today and my flight leaves in a short while so I can't do anything. And to be honest, he doesn't deserve anyone's help.'

'So nobody from your company can come?'

'No, I'm afraid not. You'll have to ring the Vice-Consulate.'

Eve went back outside and sat down again on the terrace, took out her iPad and quickly typed up an Incident Report Form on what she had just been told had happened. She thought that she perhaps should have gone along as requested but she couldn't risk anything that might mean she'd miss her own flight.

No way, Jose!

She could have rung the local agent but why should they have to get involved defending an idiot like Leggo? She really did believe it was true that when some people picked up their passport they left their brain behind. She shrugged. It was a job for the Vice-Consul.

And the best of luck to him or her!

She closed her iPad and ordered one final Diet Coke which she hoped she'd be able to sit and quietly enjoy in the sunshine before her taxi arrived.

✦ ✦ ✦

JACKIE HAD NEVER been happier than she was seeing the board announcing her flight was on time. She'd had a coffee with Charlie but they weren't sitting together on the plane, which she was quite glad about. She wanted to have the two hours and fifty minutes to herself to gather her thoughts and go over her plan. And since then everything had gone smoothly; the meet and greet car parking attendants had been there waiting for her and by half past two she was letting herself into her pretty terraced house.

It is my house again now. He's going to get such a surprise.

She picked up the post from the mat and put it on the hall table and went through to the kitchen. She sat at the table and turned on her phone. There were dozens of voicemail and text messages from him. She deleted them all without reading or listening to them. She'd had enough of his lies. Then she made a phone call to the locksmith who confirmed he would be with her just after three. She logged onto the Emirates website and saw that Scott's plane was due to land in Manchester at six o'clock. She smiled. That gave her plenty of time. She opened the back door letting a welcome blast of fresh air into the house then made herself a cup of tea determined to relax while she waited for the locksmith.

Two hours later the locks had been changed and every trace of Scott – his toiletries, clothes, DVDs, books, laptop, shoes, tennis racquets, photos and foodstuffs – had been removed from the various rooms of the house and now languished in several bin bags which were sitting next to the front door. And mixed in with the curry powder and gravy browning were heavy doses of the strongest laxatives she'd been able to find. She wouldn't witness his discomfort but it didn't matter. She knew about it.

Jackie then downloaded and printed off a dozen or so photos from Julie Clithers' Facebook page, placed them in an A4 plastic wallet and stapled it to the outside of one of the bin liners. Then with a smile of satisfaction she closed the front door and got into her car.

Sarah was right. You're worth so much more than him.

In spite of her bravado she couldn't stop a little lump forming in her throat and a tear threatening to run down her cheek.

You're going to be fine.

She nodded, knowing she would be. She'd come so far as was allowed a little wobble.

And that's all it is. A little wobble.

She couldn't help but give a little grin at the thought of watching Scott arrive home on her mobile phone via the security camera perched above the front door. She could already imagine the tantrum he was going to throw when he saw his belongings outside and couldn't get in.

He'll just have to bugger off to Julie Clithers's house. And she's welcome to him!

She deleted and blocked his number on her phone. With an air of determination she started up the car. Scott could kick and scream all he liked. She was looking forward to spending the rest of the weekend with her sister in Sheffield.

✦ ✦ ✦

RON CHATTED TO Del all the way from Southend Airport giving him a lively version of the week he'd just spent in Ibiza, making the taxi-driver laugh. The fifteen-minute journey passed quickly and soon Del was pulling onto the driveway of a large house which lay back from the main road, hidden from prying eyes by a tall, beautifully sculptured hedge.

'I'll be about half an hour if you wanna go and get a cuppa.'

'No problem. I'll wait up the road in the caff at the industrial estate. Give us a bell when you're ready.'

Ron got out the taxi carrying the huge bouquet of flowers he'd stopped to get on the way. He rang the bell and it was opened by a smart, statuesque woman wearing a pale lilac scrub-style uniform.

'Ron! You are back. How nice to see you.' She spoke with a marked West African accent.

'Afternoon, Gladys! How's my second favourite girl?'

'I am very well,' she chuckled. 'And your first favourite girl will be especially pleased you are here.'

'How's she been?'

'Very little change.'

She led Ron down a corridor he knew well, one he'd walked down almost every day for the last five years. They took the left hand passage when the corridor split in two and Gladys knocked on a door at the end of it before entering a beautiful room. It managed to be light and airy yet cosy and comfortable. Its patio doors which were ajar gave onto the garden; an immaculate lawn and bright, colourful flowerbeds.

The room was dominated by a double bed that was topped by a pink and purple duvet set and next to it, a woman, wearing a pink dress, cardigan and slippers sat in a very large wheelchair. Her blonde hair had been brushed and shone silkily. Someone had applied a little blusher to her cheeks.

'Hello, love!'

Ron rushed across the room, knelt down and wrapped his arms around his darling Veronica, holding her as closely as he could. After a while, he sat back on his heels, taking her hands in his and looking into her eyes. He stared deeply and searched but today there was no recognition in them and the disappointment cut him like a knife. She sat, staring forward, her mouth twisted in an ugly grimace in the same way that she did all day every day.

Not to be put off, he talked to her. Taking her hands and massaging them as he spoke he told her all about his holiday; the weather, the hotel, the other people, the boat trip and the tennis. He talked as if she was reacting and taking it all in. He liked to think she was. That on a deep level she knew him and understood his words. He stroked her hair and a lump caught in his throat. She'd always been consistent about getting her hair done and he made sure they still did it for her every few days. She'd always been so elegant and glamorous, too, with her passion for pink and she'd also been intelligent and smart. That was why the massive stroke she'd suffered had been such a shock. He visited every day spending a couple of hours with her, taking her out for walks round the gardens and further afield, chatting all the while, reading her favourite books to her hoping she was taking it in.

But his beautiful Veronica, the soulmate who had been by his side for almost fifty years had gone. And when he told people he'd lost his wife he was telling the truth. All that was left of that wonderful woman was a shell who spent all day lying in bed or propped up in a wheelchair while others fed, washed and bathed her, changed her clothes and made her look pretty.

Gladys put the flowers into one of the many vases that were spread around the room. Veronica had lots of vases because she loved flowers and he brought some with him most days.

'Aren't they beautiful, Veronica?' Gladys said, standing back to admire her own handiwork as well as the flowers themselves. 'And aren't you lucky to have such a loving husband?'

Ron thought it was probably time to leave as tea would soon be served.

'Bye, darling. I'll come and see you in the morning. Probably be here by about half past ten. Just wanna pull up a few weeds first. I expect the garden's in need of a bit of attention as I've neglected it for a week. I love you.'

Gladys watched as he placed the gentlest of kisses on his wife's cheek and thought it was tragic that a couple who loved each other so much should be separated by this cruel, demeaning condition while others who merely tolerated each other lived together for years in contempt and dislike.

With a final glance back Ron blew her a kiss and left the room, rang Del, and made his way back to his empty bungalow in Rochford.

✦ ✦ ✦

AT THE OTHER end of the country, more than four hundred miles away, Katrina let herself through the gate of another care home. This one was large, like a luxury country hotel and both Katrina and her mother had small, separate bungalows in the grounds, so they were on hand yet quite independent and they had their privacy. She looked around with pride and smiled as she wheeled her case along the path that wound its way around the garden and led to her little home. The house and the grounds were immaculate. Her mother had worked so hard to make Aileen Court one of Edinburgh's, and Scotland's most successful residential care homes. She let herself in and gave a huge smile of happiness as she stepped inside.

'Is that you already?'

Her smile became even wider when she heard the voice coming from the bedroom.

'Weren't you expecting me?'

'Not so soon. It's a good job I'm ready and waiting…'

Katrina dumped her case, threw her bag and keys onto the table and headed for the bedroom. Stepping inside her heart lurched at the sight of Steph lying on the bed with champagne on ice and a box of chocolates at the ready. Katrina climbed on next to her, smothering her with kisses.

'God! I've missed you. I wish you'd have come with me.'

'I'd've hated it, wouldn't I? I don't play tennis and I don't like the sun…'

Steph stopped talking as Katrina kissed her long and hard and ran her hands over her naked body. And later, as they lay together in each other's arms, Katrina thought about what had happened with Alex and Charlie and Ros. She knew some wouldn't have approved the way she'd laughed off being gay and pretended she wasn't but she thought it unimportant. Those who mattered knew who she was and who she was with and quite frankly who she decided to spend her life and her bed with was nobody else's business.

And that includes a group of people I'll never meet again.

✦ ✦ ✦

ESTELLE HAD DONE two lots of washing, had a bath and phoned for a take-away and was sitting enjoying it with one eye on game show on TV when her phone rang.

'Hello. It's James.'

'Who?'

'Spizz.'

Her stomach lurched. He'd said he'd phone but she'd thought he'd meant sometime next week.

'Been in about an hour and a half,' he continued. 'It took ages getting out the airport and driving home. It's pissing down here. Leggo missed the flight…'

There was a moment's silence.

'Have I called at an inconvenient time?'

'No! Not at all. It's really nice to hear from you.'

'Only I was wondering if you'd fancy meeting me in London next weekend. I could book a show, a meal, a nice hotel… Would you like that?'

'I'd love it,' she said.

✦ ✦ ✦

SARAH SLOWLY LOWERED herself into the deep, warm bathwater that was laced with lavender essential oil. She let out a long groan of relief as she leaned back and let the soothing water work its healing magic. The hundreds of small, sharp cuts throbbed as did her head that seemed to be drumming out its own heavy metal number. One thing was certain, she wouldn't be going to the new young partner's barbecue. She didn't even think she'd be going into work for a couple of days, at least not until her face had calmed down a bit. She could always work from home. She'd make up an excuse; at the moment she was too exhausted to think of one.

It was a funny old week. But I think I enjoyed myself.

She'd save the analysis for later, too. Right now all she wanted was to wrap herself in a huge bath sheet and sleep right through until tomorrow.

TEN DAYS LATER

✦

IN VALLEY CHURCH there was standing room only and by Eve's reckoning at least another hundred people stood outside. There was the buzz of murmured conversation and music she didn't recognise being played on the organ as the congregation sat and waited. The thick, cloying heat stuck her blouse to her skin and she could feel a trickle of sweat running down the back of her right leg, inside her black, linen trousers. She thought it disrespectful to fan herself with the Order of Funeral Service but she just had to. She was at the end of a row halfway down the church sitting beside Carlo, a receptionist at the Mango Tree Resort, who in turn was with several members of staff who had all come to support their General Manager and pay their last respects to his son.

She looked at the Order of Funeral Service, her throat catching at the photo of Radley taken a few years earlier, before his accident. She immediately saw the likeness to his father and to Michael. Michael had wanted to come to the funeral but Natalie had given everyone a scare when she'd slipped stepping into the garden and he had decided not to leave her. She wished he was there beside her, then immediately admonished herself for being selfish.

She looked at her watch. The funeral should have started almost twenty minutes ago, but this was Antigua; things ran at their own time. Just then there was a stir outside as the funeral cortege pulled up. The congregation rose as the pall-bearers, Melv, three of Radley's closest friends and two cousins, carried his coffin into the church. Mary and Juliet, sobbing, clutching each other's hands followed behind. There were two men walking closely to them who Eve knew to be Mary's husband and Juliet's boyfriend and then a couple of people she didn't know, followed by Hugo, Rowan and Rosetta all crying quietly.

After an hour of music, prayers, sermons, eulogies and readings Melv helped carry his son outside and for the long fifty yards of his last ever journey. Eve thought her heart would break for him and for Mary, who was visibly shaking.

No parent should have to bury a child.

She kept back as they neared the graveside, letting family and friends stand close. She looked across the road and above the treetops where large, dark grey clouds gathered over the sea threatening to drop their water over the mourners. As the priest intoned prayers and blessings a welcome breeze blew through the cemetery carrying Mary's wail which pierced the air and the hearts of everyone there. Eve saw Melv put his arm around her, tears pouring down his face as he drew Juliet to him, too. Her face was wet, too and she offered up a prayer of her own to a Greek Orthodox God she really didn't believe in as the casket was lowered into the ground and Radley was laid to eternal rest.

✦ ✦ ✦

EVE SAT ALONE in the bar of the Mango Tree Resort later

that night, her thoughts going over the events of the day and of the week since she'd arrived. It hadn't been the week she'd been expecting, though she couldn't have even put into words what that was.

A week earlier Eve's heart had been pounding like a pan players sticks and the flutter in her stomach became a pummelling as she collected her case from the luggage belt, knowing that Melv was just seconds away. Impatiently she'd joined the queue of eager people all anxious to get through Customs at VC Bird International Airport hoping they would move quickly.

'Nothing to declare, Miss?'

'Nothing.'

'You haven't brought anything for anyone? Any gifts? I see you're a frequent visitor.'

'No gifts. I'm here for a funeral.'

'My condolences. Go ahead.'

The Customs Officer waved her through. The automatic doors swished open and Eve walked through, her eyes searching for the tall, elegant, dark-skinned love of her life. A man raised his hand and after staring for a moment to check it was him she ran into his arms. They held each other tightly and Eve swallowed hard, determined to keep the promise she'd made to herself that she wouldn't cry; that she'd be strong for Melv. They relaxed their embrace and Melv planted a long, lingering kiss on her lips that felt so good. She took a step back and looked at him. His pain was plain to see; grief etched deep lines in his face and the sparkle had gone from his eyes. His shirt appeared a size too big; the collar swam around his neck revealing his weight loss. He seemed stooped, his shoulders rounded, shorter than he was. He was unrecognisable.

'Come on, let's get out of here,' he said, taking her case

as she took his arm.

They had driven along in almost silence. He had thanked her again for coming out; she had said she had to be there; they admired the hundreds of flamboyant trees that daubed the countryside with beautiful, bright red splashes; he said the resort was emptying out now as Carnival was over and then they'd both gone quiet. Eve didn't want to ask him about Radley. She knew he'd talk to her when he was ready.

'I wasn't sure whether I'd be staying here or with you,' Eve said as Melv's 4x4 swept through the gates, past security and down the long drive that lead to the Mango Tree Resort.

'I thought here would be more convenient for you. I'm here, too, at the moment,' he said, his voice quivering. 'I'm finding it hard to be at the house…'

Oh, nice one, Eve! Insensitive or what?

She was mad with herself and wished she'd kept quiet.

'I'm sorry, Melv. I didn't think…'

'No worries,' he said, covering her hand with his. 'I've put you in a suite.'

Ten minutes later they were inside it.

'I've missed you so much, babe,' Melv said, pulling her to him as soon as the door closed behind the porter and kissing her face and neck as he pulled her jacket from her shoulders and unzipped her dress.

Within seconds they were writhing together on the king-size bed. Eve's body trembled as thrill after thrill ran through her body at Melv's touch.

'Oh, baby, I do love you. I do love you!'

His words became increasingly louder as his passion made her gasp and groan as waves of ecstasy swept over her. It had been a long time since their love-making had been like this and Eve realised how much she had missed it and that she never wanted it to end.

But it did end with them both wrapped in each other's arms, their bodies curled together, legs entwined.

'Welcome back to Antigua,' Melv said, kissing her forehead.

'It's very nice to be here,' she replied, snuggling against his chest. 'With you.'

His breathing became relaxed and she realised he had drifted into sleep. She smiled and held him tighter, happy that she had been the conduit for the release of his emotions; that in the face of grief and with his world collapsing around him he had sought solace and confirmation of life with her. The intensity of their love-making had taken her by surprise; it had been years since it had been that good.

The jangle of his mobile interrupted their peace and silence. Melv was instantly awake. He reached across her, caressing her breast with his hand before it picking up the phone. He barked a couple of short, terse answers before hanging up.

'Problem?' Eve asked.

'It was Rosetta reminding me about the undertakers,' he said, laying his head on her chest. 'Mary and I have to see them in a while.'

'It must be so hard for you both,' she said, taking his hand and kissing it and lifting it to her cheek.

'I guess you never imagine post-divorce that any dealings you'll be having with your ex-wife will be to arrange your son's funeral. But we're both big people and we have to do it. For Radley.'

Eve nodded silently.

'And you know she never could handle what happened. She only came to see him because she had to be seen to visit him. I know that sounds harsh,' he quickly added, 'And I'm not criticising her. You know what it's like here. You have to be seen to do things and so she visited him so that people saw her visiting. But every time she came she couldn't wait to leave. She found it hard. Seeing him like that.'

How hard did she think it was for him?

Eve bit her tongue. Now wasn't the time to criticise Mary's parenting skills. And besides, Melv had been both father and mother to the boy; Radley had been taken care of and looked after. He'd been loved, not just by his dad but by his carers and his sister, too.

And Eve knew that she was nobody to condemn another mother's behaviour.

'I'd better go.'

Melv gave her a long kiss and then stood up from the bed and took a quick shower.

'Sorry to walk out on you.'

'Well, it isn't as if I don't know my way around, is it?'

'How're you gonna spend the rest of the day?'

'I'll unpack and I'm sure I'll find something to do. Is there anything I can do for you?'

'Things are taken care of, thanks. I'll try and come back later but whatever happens I'll call you. Okay?'

'Sure.'

'And thanks again for coming. I'm so glad you're here.'

Eve watched him go and then lay back down on the bed. She thought about their sex-session and exhaled loudly.

Who said you went off sex after fifty?

She gave a little giggle. She looked down at her naked body; she saw the stretch marks, the beginnings of varicose veins, the bunion, the boobs that were drifting south, the wobbly thighs, the bingo wings, the love handles and the little roll of fat that seemed to have found its home just above her knicker line. And she gave a great big grin because she knew that Melv didn't care about any of that and she was totally at ease and comfortable being naked in front of him and that was a wonderful feeling.

Her stomach growled and she looked at her watch, surprised to see it was almost five o'clock. She decided to go and have afternoon tea and then perhaps have one of Elvis's cracking cocktails and watch the sunset. Her unpacking could wait until later.

✦ ✦ ✦

'EVE! IT'S GREAT to see you!'

Elvis came from behind the bar and gave her the biggest bear hug.

'You here by yourself?'

'Yes. No group.'

'I guess you're here to support the Boss, huh? Terrible business. Terrible business,' he shook his head in disbelief. 'May the Good Lord take care of him. He's safe in the arms of Jesus now.'

Eve nodded. She envied Elvis the strength and simplicity of his faith.

'So, what can I get you?'

'I'll have a rum punch, please, Elvis.'

'It does m'heart good to hear you say those words. You drink so much Diet Coke.'

'Well, as I'm here without a group I can indulge myself a little.'

'You indulge yourself a lot, baby. Enjoy!'

He stuck a cocktail stick of exotic fruits into the drink and handed it over to her.

'You going by the beach?'

'Yes. I'm going to watch the sunset.'

Eve made her way along the pathway and onto the beach. In some ways the layout of the Mango Tree Resort wasn't so different from the Dunas Blancas, except that it was larger. She couldn't believe it had only been a week ago when they'd spent the evening on Sunset Strip in San Antonio watching the sun go down over the Mediterranean Sea. And now, here she was watching it set over the Caribbean Sea. She'd smothered herself in insect repellant as those pesky mosquitoes loved this time of day and she stepped onto the beach and found an empty sun lounger. She wondered where her group were now and what they were doing. She supposed they'd all be back to work. Except Ron, perhaps, although she seemed to remember him saying he was running some tennis camps for kids over the next couple of weeks before the schools went back. She'd liked Ron, admired his zest for life and the way he wasn't afraid to enjoy himself.

Be more Ron!

They had been a nice enough group on the whole, apart from the Fourth Form, of course. Well, Leggo really. For a moment she let herself wonder what had become of him then she quickly dismissed the thought.

Vile, nasty man! Quite frankly, I couldn't care less what happened to him.

She gave a sigh of satisfaction at how nice it was to be at the Mango Tree Resort with no group. She had nobody but herself to think about. Well, nobody except Melv. She was already looking forward to seeing him again later.

✦ ✦ ✦

MELV HAD CALLED her just before eight o'clock.

'I should be back in resort within half an hour or so. I thought we could have dinner together.'

'Sure. That sounds good.'

Over an hour and a half later she was still waiting for him. She'd gone down to the foyer and made herself comfortable in one of the big bamboo rocking chairs enjoying the breeze that always seemed to pass through. She looked at her watch and wondered what might be keeping him. Just then she saw him hurrying towards the main entrance from the car park.

'Sorry I'm late,' he apologised without giving her any explanation why.

He planted a fleeting kiss on her cheek as she stood up.

'Shall we go to the Crazy Conch? It'll be quieter there than in the main dining room,' he said, leading her along the path towards the seafood restaurant without waiting for her to reply.

They were shown to a table in an alcove and placed their orders. Eve couldn't help noticing Melv had hardly any appetite, his order consisting of only a shrimp salad. He looked at her and gave a sad smile.

'How did things go?'

'Oh, as well as you'd expect. The funeral is set for three o'clock next Tuesday. At Valley Church.'

Eve reached across the table and took his hand. It felt cold and clammy not like his hand at all. They sat in silence while their drinks were served. Eve understood if he didn't want to talk; she was happy to sit quietly with him if that was what he wanted. But he seemed on edge which she supposed wasn't surprising. He was grieving and grief was a very unique and personal thing. She remembered the weeks after she'd given up Michael for adoption and the deep hole she'd fallen into, spending days lying in bed, staring at the wall and crying. However Melv was dealing with his grief she had to go along with it and just be there to support him.

'So, what did you do for the rest of the afternoon?'

His words made her jump as they broke the silence.

'I stayed in my room for a bit and then took a rum punch down to the beach to watch the sunset.'

'Sounds good.'

Their meals arrived and after commenting on how good they were they ate in silence.

'Are you sure there's nothing I can do? To help you, I mean,' she asked after their plates were cleared away. Melv had barely touched his dinner.

'You are helping by being here,' he said, taking her hand again.

He looked at her face, studying it.

'What?'

'Nothing. I can't look at you?'

'Of course you can. But you look like you're… I don't know…'

'I have to tell you something.'

She nodded and waited for him to speak. But before he could say anything her phone rang.

'It's Michael!'

Both Eve and Melv smiled as she answered the call.

'Michael, I'm so sorry!'

'I take it you arrived okay and that you're well?' His tone bordered on the acerbic. 'What happened to text as soon as you land?'

'Sorry!'

'So caught up in seeing Melv again you forgot about me,' he teased, not knowing how true his words were. 'How is he?'

'I'm with him now. Hold on.' She passed the phone to

Melv who spoke to Michael for a few minutes before handing over to her again. As she continued the conversation with her son, Melv's phone rang. He mouthed *'Just a minute'* and walked away from the table out of earshot.

Michael told her that Natalie was fine after her fall.

'I should be at the funeral,' he said.

'No, you shouldn't. I know he was your half-brother but it's a long way for you to come, not to mention the expense and what with Natalie being pregnant and I'm not there to look after Felicity,' she said.

'I'll send flowers if you give me the details of the funeral.'

'I'm not sure if they use fresh flowers here or not. Because of the heat. But don't worry, I'll talk to Melv and if it's appropriate I'll sort out a wreath from the two of us.'

'And how is he? Really?'

She looked across the restaurant and thought Melv looked very worked up. He was pacing up and down, his arm flailing as he appeared to be having a heated discussion with whoever the caller was.

'He seems numb to be honest. He's quiet, yet on edge. But I suppose that's to be expected.'

Michael made Eve promise to keep him abreast with events in Antigua and they said their goodbyes. Melv had seen she was no longer talking to Michael and after appearing to say something curt and forceful he, too, hung up and made his way back to her.

'Everything okay?'

'Resort shit.'

He let out a long sigh and rubbed his hands over his face.

'They shouldn't be bothering you at a time like this,' Eve retorted. 'Can't you take some compassionate leave?

Surely Anderson or Kemal can run things for a while.'

'I'm better keeping busy at the moment. I'll take some time once the funeral is over. Once it's all over.'

'You know you can always come and stay with me.'

'I know.' He stood up. 'Come on. Let's go back to yours.'

They went to Eve's suite. Once inside, Melv helped himself to one of the bottles of water in the minibar that he downed in one. And then they had an action replay of that afternoon's session. He told her repeatedly that he loved her as he thrust into her making her cry out until they collapsed holding each other tightly, both panting and gasping for breath.

✦ ✦ ✦

AND THIS HAD been the pattern for the rest of the days leading up to the funeral. Eve spent most of her time alone, on the beach or by the Spa Pool, reading and relaxing. On Saturday morning she'd taken the bus into St John's and spent a couple of enjoyable hours wandering through the streets, window-shopping and having a delightful lunch in Redcliffe Quay.

Twice Melv came and had lunch and a siesta with her and every evening they had dinner together before strolling through the grounds of the resort back to her room for another marathon love-making session. But he never stayed the night, which she found odd.

'I'm not sleeping. I'm so restless I'd keep you awake all night,' he said when she asked him about it.

'You don't seem to have any trouble sparking out after sex,' she said, smiling.

'That's temporary euphoria and exhaustion,' he replied.

'Once I get into bed, my eyes are wide open, my thoughts are racing and I toss and turn the whole night through. I would disturb you.'

She hadn't insisted. He knew where she was if he needed her. She had woken up early each morning and was going for a power walk around the Resort gardens while it was still cool. Once the sun was over the horizon the humidity seemed to double and she felt too hot to do anything other than lie in the shade or the water. On the morning before the funeral she was walking across the main entrance when she saw Melv pull up in the car park. She waved at him as they drew near to each other.

'What you doing up this early?' He planted a kiss on her cheek.

'Just getting in some exercise. And you? Did you go back to the house last night?'

'Yes.' He looked away from her. 'I thought I should go back for one night. I have to sooner or later and the longer I leave it the more difficult it's gonna get,' he explained. 'Want to have breakfast together?'

'If you can give me fifteen minutes. I just need a quick shower.'

'For sure. Call me when you're heading for the restaurant and I'll meet you there.'

Twenty-five minutes later they sat down on a terrace table at the main restaurant. Eve had worked up an appetite with her power walk and tucked into yoghurt with fresh mango and papaya and then scrambled egg on toast. Melv picked at a Danish pastry.

'The first night I was here you said you had to tell me something,' Eve said, suddenly remembering. 'Then Michael rang and you never mentioned it again. What was it?'

'Really? I said that?'

'Yes. You seemed quite serious. And then you got agitated on the phone about work…'

'I have no idea what that might have been,' he said. 'Other than to tell you how much I love you and how grateful I am for you being here.'

Eve felt a lump in her throat as he took her hand and raised it to his lips. In her heart of hearts she just wanted the funeral to be over. To her, it was a mountain between them; something that kept them in a sort of twilight zone where nothing was real. Even their love-making had an ethereal, illusionary quality to it.

Nothing is as it seems.

She didn't know where the words had come from but they seemed to sum up the situation and her feelings exactly. And they seemed to have lost the easy, natural relationship they'd once enjoyed. They had little real conversation. To Eve it felt like the old Melv had slipped away from her.

✦ ✦ ✦

AND NOW THE funeral was over.

She had gone along to the wake, which had been held at Mary's house, an imposing building at Paradise View with possibly the most exquisite tropical garden Eve had ever seen. Hugo had given her a ride alongside Rowan and his wife, Cheridee. They had made polite conversation on the journey as there was little else they could talk about.

'Are you staying by Melv?' Cheridee asked her.

'No. I'm at the Mango Tree. He's staying there, too.'

'He is? I didn't know that. How long are you here for?'

'Cheridee, nuh trow questions at she!' Rowan chided his wife.

'Oh, another week or so. I'm not too sure. Melv might

come back to England for a while with me.'

'True dat?'

'Well, he had a good turnout,' Hugo said, changing the subject. 'Nice to see so many people there. I wish he'd known how loved he was.'

'Amen!' Rowan and Cheridee chorused.

It seemed that most of the mourners had gone to Mary's house. Melv sought her out as soon as she arrived, pushing his way through the large crowd gathered on the patio.

'Sorry you couldn't ride with us, babe,' he said, giving her a kiss on the cheek.

'I understand.'

'Let me get you a drink,' he said, leading her towards two catering staff who were holding trays of drink. 'Oh, you know, Mary,' he said as his ex-wife appeared alongside them.

'I am so sorry for your loss. My deepest condolences,' Eve said, leaning forward to place a kiss on Mary's cheek.

To her surprise, Mary pulled her into a hug and held on tightly.

'Thank you, Eve. Thank you. And thank you for coming today.'

Both women pulled back with tears in their eyes. Mary had been extremely cool towards Eve on the previous occasions they had met. But today was a day to put differences aside. It was a day for support and solidarity. Eve squeezed Mary's arm and Mary gave her a gentle smile.

'Your son was a fine young man.'

'Thank you. I always thought so, but then I'm his mother. It's nice to hear it from others.'

'And your house is beautiful…' Eve swallowed not knowing what else to say.

'You're welcome here. Please help yourself to food and drink,' Mary said as three women approached her.

'Excuse me,' she said, moving off to talk to them. Melv touched her shoulder as she passed by him and she placed her hand on his. Eve was pleased to see they, too, were putting all animosity behind them.

'Don't think I'm abandoning you if I have to talk to people,' he said.

'Of course I won't. You don't have to babysit me, you've got hundreds here. I'll be okay.'

'I'll be back as soon as I can,' he said, giving her a peck on the cheek and moving towards a group of young people.

Eve wandered down the crazy paving path that bisected the immaculate lawn, admiring the biggest most glorious orange and fuchsia bougainvillea bushes she had ever see. There was a marble table with four chairs nestled on a small patio at the end of the path. A couple were sitting there. They looked at her and gave a half smile as she took a seat there, happy to be in the shade and watch the mourners at the wake from afar.

The couple spoke to each other in whispers making her feel a bit like a spare part. She realised that in spite of being with Melv for over five years she hardly knew anyone there and if anything this funeral had served to show her just how much she wasn't part of his life. She thought she had been before Radley's accident and she wondered if she might be again. But this afternoon she felt like an outsider. She sipped her drink and saw Cheridee talking animatedly to Rosetta on the edge of the crowd of people on the patio. Seeing them together she wondered if they were related, sisters even. They had oval faces with high cheekbones and big, wide eyes and both were short and slender, although now she got a proper look at her Rosetta looked as if she'd put on a little weight since the last time Eve had seen her a couple of months earlier. She noticed the way both women held themselves and the angle of their heads and decided they were definitely sisters.

Nosey Parker Cheridee!

Eve accepted that perhaps she'd just been nervous or naturally curious, or was trying to be friendly in an awkward moment when she'd bombarded her with questions in the car. Then, as if on cue, as if they knew she was thinking about them both women spun round and stared at her for several moments before turning back and walking away.

She shrugged not knowing what all that was about. She felt a little awkward if she was honest and decided she wanted to leave. She'd come to the wake to support Melv but he was obviously managing without her.

And why wouldn't he? He's surrounded by his people, those that knew and loved Radley and he'll want to talk about him and remember him and stories and anecdotes that I know nothing about.

Suddenly from out of nowhere a strong breeze picked up and heavy raindrops began falling. The couple sitting beside her ran back towards the house, the woman squealing as she went. Leaving her drink Eve made her way across the lawn and up the steps to the wide, sweeping patio where the majority of the guests were gathering under huge umbrellas to shelter from the rain or trying to squeeze inside the house. Her eyes searched for Melv but she couldn't see him. She went from parasol to parasol trying to keep dry as she made her way around the patio; several people smiled at her and she smiled back. But Melv was nowhere to be seen. She decided to make her way towards the front of the house in the hope that someone would be leaving soon who could give her a lift at least back into St John's or even Jolly Harbour where she could then take a taxi or the bus back to the Mango Tree Resort. She found herself by the imposing front door that was ajar and after just a few minutes a taxi pulled in and a couple got out. She splashed through the rain to the driver's side.

'Are you free?'

'Yes, ma'am. Where you going?'

'The Mango Tree Resort, please.'

She got in and sent Melv a text.

Looked for you but couldn't find you.

Have gone back to the resort. Call me later. Xxx

✦ ✦ ✦

AND HERE SHE was, at eleven o'clock still waiting for him to call her. She felt headachy and tetchy and while there was no way she was going to criticise Melv for his apparent abandonment of her on the day of his son's funeral, she was just a bit peeved that he hadn't taken even ten seconds to send a reply to her text.

And she had so many questions about them and their relationship. They really needed to talk.

So what happens now? What happens to us?

Eve wanted to ask Melv what his plans were but at the same time didn't want to bother him when his feelings were so raw. To be honest, she was hoping he'd decide to go to England with her for a few weeks. Hanging around the Mango Tree Resort, as pleasant as that was, hadn't been what she'd had in mind when she'd come out to support Melv a week earlier. She'd imagined she would be of practical help to him with the funeral arrangements or taking care of the house. But she'd had no hand in any of it. Instead she'd been like a holiday-maker, resting and relaxing and having wild sex sessions with him. She wondered if it would even be possible to pick up where they'd left off before Radley's accident. Then they'd been talking about her moving to Antigua permanently so they could be together. Even marriage had been mentioned. But now she wasn't sure about any of that. She wasn't sure of her own feelings. She loved him but something was missing. And she had no idea about Melv's feelings towards her. And if she was honest the idea of living permanently on Antigua had lost its appeal.

And in spite of their heightened physical intimacy Eve knew that their relationship had changed. There wasn't the closeness there used to be in the earlier years when they had rediscovered each other and reconnected. It felt like two strangers enjoying a holiday fling.

How can that be possible when we've been through so much together?

And he continually told her that he loved her. All through their love-making he repeated it like a mantra. But even so…

She decided to let another couple of days pass and then she'd talk to him.

✦ ✦ ✦

EVE WOKE UP with a start. She was in bed, the light was on and her book had fallen to the floor. She checked her phone. It was twenty-five past three.

'Shit!'

She spoke out loud as she slowly moved her neck that had become stiff as the air conditioning had been blowing right onto it and rotated her shoulders. Picking the book up from the floor, she padded across the room in bare feet and switched off the AC unit before going into the bathroom. She had a wee and brushed her teeth as her mouth felt stale and then got back into bed and picked up her phone again but she could see there were no missed calls and no messages. She wondered for a minute if Melv was sulking because she'd left the wake and was giving her the silent treatment, but that wasn't like him at all. Melv usually said what he was thinking and he didn't play games. She lay down and decided he'd probably drunk a lot of rum as the memories flowed about his boy. She certainly couldn't begrudge him that. They would have plenty of time to talk later that day. She turned off the light and pulled a pillow into her arms and laid her head on it, imagining it was Melv's chest. She gave a deep sigh and slipped back into sleep with a smile on her face.

THE DAY AFTER THAT

✦

EVE WAS FINISHING her breakfast just before ten o'clock when Melv finally rang her.

'Sorry I didn't see you yesterday. Before you left. You understand…'

His voice sounded tired, weary.

'Yes, of course. I just hope you didn't think me rude for leaving.'

'Not at all. Look, why don't we go somewhere today? In the boat. Somewhere quiet. Take a picnic…'

'That sounds good,' she said. 'I'd like that.'

'I'll go by Epicurean for food on the way to call for you.'

He picked her up from the beach at twelve and they headed north along the coast towards Five Islands. It was a place they were particularly fond of as there were several small beaches around the island-rocks that were totally private. Just the occasional passing speed boat was their only company. It felt good to have the sun on her back and feel the warm breeze against her skin as Melv expertly took the wheel. Studying him from behind her shades Eve saw him start to physically relax. The strained, haunted look disappeared from his face as they got underway. Being on the sea was working its magic. Sensing her eyes on him, he turned to her and smiled.

'Feels good to be back on the boat, huh?'

'Very good. Do you want something to drink?'

She delved into the ice box and pulled out a diet coke for herself and a beer for him. They passed a large catamaran full to the top with cruise ship tourists that was heading towards Cades Reef. The Captain sounded the siren and everyone waved at them and they waved back. Eve always got a childish thrill doing that. Within a short time they were dropping anchor off one of the rocks. Once the boat stopped the sheer heat and humidity of the day hit them with full force.

'If feels like there's a storm coming,' Melv said. 'I haven't listened to the radio so I don't know. But this is tropical storm heat.'

They both slid into the warm, welcoming water.

'Remember the tropical storm that raged on the night we found out about Michael?'

'How could I forget? That was the storm that was raging when you had your wicked way with me again,' she joked.

'Like this, you mean?'

He drew her to him, kissing her mouth slowly and passionately while his hands ran over her body and lifted her legs around his waist before lowering her swimsuit freeing her breasts. She gasped in delight as his mouth took each nipple in turn, sucking it and caressing it with his tongue before his hands slid down her body removing her swimsuit in one fell swoop. She floated spread-eagled; he pulled her to him, her legs over each shoulder as his tongue brought her to her first climax of several that quickly followed one after the other. When she was sated and panting and trembling he gently guided her onto the tiny beach, and thrust into her until she cried out again and he collapsed on top of her. They lay breathless, gasping together until slowly their breathing became synchronised and returned to normal.

'The sun's burning my back,' he said after a while, 'And you're covered in sand.'

He pulled her to her feel and kissed her again before leading her into the water. They floated on their backs, naked, side by side, linking fingers, chatting occasionally about everything and nothing until Melv decided he was hungry. They climbed back onto the boat and put on their swimsuits to protect their modesty against any passing boats and opened up their picnic.

Eve suddenly realised she was ravenous.

'Hmm! That looks good and it smells amazing,' she said, looking at the ribs and chicken and potato salad that was in the ice box.

They both tucked into their feast, licking jerk seasoning from their fingers with relish. Then Melv produced a bottle of champagne.

'What are we celebrating?'

'Do we have to be celebrating something to drink champagne?'

'Of course not!'

'We're going to drink a toast to the memory of my son. And then we're going to drink to us,' he said, filling two flutes and passing one to her.

'To Radley! May he sleep in eternal peace!'

'To Radley!'

They both raised their glasses and then took a sip.

'And to us!' Melv continued.

'To us!' Eve echoed, wondering what *us* might actually be.

'And I've arranged to have a couple of weeks off work. Compassionate leave. I'll be spending a lot more time with you now.'

'That sounds good. I like it.'

Checking she'd finished eating, Melv collected the remains of the picnic and put it back in the cooler, then sat opposite her and took her hand. A small cloud appeared from nowhere and covered the sun. Melv's face had become serious and Eve suddenly felt apprehensive and uneasy.

'Eve, I think we should talk…'

'Talk?'

'Yes. Look, babe, you know I love you, don't you? You know that I wanted us to be together before Radley's accident. Well, I think we both did. We talked about it a lot, right?'

Eve nodded unsure where this monologue might be leading. He squeezed her hand tighter.

'Well now that Radley is no longer here, God rest his soul, we need to talk about us and how we can be together and make our relationship work.'

'But we've changed, haven't we? Not just because of Radley. We're not the same, our relationship isn't the same as it used to be.'

'What are you saying?'

'We don't talk, Melv. We make small talk. We pussyfoot around each other, or rather I've been pussyfooting around you because your son died and I didn't know what to say to you. And I should have done. We've been like two polite strangers…'

'What? You lie. We've been intimate like never before. The sex has been the best ever. Better than when we first met.'

'And that's just the problem, isn't it? *The sex*. We used to make love. And what about everything else that goes into a relationship?'

'That's what I want to talk about. That's what we can work on now. Together. We've spent too long apart. Too far apart.'

She had spent the last five years wondering what the best way for them to work might be. She hadn't been averse to living in Antigua but she knew now how much she'd miss Michael and Natalie and Felicity and the new baby.

'But there's something else you need to know… Before we make our plans… But I want you to hear me out. Okay?'

He was now gripping both her hands in his and staring at her intently, silently.

'Go on,' she said, her stomach flipping.

He took a deep breath and exhaled noisily. She could feel his palms sweating as his fingers held hers even tighter.

'Rosetta's pregnant.'

She heard the words without understanding them, without being able to process them. For a split second she couldn't even remember who Rosetta was. And then the cogs slowly turned and everything fell into place. She understood not just the words he said, but what he was actually telling her. She felt sick; she thought she was going to vomit.

'You're Rosetta's baby-daddy?'

'Yes.'

She pulled her hands from his and when he tried to grab them back she sat on them.

'Then there's nothing to discuss, is there?'

'Of course there is...'

'Come on then! Let's talk! Let's hear the truth, the whole truth and nothing but the truth. Has she been living with you?'

'Well, she's staying at the house at the moment. Clearing things up...'

'So, you're living together?'

'No! Yes... But not like you're thinking.'

'Don't you dare tell me what I'm thinking. You can't come close! I'm sitting here about to discuss my future with you and then you drop into the conversation that you and your son's carer are living together and having a baby. And I'm supposed to be okay with that? Am I missing something?'

'Eve, please, just let me explain...'

'There's nothing to explain. You've found someone else and you're having a child with her. And that's it. There's nothing else to say.'

'It wasn't meant to happen.'

'You were having unprotected sex so what were you expecting was gonna happen? And please don't tell me she tricked you by pretending she was on the pill!' Eve spat at him.

'But it's you I love, Eve. Rosetta knows that. She knows our story.'

'Well, bully for Rosetta! What exactly were you thinking when you asked me to come here, Melv? Are you planning on the three of us living happily together? I wouldn't even be Number One Woman if she's got the kid!'

'No! I've told her I want to be with you, but she's acting up. She won't move out...'

'And I don't blame her. She's pregnant, she's hormonal and she's vulnerable. How can you even think about throwing her out?'

'I'm not throwing her out…'

'Is she related to Cheridee?' Eve suddenly asked.

'They're sisters.'

'And does everyone know she's pregnant and that it's yours?'

'Just a couple of people. Eve, please! Let's talk about us. She wasn't meant to get pregnant, it was an accident…'

'Ha! *An accident?* Reversing your car into a lamppost is an accident not getting pregnant. And anyway, she IS pregnant. And you're going to be a father again. You have a live-in girlfriend. And I don't fit in the picture anywhere. So there's nothing more to discuss. Take me back to the resort!'

She stood up, pulled her sarong around her body and sat down at the back of the boat.

'Eve, you're behaving like a child. Listen to me, please!'

He came and sat next to her.

'I know you've had a shock and believe me I understand you're upset. But I want us to find a solution not hurl abuse at each other.'

'I'm not hurling abuse. Do you hear me hurling abuse?' She could feel herself bordering on hysteria. 'I have nothing more to say. Please take me back.'

'I just want a chance for us to be together. Rosetta knows I don't love her. She knows you're my woman, the only one I want to be with. I've told her she has to move back to her own place. I'll take full financial responsibility for the child and I'll be in its life. I want my son or daughter to know I'm their father…'

'And you're going to do all that without being involved with Rosetta?'

'Of course! Thousands of parents who never got together bring up kids…'

'You really are something else! You just assume that I'm going to slot into this Caribbean version of Modern Family and you couldn't be more wrong, let me tell you. I have a life in England with our son and his family,' she spat at him. 'I have no wish to live here in Antigua. And I have no wish to live with you.'

Melv hung his head. He had never seen Eve so quietly yet so seriously angry.

'Eve, you've gotta understand,' he tried again. 'She's been playing up since you arrived. Calling me all the while. Threatened to come to the Mango Tree and tell you herself if I didn't…'

'You were considering not telling me?'

'No! She's saying she's going to take the baby overseas once it's born and I'll never see it again. I've been through all that once with Michael…'

She stared at him, stunned by the cruelty of his words.

'That was a low blow, Melv.'

'I'm sorry! I didn't mean it to come out like that. But I want to know my child.'

'I didn't think you'd want more children at your age,' she retorted.

'I didn't. I didn't set out to have a child with her. But an innocent child is on its way and as its father I'm happy about that.'

A knife twisted in Eve's gut. She grabbed the rail with white knuckles.

'A child is always a blessing, Eve. Always,' he continued. I didn't plan a child but I'm not gonna walk away like some irresponsible *rass*.'

He reached out to touch Eve's arm but she flinched it away from him. He gave a deep sigh.

'I didn't even want to get involved with her…'

'But you just couldn't help yourself,' Eve mocked.

'You weren't here and Rosetta was always around, taking care of Radley and…'

'Oh, well that's all right then! I wasn't here and you couldn't possibly have had a wank or even gone without. Or are you going to tell me she forced you? Made you have sex with her against your will?'

He couldn't answer her; he saw that an abyss was opening up between them.

'I knew something was going on. All the phone calls that made you angry. The long silences. People looking at me sideways yesterday. How could you let me be at your son's funeral when everyone knew she's taken my place?'

'They don't all know. And besides, she hasn't, Eve…'

'And all the sex… Did you think if you screwed me senseless I'd forgive you everything else?'

'You know I love you, Eve. My life would be nothing without you. Making love to you is wonderful… And I know you feel the same…'

'You don't know shit about what I feel. And I think you've humiliated me enough. Now for the last time of asking, take me back.'

Melv slowly shook his head, exhaled noisily then sprang to his feet. The wind had suddenly got up and huge rain clouds threatened. He raised the anchor and started the engine. The boat roared into life and he sped away from Five Islands heading south to the Mango Tree Resort. He stared ahead as he steered and Eve's eyes looked at the coastline without actually seeing it. Their silence was tangible. Lightning flashed above them, thunder crashed and the sea turned grey. He was still tying the last rope at the jetty when Eve stepped over the side and onto the wooden boardwalk.

'Eve! Eve!'

His words, whipped by the wind, followed her onto the beach but she didn't look back at him. She strode ahead through the pouring rain without acknowledging him, tears teaming down her face.

THE FIRST DAY OF THE REST OF HER LIFE

✦

EVE GENTLY KICKED her front door closed and leaned back against it, shutting her eyes, locking out the world. She allowed herself to wallow in the relief of being back in the privacy and the silence of her own home in Horndon-on-the-Hill after the longest two days of her life. She breathed deeply recognising the familiar aromas; the plug-in air freshener just inside the kitchen and the deep, sweet smell of her beloved jasmine plant that had pride of place on the hallway table. Kicking off her shoes she appreciated the coolness of the dark grey marble tiles that eased her throbbing feet, slightly swollen as always from the flight. She breathed slowly, deeply and purposefully, appreciative of being back where she belonged. Home.

She didn't know how long she stood there, but gradually tiredness and jet-lag began to creep up on her. She hadn't slept a wink on the overnight flight, spending it watching yet not really seeing one silly film after another. A wave of exhaustion rolled over her. She kicked aside the post, too worn out to pick it up, pushed her suitcase to one side and made her way into the living-room. She took off her linen jacket and sank onto the sofa. She turned and rested her head against the gentle velvet fabric and within moments sank into a deep, dreamless sleep.

✦ ✦ ✦

SHE JERKED AWAKE by the shrill ring of her phone. She lay there, disorientated, trying to work out where she was. She was relieved to see the familiar surroundings of her own living-room. The phone was in her handbag which she'd dropped on the floor. A glance at it revealed the caller was Michael. She let it ring out. She loved her son dearly, but at the moment she wasn't up to explaining to him what had gone on with Melv and why she'd come home early. She saw it was just after two o'clock in the afternoon. She'd been asleep four hours yet she still felt shattered. Turning her phone onto *silent* she lay down again and pulled her knees up curling into a foetal position. But sleep evaded her now and after a few moments she went into the kitchen, made herself a coffee and took it into the conservatory to drink. The conservatory was her favourite room; bright, light and airy. She sat down and put her feet up on the pouffe and as she inhaled the coffee's deep aroma she finally allowed herself to think about her decision and actions.

As soon as she'd got back to her room after leaving Melv on the boat she went on-line to activate her ticket for the following day as that evening's flight was full. Melv rang her continually but she didn't pick up. He left her a couple of voice messages which ranged from pleading with her to talk things over and not to throw everything away to anger with her for ignoring him. She kept the safety lock on the door just in case he got a pass key to get in. He didn't go that far, although he did knock more than once. Each time she sat in silence in the room waiting for him to tire and leave her alone. He'd pushed a note under the door begging her to call him, but she quietly ripped it to shreds and dropped it into the bin. Then sat hugging her knees and listening to the rain tattooing against the window.

She didn't sleep that night and by six o'clock the following morning she'd packed her case and was dressed and ready for the airport. She hung the *Do Not Disturb* sign on the door and went into breakfast as soon as the restaurant opened at seven o'clock but barely touched what she'd served herself from the buffet. She had a coffee and took another one back to her room, leaving the sign in place so that the maids wouldn't bother her. The calls from Melv started again from eight o'clock. The day crept by slowly. Several times she considered meeting and talking to him but then decided against it and let the call go to voicemail.

There's so much to be said, yet nothing more to say.

Every time she thought about Melv and Rosetta and their baby a dagger pierced her heart.

At half-past three she left the room. Mindful that Melv had probably asked the reception staff to let him know if she checked out, she avoided the front desk. They had her credit card details so they could deduct whatever the bill came to. She no longer cared. She wanted to be as far away as possible. She pulled her case through the gardens to the taxi stand, avoiding the main pathways where she might be spotted. The taxi-drivers all knew her but today she had few words for them and Mikey who was driving her seemed to sense something was wrong and kept unusually silent. She felt sad as she looked out on the Mango Tree Resort for the last time.

So many memories. So many hopes and dreams. All shattered.

At VC Bird Airport she checked in and immediately took the escalator to the first floor joining the queue for Immigration. She seemed to be shuffling forward for an eternity, although it was in fact less than ten minutes and just as she reached the head of the queue she heard her name called.

Melv was at the top of the escalator, trying to get past the security guard who was checking boarding passes.

'Eve! Eve! Wait a minute!'

She turned and stared at him. The security guard was now holding his arm to restrain him and another was rushing to his colleague's aid. Her heart was thumping like mad; the blood was pounding in her ears.

"Please go to Agent Number Six"

The American behind her leaned forward impatiently.

'Number six is free.'

She stumbled forward and offered her passport to the officer behind desk six, concentrating on him and trying to blot out Melv's cries.

'You okay, Miss?'

The officer's kind eyes were full of sympathy. He realised her name was Eve from her passport and that she was the one the guy was shouting at.

'Thank you. Yes.'

She nodded, embarrassed.

'You have a good flight, now. Come back and see us soon.'

She swallowed hard. She couldn't envisage ever coming back to Antigua again and that really did fill her with sadness. Without looking back she walked ahead and Melv's cries and shouts faded behind her. She went through security on automatic pilot, taking out her iPad and Kindle, taking off her jacket and shoes and placing them in the tray alongside her handbag.

And then she went to the Executive Lounge and ordered a double rum.

And now back in the security of her own home she was alone with her thoughts. Finally she could be deeply honest with herself. She knew that Karma, that bitch with a very long memory, had well and truly paid her back. She had waited and had then bitten Eve on the bum harder than she had ever thought possible. A tsunami of grief, loss and hopelessness swept over her. She let out a howl of pain, flung herself onto the sofa and sobbed and wailed in agony.

✦ ✦ ✦

IT WAS TEN o'clock at night and she was still huddled on the sofa in the conservatory. The whole day had disappeared after she'd wept herself into timelessness. And emerging from it now she realised it was dark. She gave an involuntary shudder. It might be August but tonight was chilly. Or perhaps it was because she was so out of sorts that she was shivery.

Her stomach rumbled reminding her she'd eaten nothing since breakfast the previous day and she hadn't been able to face the aircraft food. She opened the fridge and the freezer although she already knew a touch of the Old Mother Hubbard's was all that faced her. In the cupboard she found a long-life milk and she poured herself a bowl of muesli which she devoured, then immediately felt sick. Then she wandered into the living-room and checked her phone that was still lying on the floor next to the sofa. Six missed calls from Michael and a voice message. She listened as he asked where she was and how she was. He said he'd had a 'weird' call from Melv who'd spent most of the night in a cell at Coolidge Police Station for causing a disturbance at the airport and that they were both frantically worried about her.

She rattled off a short text message to her son.

Hi, Michael

Sorry – not my intention to worry you.
I'm okay. Just need a day or so to myself.
To get my head straight. Will ring tomorrow.

Love you! XXXX

She sat thinking for a long while and then knew what she had to do. With an air of determination she took a writing pad and pen from beside the TV set and sat at the dining table and began to write.

Dear Melv,

As we both know, I never told you about Michael. You didn't know I was pregnant, that I'd given birth or that I'd given him up for adoption. When we met Michael it was an enormous shock for both of us, but even more so for you as you had known nothing about his existence. You were angry with me – and so was Michael – and rightly so. But you came to understand that I had been young and alone and afraid, and what I did was done out of love, thinking it was best for my baby. And you understood and you forgave me. And we fell in love all over again, although as I've told you many times, I never ever fell out of love with you in the first place. All that is old news now.

And over the last five years we've both forged a wonderful relationship with our son, his gorgeous family and with each other. Finally it felt as if the life we had been meant to live thirty years ago was coming to be. You and Mary divorced, I did every Antigua trip Travel Together had and you came to stay with me at least twice a year. We were 'together'. We made plans. Marriage was mentioned. Our fairy-tale ending was finally in sight.

But then Radley suffered his accident. Things changed and I understand they had to. You watched your strong, handsome young son with his life ahead of him have his hopes and dreams snatched away from him. I know it broke your heart and it broke mine, too, not just seeing Radley but watching you put your life on hold to care for him. And our plans were also put on hold and somewhere along the line we stopped talking about US. Not that I'm blaming Radley. It's just how things turned out. He was your priority and rightly so. And, sadly, in spite of our love, you and I drifted away from each other. You couldn't leave him and come here and although I continued to visit regularly, nothing was the same. A gulf appeared between us that seemed to become an abyss.

And then there was Rosetta.

I am not going to deny that I am hurt and angry that you turned to her. I had often wondered if there were other women while we weren't together. My heart told me there weren't and my head told me there were. If you'd had a series of one-night stands, I would have understood that. At least, I like to think I would. But it hurts so much that you'd started a relationship – an actual relationship – with Rosetta who was caring for your son and who has been living with you all along. And you *didn't say a word to me about her.*

And it hurts beyond measure that she's pregnant. And that you actually WANT the child.

You see, Melv, there was another child. A couple of years ago – at the time of Radley's accident I, too, discovered I was pregnant. You and I were expecting a second child thirty-three years after the first! And in spite of all the promises we'd made to each other about no secrets and being honest; in spite of all the heartache that resulted from my first secret I decided not to go through with the pregnancy and not to tell you about it either. You had enough on your plate with Radley and little Felicity had just been born – there was so much standing in the way of me and the pregnancy.

And besides, I never in a million years dreamed you would want to be a father again because – and I'm not proud to admit this – I didn't want to be a mother. Certainly not at fifty. Selfish? Perhaps. But there was no room in my life – our lives – for a baby. Or so I thought.

And so, I had an abortion and never told you. But you have to believe me when I say that I have lived with that guilt every moment since. Each time we spoke, each time we were together I was agonising over the truth and believe me, there were moments when I yearned to tell you. But the longer time went on the more difficult it became until I saw no reason for you to know. Ignorance is bliss and so once again I had another secret I kept from you – something else to hide and bury. So how can I accuse you of lying to me and keeping things from me when I have done exactly the same?

But now, I'm being paid back. You're going to be a father again. "A baby is always a blessing," you said, and you are right. And I am being punished for what I did to you – for a second time I denied you the chance of being a father and now someone else has done what I refused to do.

You have begged me to forgive you and to give us a chance. Perhaps now you can see why that won't work. I can forgive you what's happened. But this time YOU would never forgive ME. Not a second time. And I understand that. After all, I will never be able to forgive myself.

In spite of everything, I have never loved anyone but you. And now I have to learn to live without you.

Eve.

She read the letter again, wiping away her tears with the back of her hand. Then she went through the conservatory and into the back garden. The smell of wet grass rose up to meet her as she stepped outside and she inhaled it deeply, suddenly aware she'd been cooped up in the house since she'd arrived home the previous morning. It was now after midnight. She stood by the wrought iron table and held the letter tightly in her hand, reading it one more time before setting fire to one corner with the barbecue lighter. As her fingers became hot she dropped the letter onto the table top and watched the flames engulf her words as the paper disintegrated into tiny black specs that the breeze carried off.

Finally! It's out there. The Universe knows. I have admitted what I did.

Heavy spots of rain started to fall again but she didn't move. She let the summer shower work its magic, washing over her and hopefully taking a little of her guilt and shame and anguish with it. She stood under the deluge until it began to ease and then drenched and dripping she stepped inside. She dried off and slipped into her pyjamas and finally climbed the stairs to her bedroom. But once again sleep evaded her. After half an hour of tossing and turning she got up and made herself a herbal tea and took it back to bed.

She sat up sipping the steaming liquid and opened up her iPad and for the first time in several days checked her Travel Together emails. There were a couple from her tennis group, Liz, Katrina and Ron thanking her for giving them a good time. She loved it when people were appreciative and she sent quick replies to them. She smiled at Ron's email.

> *I hope you're settled back home and have spent the last ten days doing some preparation for those books of yours. They'll be a cracking read and I can't wait to see them on Amazon.*

She found herself re-reading his words several times. Eve knew she'd had a wonderful life thanks to Travel Together. She had travelled the world and seen so many of its wonders, both natural and man-made. She'd been to every continent. She'd seen glaciers and deserts and mountains and rain forests and jungles and beaches and visited hundreds of vibrant, fascinating cities. She'd had the most amazing experiences – she called them her *Know You're Alive Moments* – and had met so many diverse, interesting people. She rummaged in the bedside cabinet for a pad to start making notes. She had so many stories and tales to tell but she knew exactly which holiday she was going to write about first.

It wasn't just going to be about any old singles' holiday.

It was going to be based on that fateful holiday to Antigua, the one where she met up again with Melv and Michael. She was proud of her wonderful son and would publicly recognise him in her book.

My book!

That sounded so good. She said the words out loud over and over.

'My book! My book! My book!'

But you've never written a book before…

The Inner Voice of Self Doubt whispered in her ear.

'But I'm going to write one now!'

She spoke her answer loud and clear.

Driven by the excitement of planning her first book she went onto Amazon and ordered a white board, a pack of marker pens and a giant pack of multi-coloured Post-It stickers, all weapons in the armoury of any budding author. She was pleased to see they would be delivered the following morning.

She made notes, jotting down anecdotes, snippets of long-forgotten conversations that now miraculously came back into her mind, events and outings, people and places and she began to feel an enthusiasm that had evaded her for the longest while. She didn't even care if nobody read it; she was writing for herself. She thought about her cast of characters – who would all be fictitious, of course. She decided on their names and then set about writing their back stories. The hours flew by; she worked her way down several pots of coffee. She was buzzing; she was actually *enjoying* herself. All signs of tiredness had completely disappeared.

And she knew her book was going to be a love story; their story, hers and Melv's.

A love story that even after more than thirty years wasn't meant to be and didn't have a happy ending. No

Happy Ever After for Eve and Melv.

She faltered for a moment at the thought.

Don't go there! Write your story and work through the pain.

The pages of her pad were quickly filling and she was just wondering what time her Amazon stationery delivery would come when the bell went.

Yes! Right on cue!

She rushed to the front door mindful that she was in her pyjamas but thought the delivery driver had probably seen much worse than her M&S floral sleepwear.

'Hear me out!'

Melv shoved his foot in the door to prevent her from slamming it in his face.

'Please, Eve. Let me come in and talk to you.'

Seeing Mr Peyton's rheumy eyes peering over the privet hedge, curious to see what was happening at his neighbour's front door, Eve grabbed hold of Melv's arm and dragged him inside, slamming the door on Mr Peyton and Melv's suitcase, which sat neglected and forgotten next to the step.

They stood at opposite ends of the short hallway; both breathing hard, staring at each other. Eve wondered if she looked as dreadful as he did. Deep shadows underscored his eyes and he appeared even gaunter than before. Agony was etched onto his face.

'We have to talk, Eve. We've got too much going on, too much… All these years of love… We have to find a way of going forward. Together. Please, Eve… I am nothing without you.'

Her stomach flipped and her heart thumped as she looked at him. Tears leaked onto his cheeks. She reached and brushed them away with her thumb. She was overcome with love for him and she, too, began to silently cry.

'Oh, baby, don't.'

He pulled her into his arms and they held each other, both quietly sobbing because they knew there would never be anyone else for either of them and their love was far too great to simply throw away. A quote from one of her favourite books Wuthering Heights flashed into her head.

Whatever our souls are made of, his and mine are the same.

Slowly, she released herself from his embrace. She raised his hands to her lips and then led him into the living-room. She sat on the sofa, gently pulling him down next to her. She took a deep breath and turned to face him.

'I have something to tell you,' she said.

The End

Author's Notes

Writing the Singles' Series has possibly been the most enjoyable and satisfying of my accomplishments as an author. It was such fun revisiting Antigua (Singles' Holiday), India (Singles and Spice), the Essex village of Tolleshunt D'Arcy (Single All The Way), Amsterdam and the Norwegian Fjords (Singles At Sea) and Ibiza and Antigua again (Singles, Set and Match) some of the wonderful places I went to during my twelve and a half years as a tour manager.

It is no secret that writing the first book got me fired, but to be honest, I haven't looked back since. Life has been good and I have branched out with my writing. In 2017 I co-wrote a short film Only the Lonely, which recently won the prestigious Groucho Club Short Film Award and I have more screen-writing plans coming to fruition. Watch this space!

I want to thank all the fabulous book bloggers – too numerous to mention – who have come forward so willingly to help promote my books. I thank you from the bottom of my heart for your time and generous observations.

A huge *Thank You* also has to go to Rachel Gilbey of Rachel's Random Resources for organising the most amazing cover reveal and blog tour for Singles, Set and Match; to Kim Nash, aka Kim the Bookworm, for her never-ending support and friendship and to Nicola May who is always so generous with her time and advice. You are three wonderful women!

My thanks, too, to Lisa Morena for the wonderful cover design of all five books.

And my undying love and thanks to my readers – thanks for sticking with me and for continuing to ask "What happened to Eve and Melv?" That spurred me on to keep writing their story.

And if you're asking *'Is this really the end?'* may I suggest you check back with me in late January? I *might* have a little surprise for you…

And if you've enjoyed reading any or all of my books, please do leave a review on *amazon.co.uk*. Reviews are a writer's oxygen supply and it's the way other people find our books.

Thank you all so much.
Elaine xx